Francome, John.
False start

When Charlie Patterson and Nick Ryder begin training together they strike gold in their first season. They have been sent a yearling by Kate Scanlan, the attractive boss of a local animal rescue centre. Willow Star, as the scrawny filly is named, is sold to Major Patterson, Charlie's step-father, and the youngster quickly defies her looks by establishing herself as one of the fastest of her age. A stab at the following year's classic races is about to begin when Major Patterson informs Charlie and Nick that he is selling Willow Star to another yard. The ambitious trainers see their chance of hitting the big time disappear when their attempts to deter the sale fail. What ensues is a tale of mystery that finds Charlie cornered, facing the impossible dilemma of having to choose precisely where his loyalties lie—with his best friend Nick or with his family—and needing to solve a murder to stay alive...

FALSE START

John Francome

Thorndike Press
Thorndike, Maine USA

This Large Print edition is published by Thorndike Press, USA.

Published in 1997 in the U.S. by arrangement with International Creative Management, Inc.

U.S. Softcover ISBN 0–7862–1126–1 (General Series Edition)

Copyright © 1996 John Francome and Peter Burden

The right of John Francome to be identified as the Author of the Work has been asserted by him in accordance with the Copyright, Designs and Patents Act 1988.

All characters in this publication are fictitious and any resemblance to real persons, living or dead, is purely coincidental.

The text of this Large Print edition is unabridged.
Other aspects of the book may vary from the original edition.

Set in 16 pt. New Times Roman.

Printed in Great Britain on acid-free paper.

British Library Cataloguing in Publication Data available

Library of Congress Cataloging-in-Publication Data

Francome, John.
    False start / John Francome.
        p.   cm.
    ISBN 0–7862–1126–1 (lg. print : sc : alk. paper)
    1. Horse racing—England—Fiction.   2. Large type books.
I. Title.
[PR6056.R282F35   1997]
823'.914–dc21   97–13098

CHAPTER ONE

Kate Scanlan peered through the window of her warm office into a dark, blustering night. Raindrops drummed on the glass, making it difficult to see what was happening outside. She leaned forward. In the weak glow of an old security light, she could just make out the figure of her head girl, Sandy Jennings. It was six o'clock, going home time, and Sandy was heaving shut the large sliding door to the stable block.

Kate sat back and looked at her reflection in the window. She wasn't sure if she liked her new short bobbed hair. It made her look older, more like the twenty-six she really was. She became nostalgic and thought longingly of the time when closing up had been her job. She'd been happier then, taking hands-on care of the animals at the Rescue Centre. Organising the staff and the day-to-day admin was much more of a chore, but when the chance of promotion had come, she couldn't turn it down; the mortgage on her recently purchased small cottage had decided it for her.

The North Wiltshire Animal Rescue Centre (or NOWARC, affectionately known as Noah's Ark) was part of a highly efficient national charity with an annual turnover of tens of millions. It had been set up originally to deal with the thousands of farm animals which were found each year abandoned or abused by their owners. The centres were called in by the public and other agencies to house, cure and find new homes for a wide variety of victims, though NOWARC dealt mainly with horses, cattle and sheep.

1

While the animals always came first, the trustees of the charity were adamant that their donors' money should not be wasted and they demanded thorough accountability from the leaders of the centres, which meant showing where every penny had gone. Maths had never been one of Kate's strong points and she loathed this side of the job.

She'd had enough office work for one day. She closed the accounts book in front of her and rummaged in her bag for a packet of Marlboros. The girl who helped in the office hated the smell of tobacco smoke, but she'd already gone home. Kate lit her cigarette. She had taken a couple of contented drags when the phone rang. She glanced at it, prepared for a moment to ignore it, but she couldn't. Working at the Rescue Centre was a vocation, like being a doctor or a priest; being needed was the point of your existence.

She picked up the phone. It was Richard Stanley, head of the local branch of the RSPCA.

'Kate, I'm sorry to do this to you on a night like this, but I've got three men off with some bug and it's pandemonium here.'

'You're sorry to do what?' Kate asked as she looked out at the blustering rain with a sinking stomach.

'The police have just phoned. They've had a call about some cattle making a hell of a racket on a farm a mile or so up the hill above Ramsbury. They want someone to take a look...' He left the sentence hanging in the air.

'And you haven't got anyone spare,' Kate said helpfully.

Richard Stanley uttered a guilty sigh. 'I suppose you couldn't send someone over, could you?'

2

'Yes, I suppose I could,' Kate said with a grin. Through the window she caught a glimpse of the tail lights of Sandy's car disappearing through the gate of the small car park. 'Damn!'

'What's the matter?'

'Oh, nothing,' Kate said. 'I've just missed Sandy, that's all. I'll go myself.'

'Great. Thanks, Kate. I owe you one.'

'And I won't forget it. What's the farmer's name and how do I get there?'

'Cyril Barton. Apparently he's in his eighties, lives on his own.' He gave Kate the name of the farm and rough directions. 'Give me a ring if you have any problems.'

When she'd put the phone down, Kate got up and walked across to look at the Ordnance Survey map on the back wall of the office to see exactly where she was going. She knew most of the farms within half a dozen miles of the centre, but she'd never had any dealings with this particular one. When she'd worked out the best route, she locked up the office and went out to her old Renault in the car park.

Twenty minutes later, her car headlights picked out a rotting sign on which the words 'Lodge Farm' were just discernible. The post from which the sign hung had long since broken off at the bottom; now only a thick, black hawthorn hedge supported it.

It was surprising that anyone had complained, she thought. The farm—more of a smallholding—was a good quarter of a mile from the metalled lane and, as far as she could tell from the map, some distance from the nearest neighbour.

Kate's headlights lit the muddy, puddled track beyond the entrance. She shivered. She dreaded what she might find. Once on a similar mission, she'd

3

discovered fifteen starving horses. She had wept hopelessly at the sight of them and the memory still haunted her.

Without much enthusiasm, she drove her car through the entrance and cautiously along the deep ruts. She had covered three hundred yards and was beginning to wonder if she had somehow gone wrong, maybe missed a turning off the track to the house, when round a bend her headlights swept across a three-sided courtyard and reflected off the wet stone of a dilapidated house and the ancient buildings clustered round it. She drove into the yard and parked her car just inside the gate. The house loomed darkly, unlit on the far side. She turned off the engine and waited, wondering what to do. Something about the place gave her the creeps. She locked the car doors and picked up her mobile phone to call Sandy, but the orange light showed she was out of signal.

The wind had dropped and the rain diminished to a silent drizzle.

Abruptly, the quiet was shattered by a furious bellow from one of the barns. Kate froze, startled out of her normally collected wits. She knew almost at once that the noise wasn't human, but it took her a few seconds to register that it was an angry, probably very hungry bullock.

The bellowing was joined by a rasping regular bark of an old dog. Kate looked at the house for a reaction. No light, no human sound marked the owner's presence. He could have been out, or asleep, or ill. But that wasn't her problem; at least, it wasn't her priority. Her job was to look after the animals, and by the sound of it, they needed it. Every instinct told her to drive away, but instead she leaned over to

4

the back seat and found her torch. She got out and directed its powerful beam into a large, ramshackle timber-clad barn. The big wagon door had been blown open, and inside she could see a jumble of straw bales, muddy farm tackle and empty paper feed bags. She picked her way across the remains of the cobbles that had once covered the yard until she stood in the doorway.

The dog's barking crescendoed to a manic yelp as her torch picked it out, crouched, too arthritic to want to move from a bed of filthy sacking under a long-abandoned Ferguson tractor. She moved cautiously into the barn, flicking the torch's beam into every crevice, searching for hidden danger. When she reached the dog, she looked behind her, then bent down to offer it her hand to smell. The bark became a pleading whimper as she stroked it and murmured gently until the silence was fractured again by the angry bellowing.

Kate looked around and saw the source of the noise. In an old stable to her left, behind high iron bars, were two half-ton bullocks. She left the dog and went across to them. She hauled back an ungreased bolt which squealed in protest. Cautiously, she let herself in. The animals nuzzled her roughly, desperate for food, as she searched around their quarters. The manger was empty; the water trough was bone dry.

What these animals needed most was water. There didn't seem to be any reaching the inflow valve of the troughs. Filling them would be a tap and bucket job. She searched the yard until she found them both outside the back door of the house. Carrying her torch under her arm, she trekked back and forth until she'd heaved five bucketfuls which the big beasts sucked up almost as fast as she could pour the water into the iron tank. Filling the buckets eased her earlier fear, and she began to move about with more confidence.

In another stall, she found a ewe with a pair of weak, spindly lambs. She watered them all, then the dog. There were no more animals in the first barn so she crossed over to the next.

It seemed colder and wetter in this one. A sweep of the torch among the trusses and bearers showed large gaps between the roof slates which looked as though they had been letting in the weather for years. Under this scanty protection was a suckler cow with her two-month-old calf. The cow was lying on her side, weak from lack of food and liquid. The water trough and manger were empty. The straw had been trampled into a filthy paste of mud and slurry. The calf could barely open its eyes. Kate made a few more drenching trips with the buckets across the yard then looked around for some food. Besides the hay in the first barn, she could find nothing else. She'd have to come back up in the morning with some supplies.

As she worked, she wondered angrily how things could possibly have reached such a state and rehearsed the lecture she was going to give the owner.

Where the hell was he, anyway? He had no right just to go off and leave his stock unattended.

She marched back across the yard and shone her torch on a back door which hadn't seen a paintbrush for forty years. She looked for a bell. There wasn't one. She hammered and heard only the hoot of an owl for an answer.

She waited half a minute before she turned the old iron ring handle and pushed impatiently. The door creaked open.

She considered leaving; after all, she'd done her job for the moment. Then she found herself calling out, 'Hello! Anyone in?'

She was answered by a profound silence. She shivered, gritted her teeth and stepped through on to a cold, flagstone floor. Her nostrils were filled with the damp, musty smell that belongs only to very old houses which have never known central heating or damp-proofing. It was a smell which in her line of work she associated with old people—people who had grown too weak or too crippled or too poor to look after the animals which they'd been used to having around them all their lives, and which they refused to give up.

She flashed her lamp around a messy hall, cluttered with old yellow newspapers, Wellington boots, stout hazel thumbsticks and decrepit furniture. A dusty, unshaded bulb hung on a length of fabric-covered flex. After some searching, she found a switch. She wasn't surprised when it produced no light.

There were four closed doors off the hall. Kate opened the first and shone her torch into a large room, some kind of formal sitting room, tidy and furnished with good, solid old pieces. It looked as though no one had sat in it for years.

She tried the door at the back of the hall. A short passage led to a room which her nostrils told her was the kitchen. On a large pine table, among stacks of unopened *Farmers' Weeklys*, there was an old oil lamp with a box of Swan Vestas beside it. Kate lifted the glass, turned up the wick and lit it. In the more general glow that it cast, she saw a bowl of rotting fruit and a loaf of bread that was growing a thick coat of grey-green woolly mould.

Wrinkling her nose, Kate carried the oil lamp with

7

her back to the hall. The silence and the lack of response were beginning to make her jumpy again. She tried another door, this time opening on to a flight of steep, narrow stairs. She called out again, not really hoping for a reply, and, summoning all her courage, started up the creaking steps.

They led her to a wide, bare-boarded landing. Ten feet from the top of the stairs, in a heap of crumpled old pyjamas and a threadbare dressing gown, a very old man lay curled up like a baby.

Kate's heart thumped as she took a few steps towards him. Holding the lamp high, she looked down at a small, white face then she jerked backwards, transfixed by the face's expression cast in complete and utter terror.

Holding her breath, Kate knelt down to listen. Not a whisper of air escaped the wrinkled, slightly parted lips. Trying to control her fear and revulsion, she stretched out a hand to touch the white forehead. It was dry and as cold as stone.

Kate snatched back her hand and wiped it on her jeans. In twenty-six years of rural life, she had never seen a human corpse at first hand. This one certainly hadn't died peacefully. As she looked closer, she noticed the purple-brown bruises round the loose-skinned turkey neck. Her heart missed a beat.

Instinctively, she glanced over her shoulder with wide horrified eyes in the lamplight, although she knew that the man must have died hours, days before, and the killer would be long gone.

She scrambled to her feet, tilting the lamp in her haste. The glass fell to the floor and shattered, snuffing the light as it fell. The torch and the matches were in the kitchen. Kate stood rooted to the ground in panic and total darkness. Clenching her fists she

8

tried to pull herself together.

She forced herself to breathe normally. When she was ready, she felt her way back to the top of the stairs. She stopped and listened, ignoring the calm voice of logic trying to tell her that no one would still be in the house. She forced herself down the narrow stairs and groped her way into the kitchen, to the table where she had left her torch. Gasping aloud with relief, she found it and flicked it on.

Nervously, she flashed it around the filthy room, vaguely looking for a telephone. She must get someone up here, quick—the police, anyone, to deal with the wrinkled, strangled corpse upstairs.

She began to search in earnest but she couldn't find a phone in any of the downstairs rooms. She couldn't bear to go upstairs again. Maybe the old man simply didn't have a phone. She went outside into the still drizzling night and shone her torch around the gables of the house. There wasn't a sign of an incoming telephone line. She'd have to go for help. But where? Drive to Marlborough, or find a phone-box?

There must be someone living near enough to have heard the distressed bullocks and alerted the police. She ran out of the yard and looked south, down the hill towards the river valley. At the bottom of a grass field was a belt of woodland and through it, like a beacon of welcome, glowed a light from a cottage window.

She clambered over a gate into the field. She slithered down the wet grassy hillside, unconcerned about scratches and bruises as she slipped and stumbled between thistles and molehills.

It was further than it looked, five or six hundred yards, and when she reached the bottom, she had to get herself over a barbed wire fence between the

9

pasture and the woods beyond. Panting, scratched and soaked to her skin, she pushed her way through a thicket of rhododendron until she reached a clearing in the birch wood where the cottage stood.

She had approached it from the back where there was no entrance. She ran round, found the front door and rapped a tattoo on it.

A moment later it was opened by a small, neat woman who looked with alarm at the soaking, bedraggled young woman on her doorstep.

Kate gasped with relief at the sight of a kind, normal-looking woman, not unlike her own mother. 'I'm so sorry to burst in on you like this, but I need to phone the police.'

'My goodness! You'd better come in.' The woman opened the door wider and beckoned Kate. 'What's happened? Are you all right? Is someone after you?'

'No, no. I've just come from the farm at the top of the hill. There's no phone. I found the farmer there. He's dead. I think someone killed him!'

'What? Old Cyril Barton at Lodge Farm?' The shock in the woman's voice conveyed that she'd known him.

Kate nodded urgently. 'Yes. I nearly fell over him lying there. Please, let me use your phone.'

They were in a small, brightly lit hallway. As Kate was speaking, a door opened and a tall, grey-haired man in his sixties appeared. 'What's happened?'

'Oh, David. This girl's found Cyril Barton dead in his house. She thinks he's been murdered!'

'Why do you think that?' the man asked without any sign of panic or alarm.

'He's just lying on the landing, in his pyjamas ... It's the look on his face, and there are horrible bruises on his neck.'

10

The man nodded. 'Right. Don't worry. I'll call the police.'

He went back into the room he'd come from. Kate and the woman listened through the open door while he gave an operator precise details and directions to the farm.

When he had put the phone down, the woman asked Kate if she would like anything—a hot drink, a change of clothes?

'No. I need to get back up there. I was called in to check the animals. Someone complained.'

The woman nodded. 'That was me. I should have gone up to check first, but my husband wasn't here.'

'I've dealt with most of them but on my way down here I thought I heard something in the field—a horse cantering around making a fuss. I didn't see it, but I really ought to check. None of the animals had been fed or watered for days as far as I could tell.'

'I'll run you back up there,' the man offered.

'That would be great. Thanks.' Kate had been having serious second thoughts about going back on her own.

When they were in his car, the man told her he was called David Patterson and that he and his wife, Pru, stayed in the cottage most weekends.

'I'm Kate Scanlan. I run the NOWARC centre.'

'Who called you in?'

'The RSPCA. They hadn't anyone spare.'

'And you dealt with the animals before you went looking for the farmer?'

'Yes. They were making such a racket when I got there, I had to get on with it. Besides, there weren't any lights on in the house. But I went to look for the owner, to give him a piece of my mind.'

'That must have been quite a shock for you.'

11

'God, yes. I've never seen a corpse before and I'm sure he was murdered.'

'So you said.'

Kate considered what the man had said. She was struck by his lack of any sense of crisis. There was a certain confidence about him, yet his eyes were cold as ice.

'You're not a policeman of some sort, are you?'

'No, though I was a soldier once. This won't be the first time I've seen a corpse.'

When they reached the farmhouse, a mile or so by road and track, Kate didn't want to go in again. 'I really just want to see what's in that lower field. Do you think you could wait up here while I have a look around?'

'Of course. Do you want me to come with you?'

'No, that's okay. It shouldn't take long to see if there's anything there.'

She didn't relish the thought of wandering around an unfamiliar field in the rain on a pitch dark night, but knowing this very calm ex-soldier was watching, she felt happier about it.

She found a rope in the big barn and clambered back over the gate. She cast her torch around the field. It wasn't large, six or seven acres, and hedged with untrimmed hawthorn.

She had been right. Within minutes, she picked out the shape of a nervous horse with a tattered jute rug half twisted under its belly. Using all her skill and persuasion, she managed to get near enough to loop the rope round its neck. Close to, she saw that the animal, although it was muddy and out of condition, was an obviously well-bred mare. Looking at the shivering horse, Kate decided to bring it in out of the cold for the night. She could have a proper look at it

in the morning. The mare fretted and ⌐⌐⌐⌐ ⌐⌐
unwilling at first to come, but Kate gently le⌐⌐⌐
to the yard and into the stable next to the c⌐⌐⌐
calf.

David Patterson was waiting by the gate. 'Well done! Can I do anything to help?'

'No, thanks. If there are any more out there it's too bloody bad.' She settled the horse on to some clean straw, filled its water trough and stuffed a hay net. As she came out, the shrill wail of a police siren was carried up on the breeze. A moment later a blue light flashed round the bend in the track.

'Do you want me to stay around while they deal with the old boy?' Patterson asked.

'Would you? That'd be great. I've got to get back and change out of these clothes.'

'You'd better just stop and tell them how you found him, then I'm sure they'll let you go.'

*   *   *

'Who was the old geezer, then?' Jason asked from the back of Kate's Renault.

'A farmer called Cyril Barton. Lived alone in the farmhouse. Really squalid.' The cloud and rain from the previous night had completely blown away. Kate was peering into the rising sun ahead. Although she'd found it in the dark the night before, it would be easy to miss the narrow turning up to the farm.

'How big's his place?' Darren in the passenger seat beside her asked. He came from a farming family himself—measured people by their acreage.

'Not much. Thirty, forty acres, maybe. I went round one of his fields with a torch last night. Most of the animals were already in, but I found a lovely mare

13

ull out.'

Jason and Darren were on a work experience scheme at the Rescue Centre. Kate had brought them along to help with the feed bags and to make up the animals' bedding.

'Who rang up, then?' Jason asked.

'His nearest neighbour. She told the police she could hear some cattle bellowing. They rang Dick Stanley, and he rang me.'

'Did you go up on your own, then?'

'Yes,' Kate nodded.

'And you found the old boy, like?'

'Yes, I did,' she said with a shudder.

'Bloody hell! Wasn't you scared?'

'Of course I was—bloody terrified. I've never seen a real live corpse before.'

Jason laughed. 'Well, you wouldn't, would you,' he said, labouring the joke. 'What did he look like?'

'Like a piece of wrinkly old putty. I touched his face to make sure he was dead. It was all cold and dry. Ughhh.' Kate spotted the old sign to Lodge Farm and turned on to the muddy cinder track, driving carefully over the ruts. They rounded a corner and she had her first daylight view of the farmhouse and its outbuildings.

'Is that it?' Darren asked. 'What a dump!' Darren's grandparents lived in a similar house; most of their lives they had looked forward to moving into a tidy little bungalow.

'It's got loads of character—three or four hundred years old, I should think,' Kate said. 'It could be really nice with a bit of money spent on it.' She hoped she'd end up in a place like this.

They reached the top of the track where a pair of lopsided gateposts with no gate marked the entrance

14

to the yard. On the far side, the house loomed with its back to the sun.

Kate turned off the engine. She and the two boys got out into a deep rural silence. Even now, at the start of a bright winter's morning, there was an eerie, other-worldliness about the buildings.

Jason shivered. 'What a creepy place. When's this vet coming?'

'He should have been here by now,' Kate said. She had phoned Mike Pengelly before she left at eight that morning, and he had less far to come. 'Anyway, we'd better get on with it. Start with watering them. It's a tap and bucket job, I'm afraid; there's nothing reaching the valves in the troughs.'

The rasping bark of the arthritic dog echoed from the big barn on their left. This was joined by the furious bellow of one of the bullocks. Jason jumped. 'Christ! He sounds pissed off.'

'Start with him, then,' Kate said. 'There's the tap, by the back door.'

Jason nodded and walked off to quench the thirst of the angry bullock.

Kate told Darren to unload the bags of cattle feed, corn and beet they had brought up from the centre while she made a more thorough search for food among all the buildings, under every lean-to and tarpaulin. She found nothing. She was surprised. She had expected to find something special for the horse, at least. She had been impressed by it, even in the dark and covered in mud. It was unusual for anyone with quality horses not to look after them.

Kate shrugged philosophically. After two years at the refuge, she had seen more than enough evidence of people's callousness and stupidity where livestock were concerned. She would arrange transport for all

15

the animals to the centre later that day. In the meantime, they'd get as good a feed as she could give them.

She walked into the smaller barn. The cow looked up brightly. Darren had already refilled her trough and manger and the calf was on its feet, sucking happily. Kate smiled at the fruits of their efforts. 'Well done, Darren. They're looking a lot happier than they were last night. Have you had a look at the mare yet?'

'I have. I've done her water but she still looks miserable.'

Jason and Kate walked across to the box which contained the mare. She gave them a wary glance and carried on pacing around the box, apparently anxious and distressed.

'I wonder what's wrong with her,' Kate said.

'Maybe she's missing a friend,' Darren suggested.

Kate looked at him sharply. She knew from experience that his intuition as far as animals were concerned was highly developed and often right.

'But there weren't any other horses around last night.'

'It was dark, wasn't it, and you didn't check all the fields.'

'I was going to have another look this morning anyway. We'll do it now.'

Kate and the two boys walked out into the yard. Kate sent the boys to look down the hill and headed for the field above the house. When she reached the gate, she clambered over the five bars into a four-acre meadow hemmed in by a ragged hawthorn hedge. The grass was well-grazed but dotted with patches of docks and nettles. At first glance it appeared empty. She walked along the hedgerow, looking for holes or

16

gaps. But despite its unruly appearance, it was well wired. At the first corner there was a ditch, damp at the bottom. Kate worked her way along it, parting the lower branches where they were splayed across it. She found an abandoned plough and a few oil drums, but no sign of a horse.

She approached the next corner where a group of pollarded willows marked a larger watercourse. The ditch widened to meet a permanent stream which ran off the chalky downland behind. Water had backed up to make a patch of boggy ground between two fallen willow boughs which had sprouted new wands of their own. On the far side of the ditch the mud was churned up and there were long marks where horse's hooves had slithered and dug in. Beyond it, a rotten post and wire fence lay flat on the ground.

Kate drew in a breath and looked at the uninviting muddy slope.

'Katie, come quick! For God's sake!'

She turned sharply and looked back towards the gate by the house.

Darren was standing on a lower bar, waving frantically. Kate set off at a run across the meadow. When she reached the gate, Darren was hopping around on the other side of the yard at the entrance to the lower field. When she caught up with him, she found she was in the field she'd run through in the dark the night before. It was below the one she'd been searching, with the fallen fence visible at the top of a steep slope. Darren headed for the lower corner where a drinking bay had been carved in the bank which dropped down towards the brook, partially hidden by a group of three whiskery old willows.

Only when Kate reached this crude access point to the stream could she see the young horse which had

17

become trapped there. The animal, no more than a yearling, had tangled its legs in two strands of barbed wire and the pig wire below it, which was intended to stop any animals wandering off up the brook. The posts had collapsed and left the wire suspended a few inches off the ground.

Kate slithered down the muddy ramp. As she came within a few yards of it, the horse panicked. The whites of its eyes rolled up, its ears flattened down its neck and it struggled frantically to release itself.

Kate stopped short and stood a few feet away, talking gently, trying to calm it. Darren watched with admiration from the top of the ramp, impressed by Kate's capacity for winning the animal's trust with just a few words. When he had tried to get near it, the creature had flailed around so that it was now held even tighter by the brutal wire.

Kate could see fresh blood oozing over the congealed remains from the savage lacerations in the fine-boned legs. The young horse stopped thrashing long enough to let Kate lean forward and offer her hand. Its ears twitched forward tentatively and its large eyes settled in their sockets. Kate moved another couple of inches and softly stroked its nose with the tips of her fingers.

Ignoring a thick layer of sticky mud on the ramp, Kate settled on her haunches to talk to the horse where it lay on its side. She was grateful for the sunshine; waiting for the animal to trust her sufficiently to let her unravel the wire round its leg could take a long time.

Slowly, she eased herself down the slope towards the brook and the collapsed wire fence. She could see that the horse had somehow got its leg between the two barbed strands and, hopping around, had put a

18

slender hoof through two squares of pig wire, tightening it every time it struggled.

Kate turned to Darren who'd been joined by Jason and was still watching from the top of the ramp. 'One of you go and see if you can find some wire cutters. And bring some feed.'

Jason ran up the field and came back a few minutes later with a pair of sharp edge pliers. 'These should do the job,' he said, panting, and slid them down the slope, along with a scoop of horse nuts, to where Kate was still comforting the young horse. She picked them up, let the youngster nuzzle a few nuts, then, taking her time, she began a continuous rubbing motion with her hand over the soft brown hair of the horse's neck. Gradually, Kate worked down to the shoulder, flanks and finally to where its hind legs were trapped. All the time she talked, gaining the horse's confidence. Each time she felt it resist her hand moving to a new part of its body, she'd move backwards and start again.

There was a lot of tension in the barbed wire. Somehow she would have to move the animal back down towards the brook to slacken it and avoid the wire whiplashing as soon as she cut it. Slowly, by heaving gently, she eased the horse down until there was no strain in the wire. She cut the first barbed strand as close to the leg as she could. The horse flinched as a loose end scratched its leg. The second strand came free as easily but whichever way they moved, the pig wire was still tight round the fragile limb.

Kate decided to cut through from the top of the fence, four strands away, to give a clear opening for the horse to remove its leg.

She had cut through the first two when a pheasant,

lying low in the dead bracken on the far side of the brook, abruptly decided it had taken enough risks for one day. With a clatter of wings it launched itself from the cover into the air while its frantic honking ricocheted through the still morning air. In its eagerness to get away from the alarming disturbance, the horse tried to propel itself up the ramp with its three free legs. A flailing hind leg caught Kate a passing blow on the temple, knocked her off balance and sent her slithering down into the brook and three feet of icy water.

Ruefully, she heaved herself out, sodden, frozen and weak from the bang on her head. The horse had stopped thrashing, though, and this time it didn't take so long for Kate to talk it back into a state of calmness. Shivering now with cold and nausea, she worked her way through the rest of the pig wire. The last strand fell away and eased the tourniquet on the horse's leg. Kate could sense the animal beginning to realise that it was no longer constrained. When the knowledge had sunk in, it scrambled to its feet, slipping and sliding on the muddy ramp and barely able to make use of a weakened off-hind leg.

Kate left it to get up as best it could and shouted to the boys to give her some space. 'We'll catch her in a minute.'

The young horse scrabbled up the slope to the thick green grass of the paddock.

The two lads stepped aside and the filly trotted unevenly into the freedom of the big field while Kate painfully limped up.

'Nice looking filly,' Jason said.

'Yeah,' Kate panted. 'All yearlings look lovely. I just hope the wire hasn't done too much damage.'

'You reckon she's a yearling?'

'She's certainly too big to be this year's foal.'

'D'you think she's out of that mare, then?'

'More than likely. No doubt we'll find out. But it's going to be quite a job to get that leg right without any permanent damage. Look, she's hardly using it at all.'

'I think we should catch her now, before she runs around on it too long.'

'Yes. You're right. Go and see if you can find a head collar in one of the barns.'

Darren ran off as Jason and Kate slowly worked their way across the five-acre field to corner the nervous filly and keep her away from the damaged fence at the top.

They put the yearling in the box next to the mare. 'Keep an eye on her,' Kate told the boys. 'I'm going to see if I can find out who her dad is.' She left Jason and Darren and walked across to the house. It wasn't locked; no one had been able to find a key and the police hadn't been back to secure the place yet.

As the mare looked to be a thoroughbred, Kate thought it likely she'd been covered by a thoroughbred stallion. It would be interesting to know the father of the plucky yearling filly she'd rescued from the tangle of wire.

Kate quelled any guilt she might have felt about prying into a dead man's things as she rummaged through the piles of paper on the grimy old kitchen dresser and table. But she found nothing about the horse. She went into the front sitting room and plunged into a bureau crammed with dog-eared documents. This produced a horse's 'passport', which confirmed the registration of a mare at Wetherby's. It gave details of colouring and markings, including whorls, of a horse called Stella

21

Maris which matched the horse out in the stable. It showed that she was respectably bred by a very fast, flat-race stallion which had died some years before.

What Kate really wanted was some correspondence with a stud which would tell her the name of the sire of the filly.

Half an hour's search had produced nothing when she was interrupted by Mike Pengelly, the vet, arriving to keep his appointment with her.

Mike, dedicated, forty and innocently unaware of his own good looks, made a thorough examination of all the animals, beginning with the yearling, and pronounced them all in reasonable health. The damage to the filly's rear leg wasn't as bad as it looked though it still needed half a dozen stitches.

'I'll give her a tetanus,' Mike said as he worked, 'but keep your eye on it; keep it clean and keep her on the move to stop it swelling up. Insofar as I'm any judge of these things,' he added, standing up, 'she looks like a nice little filly.'

He and Kate stood in the box, gazing critically at the young horse. 'I'm a hopeless judge,' Kate admitted. She wrapped her arms round the animal's slender neck. 'All horses look wonderful to me at this age. I wonder why the old boy bred her. What was he going to do with her? And I wonder when she got caught in the wire. The police weren't sure how long the farmer had been dead. There's virtually no grass out in the meadows and there was practically nothing in here. I'm amazed they look as well as they do. By the way,' Kate went on, 'I tried to see if I could find out who the sire is, assuming the mare's her mother. But I couldn't find a thing.'

Mike Pengelly, used to Kate's seamless monologues, had crouched down to continue his

22

examination of the filly. He half turned and spoke over his shoulder. 'I dare say some paperwork will turn up sooner or later.' He ran his hand gently down the damaged leg. 'There'll be a bill from a stallion owner somewhere.'

'Maybe, but I'll have to find a home for all these animals and the executors will want to know we've got a fair price.'

'You'll definitely need details of paternity for that,' Mike said. 'But aren't there any relations to take them on?'

'No. According to the police, the only one they could trace was a niece who lives in Liverpool. Apparently she's coming down to identify the old boy formally, though she hasn't seen him for over fifteen years. He was a real old recluse. Even the neighbours didn't see him often and the house is like something out of *Cold Comfort Farm*.'

The vet stood up and stretched. He looked at the ill-kept, mouldering house and the buildings falling down around it. 'Not without a certain amount of charm. Certainly, no one could accuse it of being over-restored. How old was the farmer?'

'In his eighties, I think. Cyril Barton he was called.'

Mike chuckled. 'Cyril Barton, eh? I haven't heard of him for years. He used to be a bit of a force in pointing round here when I was a small boy. Fancy him still keeping brood mares. It's amazing how some people just can't kick the habit.'

'What habit's that?' It was a new voice, not one of the lads from Noah's Ark. Kate and Mike looked up. David Patterson, in a tweed jacket and burnished brown brogues, walked into the barn.

'Oh, hello, Mr Patterson. This is Mike Pengelly, the vet. We were just talking about racing. Mike was

23

saying Mr Barton was keen on it for years. He must have wanted to keep his hand in. We found this filly, tangled in wire down by the stream. I'm fairly sure she's out of the mare I found last night. Mike reckons she's pretty good.'

David Patterson walked over and looked at the quivering animal. He shrugged his shoulders. 'They all look the same to me, but what happens to them in circumstances like this?'

'Usually, after we've sorted them out, they ask us to find homes, or buyers for them if possible. This one might be worth a bit.'

'If you can discover her breeding,' Mike Pengelly interjected.

'I don't know if I'm talking out of turn, but my stepson is in the racing business, near here at Lambourn. He might be interested in the filly. Can I tell him to get in touch?'

Kate glanced at Mike. 'Why not? What's he called?'

'Charles ... Patterson, like me.'

'Tell him to ring me at NOWARC. He can come and have a look at her there if he likes. We're taking all the animals over today.'

'Right,' Patterson nodded. 'I will. Anything else I can do to help?'

'No, thanks. We're all under control here now.'

'Well, let me know if there is.' Patterson left the barn and they heard him start up his Mercedes and drive out of the yard.

'Funny him being Charlie Patterson's stepfather.'

'What about it? Do you know the son?'

'No, but I know his partner well.'

'Who's that?'

'A chap called Nick Ryder, cousin of mine.'

24

'What's his interest in horses?'

'He's an assistant trainer with Charlie at Robert Aylestone's yard. Racing mad.'

Kate, although not obsessed with racing, took an interest. Her parents were members at Newbury and had taken her regularly since she had been strong enough to hold a pair of binoculars.

'Robert Aylestone's not much of a recommendation.'

'No,' the vet agreed, 'but Nick and Charlie are trying to get some money and horses together to start their own yard. And as long as they're at Aylestone's, they'll learn a lot.'

This was true. Robert Aylestone had a fearsome reputation for gambling, among other vices, but at least he usually backed his own horses and knew how to get them to peak for the races which he cannily selected for them.

'Are they honest?' Kate asked, down-to-earth.

'I don't know about Charlie, but Nick certainly is. He'd be interested in the horses.'

'I can see why he might be in the yearling but what about the mare?'

'I think he'll like her. If he takes them, you can be sure they'll be well looked after and you could keep tabs on the filly if you wanted. You're obviously rather attached to her.'

'Okay,' Kate said. 'I'll let you know what's going to happen to them.'

Wistfully she watched Mike Pengelly go. Though he probably didn't know it, it was he who had originally inspired her to try to be a vet herself, but she'd got bogged down with all the science involved and given it up. He certainly didn't know that as far as she was concerned, he could do or say no wrong. If

Mike thought his chap Nick Ryder should have the horses, that was good enough for her.

* * *

It was a fortnight before the Rescue Centre heard from anyone about the dead farmer's animals. A solicitor in Marlborough telephoned to say that Mr Barton's sole heir, Mrs Cora Lenigan, would be coming to the refuge to see the animals and decide what to do with them.

Cora Lenigan arrived two days later. She had come by taxi from the solicitor's office in Marlborough. It was clear from the diffident way in which she dealt with the taxi driver that it wasn't a normal mode of transport for her.

Kate came out to greet her in the mild winter morning.

'Good morning, Mrs Lenigan. I'm Kate Scanlan.'

'Call me Cora, pet, or I'll feel like a granny.'

Kate smiled, liking the look of the woman and her lazy Liverpudlian drawl.

Cora gazed around at the sheds and compounds which held the various animals passing through the centre's hands. 'Which ones are mine?' she asked.

Kate took her on a short tour and showed her the dog, several cats, the cow and her calf, the ewes and their almost full-grown lambs and, finally, the horses which had come from Cyril Barton's farm.

'Crikey, they're big,' Cora said.

'She's a lovely filly,' Kate said enthusiastically.

'She certainly looks nice,' Cora said.

'You should keep her,' Kate said spontaneously. 'Put her in training yourself.'

'What? Me?' Cora laughed. 'I wouldn't know

26

anything about having racehorses. That's a bit out of my league. They wouldn't even let me have a budgie when I were a kid. It's going to be bad enough trying to get used to having a few bob when they sell that old house. It's funny really. I don't suppose I'd even thought of Uncle Cyril for months before the solicitor's letter came. And I'd never thought about him leaving anything to me—not that he did, really, he just never made a will and I'm the only relative he had left.' She shook her head with a slightly puzzled grin. She was evidently finding it difficult to come to terms with her good fortune. Kate liked her for that. 'You know what else is funny? You saying keep the racehorse when my husband, God rest him, Johnny Lenigan spent every penny he ever earned—and that weren't a lot—betting on horses that never won.'

'You're a widow, are you?'

Cora nodded. 'Johnny was a waster but he was a lovely bloke. He must be going mad up there, seeing me getting all this from Uncle Cyril when he can't get his hands on it,' she reflected without malevolence.

'Well, what would you like me to do with the animals?'

'Make sure they go to good homes.'

'That's no problem, Mrs Lenigan. If you don't want to keep them, we can arrange to sell them for you and certainly make sure they all go to good homes.'

'Would they be worth much?'

'Not the dog or the cats but we'll get a bit for the sheep, and the cattle might be worth a few hundred each; the horses a lot more probably. Of course you can always arrange for the lawyers to sell them for you.'

'Those slimy buggers? You must be joking. No, I

can see just from your face you wouldn't cheat me. You get what you can for 'em and let me know, okay, pet?'

CHAPTER TWO

'There's a gorgeous bloke here says he's come to look at your precious yearling,' Sandy bellowed across the yard at the Rescue Centre.

Kate glanced up, not expecting to share Sandy's eccentric opinion of their visitor's attractions but, she admitted to herself, the man strolling towards her with his hands in his pockets did have a particularly striking set of features.

He was in his late twenties, a shade over six foot, lean and energetic in a battered sheepskin jacket and a pair of faded jeans. Large pupils rimmed with blue in slightly short-sighted eyes gleamed a challenge from beneath a pair of dark brows. Kate sensed there was more than mere politeness in the smile that parted his well-shaped lips as he came up to her.

'Hello. Mike Pengelly told us about a yearling and a mare you've rescued.'

'Are you Nick Ryder?'

'No. I'm his partner, Charles Patterson. I think you met my stepfather.'

Kate nodded. 'Yes, I did.'

'Nick Ryder will be round later. He just asked me to have a look first.'

'As long as you know I'm supposed to dispose of these animals not only to good homes but at market price, and I promised the woman who owns them now that I'll get as much as I can, so I don't want any

28

clever tactics to keep the price down.'

Charles Patterson looked wounded. 'Do I look like the sort of man who'd do that?'

Kate appraised him frankly. 'I should think you're the sort of man who's used to getting away with plenty.'

Charles laughed. 'I'd better leave negotiations to Nick, then, but can I have a look at them now?'

'Okay.' Kate led him into the barn which held a dozen stables used to house the larger animals that passed through the centre. Cyril Barton's mare, Stella Maris, was looking out through the top door of the first box. Her ears pricked at the sight and sound of Kate and she willingly backed away from the door to allow her visitors in.

Charles raised an appreciative eyebrow. 'Mum looks quite useful. Did she ever race, do you know?'

'To tell you the truth, I haven't looked her up yet.'

Charles nodded his dark, curly head thoughtfully and turned his attention to the next box where the filly was poking her tiny nose through the bars, desperate for Kate's attention. He went in, knelt down and felt the slender legs, picked up the small hoofs and inspected them. He stood up to gaze without speaking at the nervous creature.

'Well?' Kate asked anxiously. 'What do you think of her?'

'I think she's a lovely filly. But then,' he turned to look at Kate, 'aren't they all?'

'But you're in the racing business. You're supposed to be able to judge.'

'Judging a yearling tends to be a matter of guesswork. Especially,' he added, 'when you only know half the parentage. As you may know, you can't race a horse without a thoroughbred pedigree.

Of course, if we wanted to take it eventing it wouldn't be a problem.'

'Don't worry. Cora, the farmer's niece, found the invoice. Apparently she's by quite a good jumping stallion called Nunsfield.'

'Is she?' Charles was impressed. Nunsfield had been a Group Class stayer on the flat and had sired plenty of good jump winners.

'The problem is,' Kate said, 'it looks as though Cyril Barton never paid the stud fee. There's four thousand pounds to pay.'

'That takes the gilt off it a bit,' Charles said flatly.

Kate looked crestfallen. 'But surely, if that was the stallion's fee, she must be worth at least that.'

Charles laughed. ''Fraid not. Nothing's as simple as that in bloodstock breeding. The quality of the mare and the animal itself are just as important, some would say a lot more. But don't look so worried. This filly's a nice enough looking animal, well worth a second look,' he said, genuinely appreciative and unconcerned that the smile on his face might adversely affect his bargaining stance. 'What happened to the leg?' he asked.

Kate was standing behind him. 'I found her with it tangled up in wire.' Charlie smiled at the compassion in her voice but he didn't let her see. 'It was quite badly cut,' she went on, 'but Mike Pengelly did a good job on it.'

'This was how long ago?'

'Just over two weeks.'

Charles crouched down to run his hand over the leg where it was still scarred below the hock. He nodded. 'I think it's probably over the worst.' He straightened his legs and looked at Kate with shining eyes. 'If you don't want too much for her, we'll have

30

her.'

'What are you offering?'

Charles grinned again. 'Steady. I thought we'd agree that Nick would talk terms. I'll tell him what I think, then he can deal with you.'

'What about the mare?'

'Maybe we could do a package deal, but you'll have to appreciate that it may not be much more than the outstanding stallion fee. You'd better talk to the executors, though I'm sure we'll offer you as good a price as anyone. I'll look the mare up; see what she's done and if she's ever bred anything.'

*   *   *

When Nick Ryder came to the centre next morning, Kate couldn't imagine him and Charles Patterson as friends. Nick appeared to have none of Charles's self-assurance, none of the charm or infectious cheerfulness. He was the same age as Charles, but his brown hair was already thinning, and the old-fashioned spectacles he wore did nothing to enhance his plain features. But he shook her hand with a firmness which surprised her.

She looked at him. Perhaps there was hidden substance beneath the diffident exterior.

He examined the yearling, registering no reaction. He spoke little and without embellishment. 'Have you any idea what she's worth?'

Kate shrugged, and plucked a figure from the air. 'Fifteen thousand?'

'Fifteen thousand?' Nick raised his eyebrows with no sense of aggression. 'But I understand that there's a stud fee of four thousand to be settled.'

'I meant fifteen thousand including that.'

31

'I see. I'm afraid the best we could offer is ten, all in. Her mum was only a moderate race mare and, according to the stud, this is her first foal.'

'But that only leaves six to the estate.'

'I know,' Nick said apologetically, 'and it's probably the best offer you'll get. I'm only making it because Charlie's very keen on her.' He shrugged. 'I can see you're disappointed. I'm sorry.'

'It doesn't really matter. It's not my money, but I just feel she's special.'

'I've seen dozens of better bred horses knocked down in the auction ring for a thousand or two. It's heartbreaking for the breeders, but dealing in young stock is subject to market forces, pure and unadulterated. I tell you what; as you're so keen on the animal, we'll grant you permanent visiting rights, as long as she's in our yard.'

Kate perked up. 'Where is your yard?'

'Ah.' Nick glanced away then back again. 'There's the rub. We haven't got one yet. We're both still working for Robert Aylestone, until we've got enough money together.'

'But how are you going to pay for the filly?'

'Charlie will think of something, or so he says,' Nick added with a shake of his head, and Kate liked him for his honesty and for his loyalty to his friend, obviously against his better judgement.

'Okay,' she said. 'Provided I always know where she is. It was me who actually rescued her. She was stuck so tight in some wire that she wouldn't have got out in a month, and her owner had died, and she was in a field miles from anywhere, up above Ramsbury.'

'So I hear. I'd say that definitely entitles you to special visiting rights.' Nick smiled at last. 'I promise we'll keep you posted. If she's any good, we'll be

32

training her ourselves next year.'

'She'll be brilliant,' Kate said.

'Maybe, but we'll still only pay ten for her.'

Kate looked resigned, though privately she was delighted to have got so good a price; she was relieved, too, that it was Nick and Charles who were taking the filly; she knew she'd enjoy seeing them both again. 'What about the mare?' she asked.

Nick shrugged apologetically. 'Unless you wanted to throw her in, we haven't got any more money to spend.'

'Oh well,' Kate said, making up her mind. 'I think I can get her sorted out all right.'

*   *   *

Charles Patterson—Charlie to his friends and thousands of punters who had followed his successful amateur riding career—came out of the long left-handed bend at Worcester racecourse and gave his reins a sharp tug. The big old gelding beneath him shortened his stride for a couple of paces and met the open ditch just right, standing back from it, gaining half a length in the air on the horse in front.

There were three more plain fences to jump in the final straight before the winning post. Charlie knew if he wanted to win he mustn't let his horse get its nose in front until the last moment or it would pull itself up. He had carefully saved the animal's speed for the last half-furlong of the run in. He had no doubt that the very amateur rider on the horse in front had already squeezed every bit of energy he could from his splendid old campaigner. He was happy to close the five-length gap which still separated them stride by stride until they were well beyond the final fence.

33

Charlie didn't need his whip. The old horse knew it was time to go, and he went, until he had his head in front a few yards before the post.

Charlie slowed to a trot and slackened to a walk as the favourite he'd just beaten jogged up beside him. Charlie turned to the other jockey. 'Sorry to sneak up on you like that,' he said with a grin. 'But it's the only way I can get this old bugger to win.'

The other jockey gave him a sour smile and said nothing. He wasn't looking forward to the greeting he would get from his father who'd paid well over the odds for a horse to give his son a win.

Charlie, on the other hand, could not have had a more exuberant greeting from his trainer, who was also his boss.

Robert Aylestone was a good trainer, no one denied that, but he was incurably devious. He had marred his reputation and discouraged a lot of otherwise admiring owners with his persistent urge to beat the bookies whenever an opportunity presented itself. As far as he was concerned, a hunter chase at an evening meeting at Worcester was as good an opportunity as any. The horse had been entered as trained by his permit-holding brother-in-law, but it was Robert who had got him right and knew when he would perform. Charlie was always going to give the gelding a good ride; he had the experience and the talent.

Robert Aylestone limped on the ankle he'd broken in a fall twenty years before, barely conscious of the residual pain as he stretched up to take the gelding's reins.

'Well done, Charlie! You rode that perfect! I'll have a little present for you later, after I've collected.'

Charlie wasn't going to say no to some cash, but

34

what Aylestone seemed unable to grasp was that he would have ridden the race exactly the same without any inducement or reward, because he liked to win. At least, Charlie thought, Aylestone had never been stupid enough to ask him *not* to win.

Charlie drove the lorry back to Lambourn with Kenny, the lad who had brought the gelding and another runner to Worcester that evening. Aylestone had gone off for a drink with his brother-in-law.

'The guv'nor won't be out first lot tomorrow,' Kenny remarked drily as they left the lorry park.

Charlie laughed. 'He doesn't usually let a hangover stop him.'

'No, but he'll have a hell of a hangover tomorrow. D'you know how much he had on that horse?'

'Nope.'

'Well, how much did he give you?'

'Actually, I haven't looked yet. Fifty or a hundred, I should think.' Charlie felt his pocket for a crumpled envelope. Aylestone had handed it to him in the lorry, with instructions to 'Have a drink on me, Charlie'. Charlie squeezed it between his fingers and grinned. 'Unless it's old one pound notes, you're right. He must have had a monster punt. This'll come in handy for our new yard fund.'

'How's that going?' Kenny asked.

'Slowly. But don't you worry, we'll have got enough together by the end of the year.'

'D'you still want to train flat horses?'

'Yes. That's what I've always wanted to do, since I was about twelve. Of course, it's trickier than trying to get going with a jumping yard, but I want to deal in the cream.'

'You should be so lucky,' Kenny laughed. 'But I'll still come with you. I don't know how long I could stick it with old Aylestone, the bad-tempered sod. Did you go and see that yearling at the animal rescue place?'

Charlie smiled as he remembered the guileless, flawless features of the Rescue Centre's manager, and her pleasure at their decision to take the filly. Of course, ten grand was plenty for a Nunsfield filly, but in all the big yearling sales Charlie had attended, this one would have fetched at least what they had offered. But the sales were over and that option was no longer available to Cyril Barton's executors.

'We did,' he told Kenny. 'All we've got to do now is find the money to pay for her.'

'What do you want to go buying yearlings for before you've even got a yard?'

'I just liked her. She's a lovely looking filly, already got plenty of back end. Her sire and both her grandsires were good winners. Her dam wasn't much, but she looks useful.'

'Who's the filly by?'

'Nunsfield.'

'But he's a bloody jumping stallion!' Kenny scoffed. 'I thought you wanted flat horses.'

Charlie laughed at Kenny's scorn. 'We do, and this one's dam line is all sprinters. Mike Pengelly told me the old boy who bred her always put sprinting dams to long-distance sires, and you don't get much more long-distance than Nunsfield. But this particular individual has all the characteristics of a sprinter. Anyway, wait till you've seen her before you start criticising.'

Kenny grinned. 'All right, all right.' He was the first to admit that Charlie had an eye. Besides, he certainly didn't want to be in Aylestone's yard after Charlie and Nick had gone.

36

Charlie and Nick had a room each in a cottage on the outskirts of Lambourn. Their landlady was unashamedly fascinated by their private lives, especially Charlie's. She had a clear view now, through the window of her sitting room, of the young woman walking up the path to the front door.

'Never make one of them supermodels,' she observed to herself. 'Bit too well-covered and too short, but fresh enough to get most young men excited.' There was an assertive jauntiness in the way the girl had opened the gate and walked which the old lady behind the curtain knew would appeal to her good-looking tenant.

Kate shook her short mop of glossy black hair from her round face and rang the doorbell. The old lady was there to open it almost at once.

'Oh, hello,' the girl said in a light, husky voice. 'Does Nick Ryder live here?'

'Oh,' the old lady said before she could hide her surprise. 'You've come to see Nick, have you?'

'Who else would I have come to see then?'

'Mr Patterson, I thought.'

Kate's expression became evasive. 'He lives here too, does he?'

'Do you know him?' the old lady asked.

'We've met,' Kate said curtly, in a way which made the woman think that next time she came round, she'd be asking for Charlie.

'Mr Nick's room is at the top of the stairs and turn right. They're not really allowed females in their rooms but as it's so early . . .' She waved Kate towards a narrow staircase whose walls were crammed with shelves of accumulated mementos and gifts from

37

previous tenants.

Kate hadn't stepped through the front door but she could already guess how this household was run. She shook her head. 'It's okay. Just tell him I'm at the pub, and I'll see him there.'

She had ordered herself a pint of cider when Nick came in. He was with a young golden Labrador, apparently fixed by some invisible means to a point two feet behind his heels. Nick was full of apologies about his landlady.

Kate laughed. 'I'm sure she thought I'd come round to have it off with you.' She watched with guilty satisfaction as Nick blushed.

'Would you like a drink?' he mumbled.

'I've already got one, thanks.'

'Oh, so you have. I'll just get one for me and Hercules.' Nick went to the bar and came back with a pint of beer for himself and bowl of water which he put on the floor for his dog. He turned to Kate. 'It's more likely that my landlady thought you'd come round to have it off with Charlie.'

'As a matter of fact, I think she did at first. That's what I objected to most.'

'Charlie's okay,' Nick said, evidently in the habit of defending his friend.

'How long have you known each other?'

'Since we were thirteen. I was always the brains and he was the brawn. We make a good team.'

'You don't need brawn now, though, do you?'

'No, but the confidence that goes with it is useful. Anyway,' he went on, 'have you spoken to this woman about our offer for the filly?'

'Yes. That's why I'm here. She says that's fine, and so do the executors. You have to pay them. I've got the address here and an official bill of sale.' She

38

handed him an envelope.

'Great,' said Nick. 'Now all we have to do is find someone to pay for it.'

'What?' Kate said, alarmed. 'You mean you can't?'

'No. I told you, we're trying to get enough money together to set up our own yard. Don't worry, Charlie's pretty sure his stepfather will take her on.'

'Major Patterson, you mean? God, I hope so, now I've persuaded everybody it's a fair price.'

'A fair price,' Nick protested. 'Over the odds, if you ask me.'

'Have you thought about naming her yet?' Kate asked.

'Not really. There didn't seem much point until the deal was done.'

'Well, now it is, do you mind if I make a few suggestions?'

At that moment, Hercules leaped to his feet and waved his long feathery tail across the table, sweeping a small tin ashtray to the ground with a clatter and knocking Kate's glass so that only her swift reaction and nimble fingers stopped it from smashing on to the stone floor. She glanced up with annoyance to see what had caused Hercules's excitement.

'Ah,' Nick followed her glance. 'Here's Charlie.'

Kate took a deep breath and looked down at the table as Charlie made his way across the bar, acknowledging greetings on the way. He nodded at Nick and smiled at Kate's head.

'Hello, Kate. I take it this isn't a social visit.'

Kate lifted her head. Her eyes met his with chilly reserve.

Charlie took it in his stride. He didn't know why some women took this line with him, but when they

39

did, he found that the less he worried about it, the sooner it softened. And in Kate Scanlan's case, he felt, the sooner the better.

'No, purely business,' Kate answered.

'Okay,' Charlie nodded. 'Do we get the yearling?'

'Once Cyril Barton's executors have the money.'

Charlie was standing opposite her now. 'I've been working on that. Can I get you another drink? Nick, are you having one?'

When they all had full glasses in front of them on the battered oak cricket table, Nick asked Charlie how he had got on in the race at Worcester.

'I managed to get the old boy's nose in front a few inches from the line. I didn't give him enough time to realise he was there until we'd passed the post.'

'Charlie rode in a hunter chase today,' Nick explained to Kate. 'The horse hates being in front, so you have to time your run exactly right.'

'Well done,' Kate said flatly, refusing to be impressed.

'The horse is a brilliant jumper, hardly needs any help at all and he can still produce a turn of speed after three miles,' Charlie said, disowning any credit for the win. He turned to Nick. 'Aylestone had a serious punt.'

With a faint nod, Nick acknowledged what Charles was saying, but he didn't ask for more details. 'Kate was wondering,' he said, 'if she could help us choose a name for the filly.'

'My father won't want the hassle,' Charlie agreed.

'Is he definitely buying her then?' Nick asked.

'Oh yes. I haven't had a chance to tell you. He phoned at lunchtime to ask me who he had to pay.'

'Great,' Nick said with undisguised relief. 'He was bloody surly when I last phoned. Anyway, here's the

40

invoice and all the details.'

Charlie picked up the paperwork and leafed through it. 'I'm sorry he still gives you such a hard time,' he sighed. 'You'd have thought by now he'd have accepted we've been friends for fifteen years. I wish I knew why he found it so hard to be polite to you. You're not alone, though, if that's any consolation. Right.' Charlie turned his attention to the filly's pedigree. 'The mare's called Stella Maris, isn't she?'

Kate nodded. 'Star of the Sea.'

'And you found the filly, didn't you?'

'Yes, trapped by a stream below a stand of old willows.'

'Something to do with the willows, then, or water?' Nick suggested.

'How about Pussy Willow?' Charlie said with a grin.

Kate looked at him with a dismissive toss of her head. 'I don't think so. What about Star something, after her mother?'

'Star Pussy?' Charlie suggested.

Kate ignored him. 'Why don't we call her Willow Star?'

'Sounds a bit corny,' Charlie said.

'But it rather suits her,' Nick answered thoughtfully. 'And anyway, Kate found her, so let her decide.'

'Willow Star it is, then,' Kate said. 'Even sounds like a Guineas winner.'

'An Oaks winner,' Charlie laughed. 'No. Wrong tree.'

'Here's to her, then.' Nick raised his pint of murky bitter. 'To Willow Star, the founding member of the Ryder-Patterson yard.'

41

Kate and Charlie joined the toast and there was a moment's silent harmony.

*   *   *

'Morning, Dad,' Charlie said cheerfully into the phone. 'We've named this filly for you. All we need now is your cheque.'

After only a moment's hesitation, David Patterson answered. 'Yes, of course, as you still seem determined to set up your own place. But don't go away with the idea that I'm going to buy every horse in the yard for you, if you ever get it. By the way, you'll have to make arrangements for the filly until she's ready to come to you.'

'No problem. We'll have our own yard any time now.'

'And how are you going to pay for it?' Patterson asked warily.

'We'll think of something,' Charlie said. He realised he wasn't going to get any more backing from his stepfather. Perhaps it had been a mistake to use up what good will there was from that source on a damaged, unproven filly. But it was too late to change tack now. 'I've got an invoice from Noah's Ark, on behalf of Barton's executors. I'll send it on to you today. Listen, Dad, I really am very grateful to you.'

'I'm glad to hear it,' Patterson replied drily. 'I'll leave the rest of the arrangements to you.'

'Fine. I'll look after all the paperwork. By the way, how's Mother?'

'Oh, fine. Busy with her charity work. She's taken up visiting people in prison again.'

'Has she? Why?'

42

'I'm not entirely sure. You'll have to ask her. She runs a writing class, says it's good for them, gets things out of their systems.'

'And what do you think?'

'Don't ask.' Major Patterson didn't expand.

Charlie knew better than to expect him to. His mother had always thrown herself into any good deeds that were there for the doing. Charlie suspected it was out of a perverse guilt caused by her husband's lack of overt affection. He wished his stepfather a brief goodbye and put the phone down.

Nick was standing beside him. 'Well?'

'He says he'll do it, but he didn't sound as enthusiastic as I'd hoped.'

'Can he put his hands on ten grand easily?' Nick asked.

'Yes, I'm sure he can. He's just naturally very cagey. He's never told me anything about his affairs, but I think he's made a fair bit of money in his time. Especially when he was out in the Middle East.'

'After he left the army?'

Charlie nodded. 'He was on a massive tax-free salary out there.'

Nick pondered this. 'I suppose if he wasn't spending much, it could have grown quite impressively. But when I last saw him, in that shop of his in Kensington, he didn't strike me as being all that happy about business.'

'It's his habit not to strike anyone as being all that interested in anything. At least he's agreed to buy this filly. I just hope we can win a race with her.'

43

CHAPTER THREE

'Do you know,' Nick said, leaning on a paddock rail, gazing fondly at Willow Star, 'I think we were mad to persuade your father to buy her but I'm bloody glad we did.'

Charlie, beside him, nodded. 'Yes. I think he's got himself a bit of a bargain.'

With the right diet and a bit of tender loving care, the handsome filly had thrived. Ivor Thompson, an old and well-respected trainer who was fond of both Nick and Charlie, had agreed to let them lodge their filly with him for a few weeks while they nursed her back to health and broke her in during their spare time—not that Robert Aylestone allowed them much free time these days. Ivor was sure that Aylestone suspected something and was making it as difficult as possible for either of them to fly the nest.

Robert Aylestone, short of really top-class horses, relied heavily on his skill in choosing the right races for his eighty charges. He had managed to come fifth in the National Hunt trainers' league table the previous season with eighty-five winners. He owed this comparative success in no small way to the dedication of his young assistants. Charlie had helped further by riding eleven hunter chase winners for the yard.

Aylestone had also pulled off a couple of large gambling coups and the partners had discreetly ridden on his coat tails. Charlie and Nick had managed to scrape up winnings and savings now amounting to a little over ten thousand pounds. Although this was a fraction of what they needed to start up their own yard, Ivor Thompson had assured them that his attractive set of racing stables on the edge of Upper Lambourn would be available whenever they needed it. The partners were now determined to get in there by February at the latest for the following flat season, with as many horses as they could muster.

Charlie and Nick could see the yard across the meadow where Willow Star was grazing in a borrowed rug.

'Has Ivor come back with a price yet?' Charlie asked Nick.

'Yes. It's fair enough. Thirty grand a year for the yard and these twenty acres. He's staying in the house but we can use the bungalow—the lads' hostel.'

Charlie made a face. 'I'd almost rather stay at Mrs Phipps.'

'It'll be okay; we can get someone to do it up a bit. And we've got to be on the spot.'

'Maybe we can get Kate round to give us a hand.'

Nick groaned. 'Are you still trying to pursue that one? Haven't you heard the old adage about flogging a dead horse?'

'I don't think you can reasonably describe Kate as a dead horse and I've got no intention of flogging her, but I'll get through to her some day. I know she fancies me.'

'That's just what she doesn't like about you.'

Charlie assumed an air of bafflement and shook his head. 'I'm beginning to think that the only way I'll get anywhere with her is if I get Willow Star to win the Oaks.'

'Yes, well, the way things are going, we're not going to be in business in time. I've tried all the banks. They're quite happy to put up half if we provide a

45

hundred per cent security and put up the other half, so that's no good.'

'And I've drawn a blank with my stepfather. In fact he was quite shirty about it when I asked him. Asked me what I thought he would get for the filly.'

Nick's face whitened. 'Oh no!'

'Don't worry. I talked him out of it, said she'd be worth three times as much as soon as she's had a few runs. But he certainly won't come across with any more.'

'What about the other people you went to see?'

'I've tried most of the owners we thought might come in with us. They all said we should spend a few more years at Aylestone's, then they might put a horse or two with us if we get a yard.'

'I've got a few more irons in the fire,' Nick said, 'but everyone's still bloody cautious. This recession's gone on so long.'

'Maybe we should have been bolder with our punting,' Charlie said. 'We're about five grand ahead at the moment.'

'Sure, but only on Aylestone's touches.'

'Okay, but maybe we should go in a bit heavier next time. After all, that's what keeps him in new Mercedes.'

'Let's wait and see.'

*   *   *

Robert Aylestone limped out of his office into his tidy, brightly lit yard. The light from the stable windows glowed through a freezing rain which made no impression on his hard, ruddy features. As usual, he was carrying around too many plans, campaigns, schemes, and deals in his head to worry about

46

external elements. His only concern about the weather was the effect it might have on the running of his horses. The top doors of all the boxes were closed tight. Inside, the lads groomed vigorously with their jackets off, dressing over each horse for evening inspection. By the time Aylestone began looking around at five thirty, everything would be immaculate. Hoofs would be grassed, mangers scrubbed clean and a neat twist of straw laid in each doorway.

Aylestone caught sight of Charlie coming out of the feed house.

'Oi! Charlie!' he bellowed as he might have done at a new apprentice. Charlie tensed up angrily. He stopped where he was and let Aylestone limp across to him, hoping his annoyance would be registered. It wasn't.

'Get Nick to look after tomorrow's first lot. You're going to take Percy to Newbury. I want him to have a good work-out.'

Persimmon Way, or Percy as he was known in the yard, was a well-built bumper horse which Aylestone had bought at Ballsbridge in the summer. He'd looked half starved when he'd first arrived. Nick and Charlie had both questioned their boss's sanity in buying him but then, as had often happened with similar horses that had passed through the yard in the four seasons they'd been there, the animal began to flourish.

Charlie had ridden him in his only race to date, a moderate contest at Ludlow where he'd scrambled home by a neck. Since then he'd improved almost beyond recognition and there were now few better horses in the yard.

'What time are you sending him?' Charlie didn't

disguise his annoyance. 'I've a ride booked at Warwick at three thirty; I'll need to be on my way by one.'

'I've fixed it for nine o'clock sharp.'

Since he had worked for Aylestone, Charlie had only once known him to send horses away to gallop, and that had been after a long cold spell when there'd been no racing and the gallops at home refused to thaw. He wondered why Aylestone was sending Percy now. Until something else occurred to him. 'Who are you going to work him with? The only suitable horses we've got are either running or about to run. You won't want to use one of them, will you?'

Aylestone shot him a withering look. 'No, son. I won't.' He turned and hobbled back to his office.

As Charlie started on his round of the horses, he considered what Aylestone could be up to. As much as he despised the man, he recognised that he had a rare understanding of horses, an intuition that you couldn't learn from books. If he and Nick were going to survive when they started training on their own, they would have to learn to think as Aylestone did.

Charlie thought through all the possibilities. He was sure about one thing; whatever Percy was going to gallop against would need to be very useful. He had been riding Percy out most days and the horse never seemed to stop improving.

By the time Charlie had organised the work board for the following morning and arranged a visit from the blacksmith, it was after seven. When he arrived back at Mrs Phipps' cottage, Charlie slammed his keys down on the table.

Startled, Nick looked up from the form book in his lap. 'What's the matter with you?'

'The sooner we start on our own, the better. We

48

work our balls off for that bloody trainer and the conniving little rat won't even tell us what's going on.' Charlie told Nick about Aylestone's arrangements for Percy's gallop. 'What do you think he's up to?'

'If Percy isn't working with one of ours, he's obviously working with someone else's.'

'Well done, Sherlock Holmes,' Charlie said sarcastically. 'What I want to know is who the other horse is, and why the secrecy. If he's planning a gamble, we ought to know about it. What's the point of being his bloody assistants otherwise?'

Nick put down his form book. 'Okay then. Let's work it out logically. Percy's the only bumper horse in our yard and we haven't got anything else to work him with. He needs a good gallop to put him spot on if Aylestone is planning a touch with him. So, what does he do? He works him with a good bumper horse who's already shown some decent form. And you can assume he's planning to run him soon, or he'd wait and gallop him with one of our own.'

The pair discussed several other possibilities. In the end, they accepted that they'd just have to wait until the next day to find out exactly what was going on. But characteristically, Charlie wouldn't let it go. He sat up in bed with a pen and pad on his knees, determined to figure it out. He was the same with a crossword; he'd keep on going back until it was finished.

If Aylestone was hatching a coup, there had to be a way he and Nick could make some money too. Another twenty thousand and they'd have enough to get their own yard started. With the incentive of getting away from Aylestone, Charlie was even more determined to work it out. He'd almost fallen asleep

49

when he suddenly remembered a bumper horse he'd seen win at Ascot three weeks before. He couldn't think why he and Nick had missed it earlier. The horse had trounced a number of well-fancied rivals without ever coming off the bridle. More significantly, it was trained by Aylestone's ex-head lad, Oliver Baring.

Charlie remembered now that, after the race, Baring had told the press the animal's main target for the season would be the bumper at Aintree. In between, it would run at Sandown. Charlie looked at the date on his watch. The Sandown race was a week tomorrow.

Charlie put his head back on the pillow and smiled. If he was coming to the right conclusion, there would certainly be some money to be made, maybe a lot more than he and Nick had ever made before.

In the morning, Charlie drove the horsebox into Newbury Racecourse. A light frost lit by a weak wintry sun glistened on top of the ground. Aylestone, wrapped in a bulky sheepskin coat, was already waiting beside his Mercedes. A Dutch cigar was jutting from his mouth.

'Get him tacked up, son. They'll be here in a minute.'

Charlie dropped the ramp and went up into the box. He was getting Percy ready when he heard another lorry pull in and draw up alongside. He was itching to see if his theory was right. He pulled the saddle down over the foam pad, finished tugging up the girths and stood on the tips of his toes to peer through the side window.

A ripple of excitement ran through him.

Parked beside him was a dark blue two-box. On the back, in large white letters, were the words 'Oliver

Baring'.

Charlie watched as Aylestone walked over to greet the young trainer who was jumping down from the cab. While they talked, a lad got out of the other side. Baring issued some instructions and a few moments later a tall, angular bay was being led down the ramp. It was Paymaster, the horse Charlie had seen win at Ascot.

Paymaster had travelled with his tack on and was ready to go by the time Charlie had dragged Percy down the ramp. The two geldings, glad of the company, briefly touched noses and snorted. Their hot breath billowed in the crisp morning air. Paymaster seemed almost embarrassed by Percy's immaturity and threw his head in the air. Charlie pulled Percy away and let Aylestone leg him into the saddle.

Aylestone's orders were simple enough. Charlie and the other lad, a conditional jockey called Tony Hellier, were to warm up both horses for twenty minutes or so, after which Tony was to lead them along at a good swinging canter for a mile before letting them run along up the straight.

'Make sure he has a good blow, but don't overcook him,' Aylestone added. 'If he can't get to the other horse, don't worry. I'll be watching from the stands.'

'What's all this about then?' Charlie asked Tony Hellier as they walked out of earshot.

Tony shook his head. 'Don't ask me. All I know is this horse is supposed to be running at Sandown next Friday and the guv'nor says I can ride him again. He also said if anyone gets to hear of this gallop, I'll be looking for another job.'

Charlie hadn't registered that Tony had been the jockey when Paymaster had won at Ascot. Now it

51

emerged that he looked after the horse at home and saw him as his main chance of making a name for himself. He also told Charlie that the horse had improved since his win.

The two jockeys chatted as they jogged and hacked for a circuit of the course. Despite an awkwardness in his appearance, Paymaster had a definite presence about him, a confidence which Charlie didn't think Percy had yet. The longer they were out, the less he fancied Percy's chances of winning the gallop.

He and Tony pulled up to let the horses catch their breath. After a few minutes, they set off in earnest, keeping to the outside of the hurdle course where the ground was seldom used. There was always room for manoeuvre when a trainer wanted a good, swinging gallop and it was obvious from the way Tony set off that he planned to take no prisoners.

In the past, Percy had sometimes been difficult to settle, but now it was all Charlie could do to lay up. He sat quietly on the horse, talked to him, tried to make him think he was travelling faster than he was.

They tracked Paymaster for half a mile before Charlie felt Percy gradually find his feet and his breathing became less strained. As they swung wide into the straight, Charlie squeezed Percy firmly between his legs, taking him up to join the horse in front. He shortened his reins to take a firmer hold of Percy's head, keeping him balanced, at the same time getting him to lengthen his stride.

Percy lacked experience; it took him a while to understand what he was supposed to do, but then it clicked and Charlie felt him respond.

As Percy quickened, Tony let out a reef on Paymaster and they passed the three-furlong marker both flat out, with Paymaster shading Percy by the length of his neck. The two stayed locked together for another two furlongs before Charlie felt Percy begin to lose his action; the strain of laying up with Paymaster was taking its toll.

Charlie kept his hold on Percy's head but stopped pushing. He let Paymaster ease away until he was some six lengths ahead when he passed the winning post.

Walking back towards the exit from the track, Tony Hellier had a big smile on his face. 'I told you he could go a bit. What do you think?'

Charlie reckoned that Percy could have kept within a length of the other horse if he'd really pushed him, but he agreed that Paymaster was something a bit special.

*　　　*　　　*

Charlie didn't see Nick again that day until he got back from Warwick later in the evening.

'Well?' Nick asked excitedly. 'What happened?'

'Percy got beaten. That's what happened.'

Nick's face registered disbelief. 'By what?'

Charlie took him through the whole gallop in detail.

'He must be some tool to beat Percy,' Nick said with disappointment. 'I really thought he was the best we'd got in the yard. So, what do we do now?'

'I'm not sure. Presumably now the guv'nor and Baring know which is the best horse, they'll run them both and back Paymaster.'

'And so will we,' Nick said, hitting the arm of his chair with his fist. 'I took another look over Ivor's yard today. It's perfect for us. I reckon by the time we've paid a year's rent and insurance, bought some

53

tack and rugs and paid a few weeks' wages, we're going to need at least forty thousand. At the moment we've got just over five in our punting fund.'

'Okay, let's put the lot on.'

Nick gaped at his partner. 'You must be joking.'

'Why not? Come on, let's do it. Shit or bust, unless you still want to be working for Aylestone in ten years' time.'

It took Charlie three days to persuade Nick to go for broke. It was entirely against his friend's prudent nature, but in the end he gave in to Charlie's relentless campaign. When the five-day entries appeared, Nick dived into his form book, checking which of the other runners in the race at Sandown were likely to bother Paymaster. After two hours, he came to the conclusion that unless one of the newcomers was exceptional, Percy was the only danger. And they both knew now that he wasn't good enough.

Two days before the race, Nick and Charlie worked out their plan. Charlie had ridden Percy every day since the gallop and once again had the ride on him at Sandown. Nick was worrying that the two trainers might have a different plan from their own.

Charlie tried to reassure him. 'If they were planning something else, Baring wouldn't have warned Tony Hellier not to mention the gallop to anyone.'

In the four years that Charlie had been riding as an amateur, he'd accumulated a number of punters of varying wealth and success. Common sense told him that the only punters who could get a large wager accepted were those who regularly bet in large amounts and were net losers. Bookmakers didn't keep winners on their books.

Charlie didn't know any really big gamblers, but he knew a handful who, given the right information, would bet a thousand. Normally when he had a ride or the yard a runner which they all fancied, he would tell his punters and they would put him on the odds to a hundred pounds. This time, Charlie would need to go to them with the money, but it would need to be placed as close to the race as possible so that only those who were meant to would know what was going on.

As he discussed the details, Nick tried once more to get him to halve the stake.

Charlie put his arm round Nick's shoulders and gave him a confident squeeze. 'By five thirty on Friday we'll have enough for that yard. You draw the cash out tomorrow; I'll organise the punt.'

* * *

Except for those with a vested interest, the seventh and final race on the card that Friday in January was an unimportant event: a National Hunt flat race; twelve runners, five of whom had never appeared on a racetrack before. Apart from Paymaster, those that had run didn't offer much promise of high-class sport. The rumours circulating about the débutantes were the usual unreliable lads' stories. The bookies had no strong views about Persimmon Way who was quoted at six to one; the form of his Ludlow success hadn't impressed anyone.

Charlie and Nick still didn't know for certain if their boss was gambling on the race, but the right result would mean they could phone Ivor Thompson that evening to confirm they'd be taking on Oak Hollow Stables within a fortnight.

For most of the afternoon, a damp westerly had been carrying in a cargo of thick grey clouds which had started to drop their load on the Esher track. The going had changed from soft to heavy by the time the runners for the bumper had left the paddock and headed along the tarmac road towards the course. None of them had ever raced on anything worse than good to soft. Charlie began to worry that he'd made the wrong decision. If he'd had the chance now, he'd have called off the bet; that's what a cool-headed professional gambler would have done.

But it was too late.

The lad leading Percy wished Charlie luck and pulled the lead rein from the horse's bit. Charlie and Percy set off through squelching mud downhill towards the start.

Percy floundered slightly as he tried to adapt to the new, unfamiliar conditions; Charlie kept a good hold of his head to help him to stay balanced. He looked at the horses going down in front and derived some consolation when he saw that Paymaster and the others appeared just as lost.

Nick watched anxiously as the runners walked around at the start. The picture on the screen in the bookies' shop in the village was blurred by the pouring rain, but through the clouds of steam rising off the horses he could just make out Percy's colours. Three lads from Aylestone's yard were standing beside him. He wondered if they knew that Percy wasn't supposed to win.

As they came under orders, Charlie had Percy positioned on his own, wide on the outside. Nick assumed that Charlie had walked the course and found the going heavier there—anything to make it more difficult for him.

56

The starter let them go and they set off through the driving rain with Paymaster leading them as they laboured up the hill and turned right-handed away from the stands. The palms of Nick's hands began to dry as he watched Paymaster bowling along some five lengths clear of the pack, with Percy not even in the picture.

The camera angle changed as they swept wide into the long back straight, giving a view of the whole field. Percy was still wide of the others with only a couple behind him. Three or four of the jockeys were already beginning to scrub away at their horses, trying to lay up with the leader. They made no headway; if anything, Paymaster was increasing his lead.

Charlie sat quiet as a mouse. Nick couldn't tell how well he was travelling, but he was a good distance behind. As the horses galloped round the long bend into the straight, it was clear to Nick that nothing could beat the horse in front; he was the only animal with any running left in him.

Nick glanced at the starting prices superimposed on the screen. Paymaster had gone off eleven to eight favourite. He calculated that would contribute fifteen thousand pounds to the kitty—not enough for a full year's rent but they'd certainly be able to pay for the yard for six months.

A burst of excited shouting beside him jolted his attention back to the race. The Aylestone lads were beginning to cheer. Paymaster was inside the final furlong, but he was staggering like a drunk.

A sudden intense nausea welled up inside Nick as he saw one of the other runners come from nowhere to mount a challenge. He gulped as the picture cleared and he realised that it was Percy, still on the

57

wide outside, catching Paymaster with every stride. Charlie was sitting motionless while Tony Hellier on Paymaster was pushing with everything he had. He went for his stick, but his horse seemed to be going backwards.

As Percy collared the leader, a raucous cheer from Aylestone's lads bounced off the drab grey walls of the betting shop.

Nick forced a tight smile in an attempt to seem happy about the result. He couldn't sustain even a vague pretence. Doing his best to cover the depth of his anguish, he left the shop feeling as if the earth had opened up beneath his feet, ready to suck him down into eternal destitution.

Why, why, why? Why had they risked so much of their funds on one race? It was absolutely crazy! He couldn't think what had possessed him to go along with Charlie's plan. He cursed his own weakness in letting his friend's absurd optimism get the better of him. 'Trust me.' Charlie's words of misguided confidence rang in his ears as he opened his car door. It occurred to him that the loss of a week's wages to the local bookie hurt him almost as much as the loss of their hard-gained nest egg. Furious, he screwed up his betting slip and drove back to the stables wondering what vain madness had driven Charlie to win the race.

Robert Aylestone struggled to hide his anger as Charlie rode an exhausted Percy into the winner's enclosure. Percy's owner, a retired banker, patently had been told nothing about the intended coup as he stood waiting under the winner's board smiling excitedly at anyone who came near and looking proudly at his horse. Ten feet away, Paymaster's connections stood in a small shell-shocked huddle.

Charlie slid from the saddle wondering how vicious his reception would be.

Aylestone sidled up to him, on the pretext of giving the winning horse a pat on the neck. He looked as if he would rather have strangled it.

'I want you out of my fucking yard by the morning,' he hissed from the corner of his mouth. Charlie slowly stopped undoing his circingle and stared defiantly at the trainer.

He was going to protest, but he snapped his mouth shut before the words came. A slanging match in front of the owner and in full view of the press would do neither of them any good. He turned away and carried on taking off the sodden tack. He gave Percy a grateful rub on his nose and after a few words with the owner, hefted his saddle off to the weighing room.

*   *   *

Nick was sitting, staring blankly at the television when Charlie arrived back at their digs a little after seven. He didn't look up or move when Charlie came in, dropped his kitbag on the floor and flopped into an armchair beside him. 'What the hell have you done?' he asked flatly.

Charlie didn't answer. He was waiting for Nick to see his face. When Nick eventually did look up, he found Charlie grinning back at him.

'What's so bloody funny?'

'You are. I've never seen you sulk before. I hope you're not going to be like this when we're running our own yard.'

Nick was feeling far too sorry for himself to be humoured. 'With you investing our funds, I should have plenty of time to cure myself of the habit,' he

59

said sourly.

Charlie laughed, a great gale of laughter as he leaped out of his chair. 'Cheer up, you miserable bugger. We've done it!' He yelled. 'We've bloody well done it!' He stooped down and put his hand into the inner pocket of his kit bag. With a flourish he plucked out an enormous parcel of fifty pound notes.

Nick's heart leaped like a salmon up a spring river. 'Where the hell did you get that?' he whispered huskily.

Charlie waved the package under Nick's nose. 'Thirty-five grand, my old son, and it's all ours! Five big ones on wonderful Percy at six to one.'

Nick's body collapsed with relief as the world turned the right way up once more. 'Jesus Christ! When the hell did you decide to switch?'

Charlie grinned with a hint of rare conceit. 'Since that gallop at Newbury.'

'But you came back and told me Percy had been well beaten.'

'He was. But considering I'd put a two-stone weight cloth underneath his saddle, he worked like a Derby horse.'

Nick got to his feet, shaking his head to convince himself the nightmare was over. 'I don't believe it,' he gasped. 'You sneaky bastard. Why on earth didn't you tell me?'

'Because I thought your highly developed and unselective sense of loyalty might make you feel deceitful towards our oafish boss and if Aylestone had been in on this, we'd have been lucky to double our money.'

Nick was grinning too now. He nodded.

'By the way,' Charlie went on, 'he sacked me in the winner's enclosure. I shouldn't think that happens often.'

They both laughed as the tension of the last few weeks drained away. Ten minutes later, they were in the pub, celebrating with the lads whose loyalty bets had brought home their weekend's drinking money.

* * *

The following evening, Charlie dialled Kate Scanlan's number at her cottage. There was no reply. He tried her parents in Marlborough. She wasn't there, but Charlie asked them to pass on a message if they spoke to her.

Kate rang Charlie at Mrs Phipps' the next morning.

'Hi,' she said. 'I got a message you'd called.'

'Just keeping my half of our deal.'

'What half of what deal?'

'When we got Willow Star, one of the terms was that we must always tell you where she is.'

'I know where she is. She's in a paddock at Oak Hollow.'

'Okay, but I thought you might like to come over and take a look at her and discuss her future.'

'But I'm not her owner; your father is, isn't he?'

'I still think of you as part owner. After all, you saved her life, didn't you?'

'Well,' Kate said with tantalising indecision, 'I suppose I could come over, tomorrow morning.'

'It's a deal,' Charlie said. 'Meet me at Oak Hollow at twelve thirty. Then we'll have lunch.'

Kate hesitated a moment. 'It'd better be a bloody good one.'

* * *

Kate checked her hair and make-up just one more time before she left to drive to Lambourn. As she turned her Renault into the drive that led down to the pretty old red-brick yard, she stopped and checked once more.

She parked behind the stables, which she noticed were empty now. Outside, it was warmer than it had been for the last few days, and quieter. She listened to the sounds of the small valley, the plaintive winter bird calls, the distant sound of a tractor rolling and the whinny of a young horse nearby.

There was no sign of Charlie or his battered Range Rover. Kate shrugged. It was just like him to be late.

While she waited, she walked round to take a look at the yard. She was always interested in other people's stables. She opened the top doors of the first two boxes. They were empty and spotless, as if they had just been swept.

She wondered idly why there were no horses in the yard. She wasn't sufficiently well up on the local racing scene to know whose yard she was in. She was aware that the owner had let Charlie keep Willow Star here for a few months and the filly had done well here. She was already broken in and beginning to canter.

Kate wandered up past the rest of the boxes and opened the door to the tack room at the end.

The tack room, like all the stables, was spotlessly clean and empty, save for two chairs and a small table. It was a moment before she took in that the table was covered in a white cloth and lavishly laid for lunch. Beside the table stood a black rubber feed bucket full of ice from which protruded the top of a bottle of champagne.

As Kate gazed with amazement at the unlikely

spectacle, a door on the far side of the tack room opened and Charlie walked in with a welcoming smile.

'Happy New Year. Welcome to Oak Hollow.'

Kate frowned. 'What are you doing here with all this? And why aren't you racing today?'

'I wanted to give you lunch. I couldn't do this at Mr Aylestone's. He sacked me.'

Kate felt suddenly guilty. 'Oh Charlie, why didn't you say so? I wouldn't have accepted lunch if I'd known.'

'I'm glad you did. I wanted to celebrate our acquisition of Oak Hollow.'

'Your acquisition? You and Nick?'

Charlie nodded gleefully. 'Yes. Poor Nick hasn't had the sack yet so he's had to go racing, but he sends his warm regards. Now,' he pulled the bottle from the bucket, 'a drink?'

Kate submitted to Charlie's skills as a host and didn't pretend that she wasn't enjoying it. Anyway, she defended her attitude, in some way she couldn't quite put her finger on, Charlie had changed.

'How did this all happen?' she asked.

'Thanks to Percy.'

'Percy who?'

'Persimmon Way, to be precise. A very handsome four-year-old, whose owner I hope will send the horse to me to run on the flat. He could be really useful—a long-distance handicapper, maybe even a Cup horse.'

'Whatever that is.'

'Don't worry, you're going to have plenty of time to get used to racing terminology.'

'Why's that?' Kate asked, already knowing.

'As Willow Star's surrogate mother, you'll be

63

entitled to,' Charlie said.

'But what did this Percy do for you?'

'Won at six to one. Unfortunately—very unfortunately, I suspect—my ex-boss backed the opposition and blamed me when it lost, for some reason or other.'

'You bet on Percy and won enough to set up your own yard?'

Charlie nodded. 'That's about it. The toast is,' he said, topping up her glass and raising his own, 'Willow Star, Oak Hollow, and Percy!'

CHAPTER FOUR

With a display of reckless confidence which he didn't feel, Charlie swung his mud-spattered Range Rover up the narrow concrete ramp of a car park near Portman Square. He found a vacant space and slotted into it. He switched off the engine and turned to Nick.

'Okay. How are we going to do this? Shall we spoof or toss a coin?'

They had to decide once and for all which of them was going to hold the licence to train. The Jockey Club wouldn't mind which of them applied, but under its rules a licence could only be held in a single name. Charlie and Nick both fulfilled all necessary conditions as far as experience and references were concerned. And thanks to Charlie's natural charm at attracting owners, they had no problem in complying with the rules regarding the minimum number of horses they would be training. For a simple flat or jumping licence, the minimum was nine. Charlie and

64

Nick were going to concentrate on the flat, but they also wanted to be able to send out a few jumpers. For that, they'd have to keep at least twelve; they were expecting over twenty horses from the owners they'd already spoken to.

Nick would have loved to have held the licence himself and seen his name alongside their runners, but it was obvious to him that it should be in Charlie's name. Charlie was already quite well known and he had the ability to draw in and encourage owners, which was a trainer's principal task. Without owners, there'd be no horses to train. And it was absolutely vital to Nick that the yard should succeed commercially; the money he was putting into the partnership represented every penny he owned.

Although Charlie thought Nick was probably right, he was reluctant to admit it. He insisted that they each had qualities which were different but of equal importance in running a yard.

Nick fished in his pocket and pulled out a ten pence coin. 'All right. Heads it's me; tails it's you.'

Charlie nodded.

Nick flicked the coin into the air, caught it and slapped it down on the back of his left hand.

'Good luck,' he said. He lifted his right hand just enough to look at the coin without Charlie seeing it. 'Bollocks! You win.' Nick shook his head and slipped the coin back into his pocket.

'Hang on,' Charlie protested. 'I didn't see it.'

'Well, I did, and I'm the loser.' Nick was offering a *fait accompli*. He was sure it was the right decision. 'Come on or we'll be late and we won't have a licence at all.'

Charlie shrugged his shoulders. He knew Nick well

enough to know when he wouldn't be budged. They climbed out of the Range Rover. It looked shabby and lacklustre between a pair of gleaming BMWs. With a dismissive nod, Charlie led the way out to the street and 42 Portman Square.

The granting of the licence to train was more or less a formality at this stage. Oak Hollow had already been visited by the Jockey Club inspector. He'd reported that he was satisfied that everything was up to standard. Access to gallops and security had been his priorities. Every stable had to be fitted with a lock so that horses could be left overnight in the certainty that they couldn't be got at. Charlie and Nick knew well enough that this was only a theoretical certainty; if someone was determined to dope a horse, there was no way, short of having a full-time guard, that it could be stopped. Besides, the ruling made no mention of securing the windows which were always left at least partly open. As for the gallops, there were communal training facilities next to the yard, which included schooling hurdles and fences. Nick and Charlie had already received a letter from the owners confirming their right to use them.

All Charlie needed to do now was to go in and convince the trio of committee members that he was a fit and proper person to hold a licence. If he could do that, they'd be in business.

The interview took place in a panelled room on the first floor. As far as Charlie could tell, it started well enough. He stood and confidently answered a string of routine and technical questions put to him by the three Jockey Club stewards.

After ten minutes or so, Charlie was aware of a slight awkwardness in the proceedings. The questions stopped and an embarrassed silence

66

developed. The senior member, sitting in the middle, was looking down, uneasily shuffling his papers. When he looked up, Charlie could see the discomfort in his eyes.

'Mr Patterson,' the distinguished old peer was finding it hard to get the words out, 'in normal circumstances we would grant your licence straightaway.' He paused. Charlie's heart thumped as his mind raced for a reason why they should be turned down. 'Regrettably, we've received a letter casting doubts on your integrity. I'm afraid we'll have to postpone the granting of your licence until we're satisfied there's no truth in it.'

Charlie was dumbstruck. Why? Who on earth would wish him and Nick any harm?

He burst out without thinking, 'For God's sake, you can't—' He caught the eye of one of the men in front of him and stopped. He'd suddenly realised who the letter must be from. 'I'm very sorry,' he mumbled quickly, 'but if the letter is from Mr Aylestone, I can explain it.'

'Mr Patterson,' the senior member cut in, 'we've no intention of revealing who this letter is from. But as soon as we've investigated, we'll let you know.'

Charlie recognised that arguing about it now wouldn't help their case. Apparently, the interview was over. He thanked them without much warmth and left the room.

Outside, Nick was admiring one of the huge equestrian paintings in the anteroom. He turned as he heard the door open.

Charlie walked straight past him to the lift and pressed the button. 'Come on. We're going.'

The lift arrived and they stepped in. 'Fucking Aylestone!' Charlie hissed as the door closed behind them. 'He's been sticking his oar in, trying to screw things up for us.'

Nick listened in silence as Charlie cursed his way through his account of the interview. He was right, Nick thought. Aylestone probably had sent the letter. No one else had a motive for doing it. But whoever it was, there was nothing they could do except wait.

The lift reached the ground floor and the partners walked out of the building into the grey morning.

'If we don't get a licence,' Nick said to ease the tension, 'Kate'll be more disappointed than either of us.'

'Kate? Kate Scanlan?'

'Yes,' Nick answered defensively.

'Why should she be disappointed? What's it to her?'

'She's really looking forward to us training Willow Star.'

The thought of Kate's interest helped to lift Charlie's depression. 'Is she? I haven't seen her for three weeks. I produced a gourmet lunch for her up at the yard the day Thompson gave us the keys but I haven't been able to get hold of her since. Have you seen her?'

Nick looked embarrassed. 'Well, yes, last week. She wondered if she could have a look at the filly. When I asked her if she wanted to have dinner with me, she accepted.'

Charlie looked away and bit his lip. He knew it was absurd to be jealous. He hardly knew the girl, and Nick was his oldest friend. 'How did you get on?'

'We had a great time.' Nick nodded his approval. 'She's a bright woman, great sense of humour.'

'Did she mention me at all?'

'Not really.'

68

Charlie opened the door of the Range Rover. 'Let's hope we don't disappoint her, then. With luck, we should have our licence within a week.'

'That depends on what Aylestone had to tell them.'

'We'll just have to hope they don't take any notice of him.' Charlie said, without convincing himself.

*   *   *

A week later, Nick found the letter on the table when he came back for breakfast in the cottage. It was addressed to Charlie but he knew at once where it was from. Although he had as much right as Charlie to read it, he didn't open it at first.

Since Charlie had told him about the letter the Jockey Club had received, Nick had made up his mind they weren't going to get a licence. There were so many accusations Aylestone could have made, however unfounded, which would be impossible to disprove and which would be bound to cast doubts in the stewards' minds. Charlie, predictably, had persisted in dismissing the whole thing as a red herring. 'Those old boys may look as though they don't know what's going on but, believe me, they know exactly what Aylestone's like. When we applied, they were probably expecting him to hit them with a bunch of sour grapes. Don't worry; they'll chew it over for a day or two, then they'll spit it out.'

Nick wished he had that kind of confidence, though he wondered whether Charlie really felt it. Perhaps he was just putting on a face. He dropped the letter back on the table and sat down to pour himself a cup of tepid coffee. He observed, as if it was someone else's that his hand was shaking. If the envelope contained the right message, he and Charlie would start moving out of Mrs Phipps' house today and their life would instantly accelerate into a faster lane. If not, they'd be condemned to a few more years as assistants to whoever would take them.

He took a gulp of coffee, picked up a knife, slit open the envelope and pulled out a single sheet of paper.

'Charles Patterson Esq ... After due consideration ... the Stewards of the Jockey Club have decided to grant you a licence, upon receipt of a list of the horses you propose to train ...'

Nick read the letter through twice, not absorbing all the details; they could be dealt with later. The main thing, the only thing that mattered, was that at last he and Charlie could set up their own yard.

Charlie had been right. Whatever Aylestone—if it was Aylestone—had said had not swayed the stewards. There were no reservations or provisos in their permission. But that didn't take away from the fact that somebody, before they had even taken the first step in their new career, wanted to see them fail.

Nick read the letter once more to reassure himself. This time, he put it down and let out a great sigh of pent-up anxiety. 'Fantastic!' He got up from his chair and ran back up the stairs to hammer on Charlie's door.

'He's not there.' Mrs Phipps' voice floated up from her kitchen.

Nick's euphoria dimmed for a moment. Sharing the news with Charlie was all part of it. He came back down more slowly. 'Where is he? Did he go out early?'

'No. I don't believe he came back at all last night.' Mrs Phipps pursed her lips at the scandal of it.

70

'I expect he went to see his mother and stepfather, and ended up staying the night,' Nick said, just to spoil her fun.

'He didn't,' Mrs Phipps said with satisfaction. 'His mother's already been on the phone.'

'Well, I'm sure he's not lost, Mrs Phipps, but if he comes back here, tell him to meet me up at Oak Hollow as soon as possible.'

*   *   *

Nick let himself into the bungalow that stood a hundred yards from the stable block where Ivor Thompson had housed his string of racehorses for the last twenty-five years. The place hadn't been lived in since Ivor's head lad had moved out before Christmas. The lack of heat and furniture had already given it a depressing, damp, unlived-in smell. The cramped little house hadn't anyway been decorated for ten years or more and the removal of pictures and shelves had left a messy scattering of brighter patches on the faded wallpaper. It wasn't much of a place to call your own, Nick thought, but he couldn't have been more pleased at the prospect of moving in.

In the still air he could hear an ominous dripping noise from the kitchen. He walked into the dank little room where the cold tap above the sink was depositing fat drops, thudding like a metronome into the stainless steel sink. A quick twist of the tap quietened it. The silence which followed was interrupted by the rasping scrape of the back door being opened. Footsteps clumped on the bare linoleum and Charlie walked in.

'Morning,' he said. 'What's brought you here?'

71

'Didn't you get my message from Mrs Phipps?'

'No. Haven't seen the old witch. I left at half six this morning. Went out to meet Charles Gordon.'

'Charles Gordon? The owner?'

Charles nodded. 'Percy's owner.' He left the statement dangling.

'Well?' Nick asked impatiently. 'What for?'

'To talk about Percy coming to us. I told him ages ago that I thought Percy should be in a flat yard. I'm sure he could win good handicaps. Now I think I've talked him into it. Aylestone will be livid.'

'You mean he's coming to us?'

Charlie nodded again.

'That's brilliant!' Nick laughed. 'And, by the way, we're in business. We got a letter from Portman Square this morning.'

'I guessed that when I saw your car out there. I knew you wouldn't come up otherwise.'

Nick grinned at Charlie's perceptiveness. 'You're right. I didn't want to tempt fate.'

'Right. Let's go over to Ivor and sign the lease before he changes his mind.'

Ivor Thompson beamed at his two new tenants. He remembered the day thirty years before when he had been granted his trainer's licence. He guessed these two were experiencing the same emotions. He looked at his watch. 'I know it's only half past ten,' he said, 'but I think we have ample excuse to open a bottle.' He walked across a fine antique Baluchi rug to a large oak cabinet in which a small fridge had been cunningly set. He opened it and took out a bottle of champagne. 'Krug seventy-eight okay?' he asked with a grin.

He eased the cork from the bottle and filled three glasses. 'The very best of luck to the pair of you.

You've got as good a chance as any and better than most of making a go of it. You've got the front and the bottle,' he said, lifting his glass to Charlie, 'and you, Nick, you've got the brain. Looking after the finances is as important as anything else. I wish I'd had a partner to do that in the early days. I'd be a much richer man by now if I had.'

Nick nodded sagely and Charlie hid his smile behind his glass. Ivor Thompson was reputed to be one of the richest men in Lambourn.

'Now, sit down and tell me what your plans are. What are you doing about staff, for instance?'

Charles and Nick had no objection to telling Ivor how they intended to set up their yard. He wasn't a rival; he was on their side.

'We've got Kenny Ford and three more of the best lads coming from Aylestone's—all good work riders.'

'The old scoundrel won't be happy about that, but I dare say you've worked that out for yourselves.' Ivor had very little regard for Robert Aylestone.

'He won't be too happy when he hears one of his horses is coming to us too.'

'But he hasn't got any flat horses, has he?'

'There's one which won a bumper for us a month ago.'

'Oh yes, I remember. Persimmon something, one of Charles Gordon's. I gather you had a bit of a touch on it.'

Nick, startled, glanced at him. No one should have known at all. 'Who told you that?' His tone confirmed what the older man had said.

'Don't worry. Just a discreet little bird. You can never have a touch without people getting to know. As long as it's after the event, you'll be all right. But

73

why do you want this particular horse?'

'I'm certain he could win a few staying handicaps, if we get him on the right mark,' Charlie said. 'I've ridden him and I know what he's got under his bonnet.'

Ivor looked doubtful but made no comment. 'What about the rest of your staff?' he asked.

'We've seen and liked half a dozen girls,' Nick said. 'Charlie's reputation helped there.'

'Reputation for what?' Ivor chuckled.

'They didn't say,' Nick said drily.

'Head lad?'

'We're not sure yet. We think Kenny may do. Though he's young, he's really dedicated. Anyway, we've only got about twenty-four horses to start with, so we can do a fair bit ourselves.'

'Just as long as you don't forget that one of you should be spending at least half your time out finding new owners and new horses. Without a steady flow of those, you'll run out of steam before you've done a couple of seasons. It may sound obvious, but it doesn't matter how much you know about training horses if you haven't got any to train. I can tell you that for the last thirty years most of the training in that yard was done by assistants and head lads.'

The two nodded, though they were not sure that they believed him. They had anyway decided between them that they were going to do as much as possible themselves.

'Any particularly promising horses to start with?'

'Apart from Percy, we've a couple of three-year-olds that might be useful. They're well bred but they've been backward and just had a couple of runs. And we've got a two-year-old filly called Willow Star who looks the part. I think there's enough to get us

74

started.'

Ivor was sceptical. 'You'll find that you need ten horses with potential for every one that actually goes out and does anything. That's why it's essential that you spend time drumming up business to keep your numbers up. And don't forget, the fuller the yard, the more you make on each horse in it. We'll have to see what others we can get for you. Several of my old owners will want my advice. As soon as you're up and running, I'll come and have a look.'

The partners left Ivor's manor house half an hour later encouraged by the older man's enthusiasm. Suddenly the whole thing was real. Horses would soon arrive to be bedded and fed; they would have to get to know them and try to assess their potential. Races would have to be studied and chosen; training programmes and diets worked out.

The Range Rover crunched over the gravel, through the high brick pillars either side of the gate. As he drove into the lane, Charlie turned to Nick. 'Well, we've done it! I think I believe it at last, now we've actually got a licence and a lease in our pocket. We ought to have a yard-warming party or something.'

'There'll be opportunities for parties when we've had a few wins to celebrate,' Nick said with his usual caution.

'At least we could have a few friends round for a drink. I guess I'd better ring my stepfather and tell him; I don't think he really believed we'd get the place. And you could ask Kate Scanlan—Willow will be one of the first horses to move in.'

'Yes,' Nick said, 'maybe I could.'

* * *

Within a month, there were twenty-six horses in the yard and they had spent almost four thousand pounds on tack alone. Apart from saddles and bridles, they had to buy rugs and exercise sheets, muck sacks, pitchforks, grooming tools, feed buckets and countless other bits and pieces, all of which were absolutely necessary. While they had been working at Aylestone's, they'd experimented with every type of bedding on the market, from newspaper to peat; they'd come to the conclusion that, provided it was disinfected every day, straw was still the best. It was warmer than paper and cleaner than most other bedding. It was also freely available and cheaper. But it was beginning to look as though this was the only item whose cost they had over-estimated. Everything else, even the insurance, seemed to have gone up since they'd made their original plans and, once they'd started, blacksmith's fees, vets' accounts, and bills for feed and saddlery repair seemed to arrive in an unstoppable flow. Their overdraft was hovering dangerously close to its limit.

On the last Friday in March, as they drove up the gallops, Nick outlined their financial problems.

Charlie was sanguine. 'Look, Nick, it doesn't matter if you and I don't make a lot of money this year. We've got no dependants, as far as I know,' he added. 'And we're going to be too bloody busy to spend any money on ourselves.'

'It's all very well you saying that, but I can't see any point in working our arses off for no money.'

'When Percy starts racing we'll make plenty,' Charlie said confidently. 'Don't worry.'

'Let's hope so.'

'I know so. You watch him work this morning.'

Up at the gallops, Nick stayed in the Range Rover

76

and Charlie climbed out to meet the string winding up from their stables. When Percy reached him, Charlie took over from Sally, the girl who'd ridden him up. 'Kept the saddle nice and warm,' he grinned down at her when she'd legged him up. She smiled back and reddened while Charlie reminded himself that he'd vowed not to get involved with any of the stable girls. He thought of Kate instead.

She had been up for a drink at the bungalow when Nick had rung to ask her, a couple of days after they'd moved in. She had seemed to want to make it clear that she considered Nick her point of contact, and while she hadn't ignored Charlie, she'd done nothing to encourage him. She'd been round a few times since, quick visits to have a look at Willow Star, nothing more.

Charlie told himself it was only a matter of time before she became interested. Just once—it only needed once—he'd caught her gazing at him with a quite different look in her eyes. She'd turned away almost immediately, but it had been enough.

Charlie took a deep breath and trotted off towards the bottom of the gallop, pushing Kate from his thoughts. Girls would always come second to horses while the likes of Percy were around. The gelding hadn't stopped improving since the day he'd beaten Paymaster. He'd be ready for his first real flat race soon. Charlie gave him a good piece of work over a mile and a quarter with two other horses, and he galloped all over them without coming off the bridle. Charlie pulled up, throbbing with excitement at the thought of Percy's prospects. And Percy was by no means the only exciting horse in the yard.

*   *   *

The day of Willow Star's first race promised to be a cracker from the moment the sun appeared over the curve of the downs, a balmy, May day, the first real summer's morning.

Kenny Ford whistled as he strolled down the lane from his digs to the yard shortly before six that morning. He was looking forward to a day out at Goodwood and seeing his favourite charge run for the first time. Not only was Willow Star a supremely good-natured filly, she was willing, quick to learn and the fastest horse he'd ever ridden. It was partly at his urging that Charlie had entered her. She had been a late foal and conventional thinking suggested she should make her debut later in the season. But though she was quite small, she was well-developed and a six-furlong gallop wasn't going to do her young limbs any harm.

Kenny reached the yard before any of the other staff. He took each horse a small feed and checked their legs and temperature, part of his duties as head lad. When he was satisfied there were no problems, he walked down to the bungalow where he knew Nick and Charlie would be in the kitchen. He let himself in through the back door.

'Do you want Willow to go out for a walk this morning, Charlie?' he asked.

'No. I don't think so. But when you get to the races, just remember to get her out in plenty of time before you take her into the parade ring.'

At that moment the door from the small hall opened. The three men looked up. Kenny gave a knowing grin and Nick looked startled as Kate Scanlan walked in.

'What on earth are you doing here so early?' Nick asked.

78

'I just wanted to wish you all luck with Willow today. I'm going to give her a big kiss.'

'Aren't you coming?' Nick asked.

'No. I can't. Sandy's going to a funeral so I've got to be on duty. I'll listen to the race on the radio.' She leaned over and touched Charlie's forehead with her lips before she left in her habitual rush.

Nick looked after her. 'I didn't hear her car this morning,' he said, sounding defeated.

'No,' said Charlie. 'She followed me back after dinner.'

Nick raised an eyebrow.

'Cracked it at last, eh, Charlie?' Kenny chuckled.

Nick clenched his fists and stared at the entry forms on the table in front of him.

* * *

Nick travelled to Goodwood in the lorry with Kenny. Charlie was picked up later by his stepfather in his Mercedes, a twenty-year-old model but still gleaming.

Major Patterson was handsomely correct in a linen suit and regimental tie. He opened the passenger door from inside for Charlie and greeted his stepson with a brief smile. Opaque grey eyes shone guardedly from beneath his carefully groomed grey-blonde hair. His handsome, clean-shaven features give away as little as possible. Beyond a few formal words of greeting, he didn't utter a word for the first half-hour of the journey and seemed to feel no discomfort at the silence.

Charlie had never had a communicative relationship with him. For most of his young life, his stepfather had been away, posted abroad. He had

79

never felt any affection for the man, but he respected him and was grateful to him for giving him a home and his name. He knew nothing about his natural father; his mother had offered no information. Patterson had agreed to take him on, completely and without reservation, as his own. Prudence, Charlie's mother, was unable to have more children. Charlie felt that even if he had been Patterson's natural son, he would have evoked no more affection from him and he had taught himself not to resent its absence.

David Patterson was reputed to have been a highly effective soldier. But something had gone wrong when he had reached the age of forty. Charlie had never found out what, but his step-father had left the army earlier than expected. Soon afterwards he became security adviser to a Saudi Arabian arms dealer, a lucrative but not highly respectable post. Patterson had never told Charlie anything about it. He was by nature a silent, secretive man who offered little about himself. Now, it was only after they had covered the first twenty-five miles of their journey that he made any attempt at conversation. He asked a few questions about his filly, scarcely seemed to hear Charlie's answers, and relapsed into a long silence until they were within a mile of the racecourse.

'We're in Michael and Veronica's box for lunch,' he said abruptly.

Michael Russell was David Patterson's brother-in-law, also an ex-soldier who had come out of the army to make a more than good living from his own security business. He and Patterson's sister, Veronica, had one daughter, Imogen. Despite the absence of any blood ties, Imogen was like a sister to Charlie. Both only children, they had been thrown together from an early age and had remained close.

'Good. Will Immy be there?'

'I dare say.'

'And how is Uncle Mike?'

'As prosperous as ever,' Major Patterson answered. There was a distinct sourness in his voice.

Charlie wondered why, but knew that asking would yield nothing. He extracted a little information about his cousin's activities. She had been in Italy for the last few months. Charlie hadn't seen her since he had moved into Oak Hollow.

As they joined the queue for the car park on the wooded downs behind the racecourse, Patterson asked, 'Who's riding the filly?'

'I told you, Dad. Owen Williams.'

'Yes, so you did. He's useful, isn't he?'

'He's as good as anyone on a two-year-old filly. Doesn't fuss them. He's got a very quiet pair of hands.'

'And the filly? Showing any promise?'

'God, don't you listen to anything I say? I told you, she's better than average. I'm quite hopeful.' Charlie was deliberately low key when dealing with his stepfather.

'If she made a showing at this stage, would she be worth much more than I gave for her?'

'As I got her so cheap for you, almost certainly.'

'How much more?'

Charlie was struck by the naivety of the question but didn't let it show in his voice. 'That would depend on the quality of any races that she won. If she got a good group race, like the Queen Mary, she'd be considered a potential Classic filly—worth maybe a hundred thousand.'

'You'd be doing me a good turn if you could pull that off,' Patterson murmured.

81

Charlie detected an undercurrent of nervousness which he hadn't come across before in his stepfather. But then Patterson had always been unpredictable and hard to read. Charlie mentally shrugged his shoulders and climbed out of the car.

For most of the crowd on that fine spring morning at Goodwood, it promised to be another day's enjoyable, possibly profitable racing. For Nick, Charlie and their small staff, it was the biggest day in their career so far. Willow Star was the best horse in their yard. If she didn't win or at least come close today, their chances of scoring any important victories in their first season would look depressingly slim.

Nick and Kenny had already been at the course for a couple of hours when Charlie and his father arrived. Charlie went straight round to the stables to check that the filly had travelled all right. He also wanted to be sure that Nick had declared her.

There were no problems, and Willow Star looked better than ever. With a confident bounce in his stride, Charlie made his way to the stand and to Michael Russell's box.

He walked in to an atmosphere of palpable tension between his stepfather and Michael. Imogen wasn't there. Veronica was glancing impatiently between her husband and her brother. Charlie grinned at them and sensed that they all felt some relief at his arrival.

'Charlie!' Michael said in his role as host for the day. 'Let me get you a drink. How's the filly?'

'She's travelled well. That's something. She hasn't kicked herself in the lorry, and she ate up her breakfast this morning. So far so good.'

'It's hard to tell what the opposition's like,'

Veronica said, holding the day's card in front of her. 'At least half of them are débutantes.'

As she spoke, the door opened and Imogen walked in. Charlie greeted her with a kiss and inspected her with detached appreciation. 'Immy, how are you? You look outrageously well.'

'So do you. But you look much too young to be a trainer.'

'It's a sign of age, Immy, when policemen and racehorse trainers start looking young.'

They enjoyed their customary banter as Charlie brought her up to date on the change in his status since they had last seen each other.

'Uncle David doesn't seem particularly excited about his runner,' Imogen said.

Charlie followed her eyes. His stepfather's reserve did seem more pronounced than usual. He was used to the lack of communication, but today it was worse; and there was definitely something uncomfortable between him and Michael Russell. Charlie had no idea what. He wished his mother had come to the races; it might have livened up the party a bit; but she'd gone to a meeting of prison visitors.

He made sure he sat beside Imogen at lunch but left as soon as he could afterwards to check Willow Star. Her race was the fourth on the day's card and he knew he was going to find it hard to fill in the time.

*   *   *

Charlie walked into the parade ring with his stepfather and Imogen. Kenny was already proudly leading Willow Star. The filly was walking easily with a long, loose stride. She looked in perfect condition and was undoubtedly catching the eye of the cannier

83

punters. Her price on the bookies' boards shortened steadily.

The jockeys burst into the paddock, bright splashes of shining silk against the deep green turf. Owen Williams, wearing David Patterson's colours on their first ever outing, approached Charlie.

'Good afternoon, sir,' he said, his Welsh accent pronounced. 'How do you want her ridden?'

'Sensibly. It's her first race and I want her to enjoy herself. I want her to learn something, too, so don't just sit on her.'

Kate Scanlan drove her dusty Renault into the car park as the horses left the paddock to go down to the start of the fourth race. Sandy had got back to Noah's Ark from the funeral before lunch.

'I didn't feel like hanging around,' she'd said, adding generously, 'You bugger off and watch your precious filly run.'

Kate bought herself a badge and rushed through to the Richmond enclosure in time to see the runners being loaded into the starting stalls at the far end of the straight course. She would have liked to watch the race with Charlie, but she guessed he would be in a box with his uncle, whose name she couldn't remember. While the starter was seeing the last few difficult young horses installed, Kate swept the stands with her binoculars to see if she could identify Charlie in one of the boxes.

On the second sweep, she got him.

He was standing beside what, to Kate, looked like a ravishing, slender goddess of a girl. They were both laughing, looking down towards the start, and she had an arm locked into his.

Kate tore her eyes away from the sight. She tried to concentrate on the horses down at the start but her stomach churned at the bitter unfairness of her timing. Only the night before, after months of telling herself not to, she had let herself go with Charlie, convinced that there was real depth beneath the light-weight charm and macho banter. She'd been sure she'd judged it right, and it had been a beautiful night. But what the hell was he doing, the very next day, with his arms round a girl who looked like Claudia Schiffer without a squint?

She couldn't stop her glasses drifting back to rest on the box. She winced, and her eyes clouded.

*　　　*　　　*

Down at the start, Owen Williams sat calmly on the stocky bay filly. Her manners so far had been perfect. She had walked into the stall without a hint of objection and was standing quietly but alert to everything going on around her. Her long ears were twitching like radar scanners. When the last runner was in, Owen tightened the reins and squeezed her gently to let her know they were about to go. The starter wasted no time in raising his hand and pulling down the lever to spring the gates.

Willow Star leaped out of the narrow entrance, delighted at the sight of the long, clear stretch of deep green turf in front of her. A couple of runners alongside her bumped together as they left the stalls. They had to struggle to find their balance but once they had, the race settled into a sensible pattern.

Willow Star found herself in her element. She was small and compact, ideal for the grassy switchback that lay ahead. The gentle rise of the first furlong gave her time to settle into a sharp but reassuring rhythm.

She was so much better than anything else at home

that she always worked by herself. Now she was surrounded by other horses going a really good gallop, and she loved it. As they skimmed the brow of the hill, past the five-furlong marker, the pace quickened and a gap opened up in front of her. She pricked her ears and surged forward, eager to show how good she was, until she felt the tug of the bit in the soft corners of her mouth. She eased back for a few strides, throwing her head in the air. She desperately wanted to please but now she was confused; she didn't know what was wanted of her and, throughout the next half-furlong, became unsettled.

The field was travelling fast now and Willow Star saw the grandstands looming in the distance to her left. Suddenly, she felt her jockey urging her forward. They were still racing downhill, but her balance was returning. She had never galloped so fast in her life and the effort was beginning to burn up the muscles in her adolescent legs. There seemed to be no end in sight to the uphill run to the line, but despite her tiredness, she saw that she was catching the half-dozen horses in front.

Above her she could feel the rhythm of Owen pushing and squeezing her. Helping her to maintain her balance, urging her forward. But she didn't need any encouragement. She was straining every sinew in her body. She wanted to win for herself, and also for Kenny and Kate.

The oxygen in her lungs was beginning to run short. As she raced on through the pain barrier, the months of hard training were paying off as one by one the horses in front faltered and came back to her.

With fifty yards to run, a shift in her jockey's weight told her that he'd raised his arm; a split second later, a sharp pain stung her quarters as his whip cracked down on her tender skin.

For an instant, she was going to object and dig her toes in, but an even stronger instinct made her stretch out her neck for one last effort.

As she stormed across the finishing line, with her ears lying flat against her neck, she knew for the first time what it was like to win, and she liked it more than anything else she had ever done.

Kate, almost faint with excitement, only lowered her glasses when Owen Williams had finally pulled up Willow Star a hundred yards past the finishing post and was wheeling her round to come back. For a few moments, Kate had forgotten the misery that had been tearing her apart before the race.

Now, with horrible inevitability, she raised her binoculars again and trained them on the box.

The sight that met her eyes almost made her retch.

Charlie had wrapped the girl in his arms. They were hugging each other as if they'd only just discovered it could be fun.

Kate dropped the glasses from her blurred, smarting eyes and turned away. She felt utterly betrayed, and a complete fool. Hurt, angry, confused, she came to an abrupt decision. She walked straight to the exit and out to the car park.

Robert Aylestone was feeling nauseous too. He lowered his glasses as Willow Star passed the post and allowed his dislike of Charles Patterson to reach new depths.

Everything seemed to have gone wrong at his yard since Percy had won his bumper. He'd sacked Charlie; he'd had to. His guts had told him, and gossip had confirmed, that his young assistant had worked the whole Percy episode to his own

87

advantage. Then Nick Ryder had gone.

Aylestone thought he must be slipping when he heard that his two assistants were taking Oak Hollow. He should have known weeks before. The parcel of invective he'd sent to the Jockey Club hadn't brought a result. Now, to cap it all, the cocky bastards had talked Charles Gordon into moving Percy to their yard.

It was more than humiliating, it was character assassination. Aylestone had also heard that morning that Charlie had entered Percy for a long-distance condition race at the end of June.

Nick was jubilant at the yard's first big win. He thought it only right that as a partner in the yard he should go up and congratulate the winning owner. With some misgivings over Major Patterson's reaction, he walked into Michael Russell's box. Charlie wasn't there. Nick considered backing out, but he'd already been spotted by David Patterson.

Veronica was friendly enough. Nick had known her since his school days when sometimes she had come and taken him and Charlie out for the day.

'Well done, Nick! Brilliant effort. You even managed to get a smile out of David.'

'I think you'll find,' Patterson said in his quiet voice, 'that Charlie does most of the actual training at Oak Hollow.'

Nick tried not to flinch. He'd had to deal for some time with this kind of oblique attack from his friend's stepfather. He still didn't understand why.

Veronica rushed to his defence. 'Really, David, don't be so ungracious. Nick's in it with Charlie; the licence may be in Charlie's name, but they're equal partners, isn't that right, Nick? Charlie was telling me at lunch he couldn't possibly have got it all together on his own.'

Nick nodded, embarrassed.

'Charlie always made sure Nick was on his team,' Patterson remarked.

Veronica, genuinely upset by her brother's rudeness, took Nick by the arm and led him towards the front of the box. 'Don't take any notice of him. He's one of those people who's not just a bad loser but a bad winner, too. Let me get you a drink.'

Nick wished he'd never come to the box, but as he was here he was glad to be able to get a good view of the next race, which he wanted to see. He found himself standing beside Imogen. She gave him a warm smile which made him tingle and think of Kate, then, unhappily, of her spending the previous night with Charlie.

He smiled back at Imogen, painfully aware that he held no interest for her. 'How are you, Immy? I gather you've been in Florence.'

They laughed and carried on a comfortable conversation discussing the charms and appeal of the medieval city. Nick knew that their enthusiasm would have been lost on the less erudite Charlie. The horse he had his eye on won the next race, as he had hoped. He left the box feeling less sorry for himself, acknowledging that it wasn't Charlie's fault that Kate was attracted to him and his stepfather was so damned rude.

CHAPTER FIVE

Nick couldn't get Kate out of his head. He knew he'd been a fool to let himself imagine she was attracted to him but he was still finding it hard to accept.

Being honest with himself, he knew she'd never been anything more than friendly towards him, but a few kind words from a pretty girl was all it had taken to arouse romantic ideas in his normally rational head; ideas of warm relationships, love—even marriage. He hadn't much experience of love; just two short-lived affairs with girls who didn't begin to compare with Kate.

His physical attraction to her was compounded by a mental affinity he felt they had. They shared the same dry sense of humour and taste in music; they read the same books and, of course, they both had an unquenchable fascination with horses. It seemed, just now, a terrible shame that they also shared an affection for Charlie. But at the back of Nick's mind lurked the hope that maybe, when Charlie finally lost interest in her, which on all known form he would sooner or later, he could resume his pursuit of her.

The season got into its stride and the yard became busier with more runners. Nick's hurt at losing Kate began to ebb, made easier by the fact that Charlie never mentioned her and she herself hadn't been to Oak Hollow since the day Willow Star first ran at Goodwood.

On a hot June day, when the sun baked the tops of the rolling down and no wind stirred the long coarse grass that covered them, Nick was sitting in the poky little room in the bungalow which he had commandeered for his office. Looking through the ever-changing list of the yard's inmates, he thought of Ivor Thompson's advice about the need to find new owners. Of the twenty-six horses they'd started with, only sixteen were left. Of those that had gone, just one had broken down—an older horse who'd

90

had leg problems with his previous trainer; the others had just been no good. Nick and Charlie had decided as a matter of policy wherever possible to move on any horse they thought incapable of winning a race. Their practice of being honest with owners looked as though it would pay off in the long run; they, not their rivals, were being asked to find the replacements. But good horses weren't easy to find mid-season.

As Nick turned to his current balance sheet, he reflected that having orders to buy was no help in paying the rent. Six new horses had restored the number to twenty-two, but that wasn't enough to break even, let alone pay the partners a wage for their toil.

Despite these fiscal worries, and his disappointment over Kate, Nick had to admit that he'd never been happier. He was his own boss. The horses they had were running well and prospects were bright. The advantage of weeding out the slow horses was that it allowed them to be positive about those that remained. They didn't need to believe that their geese were swans, and they could afford to aim only at goals they had a realistic chance of reaching. Each horse had its own training programme with specific targets. If one failed, Charlie and Nick meticulously drafted another.

Countless hours spent between the form book and the racing calendar had yielded other rewards. The partners had already earned tidy sums from gambling, for themselves and their owners. This, though, never showed on Nick's balance sheets; gambling winnings, as far as he was concerned, were the icing on the cake. The yard had to support itself on its training income.

The biggest encouragement to potential owners was the fact that the yard was producing winners. Charlie's high profile gave them more than their fair share of publicity and though their numbers were down, a lot of outsiders were beginning to show an interest in the new tenants at Oak Hollow. Even Nick, without Charlie's natural optimism, thought it only a matter of time before they filled the yard and really took off.

So, despite the financial knife edge along which they seemed sometimes to teeter, there was never any question of corners being cut where the welfare of either the horses or the lads was concerned. Nick and Charlie agreed that the most important ingredient of their success to date was that the yard was a happy one and discerning visitors saw that reflected in the horses as they came squealing from their boxes each morning.

Kenny and the other lads had already made a significant contribution. They never complained when there was extra work to be done, and the two young bosses weren't above mucking in with them. Because of their age, Nick and Charlie had a more informal relationship with their stable staff than most trainers. Racehorse training was generally an industry steeped in traditions of old-fashioned master-servant relationships. The lack of this obstacle to communication at Oak Hollow allowed the lads to put their point of view knowing they'd be listened to and taken seriously. The more responsibility they were given, the better they seemed to respond.

Nick leaned back in his chair, stretched his arms high above his head and let out a long yawn. He reached down and picked up the well-thumbed form book which he seemed to spend most of his life studying, searching for the easiest races for their intended runners. The dilemma facing him and Charlie that morning was whether or not they should run Flitgrove in a seller. Flitgrove was a filly moderately bred for the flat. She belonged to Percy's owner, Charles Gordon. Mr Gordon was slowly building up a small band of brood mares and had bought Flitgrove as a present for his wife, Sarah, for their wedding anniversary.

Although she had worked well at home, the filly had failed to show any form on the racecourse. After three disappointing runs, Charlie and the girl who looked after her felt she needed to gain some confidence. A selling race should be well within her capabilities and just one success, however lowly, could make a great difference to the price of her offspring when they came to be sold. The risk of running her in a seller was that someone might run the price up at the auction afterwards if she won. An even worse scenario would be that they lost her altogether to an outside bidder. Mrs Gordon adored the filly. She brought a big bag of titbits for her every Sunday morning. She was a large, domineering woman with a voice like gravel. Nick couldn't even contemplate the possibility of having to give her the news that her darling had been sold.

In the meantime, an hour's study of the other entrants' form convinced Nick that if Flitgrove ran, she would win. He was glad that the final decision to run her would be taken by Mr Gordon with help from Charlie.

Nick eased himself stiffly from his desk chair and walked out into the sunshine to find Kenny. While he was up at the yard, he saw Charlie arrive back in the

Range Rover and go into the bungalow.

When Nick got back to the office, Charlie was sitting in his chair with the phone pressed to his ear, pleading. 'I can promise you, Charles, that nobody will bid for her, but even if they do, all you have to do is outbid them. It's not a problem, I give you my word. Let her run; let her win a race and we'll see if she can win a little handicap somewhere after that.'

Nick gathered that the owner was deliberating, experienced enough to weigh the pros and cons, but Charlie was at his most persuasive, almost irresistible. After a couple more minutes of optimistic enthusiasm, Charlie put the phone down and turned to Nick with a triumphant grin. 'Another winner coming up, Nicky boy. He's agreed to let her run in the seller at Bath on Monday.'

Nick greeted the news with a wary smile. Although he agreed that the filly would probably win, he was still uncertain about running her. He doubted that Charlie had thought beyond the race. 'Let's just hope nobody does bid for her. If we lose her, I can see us losing Percy as well.'

'Bollocks,' Charlie laughed. 'You're being too bloody cautious as usual. Who's going to bid for her?'

'I don't know. Anybody could,' Nick said. Privately, he thought that Robert Aylestone might, but he didn't say so. He was still sure that it was their old boss who'd written the letter to the Jockey Club objecting to their licence application. But Charlie, after his initial anger and once the licence had come through, had pushed the event right out of his mind. Nick wished he could too. Aylestone might not notice that the filly was running, he told himself; he was only interested in jumpers. He might be away on

94

holiday. Nevertheless, in the days leading up to the race, Nick couldn't write him off as a threat when they were in such a potentially vulnerable position.

During those three days, Mr Gordon phoned constantly. Each time Charlie managed to convince him there was nothing to worry about. He told Nick that Mr Gordon had chosen not to explain to his wife what the outcome of a selling race could be, knowing she wouldn't agree to the filly running if he did. Mr Gordon, in the end, trusted Charlie and he wanted the stud to pay its way as far as possible. A win for Flitgrove would do a lot to enhance her paddock value. Once she had won, though, that would be it. No more sellers.

Mr Gordon also announced with some regret that he and his wife wouldn't be able to come to watch the race themselves. Charlie promised to take care of everything and ring them the moment the race was over.

*   *   *

Monday turned out to be a comparatively quiet day in the office. Nick had worked most of Sunday so he decided to indulge himself and go racing for a change. Besides, Bath was less than an hour away down the M4; Flitgrove's race was the first on the card. He and Charlie would be back by four.

They set off in Nick's car, a ten-year-old BMW which looked as if it had left the showroom that morning.

When they had run through the risks and returns of the afternoon's race for what must have been the twentieth time, the conversation turned to Willow Star and her next race at Royal Ascot in ten days'

95

time.

'Will your stepfather be coming to see her run?' Nick asked.

'I don't know. I told him he should, but frankly I don't think he's that interested. I think he only bought her to help us out.'

'He wouldn't have done it as a favour.' Privately, Nick didn't think Major Patterson was capable of a considerate act.

'Yes, you're probably right. He was certainly keen to know how much he might get for her if she carried on showing some form.'

'You don't think he'll sell her?' Nick asked.

'Hard to say. I don't think he needs the money, but he never talks to me about that sort of thing.'

'He was bloody rude to me at Goodwood,' Nick said reluctantly. It was the first time he'd mentioned it to Charlie.

'I know. Immy told me. I'm sorry, but that's what I mean. He's getting very tetchy lately.'

'My father told me he'd had some bad luck at Lloyd's.'

'Is he his agent?'

'I think so. He certainly introduced him to a few syndicates.'

'Anyway,' Charlie said after a few moments' silence, 'I don't know what he's thinking of doing about Willow. My guess is he'll hang on to her for a couple of seasons. At least, that's what I've told my mother to persuade him to do. To me, she's just the sort of filly that will improve as a three-year-old, and Goodwood was promising.'

'Ascot will be a better indicator. Do you suppose Kate Scanlan will be there to see her run?'

'I don't know,' Charlie said. 'Don't you?'

'Me? Why should I?'

'I thought she was such a great friend of yours.'

'The last time I saw her, she'd just spent the night with you, remember?' Nick said quietly.

Charlie didn't answer at once. He looked down at the racing paper in his lap. 'Look, Nick, I'm sorry. She's a bloody good-looking girl—I'm sorry we both fancy her. But she'd given me such a hard time, I couldn't believe it when she suddenly eased up and came out to dinner, and it all went brilliantly. Then I don't know what happened.'

For a few moments Nick stared straight ahead, concentrating on his driving. 'She said you were lousy in bed; that's what happened.'

'What?' Charlie spluttered. 'How the hell could she say that?' Stammering with agitation, he began to describe his night with Kate until Nick stopped him with a burst of laughter.

'It's all right,' he said. 'She didn't say that. At least, if she did, I didn't hear her. I haven't seen her either, to be honest.'

'You bastard!' Charlie laughed with relief. 'You had me going then.'

'I know your weak points,' Nick said. 'Did you see her at Goodwood?'

'No, but she told me she'd been. I've spoken to her a couple of times, but she's been ice-cold, said she was busy—you know, washing her hair.'

'Maybe she's embarrassed; I mean, she knew I was interested in her.' Nick sighed. 'I suppose I knew she didn't fancy me but we got on so well; she knows a lot about music, and we've read the same books.'

Charlie laughed. 'She didn't tell me that.'

'Well, she wouldn't,' Nick said with the ghost of a grin. 'Anyway, it looks as if we've both blown it.' He

97

seemed satisfied that this was, if not ideal, at least fair.

'Yeah,' Charlie nodded, only half-agreeing but relieved that the air had been cleared. He looked back down at the day's runners. 'I hope to God we've done the right thing, putting this filly in a seller.'

'It's not too late to take her out. You could always say she's off colour.' Nick knew this wasn't what Charlie wanted to hear. He sensed that his partner was getting cold feet and wanted reassurance which he couldn't honestly offer.

Charlie stared out of the window, hoping for some flash of inspiration. He wanted winners and Flitgrove should win. Even if the unthinkable did happen and they lost her in the auction, it wouldn't be the end of the world. As far as he could tell, she would never be more than a moderate horse. But he didn't want to lose Percy. He was certain there were plenty of good races to be won with him. His problem was that he could judge a horse's reaction to a situation better than a human's. He didn't know how well he would manage Mr and Mrs Gordon if things went wrong. He wound down the window and leaned back to let the cool air rush over his face.

After a while, he turned to Nick. 'Let her run,' he said decisively. 'We'll never get anywhere if we don't take a few chances.'

'All right,' Nick nodded. 'But I tell you what. I'm going to ring Aylestone's yard to find out where he is.'

'Aylestone's? Why?'

'Because if he's away on holiday, I think we'd have a lot less to worry about.'

Charlie didn't answer at once. He looked at Nick, knowing what he was saying, reluctant to admit its relevance. Slowly, he reached out and picked up the phone. 'I'll do it,' he said, starting to dial Aylestone's number. The trainer's secretary answered and recognised Charlie's voice at once. It took only a few flattering words to discover that the boss was out for the day but she didn't know where.

*　　*　　*

Bath racecourse is the highest in the country, perched over the small city, nearly eight hundred feet above sea level. On a fine day like this it was possible to see across Somerset to the Mendips. As Nick drove into the racecourse, with two hours to go before the first race, the vast green car park was already filling up with picnickers taking advantage of the sunshine for a pre-race lunch.

Charlie went off to check that Flitgrove had arrived safely and that she'd been properly declared. Nick sat and read the papers.

The conditions for Flitgrove's race stated that the winner was to be sold for not less than two thousand guineas. The race itself carried a two thousand pound prize to the winner so if someone did decide to have a go at buying her, they could bid at least that much before the expenses began to mount. Above the minimum selling price, the racecourse kept fifty per cent, which meant that if Flitgrove sold for four thousand, Charles Gordon would receive only three. Or if they had to bid four thousand to buy her in, it would cost them a thousand to keep the filly. It would be money well spent. The value that winning the race would add to Flitgrove's progeny at the sales would be much more.

Nick dozed off in the warm summer sun. He woke

with a start only twenty minutes before the filly was due to run. He half ran to the course and made his way to the front of the stands where the bookmakers were doing their best to drum up some business over what looked no more than a moderate contest. The best price he could find for Flitgrove was six to four. While Nick cursed that he couldn't find anything longer, he knew that if he were a bookie, he wouldn't have been as generous. He and Charlie had planned to put a thousand pounds on the filly, provided she wasn't odds on.

Discreetly, Nick pulled a wad of fifty pound notes from his pocket, split them into five bundles and placed two hundred pounds with each of the biggest firms on the rails. Satisfied that he'd done the best he could, he walked to the owners' and trainers' stand to wait for Charlie.

The runners emerged on to the course down to his right. There were fourteen in all. Flitgrove came out in a small group of three. Her dark brown coat glistened as she strode on to the course. She looked, Nick thought, in a completely different class to the rest of them. As the field turned and cantered back towards the one-mile five-furlong start, he lifted his glasses to take another look at the bookies' boards.

'What are you grinning about?'

Nick lowered his glasses and turned to Charlie who had slipped in beside him. 'I'm grinning because we've got six to four about an odds-on shot.'

'I've told that little jockey not to win by too far,' Charlie leaned over and whispered. 'And to make sure he jumps straight off her and leads her back in as if she was totally knackered. I think if we get away without having a bid for her, we'll have had a result. The rest of these look rubbish.'

Almost as soon as the horses had sprung from the stalls, there was never much doubt about what was going to happen. Flitgrove was always travelling easily and from the turn into the straight the only question was how far she would win by.

Charlie wanted to kick himself as she romped home by an easy five lengths with the jockey unable to make it less. On that performance, she looked as though she could have won just about anywhere. As he and Nick climbed down from the stands, he made a quick reappraisal of her value.

Although he'd convinced Charles Gordon that no one would make a serious bid for her, he had privately estimated that the most anyone would go to was five thousand. After such a convincing and obviously effortless win, it could well go to a lot more. If the worst came to the worst, he and Nick would have to help out on the repurchase because, whatever happened, they had to hang on to her now.

Despite the jockey's pantomime of jumping off her as she came to a halt, there were plenty of people pushing against the rail of the winner's enclosure to get a better look at her and see what promised to be a good, active auction.

As soon as the 'weighed in' had echoed from the tannoy, the Clerk of the Course, who doubled as auctioneer on these occasions, climbed on to a rostrum to deliver a crisp, upbeat summary of Flitgrove's racing career and breeding. Charlie bit his lip and shook his head angrily as the auctioneer eulogised over the filly, making her sound like the best thing on four legs since Pegasus.

Nick had slipped away somewhere quieter where he frantically tried to get hold of Charles Gordon on the phone. He wanted to tell them that the horse had won. More important now, he wanted to be in contact in case the bidding escalated to silly money.

'Who'll start me off at two thousand?' the auctioneer began confidently. 'Come on! You all saw her win. There are plenty more races in her—and not sellers either.'

Charlie cringed at the accuracy of his words. A coating of clammy sweat seeped through the pores of his neck and forehead.

The auctioneer was looking around, waiting, not too impatiently, for the first bid when a man—a farmer by the look of him—thrust a hand in the air and offered one thousand. The bidding was slow to start, rising in increments of two and three hundred. The farmer dropped out after two and a half thousand. Someone else had taken it up, but Charlie couldn't spot the other bidder. When the price reached five thousand, he thought he had the filly.

'All done then?' the auctioneer asked testily. 'She's bought in and you're letting a bargain go, I'm telling you.'

'I'll shoot the bastard if he doesn't hurry up and sell her,' Charlie hissed at Nick. 'Haven't you got hold of those bloody owners yet?'

Nick didn't reply. He'd just seen Robert Aylestone.

The trainer had appeared from nowhere. Now he was standing directly opposite them. He nodded at the auctioneer.

'Thank you, sir. Five thousand five hundred; that's more like it.'

Charlie gritted his teeth as the Clerk of the Course stared straight at him.

'Come on now, you don't want to let her go for the sake of a bid,' he cajoled. 'She's better than you

102

thought, I'll wager.'

Charlie raised his index finger for one last bid as the auctioneer's gavel reached its zenith, ready to knock the filly down to Aylestone.

Aylestone gave a short, quick nod and a bland smile spread over his craggy face. He looked at Charlie and Nick with an insolent shrug, daring them to take him on.

At fifteen thousand pounds, Nick still hadn't made contact with the Gordons. Swallowing bitterly, Charlie turned away. The filly just wasn't worth that much, even allowing for Mrs Gordon's extravagant affection for it.

'What the hell do we do now?' Nick said, close to panic.

Charlie was about to launch into a vicious verbal slating of Robert Aylestone when the auctioneer's excited voice rose in pitch. 'Fifteen thousand five hundred guineas. A new bidder. Thank you, sir.'

Charlie and Nick looked at each other in astonishment. Charlie glanced across the ring. Robert Aylestone's weatherbeaten face was creased with uncertainty. The bidding had been rising by a thousand pounds a time. Aylestone pondered a few uncomfortable moments before nodding again. The auctioneer turned to his right. Charlie and Nick followed his eyes. They were resting expectantly on a well-known blood-stock agent. Mike Dubens was still in his early thirties but he had already made a name and a lot of money by constantly being one step ahead of the rest of the pack. With a barely perceptible movement of his head, the bidding jumped again.

'Come on, don't lose her now,' the auctioneer gleefully urged Aylestone.

'What the fuck is Mike Dubens doing?' Charlie muttered hoarsely to Nick. 'She's stones below the type of animal he deals in.'

'I don't know, but he's going to get her. Aylestone's just walked away.'

'All done then at sixteen thousand?' The auctioneer's voice suggested he was more than pleased, in fact rather bewildered at the price he had achieved. His eyes made one last sweep around the small crowd and he brought his gavel down firmly on the front of his rostrum. 'Mike Dubens. Thank you.'

Charlie grabbed Nick's sleeve. 'Come on. Let's go and see what the hell that was all about.' He turned and made straight for the young bloodstock agent who was signing the sales docket.

Charlie and Nick knew Mike Dubens, but not well. If they'd known him better, he'd have let them know beforehand that he was planning to bid for the filly. It was a recognised courtesy.

Mike looked up and smiled as they approached. Charlie brushed aside his friendly greeting.

'Look, we know why Aylestone was bidding, and it had nothing to do with wanting the filly at that price. But I can't see any reason why anyone as sharp as you should want to pay way over the odds for her.'

Mike looked embarrassed and put his hands in the air. 'Look, I'm sorry. I didn't know you were that keen to buy her. I wanted her, but I wouldn't have bid if you hadn't dropped out. I thought Aylestone was going to get her.'

'Aylestone was trying to run us up just to make life difficult,' Charlie said. 'The bastard's pissed off at us setting up on our own. But why the hell do you want her? It's not as if she's related to anything special.'

Mike's eyes slithered uncomfortably to one side.

Charlie and Nick stared at him for an answer.

He shrugged his shoulders. 'Until three o'clock this morning you'd have been right about that.' Charlie felt as if someone had punctured his lung. He had a horrible feeling he knew what was coming. Mike went on, 'Her full brother had his first run on dirt at Santa Anita last night and knocked nine-tenths of a second off the course record. The trainer says he's the best he's ever had. It was just lucky for me I heard about it, knowing his sister was running here today.'

Nick and Charlie shook their heads in resignation. They recognised that they'd been pipped by a pro who did more homework than any other agent on the circuit. Mike seemed genuinely sorry when Nick told him that Flitgrove had become Mrs Gordon's special pet, and Charles Gordon also owned Persimmon Way.

'Look, I'd normally let you have her back for a small profit but something tells me she's capable of a lot more than she did today. She might even be like her brother and improve again once she gets on the dirt.'

Charlie heard from a distance. He was grappling with the problem of how to break the news to Charles Gordon. It was bad enough to have lost the filly but then telling him she was closely related to a potential star in America, just as he was expanding his stud, would make him justifiably furious.

'I'll tell you what I'll do,' Mike was saying. 'I don't want to sell her to you, but you can go on training her. Mind you,' he added with a grin, 'I don't want her running in any more sellers.'

This didn't do much to ease the partners' concern about the Gordons but they thanked the agent and had a brief discussion about training fees and future plans. When Mike had gone, Nick and Charlie went to the stables. They told the lads what was happening and walked back to the car park.

Nick was pulling away when they saw Mike Dubens again. He didn't see them; he was too preoccupied. He had an arm wrapped round Kate Scanlan's waist.

'I don't believe it!' Charlie spluttered. 'First he nicks our horse, then he nicks our girl as well.' He burst out laughing. 'Oh well, at least we haven't got anything to fall out over now.'

Nick didn't laugh. 'We wouldn't have done anyway.'

*   *   *

On a sunny Thursday, two weeks after Flitgrove's race at Bath, Willow Star was entered to make her second public appearance in the Chesham Stakes at Royal Ascot. The Chesham was traditionally one of the weaker two-year-old races of the meeting. Nevertheless, it carried Listed status and was a coveted prize. The form of her first win at Goodwood had worked out well. A couple of those who had finished well behind her had won since. And a win at Ascot in any race would do Oak Hollow's reputation a lot of good. Everyone involved was getting excited at the chance to show what they could really do— everyone, that is, except the two people Charlie had most expected to show interest and enthusiasm.

David Patterson gave no sign of pride or pleasure in his first racehorse, and Kate still hadn't been near Oak Hollow since Goodwood. Charlie had wanted to ring her, prompted by the thought of Mike Dubens moving in on her, but pride wouldn't allow it. Privately, though, he hadn't given up hope. He was bound to run into her sooner or later and get a chance to advance his cause. He would admit only to himself that he found her rejection and decamping to the bloodstock agent a lot harder to handle than he'd thought he would.

He refused to let it get him down. Everything at the yard was going well. He had managed to placate Mrs Gordon over the loss of Flitgrove with a lot of heartfelt apology, throwing himself at her mercy and promising to find a replacement soon. Charles Gordon had been less easy to deal with. Although in the end he'd been persuaded to leave Percy at Oak Hollow, a definite rift had opened up between them, which wasn't going to be cured in a hurry.

Besides this, they'd managed another two wins which brought their total so far to thirteen. For the size of their yard, at that stage of their first season, it was a perfectly respectable score, with the chance of a listed winner with Willow Star.

Charlie had booked Owen Williams again to ride her. This was Oak Hollow's only runner at the meeting. With runners elsewhere, Charlie had missed the first day. On the Wednesday he had treated himself to a day out and took his cousin Imogen.

She didn't have to make much of an effort to stand out, even at Royal Ascot. She was a natural target for the army of photographers and TV cameras who had come to cover the fashion rather than the racing. On a hot day, in deep maroon silk and a pink straw hat, she was a picture editor's gift.

Kate stared at the photograph in the *Daily Mail* next morning as she drank a cup of coffee in her cottage kitchen. She picked up the telephone and

107

dialled the number at Oak Hollow. To her relief, it was Nick who answered.

'Hello,' she said. 'It's Kate here.'

'Kate who?' Nick asked.

'Scanlan,' she started to say, before she heard Nick laughing.

'What's made you break your silence after so long?' he asked. 'We thought you'd forgotten all about us.'

'Of course I haven't. Look, Nick, I just wanted to ask you something. Who is Imogen Russell?'

'Immy? Oh, I suppose you've seen that very flattering shot of Charlie with her in the *Daily Mail*.'

'Yes, I have.'

'And you'll have noticed how, with typically shoddy reporting, they haven't wanted to spoil a good story with the detail that Charlie and Imogen are first cousins and like brother and sister to each other.'

There was a silence at the other end of the line, until Kate asked quietly, 'If they're like brother and sister, why were they hugging and kissing at Goodwood?'

'When?' Nick asked, genuinely astonished.

'After Willow won.'

Nick really laughed now. 'Didn't you want to hug and kiss the person nearest to you when she crossed the line? I certainly wanted to.'

'I bet you didn't though.'

'No,' Nick admitted, 'I didn't. But anyway, who says brothers and sisters can't hug and kiss?' He paused a moment. 'Is that why we haven't seen you at the yard since then?'

'Yes,' Kate said in a small voice.

'Does that mean,' Nick asked kindly, 'that we

108

might start seeing you again?'

'Maybe.'

'God, I hope so. We might get Charlie back to normal. Are you going to come racing today?'

'Mike Dubens invited me but I didn't want to come so I haven't got a badge.'

'No problem, I'll leave one for you. It won't get you into the royal enclosure but at least you'll be able to see Willow in the flesh.'

'How is she?'

'I don't think you'll be disappointed.'

*　　*　　*

Although he was head lad and responsible for the overall running of the yard, Kenny Ford still managed to look after Willow Star himself. In his eyes, the filly could do no wrong. He knew the time would come when he'd have to let someone else do her, but for the moment he was making the most of it.

The filly's race at Ascot was the last on Thursday's card, at five thirty, which meant that after he'd ridden out first lot, he'd had time to lead her down the road for half an hour to stretch her legs. Away from the gallops she behaved like an old hack and ambled along quietly at his side. Occasionally she would nuzzle his arm and pocket, looking for a mint, but for the most part she seemed glad just to be out in the open. Kenny had given her a small feed of oats first thing that morning. He'd let her have a few fistfuls of hay and, apart from water which she could drink until two hours before her race, that would be all until she arrived back home for her supper.

The horsebox was due to leave at one o'clock. At midday, Kenny gave Willow a thorough brushing and greased her feet. When he had dealt with the others' lunchtime feeds and checked that there were no problems in the yard, he went home to change into his best suit. He groomed himself with a perfunctoriness he wouldn't have tolerated in one of the horses and rushed back to the yard.

He wrapped Willow in a light travelling sheet and loaded her into the lorry with his kitbag and a hold-all containing Major Patterson's silks. When he was sure she was happy and comfortable, he clambered into the cab beside the driver. They set off far earlier than they would normally have done, to allow for any delays they might meet.

At two fifteen, Willow Star walked safely into her stable at Ascot, overlooking the lawn beside the driveway. It was hot and airless in the confines of the stableyard. Even with her sheet off, it was too hot to keep the door closed. Kenny heaved a bale of straw from the lorry and put it against the stable door, where he sat for the rest of the afternoon, keeping watch over her as the other lads and horses came and went.

Results from the earlier races filtered down from the canteen nearby. The first three all went to horses trained at Newmarket. A lad bringing news of the fourth shouted to him, punching his hand in the air. 'Four out of four, Kenny,' he jeered. 'I told you, Lambourn's only got slow old jumpers.'

Kenny smiled and lifted his hand to stroke Willow's nose. She had her head over the door, taking in everything that was going on. 'You'll soon show 'em who's best, eh?' Kenny's fingers tickled her delicate skin. She lifted her nose high in the air and curled back her top lip, baring her teeth and gums. It looked for all the world as if she was smiling. Kenny wondered if they'd both be smiling after the race.

At four forty-five, he gave her a final rub over with a brush and cloth and greased her feet again. He pulled on her racing bridle and clipped on the leading rein with its smart brass chain. He led her from the stable and joined four other horses from her race on their way up the hill and across the main road into the racecourse.

Of the nine horses declared to run in the Chesham, only two were fillies. As they walked quietly round the pre-parade ring, Kenny and the other filly's lad were careful to keep them at the back, away from the randy advances of the colts. It was hot and there was no shelter where they were. A few flies were buzzing around Willow Star's eyes and she started to sweat. Kenny kept talking to her, keeping her as relaxed as he could, but he was relieved when Charlie arrived to put on her saddle. Once it was on and he'd sponged her mouth out with cold water, Kenny was able to lead her down into the main paddock. It was much cooler there in the shade of the tall beeches. By the time the jockeys came strutting into the parade ring, Willow had dried off completely.

'How is she?' asked Owen as he leaned down from the saddle to adjust the length of his irons.

'I'd say she's improved at least ten pounds since Goodwood. She knows what the job's about now.'

Willow Star had woken up. She knew she'd soon be racing. She was too well-mannered to jig-jog but the excitement was almost too much for her. She began walking with an exaggerated movement which made Kenny laugh and pat her neck. Owen cracked her smartly down the shoulder to stop her.

Kenny reached up sharply and squeezed the jockey's leg angrily so that it hurt. 'Do that again and

111

I'll drag you off and slap you.'

Owen tried to justify himself but Kenny cut him short. 'All she's doing is letting you know how well she's feeling. In the next ten minutes she's going to run her guts out and earn you the best part of two grand. So keep your whip to yourself.' Kenny forced himself to wish the jockey luck as he released the lead rein. He watched Willow Star bound away across the green turf, eager to get on with things.

When she'd passed the Silver Ring, Kenny walked the short distance to the small concrete stand reserved for stable staff. It was a good viewing point and there was a large TV set in front of the guard rail to let the lads watch the proceedings until the last few furlongs when they could follow the race with the naked eye.

Kenny found himself sitting next to a lad with whom he'd once shared digs. The lad's horse had run poorly in an earlier race and he'd lost all his week's wages. He was anxious to know if he could recoup them on Willow Star.

'You could have done, but you're too late.' Kenny pointed to the screen as the commentator's voice calmly let spectators know that the race had started. Kenny leaned forward eagerly. He watched as Willow Star broke quickly from the stalls. She was the least experienced in the field but while most of the others struggled to find their feet, she began burning a trail up the middle of the course. She led for over three furlongs with her ears pricked, until a horse with a big white blaze pulled its way alongside her. His long easy stride contrasted starkly with hers. For a few moments it looked to Kenny as if she'd been headed. He could see her struggling to hold her place. Owen started to pump away on her, head down and hands running up and down her neck like someone using a washboard. For a brief spell it looked as if the whole field would swallow her up.

'She's had it now,' said the lad beside Kenny, thankful he hadn't got a bet on. Kenny told him to shut up and moved in closer to the screen. He heard the large crowd packing the stands beginning to bellow. He switched his view down the course where a multi-coloured blur was galloping towards him. He picked out Major Patterson's bright red silk, but couldn't judge how Willow was travelling. He darted back to the TV and a side view. His heart suddenly thumped with excitement when he saw she was almost upsides again. Both his feet left the ground as he launched himself into the air, bellowing his lungs out. 'Come on, Willow! Come on, my girl!' His head flicked from the screen to the course and back again as he watched her battling her way to the front. There were three horses in a line and everyone around him seemed to be shouting for a different one. With only fifty yards to run, a photo finish looked certain, until a brave little nose began to edge ahead of the rest.

Kenny didn't care who saw the tears which trickled down his face. It was the proudest moment of his entire life. Watching her outfight the others right up to the line was something he would never forget. He leaped from the stands amid shouts of congratulations from the other lads and ran to greet her.

'This is one tough filly,' beamed Owen.

Kenny forgot their earlier friction and heaped praise on the pair of them. He threw his arms round Willow's neck and gently pulled her ears. 'She's the best bloody filly in the whole country.'

*   *   *

In the morning, Charlie woke without the thumping hangover he deserved. He opened his eyes, took in the morning suit scattered around the floor of his bedroom, the simple white cotton frock and Kate's gentle features, serene in sleep, a few inches from his face. He closed his eyes and refused to think about his duties for the day just yet. After yesterday and last night, there didn't seem anything else left to achieve.

He eased himself closer to the soft, warm body beside him and felt a pair of arms wrap themselves round him. As he and Kate snuggled closer and her fingers crept up between his thighs, something told him he was going to be late for work.

*   *   *

After the autumn sales at Newmarket, twelve yearlings arrived at Oak Hollow ready for breaking in. The owners of the seven two-year-olds they had run that season confirmed they would be leaving them there. Only four horses moved on.

Kenny was now too busy as head lad to give Willow Star the attention she merited and a young Scottish boy called Titch had taken her over.

Willow had come home from the Chesham Stakes with sore shins. Charlie and Nick decided to rest her for the remainder of the season. For the next two months she did nothing more than light exercise. Each day Kenny smoothed soft clay on to the front of her canon bones to keep them cool and gradually she returned to total fitness. By late October she'd resumed a normal training programme with the others. Titch now rode her out every day—a

114

responsibility he relished. He rode well but had never 'done' a really good horse. For him, it was a thrill just to canter her and he spoiled her as much as Kenny had. As 'stable star', she was now housed in the best box in the yard, next to the feed house where the lads all congregated, and she was guaranteed plenty of attention. If no one took any notice of her at feed times, she would bang her feet on the door until they did.

Throughout the winter she developed well and though they were reluctant to admit it even to each other, Charlie and Nick both thought she had real Classic potential. It was a lot to hope for, and there was always the danger that she wouldn't train on or wouldn't stay beyond the six furlongs at which she had already won. But, if anything, she looked as if she'd improve at a longer trip and as the year opened, everything was in front of her.

Willow Star's first major target was the One Thousand Guineas at Newmarket. Nick had spent many long winter hours absorbed in the form book and calculated that she had to improve by at least five pounds to have a realistic chance of a place. The top fillies' race at the back end of the last season had produced some talented youngsters. One in particular, a filly called Lightbeam, had been very impressive winning at Newmarket and was already three to one favourite for the Guineas. As Willow Star hadn't run since June, she could be backed at almost any price and Nick and Charlie were worried that she might have become ring rusty after such a long lay-off.

The main prep races before the first Classic of the season came only a couple of weeks before it. It would be taking a risk to let Willow have her first run in one of them. If they found she needed another run for experience, it would be too late then.

They thought about taking her to a racecourse for a full-blown gallop but that was never quite the same. The cut and thrust of a race could never be simulated. In the end, they opted for the unusual step of taking her to the south of France, to Cagnes-sur-Mer on the Côte d'Azur where competitive racing and good ground happened earlier. They phoned to find that the going was good and there was a suitable race for her. What was more, if she won, she would more than cover the expenses of getting there. And, just as important, she seemed to love travelling.

To save money, Charlie went as a groom with Titch and flew in the plane with the horses. They arrived with their own supply of hay and water two days before the race, to give her time to settle down. The following morning, Titch took her for a spin round the outside of the track while Charlie stood on the rails and watched through his binoculars.

'How did she go?'

Titch shrugged his shoulders. 'I don't know. It's difficult to tell. I couldn't say that there's anything wrong with her.' He hesitated slightly. 'It's just she doesn't seem as perky as normal. Maybe it's being in a strange place.'

'Oh hell,' Charlie muttered. 'I hope this wasn't a bad decision. My father'll be livid if I've brought her all the way here and she doesn't win anything.'

Titch jumped down and plucked a handful of grass and offered it to the filly. She took it, then, uninterested, let it fall to the ground.

'Maybe she'll be better tomorrow,' the lad said doubtfully.

When he returned to the lads' hostel where he and

116

Titch were staying, Charlie phoned Nick. He needed reassuring that they were doing the right thing for the filly. He couldn't decide whether he should withdraw her or not, or how much damage she might do to herself if he let her run when she wasn't well. Her temperature was normal, but as Titch had said, she just didn't seem a hundred per cent.

After a long, rambling discussion, they decided to let her take her chance.

In the morning, a warm drizzle drifted in off the Mediterranean. Charlie felt as grey as the thick clouds above as he and Titch ate their breakfast in the canteen.

'She seems a bit perkier today,' he said.

'I wonder if they'll even run if this rain keeps up all day.'

'I bloody well hope so. Having come all this way, I'd like us at least to have a crack.'

Willow Star had eaten up well. Charlie gave her a little water and a couple of scoops of rolled oats first thing. 'That's your lot, darling, until you've gone out and won this poxy race,' he said.

At eight thirty, Titch led her out to stretch her legs.

Ideally, Charlie would have chosen Owen Williams to ride the filly again, but the Welsh jockey was committed to a winter riding contract in India. Instead, Charlie had booked Jean-Yves Ribello, a swarthy native of the Midi who specialised in the southern French tracks. Charlie had seen him ride a few times and despite the Frenchman's lack of finesse, he was confident he would give her a good ride.

Charlie spent the morning at the stable yard with Titch. He wasn't interested in going anywhere else or out to lunch. By the time the race was due to be run,

117

he felt as if they had been on the racetrack for a week.

Jean-Yves appeared in the parade ring looking dapper in Major Patterson's colours and leaped on to his mount with a confident grin. Willow Star left happily for the start with her short, energetic stride and her two connections began to feel more hopeful.

Two furlongs from home, their hopes collapsed.

Jean-Yves Ribello had put her in front, as instructed, and she had pulled two lengths clear at five furlongs. In the next three, the rest of the field had moved up and eclipsed her. Major Patterson's red and gold diabolo was clearly visible at the back of the field.

Before the winning horse had reached the post, Charlie and Titch had lowered their glasses. The race had ceased to hold any interest for them.

CHAPTER SIX

A misty March sun rose over the Berkshire Downs as Charlie, Nick and Kate walked towards the crest of a treeless hill. They stopped and turned. A distant rumble, a sound which a hundred years before might have augured the advance of a hostile army, floated up the empty slopes through the still, spring air. Growing in volume, it wasn't yet loud enough to drown the long liquid trill of a curlew circling above his nesting ground in the valley below.

Kate, ankle-deep in dewy, dark green grass, shivered in her sheepskin coat; the sound of galloping hooves still thrilled her. She raised a pair of binoculars to her eyes.

A moment later, the first horse broke the skyline,

118

moving in a fluid, unrelenting gallop. A bright red exercise sheet flapped lazily over the shining golden bay of its rippling quarters. Kate shivered again. She shook her crop of short black hair and a smile spread across her face. Charlie had been right. Willow Star was back to her best. She had arrived home from France with a temperature, though nobody knew what had caused it. Within four days she'd recovered. As they watched her now, she was pulling away from her galloping companions while her jockey struggled to hold her.

They didn't speak as seven horses thundered close by them, past the six-furlong marker and on to the end of the broad strip of mown turf on the grassy hillside.

As the horses began to pull up into a steaming circle, Kate lowered her binoculars. She turned to Charlie and grinned.

'She's brilliant! I've never seen her work so well.'

Charlie nodded. His blue eyes gleamed confidently, but not complacently. 'And she'll get quicker. Maybe she'll peak in May, at York.'

'Let's hope,' Kate said, breathless in the crisp air. 'You're still sure she likes six furlongs best?' Over the last few months, Kate had been following Willow Star's career much more closely. She hadn't actually moved in to Charlie and Nick's bungalow, but she was there more often than at her own cottage. She got on well with the lads and knew the form of every one of the thirty-two horses at Oak Hollow.

Charlie put his arm round her shoulder. 'I'm not sure of anything now; I don't think she'd mind ten furlongs, but she'll shine more at six.'

Nick, silent until then, joined the conversation. He'd been meaning to say what he was thinking for weeks. 'I hope she wins something big soon, then maybe your stepfather will settle his bills.' The words sounded harsher than he'd intended.

Charlie was astonished. 'How much does he owe?'

'About six months' worth.'

'Including Cagnes?'

Nick nodded.

'Why the hell didn't you tell me before?'

'I didn't want to embarrass you, and anyway, people like him only don't pay if they can't.'

Nick was right, Charlie reflected. It was very out of character for Major Patterson to owe money to anyone—especially his stepson. For her first six months' training the previous year, Willow Star had paid for herself with her winnings.

They made their way back to the yard. When the horses filed in, wrapped in a misty haze of sweat and hot breath in cold air, Kate held Willow Star while Titch washed the mud from her feet and sponged off the sweat marks around her girth. When he'd led her into her freshly strawed box, he stripped her off to let her roll.

The next lot were only cantering, not working. Charlie, Kate and Nick walked the hundred yards from the handsome three-sided brick yard to the unprepossessing pebble-dashed bungalow.

Inside, the place was beginning to look more like the country cottage they wished it was. Nick had always had a good eye at an auction and in his spare time, he enjoyed stripping down and restoring old pieces of country furniture. Although Charlie's stepfather dealt in high quality antiques, he had given them nothing. His mother, though, had produced a few handsome old kilims, and the walls were crowded with undistinguished equestrian oil paintings in

120

battered frames, photographs of horses racing, rugby teams, college groups—an edited pictorial history of their lives. New curtains and well-chosen paint had transformed the feel of the place and when the wood-burner in the kitchen was going in the early morning, it was positively cosy.

Soon the kitchen was filled with the smell of fresh coffee and grilled bacon. Nick, with Hercules his dog weaving hopefully between his legs, cooked and served up breakfast on the worn elm table which doubled as their office desk.

They were discussing plans for one of the two-year-olds when the phone rang. Nick leaned back in his chair and picked it up from among the clutter on the oak dresser behind him.

'Hello?' He was still munching a piece of toast. 'Oh, good morning, sir . . . I'm sorry to hear that.' He choked slightly on his toast and a worried look spread across his already serious face.

Kate glanced at Charlie, asking with a gesture what it could be about. Charlie shook his head and shrugged.

'Oh . . . Oh. I see,' Nick said. 'Do you really think that's a good idea? It might be helpful if I ran through the likely outcome if you keep her in training with us for the rest of the season . . .'

Nick sounded calm enough but Charlie noticed with sudden alarm that his face was reddening and the pencil he was holding snapped in his hand. Charlie hadn't seen his partner look so angry since they were both at school, when a notorious bully had picked on him all term. On that occasion some inner force that had never shown itself before seemed to burst out of Nick. He'd flung himself on his tormentor and thrashed him senseless. It had taken

121

four boys to pull him off, and no one had ever pestered him again.

He was angry now but he hadn't lost control. He was speaking in a quiet monotone whose menace might have been lost down a telephone line. 'If you don't mind my saying so, I think you're making a serious mistake.' Nick waited while the other party apparently ranted at him. 'Yes, sir,' he went on as if he was talking to a dim child, 'but at the end of this season she could be worth twice that. And of course we could come to some arrangement about your outstanding fees.'

Charlie, beside himself with impatience, got up and walked round the table to switch on the telephone loudspeaker. He immediately recognised the angry voice that burst into the room. 'How dare you patronise me. For a start, I've agreed terms with Jarvis. Secondly, she's my horse; I paid what I was asked, to help out my son, and you too. Now I think I have the right to do what I want without seeking your permission. I've done quite enough already, and I did it for Charlie, not for you. I'm sorry if you're having trouble making ends meet, but I blame you for leading Charlie into it when he's too young, not ready for the responsibility of looking after other people's expensive horses.'

Nick, shaking with anger, was holding the phone with a white-knuckled fist. All the colour had drained from his face, he was sweating and breathing in short gasps. He tried to speak but the disembodied voice went on. 'You've always had too much influence over Charles. You're brighter than he is; you've always known it and taken advantage of his good nature and loyalty, riding on the back of his personal popularity, using his gifts to supplement your own weaknesses.

122

Now, I've told you what's happening. I don't want to discuss it further.'

A click followed by a dialling tone echoed from the phone's speaker. Nick slowly lowered the receiver, placed it back in its cradle. He let out a long hiss. 'Fuck you, you arrogant bastard!'

'For God's sake,' Charlie barked. 'What did he say first?'

'He's sold Willow Star to Robert Jarvis—for eighty grand! And you know Jarvis won't let anyone but his brother-in-law train for him.'

'Shit!' Charlie thumped the table and stared angrily at two fried eggs on his plate. He glanced up at Nick. 'Eighty grand for a filly that cost ten! And he didn't even have the decency to tell me himself.'

'But surely,' Kate joined in, 'she'll be worth much more than that if she goes well this season.'

'Of course,' Charlie said, 'if she does. But there's a school of thought that advises taking a profit on a horse whenever it's on offer. And if my stepfather hasn't been paying his training bills, he must be desperate.' He shook his head. 'It's pathetic. There's a man who commanded a squadron in the SAS, must have been responsible for taking out dozens of terrorists and other human dregs, probably not giving a shit for his own life. And now he's being eaten alive by a bunch of grasping hyenas at Lloyd's.'

Nick nodded, resigned. 'He says Willow will have to go some time in the next couple of weeks. He'll let us know and settle any outstanding bills from the proceeds. You'll have to try and persuade him to hang on to her. Tell him how much more she'll be worth.'

'He's not going to take any notice of me.'

'Maybe he'd listen to your mother.'

Charlie was doubtful. 'He might, I suppose. But he's almost impossible to turn once he's made up his mind.'

'I'll go and see him,' Nick volunteered. 'See if I can patch things up.'

'Don't be crazy, Nick. You've done enough damage already. You just couldn't stop yourself trying to lecture him, could you? You really should know by now how he'd react.'

'For God's sake, Charlie. What was I supposed to say?'

'You should have handed him straight to me.'

'He didn't want to talk to you. He didn't want to be the one to tell you he was taking away the best bloody horse in the yard. And I don't know what the hell you think you could have done better.'

Charlie glared back at Nick. In the fifteen years they'd known each other they had seldom argued; when they did, it seemed all the harsher. 'You pompous arsehole! You always think you're bloody right!'

Kate looked on, horrified. She'd never heard the two friends insult each other like this. 'Charlie, for heaven's sake, calm down.' She grabbed his arm. 'Come on. Come outside with me before you say something you'll regret.'

With an angry snort and a toss of his head, Charlie followed her through the back door and slammed it behind him.

Nick looked after him, quite still.

Patterson's words had cut him more deeply than his friends could have guessed. Charlie's lack of support had made them worse. And besides all this, just as the yard was looking as if it had a real chance of succeeding, their best animal was going.

124

Nick leaned over and pulled a bottle of whisky from the back of the dresser and sloshed a long measure into a glass.

He blamed himself. He'd panicked and completely mishandled Major Patterson; Charlie was right, he'd been ridiculously pompous and put the man's back up. Now it was up to him to put it right. It would take guts, patience and a helping of humble pie.

He took another swig of whisky and gagged. The phone rang on the dresser behind him. He leaned over and grabbed it.

'Hello,' he said with gruff curtness.

'Hello. Mr Patterson or Mr Ryder?' An ingratiating, nasal male voice. Nick wondered what it was trying to sell.

'This is Nick Ryder.'

'Oh, great. Geoff Haslam here, *Racing News*.'

Nick was immediately on his guard. He said nothing.

'I was wondering if there was any decision over the filly, Willow Star?'

Nick guessed the journalist wanted to know if she was still aiming for the first of the Classics.

'About the Guineas?'

'Yeah.'

'No.' Nick said.

'There's no decision or no she's not running?'

'No decision,' Nick said, wanting the man to get off the phone.

There was a moment's pause before the next question. 'Is she staying in your yard?'

Nick felt a nasty lurch in the pit of his stomach. 'What are you talking about?'

'I've heard she might be going.'

'Who from?'

'From her owner—her ex-owner.'

Nick couldn't believe Charlie's stepfather had compounded his disloyalty like this. 'What do you mean? Who told you?'

'Major Patterson. I heard a rumour, I phoned the major. He confirmed it.'

'The bastard!' Nick spluttered before he could stop himself.

'Oh dear,' the journalist murmured gleefully. 'Been a bit of bust-up then?'

'I'm not going to talk about it.'

'You don't need to, Nick. Thanks for your help.' The journalist put the phone down before Nick could.

Nick crashed the receiver back into its cradle, furious with himself, with Charlie, with Patterson, and with the nasty little shit of a journalist who was going to make Willow Star almost irretrievable for them.

*　　　*　　　*

Willow Star took her nose from her manger for a moment, glanced up and gave a quick snort of recognition.

Kate leaned on the bottom door of her stable and gazed at the small, robust filly. She vividly remembered the misty morning, eighteen months before, when she had first set eyes on her, trapped in the wire by the brook on Cyril Barton's farm. And it was almost as long since she'd first set eyes on Charlie Patterson. Now it was hard to imagine there had ever been a time when she hadn't known him. She still thought he was vain and devoid of any intellectual ambition, but he was also optimistic, vital, kind-

126

hearted, funny and a good, strong lover. On balance, she thought she was lucky.

The filly nuzzled her. Kate gave her another carrot and stroked her nose with vigorous affection. It was, after all, Willow who had brought her and Charlie together. Kate wished it was in her power to do something, anything, to keep the animal at Oak Hollow.

* * *

Prudence Patterson stepped down from the double-decker bus which had carried her from the grey-brown, windswept open spaces of Wormwood Scrubs to the pulsing, vibrant-hued crowds swirling around Notting Hill Gate.

A session at the prison always left her in a confused state of elation and depression. There were moments of triumph to be gained from the occasional successes she felt she had achieved, when she could see the light of new hope and aspiration beginning to spark in the eyes of one or other of the inmates she had been working with. Sometimes, she would be rewarded with a piece of writing so remarkable it would have made the hardest of hardened publishers cry. But too often these turned out to be flashes in the pan, unrepeatable one-offs. She wondered, not for the first time, why she did it and as usual failed to come up with a thoroughly satisfactory answer.

A quiet, grey speck among the cacophony of colour and energy all around her, Pru was just fifty, small, neat, sturdy and easy to look at. She turned off the main road into one of the back streets which led up the gentle hill towards the upper part of Kensington.

127

In a road that lay parallel to Church Street, near its highest point, she let herself through a door in a dun brick wall. It gave into a small yard which someone had attempted optimistically, perhaps twenty years before, to turn into a garden. Now it contained a rusty bicycle, some discarded pieces of Formica kitchen furniture and a rotten hammock strung between the single small horse chestnut tree and a ring in the wall. Facing her was the disorganised paraphernalia of additional plumbing and central heating flues that had been tacked on to the back wall of the large, mid-Victorian terraced building in which she and her husband lived.

The building faced Church Street and the ground floor had been converted into a shop, or showrooms, as people in the antique trade liked to call their premises. The basement served as an extra stockroom, which meant that in the ten years Major David Patterson had been in business it had become stuffed with his mistakes.

Pru opened the back door of the house, planning, at first, to creep upstairs without disturbing her husband in the showroom. But she heard his voice, and paused to listen.

'Well, I'm sorry, too,' he was saying. 'But there it is. I can't magic the money out of thin air, and you people have already had nearly everything I own. I'm afraid you've reached the bottom of the barrel. There's nothing left but the dregs.'

There was a pause in his voice as the other person replied. Then he spoke again. 'The cottage is rented to me for a peppercorn by an old regimental friend. This building's on a lease, with no capital value. Most of the stock in the shop belongs to clients, in here on sale-or-return. The only stock I own is more or less

128

worthless. Frankly, you might just as well write me off as a lost cause—a burnt-out case. There's nothing else to take.' Though he spoke quietly, there was no escaping the bitterness in his voice. 'I wish to God I'd never given you anything. I know now I should have struck out like all those other Names. I thought they were whingeing and dishonouring their pledges at the time but, I have to say, if they get you shown up for the bunch of crooks you are, I'll be right back in there with them, suing for every penny you squeezed out of me . . .'

Pru had sidled up the corridor to the door which opened into the showroom by the bottom of the stairs. She couldn't see her husband directly where he sat at an inlaid escritoire towards the back of the shop, but she could see him clearly reflected in a large ormolu-framed mirror. He had stopped talking and from the way he was staring at the telephone she guessed that the other party had hung up. He put the phone back and leaned forward on his elbows with his head in his hands.

Pru tiptoed up the stairs to the flat into which they had moved when David had been forced to sell their London house the year before. She longed to help him, but he wouldn't allow it, wouldn't even discuss it. She knew from hard experience that she couldn't push him into revealing any more than he wanted to. It had been a regular feature of their strange life together that when he felt the world closing in on him, he would simply disappear, sometimes for a day or two, sometimes for weeks without giving her a clue where he was. When it had first happened, Pru had been hurt and wanted to be angry. She worried that he was being unfaithful but in time she had convinced herself this wasn't the reason for his absences and she

129

became used to them, even understood them. He always came home calm and free of whatever demon had been pursuing him.

David Patterson lifted his head to gaze at the framed photographs propped on the desk in front of him: Pru, who had made only the smallest demands on him throughout their marriage, and who never complained now that even these small demands could not be met; Charlie, his adopted son and only child, whom he had brought up at long distance while the army, then the job in Saudi Arabia, had kept him away from England. Charlie who had gratefully accepted a substitute father, called him 'Dad' and, as a boy, had treated him with the informal affection of a real son.

Next to the picture of Charlie was a photo he had sent of the filly, Willow Star. She was a very handsome animal, Patterson thought. It was a shame she had to go. Charlie would be shattered, let down again. Patterson knew perfectly well that the filly had provided the only real taste of success in Charlie's first year as a public trainer. It was a cruel irony that this success had made the filly already worth appreciably more than he'd paid for her. If she had performed only moderately, or inconclusively, she wouldn't be worth selling.

He was deeply ashamed of himself for telling Nick but he just hadn't been able to break the news to Charlie himself. Besides, he admitted to some satisfaction in hearing Nick so uncomfortable. It was as if in hurting Nick, he was hurting his father. And it was Nick's father, Roland Ryder, who was responsible for much of his troubles. It was Roland Ryder who had suggested he should join a number of Lloyd's syndicates in which he had an interest. The

130

Ryders had invited him and Pru to lunch, shortly after the boys had left school and he'd come back from Saudi. At the time, and on Lloyd's past record, it seemed madness not to join and you didn't even have to put up much of the money, leaving your capital free to work twice for you.

Now he despised Ryder senior for making a fool of him, for standing by while he went bust. And that spite had spilled over on to Nick whom he had never liked anyway, and who had always had far more influence over his stepson than he had himself. He knew Nick had done nothing wrong and sometimes cringed with guilt that he should be so unpleasant to Charlie's oldest, most loyal friend.

And he hated letting Charlie down. There had been a time, he knew, when his own code of personal conduct wouldn't have allowed it. He just hoped that Charlie would understand. He and Pru had to survive.

*   *   *

Charlie rattled home to Lambourn through the late spring sunset in his rusty Range Rover. Despite the looming crisis over Willow Star, he was pleased with himself; it showed in his handsome, honest face, and he didn't mind who saw it. He'd saddled two of their three jumpers at Stratford and sent home a winner and a third. If the tapedeck in the car hadn't been broken, he would have played something festive on it. The yard still wasn't making much of a profit yet but at least it was, as they say, washing its own face and providing him and Nick with a sort of living. There was the real prospect of a future shared with Kate and he was even prepared to kid himself that

131

they might find a way of hanging on to Willow Star.

Nick had obstinately insisted that it was up to him to make amends for the disastrous phone call. Charlie had half convinced himself that Nick could persuade his mother to talk his stepfather out of selling the filly. Surely it was obvious that the potential long-term profit to be made was far too great to cash her in now.

Charlie parked his Range Rover behind the red-brick boxes and walked round into the yard. Evening stables were just finishing. Heads of horses eager for their supper protruded from most of the thirty boxes.

Charlie strode across to a storeroom in one corner where Kenny was mixing the evening feeds. When he'd checked that nothing in the yard needed his urgent attention, he walked down to find Nick in the office.

Nick looked up as Charlie's cheerful face appeared and regretted that he was going to have to dowse the sunbeam smile.

'Well done,' he said first, acknowledging their winner. 'Did you have a punt?'

Charlie nodded. 'I did, as a matter of fact. They both looked absolutely outstanding so I had some on each. But we still made a profit.'

Nick nodded his older, wiser head. He wasn't in fact older but he thought in a more responsible way than his partner. It was his function to provide financial stability in the business. 'I think we've made more money punting than we have training so far this year.'

'A bit of inside knowledge is a trainer's perk. Silly not to use it.'

Nick was prepared to agree with him. 'We could do with a big hit just now. The prize money kitty isn't

132

looking great, and a lot of it last year came from Willow Star. Now I'm afraid it looks as though we're definitely going to lose her. Your father rang again.'

Charlie gritted his teeth, annoyed at having his day's success soured by the reality of Willow Star's imminent departure. 'What did he have to say this time?'

'Not a lot. Told me I was a complete amateur for talking to the press. Thank God Haslam didn't make too much of the story. I think your father was worried that some of his creditors would pick it up, but fortunately I don't think that's happened. Anyway, he's had confirmation of Jarvis's offer of eighty grand.'

Charlie still couldn't quite believe that his stepfather was about to sell the filly. He hadn't spoken a word to him about it.

'I think I'll go and see him, grovel, apologise, do whatever it takes,' Nick said eventually.

Charlie looked at his friend and raised an eyebrow. 'I think you'll need to do more than grovel. What we need is a plan—a leaseback, maybe, that'll let him keep the horse. We really need her if we're going to get noticed this year.'

Nick got up from his desk. 'Okay, I'm not too hopeful but it's worth a try.' He walked to the door. 'I'm going up to find Kenny to check this vet's bill,' he said waving a light green invoice. 'I'm sure they've been charging us for things we haven't had.'

Charlie followed him out of the bungalow and watched him for a moment, walking away with his awkward, unathletic gait. Nick might lack charm and good looks but he was his own, secure man. He knew his weaknesses but he knew his strengths, too, and built on them. Charlie was in no doubt that Nick was a better man than he was, a good counter-balance to his own exuberance and tendency towards bad judgement.

Charlie turned and went back into the bungalow, thinking about Kate, Willow Star, and his father's cold aloofness.

*   *   *

David Patterson made one last trip to the shippers to make sure the consignment had been correctly packed.

There were twenty-eight pieces in all, one of the biggest single collections in the world of furniture by François Linke. This would be the biggest, most impressive deal Patterson had ever done, and it was happening just when he most needed it. In a way, he was sorry that no one but his client was ever going to know about it, but the client didn't want any publicity, and nor did he.

The furniture of François Linke had always been something of a speciality of David Patterson's. He had been fascinated by it ever since his father had told him about the staggering lengths to which the furniture maker would go to achieve what he considered perfection. The style was too ornate for some tastes but in the right setting and to someone who appreciated craftsmanship at its very zenith, it was in a class of its own.

Born to a poor family somewhere in Czechoslovakia in the late 1800s, François Linke eventually made his way to Paris and set himself up in a small workshop beside the Seine. He was well established by the time the Exposition Universelle was held in Paris in 1900, on which he staked his reputation and every sou he possessed to build and exhibit an outstanding collection of furniture. Each piece was made from tulip wood and mounted with sculpted brass in the style of Louis XV. The centrepiece was a *grand bureau*, measuring almost five feet in height. It was the most elaborate project Linke had ever undertaken and, as was his normal practice, he kept a minutely detailed record of the work involved. The chiselling for the cast bronzes alone took his men six thousand nine hundred hours, and another three thousand six hundred to mount them.

Like most men at the time, François Linke was in the habit of rolling his own cigarettes. When he was inspecting a piece, he would take out one of his cigarette papers and if he could pass it between the wood and the moulding, he would send it back to be refitted. In all, the *grand bureau* took thirty-one thousand eight hundred and ninety-three hours to complete. It was acclaimed as the finest piece he had ever made and was quickly snapped up by one of the Romanovs. Not to be outdone, King Wilhelm II of Prussia ordered an identical one. The castle where it stood was destroyed by German troops in 1942 and most of the furniture was destroyed with it or stolen. No one was sure of the fate of the *grand bureau*.

When Major Patterson informed his old employer, Sheikh Sala Mahmoud, that he had found an original *grand bureau*, along with a large collection of other Linke pieces, the Sheikh had agreed to buy the lot, provided the deal attracted no publicity. Patterson had been given some of the money in advance, which had paid for the goods. The balance would be paid into an account he had opened in Switzerland specifically to accommodate it, as soon as the

135

furniture arrived in France. He knew Sala Mahmoud wouldn't let him down; at least, he hoped to hell he wouldn't, but to have asked for all the money up front would have killed the deal—the only good thing that had happened to Patterson in four devastating years.

He had been the Saudi sheikh's chief security adviser for several years after he left the British army. Sala Mahmoud had taken over where men like Khashoggi had left off. He dealt in arms and military hardware with anyone who could pay. He had shown his appreciation of Patterson's skills and experience with a substantial salary and a more than generous package of perks. But, even with his well-known talent for detachment, Patterson found it hard to work for Sala Mahmoud. He had been pleased enough, though, when his ex-employer had turned up to see him in London the previous autumn. It was the first time he had seen Sala Mahmoud in nine years, but it was clear that the Arab had kept himself informed of his activities.

Sala Mahmoud was based, to the French authorities' impotent frustration, in a large estate outside Paris. Guarded like a fortress for other reasons, it also provided a safe setting for the priceless objects for which the sheikh had developed a collector's taste. He had discovered that his mansion had once housed a large collection of François Linke furniture and he was obsessed with the idea of re-establishing it. He had gone to Patterson because he knew the ex-soldier was as knowledgeable as anyone about Linke. He had asked him to get as much of it together as he could, keeping him informed of the prices as he did so. The added bonus of the *grand bureau* had completely hooked the

Arab.

The sea of Patterson's financial troubles was just about to close above his head when the deal was agreed. And this time he was going to keep the profits for himself. He had taken elaborate precautions to obscure his identity when he had arranged the purchase of the furniture and its shipment. If word got out in the trade, it might well find its way back to one of the institutions to whom he owed money. He should see a profit of a little short of a million pounds on the whole transaction. Provided he kept it to himself, he could live out his days with Pru in comfort, somewhere quiet and warm and a long way from England. If he didn't do it, there was no way out; they would be left with nothing.

He didn't have any difficulty keeping his activities from Pru. He'd never discussed his work with her, since the days when he was specifically banned from doing so by his military bosses. But now he would have to tell her certain details of his plans, or she might let something out inadvertently. In any event, he was absolutely certain of her loyalty.

The last pieces of furniture were now being wrapped for carriage to Sala Mahmoud's mansion in the Forest of Fontainebleau.

Patterson checked the documentation with the shipper, confirmed the arrangements which would trigger his payment and drove his elderly Mercedes back to Kensington through the late afternoon rush hour.

Once in the flat, he assumed the air of impecuniousness that had become habitual when dealing with creditors. Pru regarded him affectionately. Guiltily, he wondered why she put up with him and the string of financial disasters he seemed to have attracted. But she seemed to know him almost better than he knew himself and to appreciate him for qualities which he considered less than desirable—his aloofness, his total aversion to depending on others.

In the small sitting room on the first floor above the shop, Patterson opened a drinks cupboard—a good Georgian bow front—which contained two bottles of cheap Scotch, a bottle of sherry and a few bottles of Bulgarian red wine. He sighed and hoped fervently that within a week or so he'd be in a position to buy some serious claret without having to look at the price.

'Sherry?' he asked his wife.

She nodded.

He poured one, and a large Scotch for himself. 'How have you been?' he asked.

'Okay.' Pru realised he didn't want to talk about his own problems and related that she'd had a letter from one of her ex-inmates, wanting to talk about his writing.

'Who's that?'

'A chap called Brian Tennent. You may remember, he was supposed to come down and do a bit of decorating at the cottage—well over a year ago now. He never turned up though.'

'Was that the chap who rang later and said he'd got lost and gone home?'

'That's the one. He's an odd specimen but quite bright, with a fascinatingly macabre perspective on life. Not without humour, either.'

'What was he in prison for?'

Pru explained rather ashamedly that he had killed two school-children while being chased in his car by police, having just robbed a building society.

The major tutted and shook his head. 'Well, if you want to help him, that's up to you.' He wanted to add 'but you're a fool' but didn't.

Later, over a supper of pasta and Bulgarian wine, he told her about the piece that had appeared in the *Racing News* and of his recent phone conversations with Nick.

Pru's face fell. 'Oh, David. Poor boys. Did you have to? After Charles did so well with the filly last year.'

'Frankly, it's only a matter of time before one of my creditors latches on to the fact that I own the animal, especially if she does as well as everyone hopes this year. If I sell her to Jarvis, he can pay me abroad where Lloyd's can't get at it.'

'But are you sure that's safe? And is it strictly legal?'

'It's safe enough, and it's strictly illegal.'

'But David, won't you get into trouble? I mean, it's rather unlike you to do that sort of thing.'

'It might have been once, but quite frankly I haven't got much choice. I've been a complete fool up until now. I've played it by the book while the people who conned me grabbed my money and laughed. But don't worry, I won't get into trouble. I was thinking it would be warmer and a lot cheaper if we moved out to Cyprus. You liked it when I was posted there, didn't you?'

Pru sighed. 'Up to a point. But I was jolly glad to settle in England when we finally did. Still, if that's all we can afford, I suppose I could cope.'

'It just might be expedient for other reasons, too,' Patterson said.

CHAPTER SEVEN

Nick drove his new red Subaru estate car slowly between the high banks of a lane which ran down towards the River Kennet; the lane was barely wide enough to accommodate his car and, since he'd set out, he was less eager to reach his destination. He was looking for the turning to Birch Lodge, the cottage where Major Patterson and his wife usually spent their weekends.

Lying below the high grassland hills of the Downs, it was one of several houses on a small estate belonging to General Sir Peter Sheridan, ex-CO of the Irish Guards as well as the 22nd SAS Regiment at Hereford at the time David Patterson had commanded his squadron there. The general had told Patterson he would be welcome to a cottage, at a peppercorn rent, provided he kept the place in good order. Patterson, knowing he'd meant it, had taken him up on the offer without embarrassment as soon as he had settled back in England.

Nick glimpsed the general's big Edwardian house through a screen of trees, carefully planted a hundred years before. He turned in at the next entrance. There was a rough drive leading away into the dense woodland to the left immediately inside the gate. Nick drove in through the tunnel of trees as Charlie had told him to that morning.

A hundred and twenty yards along the track, round a slight bend, the cottage came into view, tucked in a clearing ringed with spindly birches.

Major Patterson's Mercedes was parked outside. According to Charlie, they had driven down separately, Pru having returned from a visit to her parents in Devon.

Nick wasn't sure that he could handle Patterson without Pru there to mediate. On the other hand, if he was going to do anything to keep Willow, it had to be done now, before Jarvis finalised the deal.

He parked the Subaru on a patch of rough ground beside the cottage and walked across to ring the bell at the front door.

It was a few moments before Major Patterson appeared. He looked as spruce as he always did, in a soft tweed jacket, crisp beige shirt, cavalry twill trousers and gleaming conker-brown brogues. When Nick saw him, his heart fell. Patterson was patently angry at the unexpected interruption.

*   *   *

As Nick was stepping into the cottage, Pru Patterson was finishing her shopping for groceries in Hungerford. Thirty minutes later, she pulled into the drive of Birch Lodge, parked her car next to her husband's Mercedes and went inside.

The moment she shut the front door behind her, she could sense that something was wrong. She put her bulging shopping bag on the table in the hall and walked nervously through to the small sitting room, calling her husband's name. There was nothing but an eerie silence for a reply. As she entered the room, she put her hand to her mouth and let out a gasp.

Papers were scattered all over the carpet, the contents of drawers had been tipped out on to the floor. The sofas and chairs had been ripped apart. Carpets had been pulled up and floorboards jemmied from their joists.

141

Then she saw the body.

The shock set her trembling.

Gazing at the blood-stained grey hair around the vicious headwound and the familiar clothes, she struggled to absorb what had happened. She wanted to be sick and forced herself to turn away.

Her first instinct was to phone Charlie. She rushed into the study, also in a state of chaos, picked up the phone and, with trembling fingers, keyed the number at Oak Hollow. Before it started to ring, she dipped the plunger to cut it off.

She started again; this time she pressed 999. 'Hello? Emergency services? Police, please...' Pru was amazed at how calm she sounded. 'Hello? Yes. My husband's been killed—murdered ... Yes. I've just found him ... Please, please come now!'

They asked for the address and, once Pru had given them directions, told her they'd be there in a matter of minutes.

Pru took a deep breath, and dialled Charlie's number again. It rang six, seven times before he answered.

'Mum,' he said, sounding out of breath. 'I was outside, on the point of driving over to see you.'

'Charlie, something awful's happened.' There was barely a quiver in Pru's voice.

A catalogue of potentially awful things ran through Charlie's head. There was silence. 'Mum, what! What happened?'

'Your father's been killed. I've just found him.'

'Good God! How? Why? What from, do you know?'

'Someone's broken in and killed him. The whole house is in a terrible mess.'

'What about you? Are you all right?'

142

'Yes, yes. I'm all right. I wasn't here. Someone must have been trying to burgle the house.'

Charlie's thoughts lurched abruptly to Nick and his planned visit. Only he knew that Nick was going to the cottage that day. They had decided it would be better if they didn't warn his mother or stepfather that he was coming.

But what had happened to him? Had he decided not to go through with it?

Or had he been and gone before the murderer turned up?

Or...

Charlie could scarcely formulate the thought.

No. It just wasn't possible. And yet...

Charlie remembered Nick's rare but very real outbursts of anger under intense provocation.

No, he thought again. Nick had neither the strength nor the skill to overcome his stepfather.

'Have you rung the police?'

'Yes, of course, they're on their way.'

A thought suddenly crossed Charlie's mind, and his stomach churned. 'Mum, whoever did it may still be hanging around. I'll come round straight away.'

'No,' his mother said, firmly. 'Don't. It's such an awful sight. I couldn't bear you to see David like this. I'll lock myself in until the police arrive.'

'Mum, what are you talking about? I'll be right over.'

'Please don't come until they've been. There's no reason why you should have to deal with this.' There was no mistaking the earnestness of her plea.

Charlie didn't press her. 'Okay,' he said, 'if you're sure. Ring me as soon as they've gone and I'll come over and stay.'

'Thank you, Charles. I'll ring you later. Goodbye,

143

dear.'

Pru put the phone down and glanced at the embers of the fire. Looking around the room, distraught but in control, she noticed a beer tankard on a table beside one of the big armchairs.

David never drank beer.

She didn't touch the glass in case it had any fingerprints on it.

To calm her nerves, she took another glass from a cabinet and filled it with dry sherry. She sat down, sipped the drink and waited. When she heard a police siren approaching, she rose to her feet and rushed through to the kitchen to rinse out her glass and leave it on the drainer.

The siren echoed down the tunnel of trees and then the police car skidded to a dust-swirling halt where Nick's Subaru had sat earlier. Two uniformed men and a plainclothes officer leaped out and ran to the front door.

Pru let them in without a word and waved them towards the small drawing room where, among the mess and confusion, a blood-stained poker lay on the carpet beside the body.

*   *   *

Nick walked in through the back door of the bungalow at Oak Hollow, looking as if he'd seen a ghost.

'What the hell has happened?' Charlie stammered. 'What have you been up to?'

Nick didn't answer at once. He walked past his partner into the kitchen and sat down at the table.

'My mother phoned. She'd just found my father, dead.' Charlie stopped for a moment. He was finding it hard to get the words out. 'He's been killed ... murdered.'

'I saw him too,' Nick said flatly, resting his elbows on the table and putting his head in his hands.

Charlie noticed that his friend's right eye was slightly twitching. 'What? Was he dead when you got there?'

Nick shook his head. 'No, he asked me in.'

'You mean you were there when it happened?' Charlie asked, incredulous.

'Yes, I was. Pass me that Scotch and I'll tell you.' He mixed plenty of water into his drink and then met Charlie's worried, doubtful eyes straight on. He took a deep breath.

'When I got to the cottage, your mother's car wasn't there. I almost turned and drove straight out again but your father would have seen me and ... well, I thought I had to go in and get on with it. He opened the door but he didn't look at all pleased to see me. I said I hoped he didn't mind me dropping in. Amazingly, he said no, and asked me in.

'We went into that small sort of study, on the left as you go in. He'd obviously been sitting there. The fire was lit and there were loads of papers scattered on the desk. He sort of shuffled them away, as if he didn't want me to see them. I don't know what they were. Anyway, he asked me if I wanted a drink. I said I'd like a beer. He told me to put some more coal on the fire and went off. He was gone for a while, looking for some beer I thought, then came back with a can of lager and a glass. He said he'd had to get it from the cellar. Anyway, he poured himself a Scotch and sat down, still looking fairly twitchy. He said, "I suppose you've come to talk about that wretched filly."

'I wish I'd waited for your mother. His manner put

me right off my stroke. I got the impression he had something very heavy on his mind. But I started blathering, like I did on the phone to him. When I suggested we might carry on training Willow for nothing, he suddenly lost his temper. He went mad. Began roaring, said I was patronising him.'

'What was he so upset about?'

'I don't know. Maybe he hated my talking to him about money. He also said the horse was already sold anyway. But not to Jarvis.'

'Shit,' Charlie exclaimed, forgetting his stepfather's death for a second. 'Who to?'

'He didn't say.'

'Hell!' Charlie shook his head. 'What happened next?'

'Well, I was pretty pissed off I hadn't managed to stop him selling Willow, so I started telling him how stupid he was. I don't know why I didn't just accept it, but I couldn't stop myself. He was furious. He leapt out of his chair absolutely ranting at me and I thought for a moment he was going to hit me. God knows what would have happened if he had, but suddenly he stopped himself, as if he'd just remembered something. He walked out of the room, closing the door behind him. I couldn't think what the hell he was doing. I couldn't hear him but I was sure he hadn't left the house. I sat and drank my beer for a bit, hoping he wasn't going to come back and start attacking me again when I heard glass breaking somewhere in the house and your stepfather yelling.'

'Who was he yelling at?' Charlie asked.

'Me. He was shouting my name and he sounded in a real panic, as if he needed my help. I rushed out of the study into the hall. I heard someone in the drawing room. The door was ajar. I pushed it open

146

and went in. The place was a complete shambles. It had been ransacked. I couldn't believe the chaos. Then I saw your father. He was lying prostrate in front of the fire. There was blood all over the back of his head and he wasn't moving. I just couldn't believe it. I must have stared at him for a few seconds, then everything went blank.'

'What do you mean?'

'I mean someone hit me from behind and I blacked out. I don't remember a thing until I came round about a quarter of an hour later. It took me a while to realise where I was, lying on the carpet with a headache. Then I saw your father's feet across the floor. I got up and took another look. The mess on his head was terrible, and there was a poker with blood on it lying beside him. Thank God whoever it was didn't use it on me, too.'

'But Nick,' Charlie was looking at him closely, 'if the guy had already killed my father, why didn't he kill you?'

'I don't know, for God's sake. Maybe because he knew I hadn't seen him. I'm not complaining.'

'How bad is your head now?'

Nick reached up and felt the spot. 'The lump's gone down already, thank God.' When he saw the disbelief on Charlie's face, his heart sank. 'Hang on a minute, Charlie. You must believe me, for Christ's sake. You don't think I did it, do you?'

'I don't know what the hell I think, but it doesn't look good.'

Nick held the palms of his hands up in a gesture of innocence. 'I know, I know. Don't think I don't realise that, but I swear I didn't do it. Why should I? You must know I couldn't have done it!'

Charlie looked at him, hating the dilemma that

147

faced him.

'Charlie,' Nick pleaded. 'You're the only person who knows I was there. The police won't ever connect me with it. Let them concentrate on catching whoever it was. It must have been a burglar. The place had been torn apart, I told you.'

'Okay,' Charlie sighed. 'I won't tell anyone you were there. But are you sure no one else saw you?'

'No, I'm not, but I don't think so. I was very careful when I drove out. I stopped and listened a couple of times to make sure there wasn't anyone else around, and there weren't any other cars about when I drove into the lane.'

'You didn't leave anything or write anything, did you?'

'No.'

'What about fingerprints?'

'I wiped the beer mug I'd used and the handle of the fire tongs in the study, and all the door handles I'd touched.'

'Was there any sign of anyone else?'

'When I came round and went back into the study, it had been ransacked as well. Somebody had been through all the drawers there while I was out for the count.'

'I wonder what they were looking for. I'm sure Dad didn't keep anything particularly valuable at the cottage, assuming he still owned anything valuable.'

'Maybe it was just a chance burglar your stepfather caught in the act. The place is fairly isolated, far enough from any other house for no one to hear or see.'

'Maybe.'

'Charlie, you still don't believe me, do you?'

'I'm sorry, Nick, God knows, I really am. It just

seems such a coincidence for it to happen the only time you've ever been there.'

'Yes, well, coincidences do happen.'

'Well, I don't fancy your chances if the police get on to you.'

'You didn't tell your mother I'd been round?'

'No. I wanted to hear from you first. But the trouble is, if someone says they recognised you there, it'll look a lot worse if you haven't told the police.'

Nick gulped down a mouthful of Scotch. 'Don't think I haven't thought about that. But if that happens I'll just have to say I knew how compromising it would look and I was frightened to own up. That's all I can do.'

*   *   *

Two forensic officers arrived at Birch Lodge. They spent three hours finding very little, besides a set of fingerprints on the handle of the poker which had killed the major.

DI Mike Ferrier who was in charge of the investigation came back when his colleagues had finished in the house. He wanted to go over the afternoon's events one more time with the victim's widow. He sat in the study with her, drinking tea.

'Let me get this right, Mrs Patterson. You went out at ten, leaving your husband here, and when you returned about midday you found him dead and the place pulled apart. As far as you know, he was expecting no one and the only casual visitor who ever calls is the general.'

Pru nodded.

The detective looked at her for a moment without speaking. He stood and walked across the small

149

room.

'This glass had beer in it; the other one whisky. Your husband's prints are on the whisky tumbler, but the beer mug has been deliberately wiped, and so have the door handles. This suggests that your husband was at least prepared to entertain whoever came here, don't you think? Though I wonder why they didn't wipe the poker handle too,' Ferrier mused. 'Anyway, the forensic blokes are just having a look around outside and then we'll be off. I'll need to see you again, I'm afraid, but I'll try not to make it too soon. The minute we've confirmed the cause of your husband's death, we'll be able to release his body for burial.'

'But surely the cause of death is obvious.'

'On the face of it, but there may be signs that he died of a heart attack or something else.'

'I see. Will you need me to make a formal identification?'

'No. That won't be necessary. I would suggest you either go and stay with a friend or relative, or have one come here.'

'My son is coming over, thank you.'

'Good. Right then, I'll be in touch with you tomorrow.'

*   *   *

The police, the mess, the body and all signs of the fatal struggle had gone by the time Charlie arrived at the cottage.

Pru told him what the police had done so far, and Charlie privately thanked God no sign had been found of Nick's visit. He was ready to console his mother. He knew she had loved her husband, despite

150

his lack of obvious affection. He also knew she'd been particularly worried about him recently, though she hadn't said why. She seemed, though, to be handling the whole business of his murder with remarkable composure. The real grief wouldn't begin until the shock of what had happened wore off.

Neither of them felt like eating much. Charlie found some bread and cheese and a bottle of wine. They were picking at the cheese when Detective Inspector Ferrier telephoned.

'Hello, Mrs Patterson. Just to let you know what progress we're making. I'm afraid it isn't much but we do have a sighting of a car leaving the top of your track at around midday, just before you got back, I should imagine. I thought you might be able to help me there.'

'Oh,' Pru said. 'What kind of car was it?'

'I'm afraid it's rather a broad description—a red estate car, possibly a Subaru. Any idea who that might be?'

The only other news was that they had still had no luck in matching the fingerprints from the poker. But, as the inspector said, it was early days.

When the policeman had rung off, Pru walked slowly back to the dining room where Charlie had finished eating and was impatient to hear what had been said.

Pru looked at him quizzically. 'Nick didn't come round to see us by any chance, did he?'

Charlie swallowed and slid his eyes from her gaze.

This confirmed her suspicions. Charlie had never been able to lie to her. She sat down. 'Why didn't you tell me?'

'How do you know he did?'

'Someone has reported seeing his car leaving the

151

top of the drive just before twelve.'

'Did they take the number?'

'No. The police only have a vague description.' There was a worried look in her eyes as she gazed intently at her son. 'It sounded like Nick's car to me. The one he bought to replace the BMW.'

'Did ... did you tell them?'

Pru shook her head. 'No. And I won't. I can't believe Nick would have had anything to do with it.' She caught the look of doubt in her son's eyes. 'Why? Do you?'

Charlie stayed the night at his mother's cottage. He rang Kate from there. He wanted to tell her what had happened, but he couldn't explain it properly. He arranged to see her the following evening.

Charlie didn't see his mother when he left at six next morning to organise the exercising of his string of horses. When he got back to Oak Hollow, Nick was up, trying to do his routine tasks as if nothing had happened.

Charlie considered whether or not to tell him about the sighting of the car, and decided against it. He told him that the fingerprints on the poker hadn't been matched and weren't Patterson's. He watched Nick's reaction carefully.

Nick seemed to be more concerned with Willow Star's likely fate. 'We'll have to find out who's bought her and contact them to make sure she's staying here.'

'Presumably whatever arrangements my father was about to make will be on hold until the will's sorted out. Maybe that'll give us a chance to hang on to her.'

'No, he was definite about that. The deal's been done, paid up.'

152

'But why didn't he tell you who?'

'The conversation didn't last long enough.' Nick paused, remembering it and Patterson's vehement attack on him.

'So Willow's a hundred per cent sold?'

'That's what he said. I guess his solicitors will tell you who owns her now.'

Charlie spent the rest of the day in a confusion of emotions, trying to come to terms with his stepfather's death and worrying about his mother. At the same time, he was harbouring a gruesome wish to know why it had happened and who had done it, hoping desperately that it wasn't Nick.

Kate came round after evening stables. Since Charlie's phone call, she'd read the reports of the murder in the morning papers.

She had just arrived when a beige Vauxhall Cavalier drew up outside the yard and two men in their thirties, casually dressed, climbed out. They strolled down to the bungalow, taking particular note of Nick's car as they passed it. They walked up to the door and knocked. Charlie let them in. The shorter of the two pulled out his warrant card and tweaked it open. 'Evening, sir. We're from Thames Valley CID. Is that your car?' He nodded in the direction of Nick's Subaru.

Charlie's heart nearly stopped for a second. 'No, it's not,' he stammered.

The detective's eyes showed more interest. 'Is the owner here?' He consulted his notebook. 'Mr Nicholas Ryder?'

'He's up at the yard. Why? What's he done?'

'We just need to eliminate him from some inquiries we're making.'

'Oh. Right. I'll come up with you.' Charlie closed

153

the door behind him and walked with the two policemen up to the stable yard.

'And who are you, sir?' the senior of them asked him.

'I'm Nick Ryder's partner. Charles Patterson.'

The two detectives stopped. 'Patterson? Was Major David Patterson your father?'

'Stepfather, yes.'

'I see. I'm sorry. We're investigating his murder. A red car, possibly a Subaru, was seen leaving the major's house shortly after the estimated time of death.'

'But there must be thousands of people driving around in red Subarus.'

'Not thousands, sir, and surprisingly few that have been bought from the local dealer recently. Do you happen to know if your partner visited your father yesterday?'

'You'll have to ask him that.'

'Or did you by any chance borrow his car to go there yourself?'

'No. I was here all afternoon, ask anyone. For God's sake, I wouldn't murder my stepfather.'

'I'm sorry, sir. But it does happen. Anyway, if you wouldn't mind hanging around for a while, we'd like to ask you some questions too. But we'll see Mr Ryder on his own first, thank you.'

Nick, coming out of the tack room, knew they were police as soon as they walked into the yard. Despite the jeans and the suede blouson, there was an inescapable air of officialdom in their manner.

He gulped quickly, before they were near enough to see, and lifted an inquiring eyebrow.

'Mr Nick Ryder?' one of them asked.

'Yes?'

'We're police officers, sir,' the other said, displaying his warrant card again.

'You want to see me?'

'Yes, sir. I take it you knew Major David Patterson, your partner's stepfather.'

'Yes. Of course I did. You're investigating his...' Nick let the word 'murder' die on his tongue.

'We are indeed, sir. And we understand you called in to see him yesterday.'

Only a small twitch at the side of his mouth betrayed Nick's nervousness. 'Yes,' he said. 'I did go round there to talk about a filly he keeps with us. His car was there. I rang the bell,' he shrugged, 'but there was no reply. Of course, now I know—it's terrible—he must have been dead inside.'

'What time was this?'

'About half past eleven.'

'And where were you at half past ten?'

Nick thought for a moment. 'I took my dog for a run in Savernake Forest.'

'Did you see anyone there?'

'No. You seldom do in the part I go to. That's why I go there. It makes a change from the open downland for him.'

'I see, sir. So you arrived and rang the bell. How long did you wait before you gave up?'

'A good five minutes. I thought if the major's car was there, he must be at home. I know he never lets himself be driven by Mrs Patterson in her car.'

'So you knew him quite well?'

'I wouldn't say that, but I knew about him from Charlie.'

'Right. Well, we may want to talk to you again. In the meantime, we'd like a set of your fingerprints—just to eliminate you from the murder inquiry.'

'Of course,' Nick said, confident that his prints weren't on anything incriminating. 'Come on down to the house. We'll do it there, not in front of the lads, if you don't mind.'

Later, when Kate had gone home, Charlie drove to his mother's cottage where her sister was already installed in the second spare room.

They were halfway through dinner when Nick rang, wanting to speak to Charlie.

'Hello, Charlie. I'm afraid you'll have to get back here and look after the horses.'

'Why?'

'The police are here again, a chap called Ferrier who's in charge of investigating your stepfather's death. It's crazy,' Nick's voice faltered, 'but he says my fingerprints match the ones on the poker that killed him.'

CHAPTER EIGHT

Nick put the phone down. He was in the small office in the bungalow; he felt like a rat in a trap. He looked up at Ferrier and his sergeant who stood in front of him, pleased with themselves for having found their man so soon.

The sergeant was fiddling with a pair of handcuffs. Nick glanced at his own hands; they should have been shaking but they weren't. He looked back at the officers; now was his last chance before they snapped the cuffs on him and took him to the police station.

He lumbered to his feet, then with a speed which his physique belied he took two steps towards the door. He was through it and had slammed it shut

156

before either of the policemen could get a hand on him.

Normally, when he was out, he kept his office locked from the prying eyes of lads or anyone else who might have come to visit with dubious intentions. The key was in the lock now. Nick turned it just as one of Ferrier's fists closed round the knob inside. It wasn't much of a door; it would give him only a few seconds' lead, but that was all he needed.

He ran through the kitchen, out of the back door and into the damp night. The scrubby paddock behind the bungalow dropped away to the brook which ran along the valley bottom. Nick vaulted a timber rail fence and loped purposefully down the bank.

The stream at the bottom was full and flowing noisily. It was lined by a screen of small alders and willows. When he reached it, he stopped for a few seconds to look back. The policemen were searching around the front of the house, shouting angrily, waving torches around.

It was half a minute before they came round to the back. Nick was already up to his waist in the stream, ignoring the chill of the water that sprang from high in the chalk downs. He waded downstream until he'd passed a thick thorn hedge on the far side and clambered up the bank into a field of permanent pasture. Grazed by sheep most of the year, the going was good despite a recent downpour.

Nick was no athlete, but he didn't smoke and he was fit. He ran with an easy stride up the rising field, tolerating the squelch in his shoes and damp cotton chinos clinging to his legs. He guessed he'd already put a quarter of a mile between him and his pursuers.

He decided that the last place the police would

expect him to hide was in the local pub. And he could position himself so that he would see their car if they did turn up.

Five or six hundred yards behind him, still on the far side of the stream, he spotted the flash of a torch. He carried on to the lane, jumped over the wire fence and travelled a hundred yards down the hill on the road until he came to a gate in the hedge on his left. He clambered over and ran easily down the gentle slope.

Ten minutes later he was sitting between the fire and the window in the front bar of the Goat with a pint of bitter in front of him while he tried to concentrate on a discarded copy of the *Sporting Life*.

No one noticed him look up sharply at the sound of a wailing police siren racing by.

There were no signs of police near the pub when closing time was called. Nick walked out with the crowd and set off on foot along the main road through the village. After a hundred yards, he slipped through a gate into a silent courtyard. As he'd known there would be, two lorries were parked there. He tried the small side door of the newer horsebox. It wasn't locked. He clambered in and quietly closed the door behind him. He felt around, knowing what to expect, grateful for the blankets when he found them in the Luton above the cab. He crawled in among them and made himself comfortable.

*   *   *

In Birch Lodge, at the moment Nick made his decision to run, Charlie put the phone down with a shaking hand. His mother looked at him with wide-eyed concern.

158

'What on earth's happened?'

'The police have arrested Nick.'

'But they can't have! That's absurd!'

'His car was seen; he couldn't deny he'd been here. The fingerprints on the poker were his. I'd say the police think they've a pretty strong case.'

Pru put her head in her hands. 'Oh my God! Why on earth did it have to turn out like this?'

'What do you mean, Mum?'

'I mean ... Nick being involved.'

'He wasn't,' Charlie said, trying to fight back his doubts. 'He wants me to organise a lawyer for him. I said I'd get a solicitor down to the police station right away. Then I've got to get back to Oak Hollow. You'll be okay with Aunt Sue here, won't you?'

'Yes, of course. You get back to your horses. I'll be all right. I'm just so worried about Nick. Will you go and see him in the morning?'

'Go and see him where?'

'Well, in prison, I suppose, if they've arrested him.'

Until then, Charlie hadn't let himself acknowledge that was where Nick was going. 'Shit! What if they don't let him out or give him bail?'

'You must go round first thing and see what you can do.'

Charlie drove his father's old Mercedes back to Oak Hollow, scarcely noticing the road as he drove. He was locked in a mental struggle over Nick. As his oldest friend as well as his partner, Nick merited all his loyalty, but the evidence against him was so damning. If only the police had found something, anything that pointed elsewhere. But with such a hot suspect, would they even look now?

Nick had sounded calm enough over the phone and didn't seem to be panicking. But that was Nick's

159

way.

Charlie was very conscious of his partner's rare lapses of control, but even allowing for that, he couldn't bring himself to believe he would kill anyone. But if Nick didn't do it, there had to be something somewhere that would point to the real culprit.

Charlie pulled up in front of the dingy little house. All the lights were still on but he went up to the yard first to check his horses.

Everything was calm there. The horses for the most part were keeping away from the damp night air outside their stable doors. Charlie shone his torch into each. When he was satisfied that there were no problems, he went back down to the bungalow.

As he took out his key to open the front door, a police siren wailed up the lane from the village, coming towards Oak Hollow. He saw the flashing blue light swing off the road on to the concrete drive that led to the bungalow. The car skidded to a halt and two uniformed police leaped out. Charlie stood and waited.

'Who are you?' one of the PCs asked aggressively.

'Charles Patterson. I live here.'

'Oh. You're Major Patterson's son, are you?'

'Yes. What are you doing here? I was told you'd already arrested my partner.'

'He escaped.'

Charlie's heart dropped to the pit of his stomach. He didn't trust himself to speak for a moment. He tried his key in the front door to find it wasn't locked. The sight of the office door hanging off its hinges seemed to confirm what the police were saying. They followed him into the house.

'Has he been in touch with you?'

160

'No, no, he hasn't. I'd no idea he'd gone. I spoke to him on the phone maybe half an hour ago. I was at my mother's house. He told me he'd been arrested and asked me to get a solicitor down to your station, which I did. I've just got back.'

'We'll take another look round anyway.'

'I can't think why he's done a runner,' Charlie went on, aware as he said it how unconvincing he sounded. 'I'm certain he didn't do it. He had no reason to and he didn't have the strength, for Christ's sake!'

'I wouldn't know anything about that. We've just been told to look for a man escaped from police custody. If you think your friend is so innocent, the sooner he produces himself, the quicker he can prove it.'

'Sure. If I hear from him, I'll try and persuade him to give himself up.'

The PC looked at him hard for a moment.

Charlie shifted uncomfortably under his scrutiny.

'Has DI Ferrier had you in yet?' the policeman asked, struggling with the temptation to show up a plainclothes colleague.

'No.'

'Well, he will.'

*   *   *

Down in the village, in the deserted yard, Nick had slept fitfully. He awakened fully when the lorry's engine started up. The vehicle trundled out of the yard. Nick moved himself right to the front, burying himself in the blankets. He had purposely chosen the newer of the two lorries. Thanks to his regular painstaking study of race entries, he had guessed it was the one that would be taking the trainer's three

161

runners to Doncaster, provided he hadn't sent them up in other transport the night before.

Nick looked at his watch and saw with relief that it was only five thirty in the morning. They wouldn't be moving off this early to get to Folkestone where the only other meeting was being held today. He guessed he was safe where he was for the time being. The lorry would be on its way up to the trainer's yard to pick up the runners.

Five minutes later, after some manoeuvring, the lorry came to a stop and the engine was turned off. Nick remained hidden. The ramp was dropped noisily. A rush of cold damp air penetrated to the front of the box. A lad and a girl clambered on board, sleepily chiding each other as they opened up the partitions to let the first horse on. Shortly afterwards, the clip of aluminium shoes across rippled concrete announced its arrival. There was a sudden cacophony of prancing hooves and rich cursing as the animal objected to going in. A moment later, with a thumping of metal on timber and rubber, the horse leaped in and was quickly confined in a stall.

With much the same performance, the other two runners were loaded. The lads tied them up and the ramp was banged home. The side jockey door clicked shut and beneath him Nick heard the driver and the lads clamber into the cab. The motor was gunned back into life and the lorry lurched out of the yard.

*   *   *

Charlie had meant what he said when he'd told the police he would try to persuade Nick to give himself up, but when he heard from him, shortly after eight next morning, he was beginning to see his point of

162

view.

'Look, Charlie, I can't give myself up. You must believe I didn't kill your father, but right now the evidence is all against me.'

'Your running doesn't help.'

'Please, do whatever you can to get the police to look for someone else. They've got to listen to you. I mean, your father was the victim, for God's sake.'

'The guys who came last night after you'd gone behaved as if they thought I'd done it. I'll do what I can, but you were crazy to run.'

'The longer I'm running, the more chance there is of someone turning up the real villain.'

'Maybe,' Charlie said, unconvinced. 'Are you okay?'

'I'm fine. I'll be in touch.' Nick cut off without giving a clue where he was.

Charlie shook his head, deep in thought. He picked up the phone and dialled Kate at Noah's Ark.

When she answered, he got straight to the point. 'Nick was arrested last night,' he told her without preamble.

'My God! What for?'

'If you can believe it, for my father's murder.'

'But that's crazy!'

'It's worse than that. He managed to get away before they could get him into their car. He's done a runner and he's still missing.'

'But . . . but surely he wouldn't have done that if he didn't—'

'Not necessarily,' Charlie said.

'But it looks so much worse, Nick taking off like that.'

'Of course it does. I'll have to see what I can find to get him off the hook.'

'What on earth can you do that the police can't?'

'God knows, but they think they've got their man; they're not interested. Look, I'm going to do it but I need your help. Is there any chance you could leave Sandy in charge for a bit and come over here to help Kenny at the yard?'

'Yes,' Kate said quickly. 'Of course I'll come. There aren't many animals in at the moment anyway. When do I start?'

'Now?' Charlie asked.

'See you at midday.'

Charlie's next call was going to be more difficult.

Roland Ryder, Nick's father, had scarcely spoken to Nick since he had left Cambridge and gone into racing. He had always expressed the view that it wasn't an occupation for a serious man. Nick, without a mother since he was a boy, hadn't even attempted to justify his decision to his father, and the two had seldom seen each other in the past five years. But Roland Ryder had to be told.

Charlie got through to his office in Lloyd's where Ryder headed a large underwriting syndicate. He was put through without any delay.

'Good morning, Charles,' Ryder said unemotionally. 'I was sorry to hear about your stepfather.'

'It's all been an awful shock, especially for my mother.'

'I can imagine. As I expect you know, he was on some of my syndicates.'

'I'd heard.'

'I'm afraid there'll be some considerable claims on his estate,' Ryder went on, without a hint of regret.

Charlie realised now why he had been put through so promptly. 'That's not why I've rung,' he said. 'I'm

164

afraid Nick's been arrested ... for my father's murder.'

A short burst of indignation spluttered down the line, resolving itself in a strangled yell.

'He only went there to talk about a horse my father had with us.'

'But how the hell could he end up killing him? It's crazy!'

'He didn't kill him, Mr Ryder. It just looks that way.'

'Where have they taken him? He'll want bail.'

'He escaped,' Charlie said, deriving some satisfaction from delivering the news.

'My God! This is going from bad to worse. Which police are handling it?'

Charlie told him. Roland Ryder rang off without another word.

Charlie took a deep breath and started to make a string of phone calls to racecourses, jockeys and owners. Most of the time he was talking, his mind was miles away.

*   *   *

Nick judged that the lorry had left the M25 and was heading north up the M1. That meant they should reach Doncaster around eleven.

The lorry's destination at the South Yorkshire racecourse was crucial to his plans for the next few days. The only place in the country where he was absolutely certain of receiving an unquestioning, warm welcome was no more than twenty miles from Doncaster.

When Nick was a boy, Harold Amory had always treated him with kindness and equality. Amory,

165

already in his sixties even then, had been his parents' gardener. Since he had retired fifteen years before, the old man had moved back to his native Lincolnshire, to live in a small cottage on his son-in-law's farm. When Nick's mother had been killed in a car crash outside Monaco when he was just twelve, he had written to Amory before anyone else and, receiving a beautifully written reply, had kept up a regular correspondence with him ever since.

After a couple of long hold-ups, it was eleven o'clock before the lorry reduced speed and swung off the M1 on to the M18. They didn't pull into the racecourse lorry park until shortly before midday.

Nick listened carefully as the ramp was lowered and his three fellow passengers were led down. When it had been banged back up, there was a period of comparative silence while Nick gave them time to move away. With luck, the lorry would be parked out of sight of the stables. There was, anyway, at least a fifty-fifty chance that the small side door from the box wouldn't be visible. If he didn't want to arouse anyone's suspicions, he would just have to get out quickly and confidently, as if he belonged with the lorry.

He clambered down from the Luton, opened the door, and jumped straight out. He took a quick look around to get his bearings, closed the door behind him and started to walk towards the back of the stables. After a few yards, confident that no one was taking any notice of him, he veered off towards the main exit to the road.

*　　　*　　　*

Charlie was giving Kate a final briefing. They had a

runner in a small race at Folkestone. Charlie ought to have been going with it, but he had more pressing plans. Kate offered to go, but he needed her at the yard. In the end, they decided their travelling head lad would have to deputise and hoped the owner didn't kick up a fuss. When he felt Kate knew enough of what was going on to cope without him, Charlie gave her a quick kiss, got into the Mercedes and went to see the police.

DI Ferrier eyed him sourly. 'And where do you suggest we start?'

'You're the detective, not me. All I can tell you is my partner was physically and temperamentally incapable of doing it.'

'I understand your loyalty to your friend, but I'm afraid he was there and he was the last person to handle the murder weapon. You've admitted it was possible he and your father argued about this horse, and he's got a history of violent anger.'

Charlie stared at the policeman. 'Who the hell told you that?'

'The headmaster of his old school.'

'For God's sake,' Charlie said, feeling he'd lost control of this conversation, 'I was there with him. He never did anything more than lose his temper now and again, and that was over ten years ago.'

'Well, there it is. And he's done a runner.' The policeman nodded with a cynical smirk.

'Only because he knew it looked so bad for him.'

'He's told you, has he?'

'No,' Charlie snapped, caught on his back foot. 'But I know how he'd be thinking. Anyway, what about outside the cottage? Did you search there?'

'Of course.'

'Wasn't there anything?'

167

'I think you'll find what there was will just confirm your friend was there.'

'Why? What did you find?'

'We've got some good clear footprints on the ground outside the front door. We haven't been able to match them yet—Ryder was probably wearing the shoes when he ran.'

'You checked all the ones in the house?'

'We did.'

'Was there anything else?'

The detective shrugged. 'Not really. A pack of Rizlas.'

'Cigarette papers?'

'Yes.'

'Nick didn't smoke; and Dad certainly never smoked roll-ups. Where did you find them?'

'Outside, where the cars were parked.' Charlie felt a lurch of disappointment. Ferrier dismissed the papers as trivial. 'Could have been anyone's.'

'Have you checked?'

'You mean have we called in everyone in the district who uses green Rizlas? Quite a few of them wouldn't want to come. Maybe your friend liked the odd bit of wacky baccy.'

'No, he never liked dope,' Charlie said as if it would help Nick's case. 'I take it you can't stop me asking questions if I want to?'

Ferrier laughed. 'As long as you don't break any laws or cause any complaints. But there's no point; there's nothing you can do to help your friend except maybe get him a good brief once we've got our hands on him again.'

Charlie found as he drove out of the police station car park that in trying to convince the cynical detectives of Nick's innocence, he'd gone some way

168

to believing that the police might be right. But until Nick's guilt was proven beyond reasonable doubt, he would do everything he could to help him.

He decided to start back at Birch Lodge, or rather, on the general's estate, by asking anyone if they had seen anything unusual.

The general himself was out. His housekeeper, a silent, unsmiling woman, was prepared to accept that the son of the victim had a right to ask questions though she pointed out that she'd already told the police she knew nothing and had seen nothing.

'Who else might have been around that day?'

'Saturday? No one, really. Tom Skyrme might have been in; he sometimes comes for an hour or two on a Saturday, but I didn't see him, and I haven't seen him today.'

'Who's he?'

'The general's gardener. Lives in the West Lodge.'

The West Lodge was on the other side of the estate from Birch Lodge. Certainly the gardener wouldn't have seen any comings or goings there from his house.

Tom Skyrme turned out to be a small, wiry man in his late fifties, with a weather-beaten face beneath a worn cap. When Charlie found him he was scraping the mud from his boots on to the top of his spade. He told Charlie he'd been among the rhododendrons by the track to the major's cottage on Saturday morning.

'Did you see anything unusual, anyone around you didn't know?'

'No, not in the grounds.'

'What do you mean, not in the grounds?'

'Well, your father had someone with him.'

'How do you know? Could you see into the house?'

169

'No. I mean in his car. I saw him driving down the track and he had a bloke with him.'

'A bloke? Who was he?' Charlie asked with much more interest.

'I don't know. Never seem him before. Didn't look much like a friend of the major's.'

'Why not?' Charlie urged, bursting with frustration at the old gardener's ponderous delivery.

'Scruffy bugger, he were. I saw him get out of the car wearing old jeans and a tatty sort of bomber jacket.'

'How old was he?'

'Oh, hard to say. Fifty, sixty.'

'How tall?'

'A good height.'

'What? Six feet?'

'Maybe more.'

'What else?'

'That's it, really. I didn't pay too much attention. Not my business who the major saw.'

'What did you tell the police?'

'I haven't told them nothing.'

'Why not?'

'They didn't ask me, and anyway I've been away for a few days.'

'But didn't you think you should go to them, after what happened to my father?'

The gardener shrugged. 'If they comes looking for me, I'll tell 'em. I hasn't got time to go sticking my nose in otherwise.'

Charlie spent another five minutes pressing for any small detail. He soon realised he'd got all he was going to get, but he drove away feeling triumphant. Half an hour into the job, he told himself, and he had something new. He was eager to inform DI Ferrier and let the police get on with it, but first he wanted to take a closer look inside his father's car.

He wasn't surprised when the ashtray yielded up the fag ends of two roll-ups.

Charlie continued his search, concentrating on the front of the car where on the evidence of the gardener and the fag ends, his stepfather's passenger had been sitting.

After ten minutes, he had found nothing. He gave up and sat back in the driver's seat, feeling deflated. But there was no doubt that there had been someone with his father, by consent, on Saturday morning. And the police knew nothing about this man. But what had he got to offer them? The gardener's reluctant evidence, and two roll-up fag ends. His mother clearly didn't know that his stepfather had driven someone to the house after she had gone out to do her shopping. She hadn't mentioned it to him or the police.

Charlie sat in the car trying to decide his next move. The dull morning had cleared and was maturing into a fine early summer's day. He started the handsome old car and, in the absence of a more constructive plan, headed for Oak Hollow. Whatever else was going on, he still had to keep his eye on the yard.

* * *

There were only six policemen on duty at Doncaster races that day. There was no tradition of serious trouble there. Only the usual drunken exuberance or morbidity caused by gambling successes or failures.

PC Mike Withenshaw adjusted his helmet more firmly on his head as he walked from the police

171

minibus that had brought them up from the station. On his way to the main lorry entrance, he was thinking about the Yankee accumulator he'd put on four of the day's races and how he would spend the money when all four horses came in. The briefing before he and his colleagues had left the police station had been the usual two-line injunction not to hit back and a message circulated to all stations with a local horse-racing connection: keep an eye out for a young Lambourn trainer called Nicholas Ryder, absconded while being taken into custody to be charged with murder.

PC Withenshaw had read a profile on Oak Hollow in the *Racing Post* and he knew exactly who Nick Ryder was—not a trainer, that was for sure. Charlie Patterson did all the training in that yard. He had produced some useful winners in his first year and a small profit for PC Withenshaw.

Why the hell anyone should think Ryder would turn up at the races if he was on the run, God knew.

The constable reached his post at the gate to the lorry park and looked across at the stables. There were already several lorries parked and horses being led to their temporary accommodation. He tried to identify a few of them, but even if he had been able to consult the *Racing Post* in the pocket of his tunic, he would have been no wiser. He envied the lads, scurrying about, doing what they loved—though not so well paid, mind, he added to himself. One of them was walking towards him now. Or maybe it wasn't a lad. He was wearing a tweed jacket and a pair of rumpled cotton trousers.

The man was walking briskly, with his head down. As he got near the gate, the policeman greeted him. 'Morning. What's happened to you? Lost your horse

172

or what?'

The man looked up sharply, barely slowing his pace. 'Looking for a phone.'

'There's some back in the grandstand,' PC Withenshaw said helpfully.

'I saw one just down the road,' the man replied, and hurried on.

The policeman watched him go and tried to remember if there was a public phone anywhere near. He couldn't think of one. And he was trying to think who the man was. He'd seen him before somewhere.

A few seconds later it dawned on him and he gasped. He looked at the man's back. This chap had already given two blokes the slip. No point him going after him alone and losing him. He reached for his radio.

*   *   *

Nick was shaking as he walked out of the gate. He couldn't believe the policeman on the gate hadn't seen his fear. But there was no shout, no challenge as he walked away up the empty road.

The further he got from the racecourse entrance, the more he relaxed. Now all he had to do was to travel as inconspicuously as possible to the small village outside Gainsborough where Harold Amory lived. Then, secure in the knowledge that none of his friends or connections were aware of Amory's existence, he would be safe to sit and watch developments from a distance.

Three hundred yards from the racecourse gates, a row of terraced houses was broken by a small newsagent-tobacconist. Nick was feeling the effects of twelve hours without food. He went in and bought crisps, biscuits, chocolate and a can of Coke to keep him going. He was anxious to get out of the busy outskirts of the town as quickly as he could.

He stepped out and had walked on a few paces when he heard a car roar up behind him and squeal to a halt outside the shop.

He turned, wondering idly who was in such a hurry, and too late saw two police patrolmen leap out and run straight towards him.

He spun round and looked down the empty road, enclosed on either side, offering nowhere to run or hide.

He turned back as his pursuers reached him, shortly joined by the PC he had seen on gate duty. 'Nicholas Ryder, you're under arrest. Don't attempt to move or we may be required to use force to apprehend you.'

Nick shrugged. He understood odds. Running last night had been a reasonable risk. This time the odds against getting away were somewhere in the order of five hundred to one.

'Okay. I'm coming,' he said.

*   *   *

When Charlie arrived back at Oak Hollow later that morning, he almost wished he'd stayed away. Kate was staring blankly at the screen of Nick's computer.

She glanced up when she heard Charlie walk into the office. 'I don't suppose you know how this bloody thing works, do you?'

Nick kept all their accounts, all their entries, form information, everything to do with selecting races, on the computer. Charlie had assumed it was just a simple database. 'Why?' he asked.

'I can't seem to get into this entries file.'

'I thought you knew how these things worked,' Charlie said, immediately regretting the irritation he showed.

'I do,' Kate came back bitingly, 'but Nick's obviously got a password which you've failed to tell me.'

Charlie reddened. Kate was right, and he hadn't a clue what the password was. 'God, I'm sorry,' he said. 'We'll just have to wait until he contacts me again. I wonder where the hell he is.'

'Ah,' Kate said. 'That's the other disaster. They've caught him again.'

'Where, for God's sake?'

'In Doncaster. I've already phoned that solicitor who was going to see him. Apparently they're bringing him back to Marlborough to charge him.'

'Oh God! Poor Nick. When can I go and see him?'

'They said he wouldn't be back until late tonight. You'll have to wait until tomorrow when they'll charge him or ask to remand him for a few more days.'

'I'll have to go and see him then. At least I'll be able to get that password for you.'

'I expect we can manage from the paper records in the meantime.'

'I can probably remember what's going on over the next few days anyway. Get the calendar out and we'll have a look. I'll go and get my diary from the car.'

Charlie had left the car up at the yard. As he opened it to get the old-fashioned A5 diary that was his lifeline, one of the more energetic lads walked over to admire the old Mercedes.

'Lovely model, that,' he said.

'Yes. My stepfather was very proud of it. He had it

175

for years.'

'It's a shame it's in such a six-and-eight. It could do with a bloody good clean.'

'Are you volunteering, Jimmy?'

'Yeah. I'll have it looking like new, in and out. I done six months' car valeting in Reading before I come here. Fiver, okay?'

Charlie agreed and left the lad going for the hosepipe they used to wash down the horses' legs. Back in the office, he sat down with Kate to establish exactly what Nick had entered where over the next seven days. But as he worked, Charlie couldn't get Nick's arrest and his stepfather's last visitor out of his head.

'Look,' he said abruptly, 'I can't handle this, Kate. Can you try and make head or tail of it? Get Kenny in to help. I've got to go and see my mother. I think we may be able to get Nick out of this sooner than we thought.'

'How?' Kate asked eagerly; she had been reluctant to talk about it while she knew Charlie was still uncertain.

Charlie told her about his chat with Tom Skyrme. 'It looks as though DI Ferrier and his men have been bloody useless, but I want to be sure of my ground before I rub their noses in it.'

*　　　*　　　*

Pru Patterson was packing a suitcase when Charlie arrived at Birch Lodge.

'Where are you going?' Charlie asked, approving.

'I'm not sure. Probably to Michael and Veronica. They've been very sweet and asked me to stay as long as I want.'

176

'When are you thinking of going?'

'Not for a day or two, but I just thought I'd get ready.'

Charlie had already noticed that the whole cottage had been thoroughly tidied—a kind of occupational therapy, he guessed, for his mother while she came to terms with her husband's death. He admired her for the stoicism with which she was handling his death and he was reluctant to probe her over it. But now that there was a real chance of an alternative suspect to Nick, he had to follow it through.

'Mum, I've discovered something the police don't know.'

She looked up sharply from her packing. 'What's that?'

'Dad was seen driving someone back to the cottage on Saturday morning.'

'Really?' The surprise in her voice was genuine. 'Who saw him?'

'The gardener, Tom Skyrme. The police never even spoke to him, for God's sake.'

'But who does Tom say he saw?'

'He just had a glimpse of a man in Dad's car. Someone scruffy and tall. I found two roll-up fag ends in the ashtray and the police had already told me they'd found a Rizla packet outside. As soon as they establish exactly who it was, it might get Nick off the hook.'

Pru straightened up and started to tidy up bottles on her dressing table. 'I'm really sorry about Nick, but I'm afraid the man you're talking about won't help. I was here when he came and when he left.'

Charlie's elation collapsed like a burst bubble. 'Oh, no! Who was he?'

'He was a chap who served in the regiment with

177

David. He was just passing and called in for a chat.'

'What was he wearing?'

'I don't remember really.' Charlie could see his mother searching for an answer. 'A type of bomber jacket, I think. David picked him up from the station, they went into the study and talked for a while, then he left.'

'How?'

'Well, I suppose he must have walked,' Pru said vaguely. 'I don't know, unless David called him a taxi.'

'But Dad didn't drive him anywhere?'

'No. I went out shortly afterwards, but he'd already gone.'

'How do you know he didn't hang around and come back?'

'I'm sure he didn't, darling. He was perfectly happy when he left. David had given him whatever he'd come for and that was that. There wasn't any question of his getting violent. I wish I could give you better news for Nick's sake, but there it is.'

Charlie sat down on a small buttoned chair and put his head in his hands. 'Bugger!' he muttered. 'I really thought I was getting somewhere; opening up a lead even the police couldn't ignore.'

'Come on, Charlie.' Pru put a hand on his shoulder. 'I'm sure they'll turn something up.'

'Not if they're not looking, they won't.' Charlie glanced up at his mother. 'God, I'm sorry. Here I am worrying about Nick, when you've lost ...'

'It's all right,' Pru said firmly. 'I can cope, and I understand your loyalty to a friend.'

'But you don't think he did it, do you?'

'No, darling. Of course I don't.'

Charlie drove back to Oak Hollow in a deep

178

depression. He couldn't rid himself of the idea that his mother thought exactly the opposite of what she'd said. And with his alternative suspect accounted for and eliminated, Nick's position looked as bad as ever.

CHAPTER NINE

Charlie shivered as he looked at his partner across the small courtroom and listened to the magistrate issuing instructions.

Nick Ryder had now formally been charged with the murder of Major David Patterson. There was no question of bail being granted. He would be remanded in custody for two weeks pending further inquiries before committal.

Nick's pale face was empty of expression as a policeman led him through a small door at the back of the dock to the cells below.

Charlie still found it almost impossible to absorb the fact that the police thought Nick had murdered his stepfather. And yet, with the *prima facie* evidence of the fingerprints on the poker, Nick's admitted presence at the scene of the crime, compounded by his attempt to abscond, the magistrate had accepted that they had a sufficiently strong case.

Charlie drove to Birch Lodge to tell his mother what had happened.

'I still think it's absurd,' she said with indignation. 'There is not the slightest possibility that Nick did it. David would have eaten him alive, even if he was forty years older.'

They were sitting in the drawing room of the small

house, the room where Major Patterson had been battered to death. Charlie looked at the fire-irons, neatly placed by an empty grate.

'But the prints on the poker? What if he crept up and hit him?'

Pru gave Charlie a look of despair. 'I don't know, I just don't believe he could do it.'

'Are you really sure about that, Mum?'

'Yes, of course. Aren't you?'

'I think so; I don't know. I was so certain he hadn't when I heard about the man who came to see Dad. Now I don't know where to look.'

'What are you going to do?'

'I can cope at the yard. Kenny's been marvellous and Kate's helping.'

'I suppose that means she's moved in.'

Charlie grinned. 'Just a temporary arrangement, I assure you, so that she's on hand if I'm away late.'

'Away late? Doing what?'

'God knows. Looking for something to help Nick.'

'Surely the police should be doing that, shouldn't they?' Pru asked, alarmed.

'But they're not. They're convinced Nick did it. Everything looks right so far and the article in *Sporting Life* describing Nick's feelings about Dad taking Willow Star away seems a good enough motive.' Uneasy about this theory, Charlie changed tack. 'What about you? How are you going to manage? Financially, I mean.'

A faint smile turned Pru's mouth. 'I'm afraid I haven't been left much. I think quite a lot of things may have to be sold to cover your father's liabilities. Things had become rather tricky recently.'

'Yes, I guessed they had when he told us he was going to sell Willow Star. Was it Lloyd's that did all the damage?'

Pru nodded. 'Lloyd's and a number of other investments he let himself be talked into. Did he know Nick was coming round that day?'

'No,' Charlie admitted. 'We thought it would be better if he turned up without any warning.'

'But why was Nick coming, not you?'

Charlie winced guiltily. 'We thought you'd take more notice of him than me.'

Pru threw him a bleak glance and shook her head. She eased herself from her chair and walked to the window where she stopped and looked out at the naked branches of the birch trees swaying in the wet March breeze. 'I've arranged the burial,' she said, without looking at her son. 'It'll be at midday on Friday, at Putney Vale. It'll only be us and a few family.'

'Won't a lot of his old army colleagues want to come?'

'I've tried to put them off, as far as possible.'

'Why?'

'I just don't think I could stand a crowd, all reminiscing and telling me how marvellous David was.'

*   *   *

'Maybe I *did* do it.' The normal pallor of Nick's face was accentuated by the stark white light of the naked neon tubes above. He stared forlornly at Charlie and heaved his shoulders hopelessly. 'I've told you, I haven't got a clue what happened. I certainly didn't have any conscious wish to do him harm, although he'd annoyed me.'

Charlie thought about the fingerprints on the

181

poker and tried to envisage Nick creeping up on his father. Somehow he just couldn't picture it.

They were sitting at a bare table in a visiting room at Bullingdon jail, about eight miles north of Oxford. A wary-eyed warder was keeping watch over them.

'What did my father say?' Nick asked flatly.

'Hasn't he been to see you yet?'

'No. He phoned to say he'd come as soon as he could,' Nick answered without any detectable emotion.

'When I spoke to him he just huffed and puffed. As a matter of fact, at first he thought I'd phoned to talk to him about my stepfather's debts at Lloyd's. He told me there wouldn't be much left of the estate. Dad was on some of his syndicates, and several other bad ones as well. And there were other deals that went wrong.'

'No wonder he wanted to sell Willow Star. Though he was too proud to mention his financial problems the day I went to see him.'

'And you didn't see anyone else while you were there?'

Nick looked blank. 'No. Not a soul.'

Charlie told him what he'd learned from the general's gardener, and his excitement at discovering the cigarette ends in the ashtray. 'But Mum said he was just some old soldier on the touch and he'd gone quite happily before she'd even left the house. But look,' Charlie leaned forward and put a hand on his friend's shoulder. The warder stepped forward, shaking his head. Charlie scowled at him and removed his hand. 'Look, Nick. I'll carry on doing everything I can to get you out of here. I know you didn't do it, and I'm not going to stand by and watch you go down for it.'

Nick looked grateful but unconvinced. 'Thanks, Charlie.' He then forced a smile on to his face. 'What's the news on Willow Star?'

'She's fine. She worked very well this morning.'

'I mean, about her ownership.'

Charlie shook his head. 'I don't know for certain, but I hope she'll be staying.'

'You mean your stepfather really *had* sold her to someone else?'

'Yes, he did, that morning. What's more, he wrote to Wetherby's at once to confirm it. They got the letter yesterday saying she was to be transferred to a nominee owner.'

'So you still don't know if she'll stay with us?'

'No, I don't. In the meantime, Dad's executors said we should keep her and run her in the normal way in their name and they'll look after the fees from the day Dad died. But I'll try and get the whole thing sorted out when I go up and see them after the funeral.'

'When's that?'

'The police have released the body. My mother's arranged his burial at Putney Vale on Friday.'

'Charlie,' Nick said, showing some animation for the first time, 'whatever happens, you must hang on to Willow, she's our best prospect. It might be a long time before we get another like her.'

Charlie shook his head with a smile. 'You're amazing. You're in the shit up to your ears and yet you're still worrying about the horses. Don't worry,' he said. 'I'll sort it out. We won't lose her.' He looked behind him at the expressionless warder, and a woman with a tear-streaked face who was leaving the room. 'Look, I'm afraid I've had enough of this place. I'll come back tomorrow. Is there anything

183

you want that I can bring?'

'A high quality solicitor would be a help.'

'It's the quality of the barrister that counts. And Nick,' Charlie said, standing up to leave. 'I know you didn't do it. I don't want you ever to have any doubt about that.'

When Charlie arrived home, Kate was still working in the office. 'How's Nick?' she asked anxiously as he walked through the door.

'As well as can be expected. Come on,' he said, putting up a hand to stem the flow of questions. 'I'll tell you everything over dinner somewhere. That prison has really got me down.'

Kate obviously had a firm grasp of what went on in the yard and what needed doing. As they ate, she told him that she'd had the vet round and he'd confirmed that two of their charges had contracted ringworm. There was a good chance that some of the others had already picked it up too, so she and Kenny had decided to isolate the six most important horses in the yard. Charlie's initial alarm was calmed by her pragmatic approach and the damage limitation she'd already put into action. 'It's good to know the place is in sound hands while I do what I can for Nick.'

'I've told my regional boss that I need a few weeks off—to learn about keeping bloodstock,' Kate said with a hint of guilt.

'Are you thinking of turning Noah's Ark into a training establishment then?' Charlie laughed.

'I might be, you never know.' Kate delved into her bag for her cigarette pack. With it she pulled out an envelope. 'By the way, this is from Jimmy.'

'Jimmy?'

'Yes. The new lad. He cleaned your father's Mercedes. He said you asked him to.'

184

'Oh him. He seemed so keen I didn't want to disappoint him. What's that, a bill?'

'No, just all the bits and pieces he found while he was doing the interior. He said he thought it was all rubbish, but left it for you to decide. He gave it to me just as I was on my way to the village.'

Charlie glanced inside the envelope before he tucked it into his pocket.

Later, when he and Kate were sitting in the kitchen at the bungalow, running through the evening's messages, he took the envelope out and tipped the contents on to the table. There was a business card from a firm of art shippers, a couple of bookies' tickets, presumably from Goodwood, a slip of paper with the message 'Hungerford, 9.37' written in Major Patterson's neat hand, and a shoe repair ticket, dated the previous week, from a heel bar in Kilburn High Road.

Charlie looked at each in turn. 'It's amazing,' he said, shaking his head. 'I thought I'd been through that car with a fine-tooth comb. How did I miss all this?'

Kate looked sceptically at the motley collection. 'Just looks like litter to me.'

Charlie shrugged. 'Probably. The bookies' tickets are unlikely to yield a lot, I admit.'

'Or the shoe repair ticket, unless you think your stepfather left a decent pair of shoes to be picked up somewhere.'

'He wouldn't have had them repaired in Kilburn.'

'Maybe it was the guy who came to see him.'

Charlie shrugged in resignation. 'I suppose you're right. And this other bit of paper must be the time of the chap's train; that fits in with when the gardener saw him.'

185

'Charlie, I don't want to discourage you, but wouldn't the police forensic people have been through the car if they'd thought it was worth it?'

'Yes, but I'm going to follow up this shoe ticket. You never know, this friend of Dad's could have seen something.'

Kate agreed but part of her remained unconvinced.

* * *

Charlie sat with his mother in the back of a long black Ford. He stared straight ahead at the hearse they were following to London along the M4. In the hearse, between dark-coated, stripe-trousered men who chatted about football and their own domestic problems, was one of the cheaper coffins from the undertaker's catalogue. Charlie thought of his stepfather's once hard, efficient body lying in it among the folds of white silk.

His mother showed little emotion. Charlie supposed this must be the result of years of marriage to a man who, if he accepted the need for human emotion at all, saw no reason to display it.

He tried to identify what he was feeling within himself. Sadness? Nostalgia? Disappointment? Grief? Nothing?

He was acutely conscious that the man in the coffin had been no more than an acquaintance to him, an acquaintance for whom he had the same awed affection he might have for a favourite view of a distant mountain. His stepfather had been aloof but, until recently, he had always been consistent. He had sometimes said that he considered it a complete waste of breath and not worth the energy required to open

186

his mouth to make statements which he wasn't completely prepared to stand by. Charlie reflected that it had made for dull conversations, when ideas and conjecture were precluded.

As they reached the outskirts of London, the hearse turned off the motorway and headed south, over the River Thames at Kew. They crossed Richmond Park in convoy. Charlie looked out, detached from the walkers, runners, cyclists and horsemen indulging in their everyday pleasures. The deer grazed gracefully at a distance while stags kept guard. The sun, making its first appearance for several days, gleamed weakly orange above the Mies van der Rohe tower blocks on the edge of the park. To Charlie, everything outside seemed part of a surreal, unattainable world.

The small gathering outside the anonymous chapel brought Charlie back to reality. Despite his mother's discouragement, a couple of dozen men—old military connections, Charlie deduced from their ties and deportment—stood a little to one side of the relations: Pru's sister, Sue, David Patterson's only sister, Veronica Russell, severe and unsmiling beside her emotionless husband. Sadly, Charlie noted, no sign of Imogen. A pair of more distant cousins, seldom spoken of, almost never seen. In the background, David Patterson's old commanding officer, General Sir Peter Sheridan, stood quietly observing, speaking to no one.

The undertakers carried the coffin into the chapel. With no great eagerness, the party followed slowly. Charlie sent his mother in ahead so that he could greet any late arrivals. He watched the last of the old soldiers walk in and was about to follow when he was stopped by the sight of a convoy of three cars, two

187

Mercedes and a Rolls-Royce, sweeping up the avenue of grey-green conifers to the chapel.

The Rolls pulled up directly in front of the door. A chauffeur got out smartly and opened the rear door for his employer—a black-bearded Arab in a Western suit of shiny mohair.

The Arab saw Charlie and acknowledged him with only the faintest narrowing of his eyes. He walked straight past him into the small chapel. From one of the Mercedes, two more Arabs in jellabas and headcloths emerged. They did not enter the building but stood outside the door with the wind flapping their white garments around their silk ankle socks.

Two more men, swarthy, Middle Eastern, got out of the second Mercedes. They were dressed in jeans and leather jackets. They stared at Charlie. One of them took a pack of Marlboros from his pocket and they both lit up and leaned against the car.

Charlie was still wondering who they were when he took his seat beside his mother in the front row, a few feet from his stepfather's coffin.

A vicar who found it hard to sound concerned about one of the constant string of strangers who were brought here to attend their last service intoned the prayers of burial, the regrets and thanks for a life past, perhaps fulfilled, possibly worthy and not too sinful. The clergyman had no idea from the scanty notes he had made in a brief discussion with Pru what the man he was burying was really like.

And, Charlie thought, not for the first time, nor had he. But while he was confused by his own emotions, he was deeply puzzled by his mother's. She stood beside him, responding to the prayers in a quiet, firm voice, with no hint of a quaver to it. As the last prayers were said, the final hymn tunelessly droned and the timber-boxed body carried out by the undertakers' bearers to a deep, neatly cleft trench, Charlie thought that at least now she would show her grief.

But there was no dampness in the corner of her eyes, no wringing of her neat hands, no trembling of her lower lip, even as the box was lowered into the ground and the vicar said the final prayers and invited the widow and son to cast a trowel of earth on to the coffin. Maybe she hadn't loved him at all.

Charlie, with his mother on his arm, led the way back to the chapel. He noticed that the three Arab cars had already gone. The man in the suit, the putative boss, had not come to the grave. Charlie wondered what a Muslim had thought of the simple, undemonstrative Christian burial. He also wondered who he was. He turned to his mother and asked her.

'That was Sheikh Sala Mahmoud.'

'David's boss in Saudi?'

Pru nodded.

'I didn't know he was that fond of him.'

'He thought a lot of David but I admit I was rather surprised to see him here.'

'Who were the others?'

Pru shrugged. 'Just members of his entourage.'

'You didn't speak to him.'

'No, but that's quite normal. He came. I suppose we're meant to be grateful for that.' Pru turned to talk to several people waiting to see her, their faces full of earnest sympathy.

Charlie walked away and nodded at one or two mourners he knew. One man made a point of walking over to him. Charlie recognised Guy Helmsley-Barret. He held out a hand. 'Hello, Charles. Very sad.'

189

Charlie nodded. The man facing him was in his late fifties, thick, grey-haired, in a rumpled but expensive suit and still good-looking in a raffish way.

'He was an extraordinary man,' Helmsley-Barret murmured. He had been a fellow officer of Major Patterson's.

Charlie nodded again, though he didn't know if he agreed.

'Look, if you don't mind,' the ex-soldier said, putting a hand on Charlie's forearm, 'I'd like to talk to you about him, get a couple of things off my chest. Could we have lunch together?'

Charlie glanced at his watch and his mother, chatting calmly to the cousins. He had planned to go to Kilburn to visit the shoe repair shop. But he thought Helmsley-Barret might well be able to shed light on some aspects of his father's activities.

'Yes,' he said. 'Why not? I'll just tell my mother.'

He arranged to go round later to the flat above the now closed shop in Kensington Church Street. She made no objection to his lunching with someone else.

Helmsley-Barret drove them in his oldish Daimler to a small, busy restaurant, halfway down the Fulham Road, where he appeared to be known by the Italian staff and by a gathering of over-ripe women who were lunching together.

They were shown to a table in a corner where, Helmsley-Barret explained, they would not be overheard.

When a bottle of Frascati and plates of antipasti had been placed on the table, Charlie's host spoke in the same quiet, confidential tone he had used earlier.

'I dare say your mother's very upset. I mean, he could hardly have gone in more horrible circumstances.'

'She's coping surprisingly well, as a matter of fact,' Charlie replied. 'I think my father had trained her for years that it wasn't the thing to let one's emotions show.'

'Well, I must admit, she did seem to be taking it pretty calmly, which is something to be glad of.' He poured more wine for them both. 'You know, your father and I had some business dealings together.'

Charlie nodded. 'Stepfather,' he corrected. 'I vaguely knew about it. He referred to it once, some while ago. I . . .' Charlie considered his words. 'I got the impression there was some kind of problem.'

Helmsley-Barret glanced away, smiled fleetingly at a woman who was trying to catch his eye and took another gulp of wine. 'He was a sort of partner in a venture of mine. He wasn't involved in the day-to-day running of it but he was a director.'

'What was the business?'

'It was a chain of restaurants and wine bars. We established a very effective *modus operandi* in the early eighties, and we wanted to take advantage of it when business really took off after that. We had fantastic opportunities for growth but not enough capital, and the banks wanted usurious rates of interest or a hundred and fifty per cent security.'

'So my father invested in it, did he?'

'Only in so far as he gave some fairly sizeable guarantees for our bank loans.'

Charlie, reading Helmsley-Barret with a sickening surge of concern for his mother, was beginning to see where this was leading. 'And what sort of state is the business in now?'

His companion lifted a shoulder to show that matters were beyond his control. 'This bloody recession. We hadn't had the time to put on any fat before it hit. And of course the banks started to run around screaming like stuck pigs.'

'What does the business consist of now?'

'Nothing. We ran out of operating capital and unfortunately we're locked into one or two long leases.'

'What exactly does that mean?'

'It means that although the company has stopped trading, we still have to pay the rent—or perhaps I should say we're still liable for the rent.'

'And was my stepfather involved in these leases?'

'I'm afraid he was but he seemed extremely reluctant to honour his commitments.'

'I suppose,' Charlie said, 'the landlords will be looking to the estate for the rents.'

'Yes, I'm afraid so. I was wondering if you knew yet what sort of estate he left?'

'Were you?' Charlie nodded. 'What happens if there's not enough there?'

'You don't think that's the case, do you?' The man sitting opposite him looked alarmed. 'After all, your father came back from Saudi a wealthy man.'

Charlie ignored the man's panic. 'Who do the landlords pursue if they can't get it from my late father?'

'Any other personal guarantors.'

'In this case you, I suppose.'

Helmsley-Barret nodded.

'And how are you fixed?' Charlie asked.

'Frankly, boracic.'

'Who the hell's paying for lunch, then?' Charlie asked.

Helmsley-Barret shifted his well-dressed frame uneasily on the rush-seated chair.

Charlie stood up. 'If I'm paying, I'd rather eat with

someone who's company I'd appreciate.'

'Hang on,' the ex-officer said with an effort at smooth bonhomie. 'I'll get it. I have a sort of arrangement here.'

'Why's that?' Charlie asked.

'It used to be one of ours.'

Charlie shook his head and glanced around the busy restaurant with a cynical grin. 'Used to be?' he said before turning and walking out.

In the crisp wind funnelling up the Fulham Road, he walked east until an empty taxi cruised by. He flagged it down and asked the cabbie to take him to the Kilburn High Road.

In the halfhour it crawled through clogged London streets, Charlie tried to piece together what his father's position must have been by the time he was killed. He knew there had been cash calls from syndicates at Lloyd's but he had no idea of the size of them. He also knew that the antiques business was doing badly, like almost every other antique shop in London; his mother had told him that much but, again, he had no idea of the scale of losses. He could only guess from Helmsley-Barret's agitation that the liabilities on the restaurant company weren't small.

Charlie sighed. He hadn't expected to get anything himself from his stepfather's estate but he had assumed there would be something left for his mother. He was certain of one thing, he was in no position to support her if there wasn't.

O'Grady's Lightning Shoe Repairs operated from a narrow-fronted shop on the High Road near the tube station. The quiet sound of a rasp and the pleasant leathery smell seemed to contradict the 'Lightning' of the shop's title.

When Charlie entered, a bell above the door

pinged and an oldish man looked up from the heel he was filing. Charlie took the repair ticket from his pocket and put it on the worn lino counter.

'What have we here?' the old man said, rising from his seat and picking up the ticket. From his undiluted west of Ireland accent, Charlie assumed it was O'Grady who addressed him.

'I wondered if these were ready yet.'

O'Grady turned to the shelves across the back of the shop and fingered his way through rows of brown paper parcels. He stopped and stood back a moment, staring at the ticket. He turned slowly and confronted Charlie. 'What is it you're trying to do? Yer man already picked these up. Friday it would have been, just as I was closing. He couldn't find his ticket, but I recognised him so I let him have them. Are you telling me they were yours?' It was clear that O'Grady didn't think this likely.

Charlie offered the Irishman a winning smile. 'No. I thought I was doing the chap a favour. I was going round to see him. He left the ticket in my car, so I thought I'd pick them up on the way round.'

'He's a friend of yours?' Clearly an unlikely proposition.

'No. He served in the army with my father, though.'

'I'd be surprised if ever he was in the army. Nasty piece of work, if you ask me.'

'Do you know his name?'

'I do not.'

'Could you describe him to me?'

'Why?'

'I just need to be sure it's the same chap.'

O'Grady shrugged. His description of his customer was very similar to Tom Skyrme's. Charlie,

194

though he couldn't have justified it, derived a tingle of satisfaction from discovering this much.

'What repair did he have done?'

'Why do you want to know?'

Charlie knew from the man's voice that he was just as curious now. 'I wish I could tell you, but it's out of the question. If you don't tell me, though, I'll have to get the police round.'

'I'd rather tell you.' O'Grady nodded. 'Let's have a think now. It was a straight re-soling job.'

'Any idea what sort of soles?'

'I'd be pretty sure it was the standard composition sole, heavy duty.'

'What does that look like?'

O'Grady turned and crouched to rummage on the lower shelves. When he stood up he was holding a rubber sole with a deep tread, distinctively patterned in diamonds and double Us.

'Can you remember what size?'

'Ten, eleven.'

'Can I buy one—a size ten?'

'Sure. Did you want me to stick it on a shoe?'

'No. I want to match it to a footprint.'

Charlie left the shop with his prize and started walking towards Marble Arch with his head over his shoulder, searching for a cab.

He was satisfied with the meagre fruits of his journey. If all he had done was find the shoe that matched the footprint DI Ferrier had found, he had removed one small piece of potential evidence against Nick. It wasn't much, but it was in the right direction.

A taxi dropped Charlie in Kensington where he rang the bell on the back door of the shop in Church Street.

His mother opened it and let him in. Without speaking, she showed him up to the drawing room on the first floor. When she went into the small kitchen to make some tea, Charlie looked around at the comparative comfort of the apartment and wondered how this could be sustained in the face of all his stepfather's business creditors.

But if his mother was worried about it, it didn't show. She seemed to be far more concerned about Nick being in prison, though she was fatalistic about Charlie's chances of finding out anything that might help him. Charlie didn't tell her about his visit to the shoe menders, or the slab of thick rubber in his pocket. He didn't want her dismissing it from the equation just yet.

'I don't see what you can do that the police can't,' she said as if she'd read his mind.

'Quite a lot, as they're not doing anything,' Charlie said. 'There had to be someone else there, besides Dad's soldier. But the police think they've got their man and they're not too worried.'

Pru sighed. 'Surely they ought to be following up other lines.'

'Of course, but it's no use telling me.'

'If only he hadn't turned up just when he did,' Pru said, mostly to herself.

Charlie stayed that night in the London flat. In the morning, he and his mother had an appointment with David Patterson's lawyers.

They were met in the Lincoln's Inn offices by a partner with a harassed, disapproving manner.

'Your late husband's will was all in order, Mrs Patterson,' he said. In the still, dusty air of a book-lined meeting room, he read aloud a document which left everything to Pru. There were no other personal

196

bequests.

'We are handling probate,' the lawyer went on, 'but I'm afraid we've already had some alarming claims on the estate. It seems your husband issued a number of guarantees to banks and property companies which are being called. On top of this there was an outstanding Lloyd's liability. We've been involved in fighting this for him, but that's all a very grey area and will be for some time to come. Did your husband make any separate, life-time provision for you?'

Pru shook her head.

The solicitor looked worried. 'Oh dear. I'll see what we can do but I'm afraid it looks as though it's a case of trying to salvage what we can from the wreckage. I do hope I'm not being too depressing when you've only just buried him.'

'That's all right,' Pru said quietly.

Charlie was disappointed to hear that the solicitor had no good news about Nick's predicament but went on to ask the question he most wanted to.

'Can you tell me what the situation is with the filly, Willow Star?'

'Ah, yes. The racehorse. Your father did have an offer for it which he indicated he wanted to accept.'

'I understand he confirmed it with Wetherby's.'

'Wetherby's only received his instruction after he had died.'

Charlie bit back his frustration. 'Have you had any other offers for her?'

'We have had one and we have accepted the best offer.'

Charlie's heart raced, anticipating bad news. 'So, who's the new owner?'

The lawyer hesitated a moment. 'It's a small

nominee syndicate.'

'But who are they?'

'I'm afraid I'm not at liberty to say.'

Charlie took a deep breath. 'What are they going to do with her?'

'I dare say it will please you to hear that they wish the filly to stay where it is, in your yard at Oak Hollow.'

CHAPTER TEN

With ten days to go before the One Thousand Guineas, Willow Star's work programme was going well, but that was about all it was for Charlie.

In the two weeks since Nick had been arrested nothing had turned up to improve the prospects for his release.

Charlie was finding it difficult to concentrate on the yard while his partner's future was still in jeopardy. Barely a day passed without some speculation in the tabloid press, and Nick's resilience was fading fast.

Kate was at the yard all the time now. Without waiting to be asked, she had taken over the bulk of the paperwork which Nick normally handled and she was completely at home with the computer programme. She understood the complicated emotions afflicting Charlie as a result of the death of his stepfather and the arrest of his partner. Having looked at the balance sheet for the yard, she also realised just how important it was for him to succeed on the racecourse. The tensions in his life were palpable and potentially self-destructive, but she was learning how to defuse them.

She appointed herself guardian to Nick's dog, Hercules, who, for a time after his master's absence, had lacked his usual spark. He still wasn't quite back to his old self, but a couple of nights spent sleeping on Kate's bed, and with some regular titbits, he had perked up no end. Kate was also riding out most mornings; she was now fitter, leaner and losing the hint of chubbiness she had carried when Charlie had first met her.

Today, Kate had gone to Salisbury with a couple of runners. Charlie was still thinking of her as he waited in his office to see a potential owner with a lot of horses and a tight diary.

His visitor, a North London property dealer, turned out to be about fifty with a narrow, neatly trimmed moustache. He wore a camelhair coat, a navy trilby and a deep tan. There were large gold rings on six of his fingers and a Rolex oyster dangled on his wrist.

It normally took Charlie about fifteen seconds to weigh someone up, and another fifteen minutes to be proved right. If he wasn't mistaken, the character sitting opposite him would be a bad payer and an even worse loser. But he needed the horses. The meeting went well enough, at least to the extent that a couple of cheap two-year-olds, in which his other, grander trainer showed no interest, would be coming to Oak Hollow.

After the owner had driven away, the yard was deserted. It was two o'clock and the lads had either gone shopping for the afternoon or were in the hostel. They weren't needed now until evening stables. Charlie wanted a few things from the village. Kenny had taken his Range Rover to collect some peatmoss, so he took the VW Golf which Kate had recently bought to replace the old Renault. He was just getting into it when he saw a large Mercedes swing off the road and creep down the drive to the stables.

Charlie temporarily abandoned his plan to go to the village and got out of the Golf to walk back to the bungalow. He didn't recognise the vehicle and watched its approach with interest. He was almost at the front door when the car swung down towards him and pulled up on the gravel.

Two men climbed out, one from each side. Charlie waited to greet them. They looked familiar. He groped a moment for their identity until it snapped into place. They had been part of Sheikh Sala Mahmoud's entourage at his father's funeral two weeks before.

Why should Sala Mahmoud be sending emissaries to Oak Hollow? Charlie barely knew about the Saudi merchant's activities but as far as he was aware the man had done little more than dabble in British racing. Maybe he had developed a taste for it.

Charlie smiled. 'Good morning.'

The two swarthy men did not smile back. They started walking towards him.

There was a hostility in their approach which made Charlie take a step back to the door, instinctively seeking the shelter of the house.

The larger of the two put his hand on Charlie's chest and shoved him with sudden violence against the partly open door. Charlie sprawled backwards into the house, he tried to save himself as he fell but before his hands touched anything, the back of his head connected with the corner of a stone umbrella stand. Lightning flashed in his head as he blacked out. When he came round a few moments later, he had been dragged down the narrow hallway into the kitchen. He was propped on one of the chairs. A handkerchief soaked in vinegar was being held to his nose, making him gag.

The older of his two aggressors was slapping his face. 'We want to talk to you,' he growled with guttural Arab consonants.

Charlie snatched the handkerchief away and struggled to regain some of his senses. 'What's the point of trying to smash my brains in first?'

'We smash more than your brains if you don't talk.'

'What the hell do you want?'

'Your father.'

'What about him?'

In a flash the man grabbed hold of Charlie at the throat. 'Your father cheated Sala Mahmoud. Where is the money now? You tell us what we need to know, or we start to do you harm. Where is your father?'

Charlie could hardly breathe, let alone talk. He'd always thought himself more than capable of fighting his own corner. But something about these men frightened him. Suddenly the hand was removed from his windpipe. 'I don't know what the hell you're talking about! My stepfather was murdered.'

The second man, who hadn't spoken at all, grabbed both Charlie's arms and brought them back behind the chair. He pulled a coil of cord from the pocket of his leather jacket and bound Charlie's wrists tightly to the chair slats. The cord sliced into Charlie's skin until he couldn't move his arms without agonising pain.

The man who had tied him leaned over him. Charlie smelled his rancid breath as he bent forward

201

and put his hands between his legs to clutch both his testicles in a vicious grip, a crude technique for extracting reluctant information which was probably as old as man and always worked. The problem was, Charlie didn't have anything to tell his torturers.

They tried burning him with cigarette stubs; they put him on the floor and bent him nearly double backwards until he thought his spine would splinter. His face was hit so ferociously and so often that he could scarcely mumble his denials through thickened, bleeding lips.

His whole body ached. He was nearly unconscious with pain when, abruptly and without warning, it was over.

He became aware that he was alone and tied to the chair again. He was dimly conscious of the sound of a car starting and skidding away. A few minutes later, he heard someone walking down the passage from the front door.

'Hello? Guv'nor?' It was Kenny Ford. 'Jesus Christ! What the hell's happened?' The head lad stared with disbelief at his boss trussed to a chair, his face swollen and bruised, his mouth bleeding. Kenny was already taking a penknife from his pocket to untie him. 'Was it those blokes in the Merc?'

Charlie nodded as Kenny severed the cords binding his wrists and helped him to his feet. He flopped back on to the chair.

'I'll get you a drink.' Kenny went out into the office and came back with a tumbler half full of brandy.

Charlie gingerly put the glass to his swollen lips. 'God,' he spluttered. 'I never touch this stuff.' He took another slug and let the warming, softening, anaesthetising liquid sting his lips, dribble down his throat, through his chest into his battered guts.

Kenny sat down on the other side of the table and watched anxiously. 'What the hell's going on, guv'nor?'

'I wish to God I knew.' Charlie ran his tongue over his teeth, checking for damage. Fortunately, none were broken. 'They work for my father's old boss.'

'What did they want?'

'They said my father had stolen some money from Sheikh Sala Mahmoud, the man he used to work for. They thought I'd know where it was. At least they know I don't now. I haven't got a clue. Oh my God!' Charlie leaped to his feet. 'What about my mother?'

He picked up the phone and rang the flat in Kensington, but a recorded message announced that the line was not in service. Then he phoned Veronica and Michael, whom his mother had said she wanted to visit, but neither of them had heard from her. Finally he dialled the number at Birch Lodge. He let it ring for at least a minute before hanging up. 'I'll have to go round there,' he said to Kenny. 'If I'm not here when Kate and the others get back, tell her I'll ring later.'

*   *   *

The lock of the front door at Birch Lodge had been forced and the door was swinging on its hinges. Charlie pushed it open and walked in. Every room had been thoroughly and messily searched. Drawers were open with their contents scattered all over the floor. Upstairs it was the same. There was no sign of Charlie's mother. The case she had been packing a few days before and all her personal things had gone. That reassured him a little. But it could be she had them in London. If it was Sala Mahmoud's men who

203

had broken in, it didn't look as though they had taken anything. And there was nothing to suggest that his mother had been here when they came.

He tidied up a little and realised he should arrange for the door to be mended. He ought also to tell someone what had happened.

He phoned a local locksmith and then drove round to the general's house.

Charlie didn't know General Sir Peter Sheridan well, but he was aware that the old soldier was one of his father's few close friends. He found him pruning roses in front of his handsome Edwardian house.

'Afternoon, sir.'

'Afternoon, Charlie. What on earth have you been up to? Fallen off one of your horses or what?'

'Nothing serious, sir. I was wondering if you'd seen my mother recently?'

'Not for a couple of days. Isn't she in London?'

'She may be, but the phone doesn't seem to be working. The cottage here has been broken into again.'

The general straightened his back. 'Really? When?'

'Within the last twenty-four hours I should think. Did you hear anything?'

'Not a thing. And there's no sign of your mother?'

'No.'

'Have you told the police?'

'No.'

'Right. Let's get down there.' He looked closely at Charlie's damaged face. 'And you'd better tell me what happened to you, too.'

On their way back to the cottage in the woods, Charlie told General Sheridan about the Arabs' visit to Oak Hollow.

'They must have been under instructions from Sala

Mahmoud,' the general said. 'I'm afraid they may be justified.'

Charlie gaped at him. 'You mean my father *did* cheat the sheikh in some way?'

'I don't know, but I'm certain he was up to something. He never told me directly, but I've known him a very long time, and I could read him as well as anyone. He was in serious financial trouble—you must have known that. He'd had a lot of bad luck and made some frankly poor judgements. I warned him before he joined Lloyd's I thought the party was over there. After all, they wouldn't have wanted to go out signing up thousands of new members when they could easily have written more business themselves and kept the profit. They knew they were in for a rough time and wanted some outside punters to carry the can. That's when I got out, after fifteen good years.'

'But it wouldn't be like him to run away from a few debts.'

'I don't think it was a question of a few debts; it was total wipe-out. Besides that, as I say, I think he pulled off a questionable deal just before he died. That's almost certainly why those Arabs wanted to talk to you.'

'What kind of a deal?'

'I don't know specifically. My guess is that it was something to do with that furniture he used to deal in. Occasionally he handled some very expensive pieces. He knew a lot about it and did quite well from it sometimes but every penny he made went to paying off his debts.'

They had reached the cottage now. The locksmith Charlie had rung was waiting in his van. The general confirmed that he should go ahead with fitting a new

205

lock. He and Charlie went inside to inspect the damage. Afterwards he urged Charlie to drive straight to London to check on his mother. 'Ring if you need me and let me know that she's all right.'

Charlie drove away trying to make sense of the day's events, unable to reach a rational conclusion.

*   *   *

The break-in at the flat in Kensington had been a lot cleaner. Charlie found no sign of the lock being forced but the place had been ransacked; as he entered each room he held his breath, half expecting to find his mother lying beaten-up on the floor but there was no sign of her. He was now desperate to discover her whereabouts.

Charlie spent half an hour going through the piles of papers in his father's desk. A lot of these confirmed what the general had said about his father's current financial state. There were dozens of letters delivering draconian ultimatums. There was a letter from Nick, pleading with Major Patterson to think again about selling Willow Star.

Charlie thought of the filly for a moment. He had now received the lawyers' written instructions about the horse. The new owners had decided to remain anonymous. The bills would continue to be paid by the solicitors, and Charlie was to communicate all news through them. He wondered if the new owners had paid as much as Robert Jarvis had offered. Not that it mattered. The main thing was that the animal was to stay in his yard. And as every day passed, he became more convinced they still hadn't seen the best of her.

Charlie brought his mind back to the present

206

problem. He found the keys to the shop below and let himself in. Apart from a few light fittings and some broken pieces in the basement, the place was empty. The landlord's 'To Let' sign was already up outside the shop.

After two hours, Charlie gave up.

He drove back to Oak Hollow, worried about his mother and wondering whether his father really had been involved in some kind of serious crime when he was murdered.

Kate was horrified at the state of his face. Kenny had told her only that Charlie had been attacked, but not to what extent. He played down his visitors' brutality and insisted that she should tell him how she'd got on at the races before he talked about the day's bizarre events at the yard.

Charlie smiled at her enthusiasm as she described each of the races, stride by stride. Neither horse had been placed, but they had both shown promise and the owners had gone home more than satisfied. Charlie was painfully trying to eat his way through a steak when the telephone rang. He picked up the mobile beside him on the table.

'Hello? Charles?'

He nearly choked on the piece of meat he was swallowing. 'Mum! For God's sake, where are you?'

'I can't tell you. But I must see you.'

Charlie immediately thought that she must have been kidnapped and he imagined someone holding a gun to her head. 'Are you all right?'

'I'm fine, but I need to see you. By the giant rhubarb.'

Charlie knew exactly where she meant. 'What time?'

'Could you manage nine o'clock tomorrow

morning?'

'Okay. I'll see you there. Are you *sure* you are all right?'

'Yes, and Charles, make certain you come alone.'

Next morning he drove into London via the A4 and didn't turn off until he had passed the Natural History Museum. He headed up Exhibition Road into Hyde Park and found a space for his car by the bridge over the Serpentine. He climbed out and looked around. He couldn't help his nervousness after the previous day's attack. He half expected somebody to know that he was arriving here, although anyone overhearing his conversation with his mother would never have guessed where they were to meet. There was a favourite spot in the park where she had often taken him as a small boy, near a clump of monster-leaved water plants which he had referred to then and always since as the 'giant rhubarb'.

She was waiting for him on a bench, neatly wrapped in a Burberry raincoat. She wore dark glasses against a watery sun. A Hermes scarf depicting scenes of implausible rustic tranquillity covered most of her head.

Charlie gave her a quick kiss of greeting and sat down beside her. She saw his battered face and gasped.

'Charlie, I'm so sorry,' she said, guiltily. 'I should have warned you.'

Charlie stared at her. 'You knew they were coming?'

'Not for sure, but I thought it was possible.'

'What's going on, Mum?'

His mother reached out a small, nervous hand and clutched his tightly. 'I'm not entirely sure.'

'But you have an idea? You knew Dad was up to something?'

Pru looked out across the placid ornamental waters. She set her face firmly. 'Yes. He felt he'd been betrayed by a number of people he had trusted. He hated the fact that he had ever relied on them in the first place. Instinctively, as you know, he was a loner.'

Charlie nodded.

His mother guessed what was going through Charlie's mind. She put a hand on his arm. 'Don't think harshly of him. He always tried to think of you as his own son, he genuinely did. He was very fond of you.'

'He had an odd way of showing it.'

'Why do you think he bought that filly?' Pru defended her late husband. 'He certainly couldn't afford it at the time. He just wanted you to know he was interested in your career.'

Charlie didn't answer for a moment. 'What was he up to, before he . . . died?'

'I can't tell you. However hard you try to make me, I shan't tell you anything for the time being.'

'For God's sake, Mum. You must tell me. I had a rough time yesterday.'

Pru dried the corner of her eye with a small handkerchief. 'I can see that, darling, and I'm sorry, but they went, didn't they, because they realised you didn't know anything. It's better that way.'

'But what about you? They've been to the cottage and the flat.'

'So I gather.'

'It's bloody lucky you weren't there. God knows what they might have done to you otherwise. Where were you?'

'At Veronica and Mike's; I told you I was going

209

there.'

'But I phoned and they said they hadn't seen you.'

'I asked them to. Oh my God!' Pru gasped. 'I hope those people don't go there.'

'Would they know that Veronica is Dad's sister?'

'It wouldn't be hard to find out, would it? I'd better warn them.'

'But what about you, Mum? You can't go back to the flat, and certainly not to Birch Lodge. You should go and stay somewhere these people will never find, at least until things have quietened down.'

Pru nodded as if she was grateful for his support for a decision she had already taken. 'Yes. I'd thought of that. I'm going up to Scotland.'

'Thank God,' Charlie said. 'Where?'

'It's probably better that you don't know,' Pru said quickly.

'But what if I want to get in touch with you?'

Pru sighed. 'I'll give you a number where you can leave a message for me but if you do ring don't say it's you, say you're...' She puckered her forehead and looked around for inspiration. 'Peter Pan,' she grinned. She took a biro and a notebook from her bag and scribbled a number.

Charlie knew he'd find out approximately where she was by looking up the code. The thought seemed absurd. 'Mum, it'd be a lot simpler if you just told me what's going on, then I could go to the police.'

'Oh, no!' Pru said anxiously. 'Don't do that. It wouldn't help at all.'

'For God's sake, what is happening?'

'I can't tell you,' Pru pleaded. 'If we just ignore these people or they can't find us or learn anything, in the end they'll go away.'

'They seemed pretty determined to me,' Charlie

said.

'But they won't press you, as long as they're sure you don't know anything.'

'I must know if there's anything that could help Nick.'

Pru looked away and closed her eyes. 'How is he?'

Charlie thought back to his last visit. 'Desperate.'

Pru turned back to face her son. She forced a look of encouragement that she didn't feel.

'Tell him not to worry. I'm sure he'll be released soon.'

Charlie wanted to question her further, but he knew it was pointless.

'I'm going now. Don't try to find me. Just ring if there's a serious emergency.'

'Mum, I hope you're not involved in whatever Dad was doing.'

She smiled with resignation. 'I'd rather not be, too. Now, are you sure no one followed you?'

Charlie got up from the bench, nodding. He had checked half a dozen times on his way from Lambourn.

'Good. I'll be in touch. In the meantime, don't tell anyone you've seen me.' She stood on tiptoe and gave him a kiss on the cheek. 'And don't worry about me. I'll be all right.'

Charlie looked at her. He knew it was probably pointless to ask her again, but he caught her arm and gave it a gentle squeeze. 'Mum, you must tell me. What did Dad do to Sala Mahmoud?'

His mother looked at him with grey eyes that held steady, despite the anxiety in them. 'All I can tell you is that just before all this happened, he was involved in a reckless scheme which he should never have started. Trust me, Charlie, and understand that I

211

must protect myself too.'

Charlie sighed.

His mother touched his cheek with her hand. 'Go now.'

Charlie turned on his heel to walk back to the car park, three hundred yards away beyond a dense shrubbery.

When he reached the far side of the bushes, he ignored the signs requesting the public not to disturb the plants and dived in to push his way back through to see what his mother was doing.

She was still standing where he'd left her. He hoped she wasn't going to wait until she saw his car drive away.

After another half minute, she started to walk briskly across Kensington Gardens towards the gate at Notting Hill. Charlie slipped out from beneath the laurels and followed her.

At first it felt somehow immoral, spying on his own mother, but then he saw himself more as a discreet bodyguard and it became a matter of duty.

Pru reached the Bayswater Road and hurried west to the tube station at Notting Hill Gate. Charlie almost had to run to catch up so that he didn't lose her in the labyrinth of passages. He managed to keep sight of her as she took an eastbound Circle Line train.

At Euston Square she got out, crossed Euston Road and made her way to the mainline station. Charlie tagged along at a distance. She walked on to the main concourse and looked at the departure board before heading for the Edinburgh train.

She didn't buy a ticket. She must either have got one earlier, or she had a return. Charlie bought himself a ticket through to Aberdeen and a *Sporting*

Life. His mother had been born on an estate some twenty miles up the River Dee from Aberdeen and Charlie guessed that she would go to ground somewhere up there.

He found a seat in a carriage halfway down the train where he could keep an eye open in case his mother got off anywhere unexpectedly. For the rest of the journey, he settled back with his newspaper and fended off a couple of approaches from self-avowed racing fans.

At Waverley Station he saw his mother get out and head briskly for the Aberdeen train, as he'd predicted. Keeping his distance, he did the same. He knew that once they reached Aberdeen, his task would be more difficult. It was unlikely that his mother would be staying at her family's house or any of the several cottages that belonged to it.

When they arrived there, he almost lost her. She walked straight from the station building to the car park and Charlie's heart sank as he watched her get into her small Rover saloon. It was like discovering that a girlfriend was cheating on him.

She must have been up here all the time, nowhere near Veronica and Mike. Why had she lied to him? Surely she knew he wouldn't have betrayed her?

He turned and walked back briskly towards the cab rank. His wounded feelings would just have to wait until he'd discovered what was really happening. There were two taxis, and two sets of customers already waiting. When they had gone, Charlie was looking around desperately for an alternative when an old black cab rattled into the station forecourt. Charlie had the back door open before it had stopped and leaped in. His mother's car had disappeared. Charlie took a calculated chance. 'Take the

213

Banchory road,' he said. 'And hurry, please.'

They were leaving the sparser outskirts of the city, driving into the thickening dusk, before Charlie saw his mother's car.

'That's it!' he shouted through the opening in the glass partition. 'Can you follow that grey Rover?'

The driver was an Aberdonian who fancied he knew the ways of the world.

'Aye, no problem. It's not motoring too quick. D'you want them to know we're behind?' He looked at Charlie in his mirror on the windscreen.

'No, not if you can help it.'

The driver grinned. 'They won't.'

At first it was easy to keep several cars between them. But it became more difficult as they headed out into the country. It was after the equinox; the northern days were already longer than in the south but it was nearly dark by the time Pru drove through Banchory and turned off the main road into the heavily wooded hills to the south. After a while, she slowed and turned east on to a narrow stone track which led up a valley through the trees. Charlie paid off his taxi and waited by the road until its lights had disappeared on the way back to Aberdeen.

A damp westerly moaned through the trees, interrupted by occasional long hoots of a tawny owl in the oak woods of the lower slopes. Beside the road, a brook gurgled noisily. There wasn't a sound of his mother's car.

Charlie walked a few yards up the track in the thick, black night, peering through the trees ahead of him. There was no sign of a light. Finding his way was as much a matter of feeling with his feet as seeing with his eyes, though he was beginning to discern the gap in the trees which marked the track.

He stumbled on, his thoughts plagued with guilt that he hadn't rung Kate to tell her what he was doing or to find out how she had got on. He couldn't guess what his mother's plan was. Taking herself out of circulation to avoid any communication with Sala Mahmoud was certainly only part of the story.

The ground was rising now and Charlie was concentrating on the way when he heard a car coming. He looked up. Between the serried trunks of young pines, he saw the flash of headlamps coming towards him down a winding track.

He left the track and pushed his way several yards into the cover of the trees. As the vehicle passed, Charlie made out a short wheel-base Land Rover such as was used on every other farm in the country but he couldn't see who was driving it. He watched it bounce on down to the road then turn north and speed off towards Banchory.

He stepped out and carried on up the track. The low clouds were beginning to release some of their moisture in a thick, steady drizzle and the rutted woodland road was doubling as a stream for the run-off.

Another twenty minutes' trudging brought a reward in the form of a light glimmering a few hundred yards ahead. Quickening his pace, he almost slammed straight into the wooden garage that marked the top of the track. Cautiously, he found the door, opened it and slipped in. He flicked his lighter and by the quivering flame saw his mother's car.

He extinguished the flame and let himself out of the garage. He cast about until he found a footpath which led up to the house.

He approached cautiously, planning to find out who was in the house before making his presence

215

known.

It was a small, stone-built farmhouse. Once, before the heavy reforestation of the last thirty years, it had stood in a dell among an open expanse of rough grazing. Several barns and animal sheds still clustered around the building, neglected and seldom used. Charlie carried on past them to the house where two uncurtained windows glowed. A mile from the road, no one had been concerned to close the shutters.

Confident that the wind and darkness would cover his approach, he walked towards the first window and peered into a sparsely furnished kitchen. As he looked, his mother walked into the room, put the kettle on the stove and started to prepare a meal. She tuned the radio to a classical station and strains of Mendelssohn seeped out through the window into the blustery night.

Charlie crept past the low doorway to the next lighted window. He stopped and peered into a small empty sitting room.

When he had worked his way round the whole house, he returned to the door and knocked on it.

From the other side he heard his mother's voice, calling above the wind. 'Who is it?' Even in the noise of the night, Charlie detected her panic.

'It's Charlie,' he shouted back.

The door was opened and his mother's face appeared. She looked at him and peered into the darkness beyond him. 'Charles! What on earth are you doing here?' For an instant, she seemed reluctant to let him in. Then, as though thinking better of it, she pulled the door wide open with a flourish.

Charles stepped over the threshold into the comparative calm of the small house. Without

216

waiting for an answer, his mother led him through to the kitchen where the gas stove had already warmed the room.

'You look frozen,' she said. 'Let me give you some soup.'

At her suggestion, he peeled off most of his damp clothes which she hung off the backs of chairs around the room. 'They'll soon dry in front of this stove,' she said. She took a jug of broth from a larder cupboard and poured the contents into a pan on the stove. Before it started to bubble, she filled a big white bowl and put it on the table with a hunk of fresh bread. 'There you are.'

Charlie took a spoonful and relaxed in the comforting warmth of the place. The house was in good order, considering its remoteness. There was no electricity and he guessed that all the lamps and the cooker were fuelled by gas bottles.

'What is this place, Mum? Is it your father's?'

'No. It belongs to a neighbour, Archie Bell. We used to come up here often when we were children. It was more or less derelict then. Archie had it done up when the first rush of oilmen arrived up here, looking for places to rent not too far from Aberdeen.'

'Why have you come here?'

'Archie's an old friend. I haven't been in touch with your grandparents, and Archie will be discreet. I told you, I have to protect myself. I don't think anyone will come looking for me here.'

'I found you easily enough,' Charlie pointed out.

'How did you get here? I mean, actually up to the house. I didn't hear a car.'

'I followed you in a taxi from Aberdeen and got it to drop me at the bottom of the track. If I'd known it was so far, I'd have got him to drive me halfway up.'

217

Charlie looked around, crossed to the window and closed the shutters. 'Okay. I suppose you'll be safe enough, but for how long? Whatever this deal was that Dad did, the guys who saw me were very serious about Sala Mahmoud wanting his money back.'

'Yes, I know, and if I knew where it was, I'd give it back.'

'Don't you have any idea?'

'No. None at all. Your father did make a transfer to my account the day before he died. But I'll have to use that to live on for the time being. What he did with the rest, I just don't know.'

The fact that his mother had lied to him already was still agonizingly fresh on his mind. 'Mum, for God's sake, come clean. I'm caught in the middle here. You *must* tell me.'

'I would, Charles, if I could, believe me.' She met his gaze steadily, defying him to disbelieve her.

Charlie took her wrists and clutched them tight for emphasis. 'You're going to have to find that money,' he said. 'Or you'll never live your life in peace.'

'That depends on where I am.'

'But, Mum, you won't be safe anywhere. And they'd still be watching me, waiting for me to come and see you.'

Pru's eyes clouded over and for a moment Charlie had a glimpse of the bleakness she was trying to hide. She had trained herself and developed the strength to subjugate her own vulnerability and sensitivity to the emotional needs of the moment. Charlie yearned for her to release herself and let it all out, but he knew how stubborn she could be.

'Charles, please don't press me,' she said firmly. 'Do you think I like being in the position your father's left me? Do you think I approve of what he

218

did?' A hint of anger crept into her voice, which she hadn't intended. 'I understand, of course, because he'd become utterly desperate. He was completely broke, and no one would advance him a penny—not that he asked many, but the banks were totally unreasonable and I hated to see him so humiliated.' She shook her head. 'He felt that everyone had betrayed him, friends, Lloyd's, the bank, the whole establishment, everyone pressing him for money he simply had no hope of getting. He felt very strongly that he'd let me down; you too, when he had to sell Willow Star. All he did was pre-empt the bank, who had already written to him asking about her,' she said resignedly.

'If I'd known, we could have registered her in your name.'

'Charlie, my name is on all of the guarantees as well.'

Charlie was momentarily stunned. Her side of the family weren't enormously wealthy, but she was due to inherit part of a large estate in Scotland. He couldn't believe she had been so naive as to risk all of it for her husband.

'It's probably hard for you to understand but privately David was surprisingly insecure. It was this insecurity and his tremendous strength of personality that made him so secretive and self-reliant. He was brave, but he was careful—careful not to expose himself to ridicule or even criticism. Anyway, I loved him and loved him more when I realised he was ready to admit he needed me. I'd have stood by him no matter what he did.'

She cleared away Charlie's plate and bowl sensing some kind of admonishment from her son. 'Now, I think it would be a mistake for you to stay here,' she

219

said. 'As soon as your clothes are dry, I'll drop you back to Aberdeen. Then you must promise me you won't come here or try to contact me again, under any circumstances. I beg of you,' she pleaded. 'Or sooner or later those people will follow you here.'

CHAPTER ELEVEN

Reggie Pymer shook his head in frustration and stood back to look at the ceiling he was working on. He didn't need his tape measure to know that the last piece of cornice lying at his feet was a couple of inches too short to finish the job.

Reggie had been in the business of repairing and fitting new plaster mouldings for most of his working life. He specialised in deep Victorian mouldings. Most of them, like the one he was replacing in this mid-nineteenth-century house in Kilburn, were handmade, using the original patterns. It would be at least two weeks before he could get hold of another length.

'Bollocks!' He blamed himself. He had left Matthew, his apprentice, to carry on without him while he'd gone to the dentist. The youngster had wasted as much cornice as he'd fitted.

He turned and looked at Matthew. 'You're a useless twat, aren't you?' he said mildly, as he pushed his worn cloth cap to the back of his bald head. 'The painters are due in 'ere tomorrer.'

Matthew shuffled his feet and his spotty cheeks twitched remorsefully. Reggie gazed from the floor to the ceiling and back, looking for a solution. For Matthew's benefit, he gave a long, groaning sigh. 'I tell you what we'll do,' he said. 'You go out to the skip. Find the best piece of cornice we chucked away and I'll see if we can mitre it in to make the job look half decent. If you can't find a piece, don't come back.'

The boy nodded, eager to make up for his mistake. He clattered out of the building. Reggie sat on his toolbox and waited. He'd run short of material hundreds of times and had always been able to make good with something. It wouldn't do Matt any harm, though, to sweat for a while.

He pulled a pack of cigarettes from his pocket and poked one between his lips. He was just about to strike a match when he heard the front door slam back against the inside wall and the thud of panicked feet racing down the hallway. Matt came rushing in. His normally bovine eyes stared wildly and his face was as white as a hospital sheet.

'Quick! Come quick!' he yelled, dragging Reggie to his feet. 'There's a body in the skip.' They both ran outside to the large iron container filled to the brim with discarded materials.

Matt leaned over it and lifted a piece of broken plasterboard. Reggie peered over his shoulder.

A man's head, grey-white, with glazed and staring eyes, nestled on the rubble in which the rest of his body was buried.

*   *   *

'Probably just a tramp,' suggested Reggie to the first police patrolman to arrive in answer to his 999 call. 'I should think he just curled up for the night and never woke up.'

The policeman shook his head. 'No. He's too tidy

221

for a tramp. Look at his hair,' he said. He fingered the man's soft melton jacket. 'I'm not saying he's dressed for the City, but his clothes are clean, and he doesn't smell like a tramp.'

A second police car drew up with squealing tyres, followed almost immediately by an ambulance.

Reggie, his problem cornice forgotten for the moment, stood back and watched while photographs were taken and he and Matt answered questions. It wasn't until the body had been slid into the ambulance to be ferried across to the mortuary that they started to rummage around in the skip for lengths of cornice. They soon found some and went back inside to finish their job.

Later, as they were packing up for the day, one of the policemen came back.

'We need to check a couple of things.'

'What for?' Reggie asked, delighted that he was still involved in the drama.

'The geezer you found was murdered.'

*   *   *

Charlie never enjoyed the constrictions of flying tourist class. He stepped from the Aberdeen-Heathrow shuttle with relief. It was half past twelve the day after he had followed his mother to the cottage in the hills outside Banchory.

Self-conscious and feeling slightly paranoid, he made two circuits of the airport terminal before he was satisfied there was no one following him. He took the tube to Hyde Park Corner and walked across to the Serpentine car park to find that his Range Rover had collected two parking tickets but not the clamp he'd been expecting.

He drove impatiently out of London, catching up on his business over the phone as he squeezed his way through the crawling traffic. To his relief there had been no dramas at the yard.

'You should disappear more often,' Kate said. 'Everything runs a lot smoother without you sticking your oar in and telling everybody what to do.'

Charlie took the banter well. Just then it was what he needed to take his mind off his worries about his mother's safety and Nick's freedom, as well as his father's activities. He was almost glad to see Detective Inspector Ferrier climb out of his car just before evening stables. At least the detective was someone to talk to about his current crisis, and he wanted to present him with the rubber sole he'd brought back from the shoe repairers.

As Ferrier strolled across the yard towards him, Charlie had the impression he was making an effort not to appear too aggressive.

'Evening, Mr Patterson. I need another chat with you. Is it convenient now?'

'Yes, sure. I've got a few questions for you, too. Come into the house and I'll get you a drink.'

The DI accepted a generous measure from a bottle of twelve-year-old malt Charlie had bought at Aberdeen airport that morning.

'So,' the detective started. 'What did you want to ask me?'

Charlie leaned back in his chair and took a brown paper parcel from the dresser top. He tipped the deeply moulded shoe sole on to the table in front of him.

The policeman looked at it, unimpressed. 'Well? How's this supposed to help us?'

'I think there's a good chance it will fit the
223

footprints you found outside Birch Lodge.'

'Been visiting your friend's cobbler then, have you?' the policeman said with a faint grin.

'No. It came from a heel bar in Kilburn—that's North London.'

Ferrier's eyes narrowed abruptly and the grin faded from his lips. 'I know where Kilburn is.'

'My father was seen driving someone else to the cottage on the Saturday morning—one of his ex-squaddies.'

'How do you know?'

'Unlike you, I spoke to General Sheridan's gardener. He told me he'd seen someone with him in the car. You found a pack of Rizla papers on the ground outside. I found a couple of fag ends in the ashtray of the car, and my father never smoked roll-ups. I also found a shoe repair ticket.'

The detective's curiosity overcame his annoyance at Charlie's tone of voice. 'Why didn't you tell us this before?'

'When I told you I was sure Nick Ryder hadn't killed my stepfather, you almost laughed, remember? I also told you I was going to make my own inquiries and you said I'd be wasting my time. I wanted to be pretty sure before I came back to you with anything.'

'How did the gardener know it was an ex-squaddie who'd come to see the major?'

Charlie suddenly didn't want to answer this. 'Well, it must have been.'

'Why?' the detective asked impatiently. 'Someone must have put it to you. Was it your partner? He never told us he saw anyone else.'

'No.' Charlie knew he was backed into a corner. 'It was my mother. She said they often came to see him.'

'Why do you suppose she didn't tell us about him

then?'

'Because he'd gone away before she'd left to go to the shops that morning.'

'I see. She didn't think it was worth mentioning to us.'

'I suppose she just thought it wasn't relevant.'

'I'd like to talk to her about it myself. Trouble is, I don't seem to be able to find her.' Charlie didn't miss the edge to the detective's voice. 'Do you know where she's gone?'

'She said she was going to stay with my stepfather's sister and her husband.'

'Mrs Veronica Russell?'

'That's right.'

'No. She hasn't been there. I sent someone from the local force.'

'I'm not sure where she is then. I had a meeting with her at the lawyers the day after the funeral but I haven't seen her since. She's rung me a couple of times, I assumed from the Russells.'

'Did you?'

Charlie knew that Ferrier didn't believe him.

'I'll tell you something else about Kilburn, shall I?' the detective went on.

'What's that?'

'Someone from Kilburn rang your mother a few times.'

'My mother?'

'Yes. After the major was killed. Do you think that's the same person whose footprint you say you can match?'

'How the hell should I know? But he obviously came from Kilburn or somewhere nearby, or why would he have his shoes repaired there?'

'Indeed. As a matter of fact, though, it wasn't the

225

same man. The chap who phoned was called Miles Latimer. He was found dead as a kipper in Kilburn, yesterday morning. Someone had chucked him in a builder's skip; half buried him in rubble.'

'How do you know it wasn't the man I was told about?'

'I'm afraid I'm not sure I believe in your man. But Latimer was real enough, and he certainly didn't wear a size ten shoe.' Ferrier nodded at the rubber sole on the table. 'He'd been lodging at his sister's. She was pretty longsuffering. He'd not been out of jail long and she'd lent him a lot of money. But he kept telling her not to worry, he'd soon be able to pay her back. He'd found a goose that laid golden eggs.'

'He was going to rob someone?'

'No. Geese lay eggs regular, not one offs.'

'What are you saying?'

'Blackmail.'

Charles could feel his mouth drying up as the pieces of the jigsaw slotted into a different pattern. Did this man Latimer know that his stepfather had been involved in some illicit deal before he died? Was he trying to extort money from his mother?

'How do you know he rang my mother?'

'The number shows up on his sister's phone bill— three times—a few days after your stepfather was killed.'

'But why should that mean he's blackmailing her? And for what, for Christ's sake?'

'If we could talk to her ourselves,' Ferrier said pointedly, 'I'm sure we could sort it all out.'

Charlie stared back at him. He couldn't see which way to go next. He took a step back. 'About this shoe. Will you check it against the print you took? If it fits, I've got matching descriptions of the man who went

226

to Birch Lodge that day, from the gardener and from the cobbler.'

'All right, Mr Patterson. We'll do that. But first you've got to tell me where your mother is.'

Charlie shrugged his shoulders and did his best to appear totally mystified. 'I wish to God I knew.'

The policeman gave Charlie another long, hard stare. 'If this other person did come to the house, only she can testify to it.'

'If I hear from her, I'll let her know.'

'If you hear from her, you let *me* know, p.d.q.' Ferrier gazed steadily at him, making it clear this wasn't a polite request. 'And are you going to tell me who came looking for you?'

'What do you mean?'

The detective tapped his mouth, nodding at the bruises on Charlie's face.

'Oh, that,' Charlie gave a light laugh. 'I just tripped on the ramp of the lorry leading a horse out and fell flat on my face.'

Ferrier raised an eyebrow but didn't comment.

Charlie looked back innocently.

Ferrier drained the last drop of whisky from his glass and stood up. 'All right,' he said. 'You can stop the amateur detective stuff now. We'll follow up your heel bar and the gardener.' He nodded and walked out of the front door. Charlie followed and watched him get back into his car.

'Don't forget,' Ferrier said before he closed his door. 'If you hear from your mother, let me know, for her own good. Thanks for the Scotch.'

Charlie watched the Vauxhall drive up the track to the gate. He guessed he wouldn't be able to make a move now without someone reporting back to the detective—or to the Arabs. But he would have to see

227

his mother and warn her that the police were as keen to find her as Sala Mahmoud was.

*   *   *

The next day dawned bright and blue-skied for the first time in a fortnight. Charlie woke alert and positive about what he was going to do.

There was no sign that he was being watched but he didn't take any chances. He rode out of the yard with the first lot, reaching the bottom of the gallops shortly before seven. He watched Willow Star cantering and then set off towards a clump of beech trees a few hundred yards away where Kenny was waiting to take over. While the head lad rejoined the rest of the string Charlie slipped through the trees to the far side of the copse where a hedge straggled along the brow of the hill. He walked quickly in the shadow of the hedge for a quarter of a mile until he found Kate's new Golf which she'd left for him the night before. She had agreed to his using it, but he hadn't told her he was planning to drive to Scotland in it.

He had the key to the car in his pocket. He let himself in and drove quietly down the track towards the Wantage road. Within half an hour he was on the far side of Oxford, heading across country for the M1, and by three o'clock that afternoon he left the A90 at Laurencekirk and headed up the road for Banchory.

He reached the gap in the woods where the track led up to the house. He didn't turn into it. He drove straight past and on to the next village where he pulled up outside a small dusty general store. Looking in the driving mirror of his car, he could see

228

no other vehicle coming up behind him, but he waited five minutes and watched two local cars drive past before he was satisfied there was still no one on his tail. He certainly didn't want to be caught now, when he was so near his destination. He got out and walked into the shop to buy a paper before getting back in and turning south.

When he reached the spot where the taxi had dropped him two days before, he drove off the road and up the stony, gullied track. He was impressed again by the remoteness of the place. He guessed that as long as his mother's own family, who anyway lived ten miles away over the hills, didn't know she was here, she would be quite safe for the time being. But sooner or later someone would recognise her and tell her family. And it would probably be only a matter of time before her whereabouts was known to everyone.

He stopped his car halfway up the track at a muddy passing place. He got out to listen. A chain saw whined faintly and intermittently somewhere across the valley. Otherwise he could hear only the emptiness of the conifer woods. Ignoring the track, he walked on up the hill through the trees. From now on caution was paramount.

He reached the barn which served as a garage without seeing or hearing anything to alert him. His mother's car was still there.

For a few minutes he remained concealed, his eyes fixed on the house beyond. There was nothing about the place to alarm him. A wisp of smoke curled reassuringly from the chimney. He took a deep breath and walked across the grassy clearing.

The front door was ajar. He was about to call out when he heard a voice from inside the house. It was his mother's, on the phone, Charlie guessed.

Something about her tone that sounded not quite right, out of place, made Charlie hold back a moment. Then it struck him—it was too light-hearted, too cheerful. He paused in the hall to listen a little longer before he let her know he was there.

From the small sitting room on his left he heard her give a quick, warm laugh. 'I'm looking forward to seeing you too,' she said with unmistakable tenderness. There was a pause while the other party spoke, then Pru's voice became more serious. 'Yes, I will take care. Apart from Charlie—and Archie, of course—no one knows I'm here and Charlie's not going to tell anyone.'

Charlie racked his brain trying to think who might be on the other end of the line.

'I'm sure he has no idea,' Pru was saying now. 'Anyway, I'll see you tomorrow morning ... No, I won't be late, midday, but I wish I could stay with you ... All right. I understand. Goodbye, my darling, and look after yourself, too.'

Charlie had to decide then and there what he should do. An appalling thought had entered his head—appalling, but a rational explanation of a lot of contradictions since his step-father had died.

Before his mother had replaced the phone, Charlie had slipped back out of the house. By the time she reached the hall on her way to the kitchen, he had run across the clearing and was already hidden among the pine trees.

That his mother should have a lover wasn't, on the face of it, so strange; David Patterson had always been a difficult man. But Charlie had never doubted that his mother had stayed loyal to him despite that and it was beyond his comprehension of her that she could have concurred in the murder of her husband.

230

Yet it explained her strange calmness and lack of emotion at the time of his death. It explained her reluctance to talk to the police or to see that Sala Mahmoud got his money back.

His mind shied away from his thoughts. The implications were too awful to contemplate. He was jumping to conclusions. First he had to find out who she had been talking to. She was due to meet him next day; he would simply wait here until then, and follow her in the morning.

Charlie managed a few hours' uneasy sleep in the reclining seats of the Golf with a horse rug wrapped round him. But he'd been awake for two hours, longing for a coffee, when finally he saw his mother's Rover emerge from between the trees at the bottom of the track.

He was parked three hundred yards away at the side of the road, confident that his mother wouldn't recognise the Golf. He took care not to get too close to her. If he lost her, he lost her; she would always come back to the cottage. But if she discovered he was following her, he might never get to the bottom of this mess.

He still found it impossible to reconcile his knowledge of his mother with the actions of a woman who could connive with her lover to murder her husband just when he had made an apparently huge illicit profit through a deal with an Arab who was prepared to torture her son to regain his money. And what about Nick? Charlie's hands tightened on the steering wheel. No wonder his mother had been so sure Nick was innocent.

Charlie had no idea how he was going to deal with her and the man she was meeting, but he had to do this himself. He couldn't simply hand his own mother over to the police.

As he drove, now seeing her, now letting her get ahead, Charlie tried to convince himself that there might yet be an innocent explanation for the phone call he had overheard, but as they crossed the snow-draped Grampians and the Spey at Grantown he still hadn't managed to come up with one.

At Inverness, Pru headed south-west along the bank of Loch Ness. The bright spring sun glittered on the narrow length of the loch as they followed the northern shore to Fort Augustus. It was half past twelve when they reached the small town. Charlie hung back, as he had in Inverness. He let a couple of cars in between him and his mother although he was confident that she had no idea he was behind her.

When she parked in the main street, Charlie drove on by and found a space further up. He stayed in his car and surveyed the sleepy high street through his rearview mirror. Pru got out of her car and crossed the road with her short, busy stride. She walked into a pub and disappeared from sight.

His heart thumping, Charlie climbed out of the Golf and crossed the road a hundred yards from the large inn. Taking care not to be seen from inside it, he sidled along until he could steal a glance into the bar.

Pru was sitting, facing the door. The man she was talking to had his back to Charlie. He was wearing a scruffy donkey jacket. His dark hair was long and untidy.

Charlie ducked back before his mother looked up. He couldn't go in and confront them there. He would have to wait until they came out. If they split up, he would follow the man.

He bought a paper and walked back to his car. He angled the driving mirror so that he could watch the

232

door of the pub; he could see his mother's car in his wing mirror. He opened the paper and pretended to read, glancing up every minute or so.

He didn't know how much later it was that he jerked awake to see his mother's car pulling out.

He was in time to see her drive past him and he frantically searched up and down the street, hoping to catch a glimpse of the man she'd been with. Angry with himself for having missed his chance, Charlie started the engine and was about to move off when the man who had been drinking with his mother appeared from the bar. At a distance of fifty yards, the man seemed vaguely familiar. Charlie was beginning to think that he was looking at the person who had been described to him by Tom Skyrme and Mr O'Grady in the heel bar. And he realised with a physical jolt that this would explain something which had been worrying him for weeks: why his mother hadn't told the police—hadn't even told him, for God's sake!—about the earlier visitor that Saturday morning. Nick turning up when he had must have been an unexpected piece of luck for them, a ready-made red herring.

The man hauled himself into an old Land Rover and set off towards the village of Invermoriston with Charlie following him. Here the Land Rover branched off to the left along a road which swooped and curved through a shallow river valley. On either side, the craggy mountain peaks stood out crisp and white against a clear blue sky and no wind disturbed the thick forests of the silent valley.

The road was empty and Charlie had to hang well back from the slowly moving vehicle. After twenty minutes, another small loch came into view. The Land Rover carried on along the northern bank on a straight, flat road. It was travelling even more slowly now. Charlie almost came to a standstill until he was about half a mile behind his quarry. The road took a dog-leg turn past a stand of Scots pines and Charlie lost sight of the Land Rover. He quickened. When he reached the trees, he was confronted by the sight of half a mile of lonely road.

He stopped and gazed at the grey strip. His lips tightened in frustration, and he swore. He set off slowly, glancing from left to right, praying for a glimpse of the vehicle. On his left there was only a thin swathe of land between the road and the loch. On his right, the ground was well covered in heather, bracken, and stunted, scrubby trees, sweeping up to a stark rocky edge. There was no sign of the Land Rover or any other human intrusion. And yet there hadn't been time for the vehicle to reach the far end of the road. Charlie drove on to a point where the road curved left again to present another empty landscape.

Angry with himself, he turned and drove back. He stopped halfway along the straight and climbed out. Nothing broke the sea of purple, green and dun that swept up the mountainside. The wind moaned gently, carrying a few bird calls which emphasised the absence of man.

Cursing his incompetence, Charlie got back into the Golf and headed back down the loch. He thought about his mother and how he should confront her. When he reached Invermoriston on the shores of Loch Ness, he still hadn't decided what to do. He didn't even know what he would have done if he had found her lover. She was obviously implicated in the death of his step-father, but whatever she had done, all his instincts recoiled from handing her over to the

234

police.

He stared at the narrow lake for a few minutes, took a deep breath and turned his car south.

* * *

It was midnight when he drove in through the gates at Oak Hollow. A few minutes later he slipped into bed beside a soft, sleepy body which welcomed him with arms that wrapped round him. Kate's body arched in answer to gentle fingers feeling the warm, damp recesses of her bushy mound. Soon, Charlie's problems and tensions had melted away, not to disturb him again until morning.

CHAPTER TWELVE

The prison visiting room smelled faintly of disinfectant and depression. Despite the authorities' efforts to soften the experience for visitors—brightly painted murals, and smiling women from the WRVS serving tea—the walls seemed to ooze anguish and the tears that had been shed here. Charlie could see that his attempts to cheer Nick weren't working. His partner's jaw was set, not with determination but with hopeless resignation to the inevitable. His depression was tangible. He'd resigned himself to his fate. Not even the news about the body in Kilburn or the man spotted in his father's car had stirred him. There was an awkwardness between them, brought on largely by Charlie's failure to mention his mother's involvement, and after a short while Charlie muttered an embarrassed farewell, leaving his friend

235

more miserable than ever. But he knew now that he had no option but to get straight back to Scotland and find the man responsible for Nick's incarceration.

*   *   *

Charlie pulled up beside the loch, turned off the Golf's engine and got out. The water shimmered in the light of a young moon. Only the distant gurgling of a capercaillie broke the deep mountain silence and there was not a glimmer of light or sign of human habitation to be seen.

Neil MacPhee, the landlord of the pub in Fort Augustus, had told Charlie that the man he was asking about was David Urquhart—a writer, he thought. He didn't know him, but he'd heard that sometimes he stayed in the croft by Loch Cluanie. The directions he gave were vague, but Charlie couldn't find anyone who could pinpoint the place more precisely.

Standing looking up at the empty, silent slopes, Charlie knew that the house, croft, cottage, whatever it was, was no more than half a mile from where he stood. The small cairn of stones by the roadside was the landmark he'd been told to look for. There was no road, just a track which might be viable with four-wheel drive. He had to find somewhere suitable to leave Kate's car. The edge of the forest was a few hundred yards along the bank of the loch. Charlie got back into the car and drove until he reached a piece of sheltered verge. He parked the car there and left it, confident that there was a negligible risk of its being stolen in such a deserted spot. Carrying a small rucksack he had packed in Lambourn early that

236

morning, he walked back to the cairn which marked the point where he had to leave the road.

In the scanty, silver light, Charlie could make out the faint track which led due north towards the Pole Star. He set off cautiously, stopping to listen every few yards. Once he heard the sharp scream of a barking fox. From several miles away to the east, the breeze wafted the sound of a car coming up the side of the loch.

After three hundred yards, when he met the rising ground, the path turned forty-five degrees and dropped down into a dell with a small copse of Scots pine and oak. The place he was looking for should be just north of the copse, sheltering in a small gully in the hillside.

Charlie reached the copse. Just behind it, in the growing moonlight, he caught sight of a building of lime-washed stone. Relieved that he had arrived, he stopped and listened again. There was no sound of the car. Reassured, he set off cautiously over the last fifty yards. He could see now that the building was definitely a dwelling—one-storey, with a fat chimney in the middle of a broad-slated roof and two small windows on either side of a simple front door.

There wasn't a hint of light from inside. Charlie approached one pace at a time, his heart thumping. Was the man away? Asleep? Alert and already waiting for him?

He stopped to listen again. He had seldom heard such silence; his own heartbeat was the loudest sound.

He took the last few paces to the front door. It had a simple wooden latch and a bolt which could be secured with a padlock.

Charlie pushed down the latch with his thumb. The

door swung open and he stepped inside, dark as pitch, but for a glimmer of orange light glowing through the blackened glass doors of a large stove. The low-ceilinged room harboured a strong smell of peat smoke. He groped by the door for a light switch until, feeling foolish, he realised there wouldn't be any electricity in a place like this. He struck a match. There was an oil lamp standing on a table in the middle of what was a small living room and kitchen combined. He lit the lamp, keeping the wick as low as he could, and pulled a pair of shutters across the window. He turned up the flame a little. The walls were white-washed stone and the floor was flagged. There were two side chairs at an old pine table and a large old oak carver opposite the peat-burning range.

He was about to start looking around, to get some idea of who he was dealing with, when a sound from outside froze his blood.

He had heard a distinct rustle, the sound of the scrubby bracken and heather being disturbed. It could have been a fox, maybe, or a deer, but all his instincts told him it was a human. He stepped across the room so that he'd be behind the door when it opened.

A second later, it flew back, letting in a gust of heather-scented evening air and two powerful torch beams. The door was pushed shut and one beam swung round and found Charlie pressed against the wall like a rabbit in a trap. He hadn't even started to make a plan.

He held his breath and in the few seconds that followed a torrent of thoughts rushed through his mind. He could see no one behind the lights but he knew there were at least two of them. The man he had seen in Fort Augustus, David Urquhart, his mother's

238

friend? And who? His mother?

It seemed unlikely that his mother would be running around the glens in darkness. He wished someone would speak.

'So.'

Charlie quaked. He recognised the voice at once. 'Why have you come here?'

The wick of the oil lamp was turned up. The torches were clicked off and the smoky room was filled with the warm yellow glow of the lamp. Charlie found himself looking at the distinctive features and glistening black beard of the man who had done all the talking when he'd been tied to a chair and tortured at Oak Hollow. Behind him was the even less forgettable face of the man who had tortured him. Both men were holding pistols, aimed directly at him.

Charlie's guts heaved and sweat prickled the palms of his hands. 'What do you want?' he croaked.

'Sheikh Sala Mahmoud would still like his money, and he is getting impatient.'

'I don't know where it is. I told you before. I know nothing about it.'

'Then why have you come here?'

Charlie didn't answer. He couldn't think of a plausible lie. The second Arab, silent up till now, grunted and stepped forward. He lifted his gun, turned it round and smashed the metal butt on to Charlie's jaw.

Charlie's head jerked back, lolled forward and came to rest on his chest, feeling as if it was filled with cement. He couldn't even contemplate what was going to happen to him. He had no experience of this kind of violence and had no idea how to cope with it. He wanted to fight back but he was a complete

239

amateur, and he knew it.

He felt himself grabbed and a hard, sinewy forearm was jammed across his windpipe as he was manhandled towards the centre of the room. For the second time he was shoved brutally on to a chair and his wrists bound with cord.

The memory of the pain he'd suffered last time surged through him. He closed his eyes and prayed that he would faint before it started again.

The bang of the door crashing back against the wall reached him with a gush of fresh air. He jerked his eyes open. He was facing the door. Standing in the frame, with a gun in his hand, was the man he'd come to find. In the time it took Charlie to form the thought, orange flame spurted twice from the short barrel of the weapon. The shots followed so close on each other they mingled into an extended single report. Without seeing them, Charlie was aware that the men either side of him had slithered to the ground. Involuntarily he closed his eyes and waited for the next shot.

Nothing came.

He was dimly aware of activity behind him and felt the cord round his wrists loosen. He flicked his eyes open and turned round to find himself staring into the eyes of his stepfather.

'Are you all right?'

Charlie blinked hard, feeling a mixture of relief and bewilderment. 'Dad? Dad! What the hell...'

David Patterson cleared his throat. 'I've never known you to be stuck for words.'

Charlie was still staring. 'But ... For God's sake! We buried you!'

There was a hint of shame in the major's voice. 'I know.' Then, unaccustomed to such guilt, he

240

reverted to his military tone. 'But what the hell are *you* doing here?'

There was a short silence as he helped his son from the chair. Charlie felt his blood begin to flow again as he walked around the small room, avoiding the still, silent figures splayed grotesquely across the floor, but unable to take his eyes from them.

It was like a scene from a film. He looked around in bewilderment at the simple room. The peat smoke was hanging like a cloud below the low roof. He coughed to clear his bruised windpipe. His father stepped over one of his victims and opened a cupboard. He reached in and took out a bottle of whisky and glasses.

Charlie gratefully took a large gulp. Patterson sat down opposite him and drank more slowly.

'What are you going to do about these two?' Charlie asked.

For an answer, Patterson stood, leaned down, grasped the first of them by the collar of his expensive leather jacket and heaved it up until he could sling the limp body over his shoulders. 'I'll get rid of them now.' Charlie was astonished by the ease with which his father hefted the first corpse outside and kicked the door shut behind him.

Charlie took another slug of whisky. He looked with horrified fascination at the remaining Arab. There was a small, neat hole, scarcely any blood, in the centre of his forehead. Charlie had never seen his father fire so much as a twelve bore in all the time he'd known him. He supposed he'd always known he was a first-class marksman—it was part of the job in the regiment—and he'd always assumed that he had killed people. But to see it happen so coolly and so efficiently had somehow made the actual event less horrific than he would have expected. Even the entry wounds were tidy. And now his stepfather was calmly disposing of the bodies.

The front door opened and Patterson came in. Without a word, he heaved the second body over his shoulder and went outside again.

Charlie felt the tension in his muscles ease now that the dead men were gone. The whole thing—his stepfather coming back from the dead, the abrupt denial of his belief that his mother and a lover had been responsible for killing him—seemed like the jumbled recollection of a crazy nightmare, until Patterson came back in as if he'd just been for a quiet walk. He gave Charlie a quick, remorseful glance. 'I'm sorry you had to see that. I really didn't have any choice. Anyway, no one will ever see them again.' He picked up his whisky and sat in the chair by the range. 'Now, I must know how you got here. I suppose you persuaded your mother to tell you.'

Charlie shook his head. 'No. She didn't even tell me you were alive.'

For the first time since he had walked in, Patterson looked worried. 'Oh my God. They must have found her,' he said.

He hastily took a mobile phone from the pocket of a jacket hanging up behind the door and keyed a number. After a few seconds, a look of relief spread over his face. 'Are you all right? ... That's great. Something happened ... It doesn't matter. We've dealt with it ... Yes, Charles is here. It's a long story. I thought you'd given directions, but he must have been followed. Everything's under control now. Stay there. I'll be in touch.'

Patterson turned to Charlie. 'She's seen no one. I'll have to get back and check out the house, though.

And this place will already be insecure if our visitors passed on their position before they came in.'

'But I don't see how they can have followed me. I checked dozens of times.'

'They could have put a bug in your car.'

'I came in Kate's car. She's using mine.'

'Okay. We'll check it out. But how did you find me?'

'I met up with Mum and followed her back to Scotland.'

'Yes. I saw you arrive. I was driving out.'

'That was you in the Land Rover?'

Patterson nodded. 'But if your mother didn't tell you, who did?'

'I came back up to Banchory again, twenty-four hours later. She didn't know I'd come. When I reached the house, the door was open and I overheard her talking to you on the phone, arranging to meet you.' Charlie laughed and shook his head at the absurdity of what he'd deduced. 'I thought she was talking to a lover—a lover she'd persuaded to kill you. I waited outside until she left and followed her over to Fort Augustus in the morning. I saw her meet up with you and when she left I followed you back as far as the loch. Then I lost you. Of course, I didn't know it was you, with the beard and the dark hair and glasses.'

'So, how did you find me? That was two days ago.'

'I went back to Lambourn and went to see Nick in prison. He was in a terrible state. He looked as if he was about to top himself. I promised myself I'd come straight back up here and try and track down the man I'd seen with Mum. I asked in the pub where you met her. They told me you were a chap called David Urquhart who rented this place, and they told me

243

roughly how to get here. I wish to God Mum had let me know what was going on; it would have saved a lot of hassle.'

'We wanted to keep you at arm's length from the whole business, but I hear Sala Mahmoud's men had already visited you.'

'Yes,' Charlie said ruefully.

'Those two?' Patterson nodded at the door through which he'd carried the dead men.

'Yes.'

Patterson looked more closely at the injuries still visible on his stepson's face. 'What did they say?'

'They were looking for money.'

'Did they sound as though they thought I was still alive?'

'I couldn't say for sure.'

'And you had no idea?'

'No, of course not.'

'Do you think the police have?'

Charlie tried to think of DI Ferrier's attitude two evenings before. 'I don't think so. The DI who's been handling your . . . case turned up at my place a couple of days ago, just when I'd got back from here, and told me they'd found some guy called Latimer dead in a skip. He'd been murdered, and they knew from some phone bills that he'd spoken to Mum a few times just after you were supposed to have been killed.'

'They did, did they? And who do they think put him there?' Patterson's eyes rested coolly and steadily on Charlie's.

'They didn't say. But presumably it wasn't the man who came to see you that morning.'

Patterson didn't answer; his expression gave nothing away.

244

'Come on,' Charlie said. 'For God's sake. That had to be the man who was dead in your drawing room. I understand, if he was threatening you or something.'

'What he was,' Patterson said quietly, 'was a man who was quite prepared to kill young children who got in his way, and never showed a sign of remorse in the fifteen years since.'

Charlie thought of a dozen retorts but it wasn't the moment for a debate on moral justice. He took a gulp of whisky. 'Dad, you've got to tell me.'

Patterson shook his head. 'No, I haven't. The less you know, the safer you'll be.'

'That's not going to stop the police looking, and they are. I think you underestimate them.'

'Do I?' his father said sourly. 'And what are you going to do about it?'

'Me? Nothing as far as the police are concerned. But somebody's going to come looking for those guys, aren't they?' Charlie waved a hand towards the door. 'Sala Mahmoud's not going to give up until he's had some kind of satisfaction from you. They said he's very upset; he's been taken for a ride, and now you've killed two of his men. He isn't going to like it. He'll want revenge.'

'He wants revenge and I wanted repayment, Charlie, I'd been swindled by people I'd known and trusted for years.' Patterson's voice cracked. He grunted to cover it up. 'I'd been brought to my knees. It wasn't going to make any difference to Mahmoud, and he got what he wanted. God knows how he ever found out the stuff wasn't right. They were the best fakes I've ever seen.' For a brief second, his despair showed. 'God, I'm sorry to have dragged you into it. I suppose it was a damn stupid thing to do, but I can't

245

go back on it; not now.'

Charlie had never seen his stepfather ready to admit a fault or so prepared to let his true emotions show. He wanted to let him know that he understood, whatever he'd done, then an image of Nick in prison stopped him short.

'Running and hiding isn't going to achieve a thing,' he said. 'There are some very heavy people after you. There's a limit to how long you can hide in a place like this.'

'Maybe not here, but I'm quite used to looking after myself in these sort of conditions.'

'Dad, it must be twelve years since you saw anything like active service.'

'Don't knock it, Charlie. There are some things which you never forget.' Charlie remembered the calculated manner in which he'd shot the two armed men. 'In the meantime, there are only three people who know I'm here. Your mother, me, and you.'

'What about the locals?'

'I've been coming here on and off for years. I pay forty pounds a year rent for this place in the name of David Urquhart. They think I'm a romantic Scottish writer who misses his homeland and enjoys a bit of quiet fishing.'

'I've never heard you mention this place.'

'I never did, to anyone, not even your mother. It was absolutely private, a place where I could assume an alternative identity when I needed it—until now.'

Charlie looked at his stepfather's handsome face beneath the beard and the glasses—strong, forceful, unassailable. He recognised more clearly than ever than there were whole areas of this man's psyche he had never known; that he had no idea what he was really capable of.

246

'Dad, what are you going to do? If they don't find you, they may find Mum, and I don't suppose they'll leave me alone.'

'Did they do that damage to your face?'

Charlie nodded.

'What else did they do?'

Charlie told him.

Patterson showed his sympathy with a curt nod. 'They were undoubtedly Palestinians. Saudis are often too lazy or too stupid or too damned uneducated to do most things in life, and though they hate it, they rely on the Palestinians to carry out a lot of essential jobs.'

'Including revenge.'

'Including that,' Patterson agreed.

'But you can't just sit and wait for it. What about Mum? What about me?'

'Nobody will do much to you, as long as they think you know nothing. And your mother's secure where she is.'

'For the time being.'

'I'll move her from there shortly. I just didn't want to risk her being here with me yet. I knew if I was found, it would get nasty and I wouldn't go without serious resistance. When I'm sure the trail has gone cold, I'll leave the UK and she can join me. Now,' he said standing up. 'As you're here, you'd better stay the night, but tomorrow you must leave, and forget you ever came.'

Charlie decided he would do better to save his arguments until the morning. He took another glass of whisky. 'How come you were outside when I came?' he asked.

'I've got trip wires all round the place.' Patterson nodded at a khaki metal box housing a row of

247

monitoring dials, a British Army surveillance field system.

'What about power?' Charlie asked.

'Batteries and a generator fifty feet inside the cave behind this place. I've also got a few microphones in the trees on the way up from the road. The bloody sheep keep triggering them every time they cough,' he added with a laugh, a sound which Charlie had seldom heard.

'What else have you got to protect yourself?'

Patterson patted the automatic in his pocket and pulled open a drawer in the cupboard behind him. 'This is a Heckler & Koch MP5 automatic assault rifle,' he said. Charlie admired the gun along with a stock of magazines and half a dozen bush knives and throwing blades. Patterson pushed the drawer back. 'Those should cover most events,' he said. 'Now, what have you done with your car?'

'I left it about a quarter of a mile west of the pile of stones, in the woods.'

'Visible from the road?'

'Not easily.'

'Okay. We'll deal with it first thing in the morning. And we'll have to do something about our visitors' vehicle. Now, we'll eat.'

Patterson produced a bowl of mutton and barley stew from the range and spooned some on to two plates. As they ate, he refused to discuss the deal he'd done with Sala Mahmoud, or why he had done it. And on the question that Charlie wanted answered most, he offered nothing. Every time Charlie tried to draw him on the identity of the dead man at Birch Lodge, he shook his head in dismissal.

'But for God's sake, Dad,' Charlie pressed. 'What about Nick?'

248

'He'll be all right. They'll let him go sooner or later, when they dig up the truth.'

'What the hell do you mean?'

Patterson raised an eyebrow. 'Just believe me, Charles. Your friend won't suffer more than a few weeks on remand. And I dare say the experience will do him good.'

Charlie looked at him, shocked by his stepfather's apparent indifference to what Nick was going through and his total lack of remorse for the murders he had committed.

Patterson produced a palliasse and some blankets from an oak chest and made a space on the floor. 'You'll be comfortable enough on that,' he said to Charlie. 'I want you up early and away in the morning so you may as well turn in now.'

Charlie was far from ready either to sleep or to end his discussion with his father, but he wasn't offered an alternative.

To his surprise, he slept well and was feeling fully restored when his father shook him at six next morning. The smell of freshly brewed coffee hanging in the atmosphere also helped to wake him.

'Go back to the road the way you came. I'll give you ten minutes before I follow. Don't let anyone see you coming out of the track. If possible, I don't want anyone to know I've had visitors. They don't have a lot to talk about round here and the smallest unusual activity will get them gossiping.'

Charlie gulped down some coffee. Before he had fallen asleep the night before, he had firmly resolved to confront his stepfather again about his activities and future plans, but as he looked into his father's emotionless grey eyes, he knew he'd be wasting his time.

At half past six, with the sun making its first appearance over the top of the mountains to the east, David Patterson unlocked the door of the simple house.

'Go carefully,' he said as Charlie walked out. 'I'll meet you by your car in fifteen minutes.'

Charlie sniffed in the intoxicating dawn smell of damp heather and bracken as he walked briskly along the track. He looked for his father's trip wires and microphones but, not surprisingly, saw no sign of them. Before he reached the road, he dropped to his hands and knees and crawled behind a bank of heather. In the still air, he guessed he would hear a motor from half a mile away, but there was no sense in being hasty. Carefully and slowly, he parted the wispy branches to survey the road beyond.

There was no moving traffic, but parked, hastily by the look of it, on a wide verge of coarse grass was a silver BMW. Charlie's heart stopped. He recognised it, he was sure. He scrolled back through his memory trying to place it. At last it came to him. He'd noticed a BMW the afternoon before in Fort Augustus. He even remembered checking that it hadn't followed him out of the town.

Coincidence was out of the question. God knew, he thought, wracking his memory for where he'd gone wrong, he hadn't seen a sign of the car trailing him yesterday. His stepfather must be right; the Golf must have been bugged.

When he was confident there was no one in it or near it, he emerged cautiously from his cover and walked across to the BMW. He put a hand on the grille. It was stone cold. The car was locked and there was no one inside. Satisfied that the only occupants had been the two dead men, he set off at a brisk walk

250

towards the forest where he'd left the Golf.

David Patterson was already waiting for him when he arrived. He was holding a small, muddy metal object. It had taken him less than half a minute to find the tracking device.

'Maybe they bugged every vehicle in your yard,' he said.

'No. I know what happened. When they first came to see me, I was just about to drive down to the village in Kate's car. They must have seen me getting out of it and assumed it was mine.'

'You should have thought of that.'

'I haven't had the benefit of your training.'

'No,' his father agreed. 'Did you see their car?'

'Yes. A Silver BMW. Just by the track down to the croft.' Charlie paused guiltily. 'Actually, I saw it in Fort Augustus yesterday, when I was asking around about you. I even checked to see if it had followed me.'

'Well, there's nothing you can do about it now. I'll get it out of here before the police find it and start asking questions.' He pulled a key on a hire company fob from his pocket. 'I'll take it with me to my next billet.'

'Do you want me to come?'

'No. You get back to your place. If you're away too long without notice, whoever takes over from our friends back there will think you know more than you did. And the police may sniff a lead.'

CHAPTER THIRTEEN

Charlie tried to analyse the expression on DI Ferrier's face as he walked into the office at Oak Hollow. It had all the smugness and elation of a hunter lining up a kill.

'We've made what you might call a bit of a breakthrough,' Ferrier said, deliberately low-key. He was leaning back in the office chair. 'You'll be pleased to hear that we've established that Nick Ryder didn't kill your stepfather.'

Charlie leaped to his feet with delight. 'I told you that two weeks ago,' he said, smiling uncontrollably. 'But what made you change your mind?'

'I think that'll become clear in a moment. You can go and pick him up as soon as you like.'

'That's great. So who killed my stepfather? The man who went to see him that morning—the man I told you about?'

'We've found him, but it wasn't him.'

'But surely if it wasn't Nick, it must have been him.'

'I doubt it, Mr Patterson. He's dead.'

'Good God! Where did you find him?'

'Where do you think?'

'Where do *I* think? How should I know? Where was he?'

'In a coffin labelled "Major David Patterson".'

Charlie gaped at him. 'Two of them? In one coffin? But that's absurd. How did they fit?'

'Major Patterson wasn't among those present.'

'You mean he wasn't there?'

'Yes. Just the other bloke, with the back of his head

252

damaged exactly as it was when we first found him at your parents' cottage.'

'Are you saying this man was killed at Birch Lodge, not my stepfather?'

'Yes, Mr Patterson,' Ferrier hissed impatiently. 'That's exactly what I'm saying.'

'But my father was identified.'

'By your mother. And I have to tell you, we're getting nowhere looking for her. We should have had her permission to exhume the body. As it turns out, it wasn't hers to give or refuse anyway, seeing as it's not her corpse. But as you may imagine, we are more anxious than ever to see her now.'

'My God, yes. I can see that you must be.'

'Well? Where is she?'

'I wish I knew. I've lost track of her. I can't find out where she went in Cornwall and she hasn't been in touch with me at all. Do you suppose she's all right?'

'I should think she's being very well looked after—by your father.'

Charlie did his best to look astounded.

'Surprised, Mr Patterson?'

'Yes. I mean, if my stepfather isn't dead, where is he?'

Ferrier looked at him for four or five seconds. 'I don't know where he is. That's what I'm hoping you're going to tell me.'

Kate appeared at the door of the office with cups of coffee for them. Neither of them spoke until she had gone.

'I'm sorry,' Charlie said. 'This isn't making any sense. As far as I'm concerned, my mother and I buried him six weeks ago. I suppose I've got to believe you when you say he wasn't in the grave, but the whole thing sounds crazy to me. I mean, who

253

killed this man?'

'Who do you think, Mr Patterson?'

'Not my stepfather.'

'Why not?'

'Why, for God's sake? Why should he kill some old soldier?'

'He wasn't an old soldier. He was an ex-con called Brian Tennent, one of your mother's writing protégés. He'd been inside with Latimer, the bloke we found in the skip. We think Latimer was the only person who knew where Tennent was going that Saturday morning—apart from Major Patterson who'd arranged to meet him.'

Charlie stared back at Ferrier. 'You're seriously suggesting Dad had something to do with Tennent's death, and that he's done a runner, with my mother? That's crazy. He's not that kind of man. He's too honourable, too conventional. There has to be more to it.'

'If there is, it wouldn't do him and your mother any harm to come in and talk to us, would it?'

'I can promise you, Inspector, if either of them contact me, I'll tell them to get straight on to you.'

'No you won't, son, unless you want to be charged with aiding and abetting. You don't mention me, and when you've finished talking to them, you get in touch with me, understand?' He banged his mug down on the table and stood up. 'Why don't you go and pick up your mate from jail? I think he's been there long enough.'

*　　*　　*

Driving back from prison in the April sunshine, Charlie told an incredulous Nick what had

254

happened.

'What are you going to do about it?' Nick sighed.

'God knows. I can't turn my father in. I can hardly believe it, but it looks as though my mother's involved, at least to some extent. She'd be up on a charge of aiding and abetting at least.'

'How the hell did she let herself get talked into it?'

'My father's a very domineering man. He thinks people like Tennent and this other guy, Latimer, are totally worthless. He wouldn't have any feelings at all about killing them.'

'But doesn't he see that in a civilised society, individuals can't dole out arbitrary justice?'

'I wish I could tell you what was going through his head,' Charlie grunted. 'God knows how this whole thing is going to end. Still, you're out of jail and off the hook.' He leaned across and slapped Nick on the shoulder. 'You can start concentrating on the horses now.'

Nick grinned. 'I can't wait. I hear they all look great and Kate's been a star.'

'Who did you hear that from?'

'Kenny came up to see me. He says all the lads really like working with her.'

'Yeah,' Charlie said thoughtfully. 'She's not going to want to go back to the rescue centre in a hurry now. I think she's caught the racing bug.'

'I'll leave that one with you, then,' Nick said with a laugh.

'Don't worry. She knew it was only a temporary job, covering for you until you got out.'

'I still can't believe it. I thought I was in there for good.'

'Can you believe what my father said? He thought the experience would do you good, and he seemed

255

certain the police would never make it stick.'

'That's not the impression I had. But what are you going to do?'

'I'm not going to shop him but I've got to try and persuade him to give himself up and let my mother off the hook. And he'll have to give the Arab his money back or they're going to be hounded for the rest of their lives.'

'Your father seems well able to hide himself away if he needs to.'

'It's okay for him. He's not a very social animal, but my mother has friends and relations she cares about, and she won't dare get in touch with them in case they get caught up in it all.'

Nick looked at Charlie's exhausted, harassed face. 'I think you should tell the police. I don't think you've got a cat in hell's chance of persuading him to go himself.'

*   *   *

With Nick out of jail, an immense sense of relief had descended on the yard. Charlie should have been sleeping more easily, but he wasn't. As his mind conjured with the seemingly insolvable problems, the night passed slowly in a blur of fitful sleep and anxiety. Should he go to the police; attempt to persuade his father to give himself up and submit himself to British justice; or do nothing and hope that his parents would get away before either the police or another gang of Palestinians got to them first?

Despite his troubled night, he was in the yard at six o'clock.

Titch was working Willow Star. She galloped freely for half a mile while Charlie watched her

256

through his binoculars. There was no doubt about it; her development had been immense since the early disastrous run at Cagnes. The sunshine would improve her yet again. He looked at Nick beside him. Hercules had been allowed up on the gallops as a treat and was still gambolling around his master like a puppy.

His partner was in a state of euphoria after sleeping in his own bed for the first time in weeks. He ought to have had a king-sized hangover from the quantity of champagne he'd drunk the evening before, but nothing could depress him this morning. He looked up at the big blue bowl of the sky edged with gold in the east and grinned at the pleasure of simply being free.

'Let's confirm her for the Duke of York Stakes,' Charlie said. 'The Guineas is too soon, but in two weeks she'll be spot on.'

Nick agreed. 'Perfect. A group race and a sixty thousand pound prize would go down very well at the moment. By the way, did the lawyers tell you how much this mystery owner paid for her?'

'No. They said it was none of my business. Our only concern is to train her.'

'Well, let's hope if they get a really good win out of her they'll have the decency to show themselves, and perhaps we can talk them into buying another.'

Driving back to the yard, Charlie found it hard to believe how normal everything seemed. Here he was watching his horses, doing his job as if he hadn't been anywhere near his father earlier that week, watching him shoot two Palestinian heavies without turning a hair.

He had been worried that someone might have circulated details of the Arabs' car, but he guessed that if anyone ever did report them missing, it wouldn't be until several days after, by which time Patterson would have got rid of the BMW or doctored it beyond recognition.

He thought of his mother and hoped for her sake she'd been able to join up with his father now. At least he would know how to look after them both. Having heard nothing from either his parents or the police, or anyone else for that matter, Charlie allowed himself to believe that no news was good news.

Then, two days later, his mother telephoned him. She used his mobile number and briefly asked him to see her again where they had met last time, in two days' time.

This meeting in Kensington Gardens was very different from the previous one.

Charlie arrived late. He noticed a blue Ford Sierra behind him as he drove out of Lambourn. He spotted it again in Hogarth Road and dived off down Earls Court Road at the last moment.

The Sierra came with him, but he slipped into a small mews, parked and walked down a pedestrian alleyway before his tail had time to back up and turn into the narrow road itself.

He went the rest of the journey by tube.

When Charlie saw his mother, he could tell at once that she was under pressure. Her face was drawn and she fidgeted nervously.

When she spoke she was close to tears. 'Charlie, I don't know what we're going to do. David told me about the people who followed you to Scotland and Glen Shiel. Thank God they didn't come up to the lodge and find me. But it's all got out of control. He has no idea I'm seeing you. I didn't dare tell him, in

258

case he moves us on again. But I can't persuade him to face up to what he's done. Do you think you could?' Her voice was pleading.

Charlie put his arm round his mother's shoulder and he felt her fight back a sob. 'I doubt it,' he said. 'I tried when I was with him, but he said the whole thing would blow over and you and he would be able to slip away somewhere where you'd never be found.'

'He just doesn't understand that I don't want to hide for the rest of my life, live like this, with the constant threat of being found and murdered in our beds.'

'The trouble is, Mum, it's second nature to him. But surely you must have known something like this would happen when he faked his own death. It's not surprising Sala Mahmoud guessed he was still alive, is it? After all, it was a bit too much of a coincidence just after Dad had ripped him off.'

'Yes, but he didn't tell me about that, he just said if he didn't disappear, there'd be even more money problems. He was adamant, wouldn't take no for an answer. I didn't want to see Brian Tennent killed. God knows, he'd done a terrible thing and he'd shown absolutely no remorse for what he did, but he'd done his time, paid his penalty.'

'He would have done it again, sooner or later. You could tell yourself that someone else has probably been saved from him.'

'Maybe, but that's not how it works, and you know it.'

Charlie nodded. 'Look, the police are keeping tabs on me at the moment. The best thing for me to do is to get on with my job for a week or so. Let things settle. You and Dad, keep your heads down. If there's a sudden change of plan, let me know; if you're desperate and you need to, ring me and I'll try and meet up with you, maybe halfway, in Manchester or somewhere.'

His mother nodded, grateful that at least her son understood her state of mind. She put her hand on his forearm. 'Charlie, don't let anything happen to you. I don't want you to take any of the blame for what your father's done.'

Charlie took a deep breath. 'I'll be fine.'

Pru shook her head slowly. If anything happened to Charlie because of her, she'd die. 'We've got to bring this to a head. David's sure that we're all right at the cottage for a while. He's set up all his surveillance stuff and God knows what, but I'm convinced we should move.'

Charlie could hardly believe his ears. 'You mean you're both at the house by Banchory?'

'Yes. There's a sort of priest-hole there, and he's got rid of the Land Rover and neither of us goes out anywhere now. He'll be going mad, I just left a note for him saying I'd be away for the day.'

'Well, he may not want to stay there when the rest of the news breaks. I had Ferrier round the day I got back from Scotland. They've dug up the coffin.'

'Oh.' Pru looked away, wondering what to say. 'I knew it was too much to hope for but David was so certain that it would work.'

'It might have done if you hadn't disappeared. When the police couldn't find you, they assumed you knew something they didn't. And then they found this guy Latimer, dumped in a skip in Maida Vale.'

The blood drained from Pru's face. 'Oh, no! David promised me he wasn't going to do anything about that.'

'About what?'

260

'The phone calls I got from Latimer. He was trying to blackmail us. He said he knew what had happened. Don't ask me how, unless he'd made some arrangement with Tennent which wasn't kept. He said he would tell the police that they wouldn't find Tennent alive, ever. I believed him. I asked David what to do. He said Latimer had no way of following it up and couldn't prove anything.' Pru's resolve was weakening. 'How on earth could he do it? I can hardly believe it.' Her voice was breaking, large tears were sliding down her cheeks.

Charlie glanced around but no one was taking any notice of them. 'And there were the two Arabs who followed me.'

Pru gazed bleakly across the glittering Serpentine. 'And what about Nick? If only he hadn't turned up that afternoon. I was very angry with David about it, but he said that they'd never convict him.'

'That's the one bit of good news. Nick's out now. They let him go as soon as they realised Dad wasn't in the coffin.'

Pru sniffed back her tears and forced a smile at the news. 'Thank God for that.' She let out a sigh and stood up to leave. 'I must go, or I'll miss my train. I'll be in touch if I need you.'

Charlie rose and hugged his mother tighter than ever before, pressing his cheek against her hair.

'Look after yourself.'

*   *   *

Charlie drove back to Berkshire, uncertain what to do. Ferrier was waiting for him in the office again. Nick had discreetly disappeared.

'Morning, Charlie,' the policeman said with a grin

261

which Charlie didn't trust. 'Heard from your mum or dad yet?'

Charlie met the detective's eyes straight on. 'I wish I had, at least from my mother. Whatever happened, it can't have been her fault.'

'I wouldn't be so sure. After all, she identified Tennent as your father.'

'Sure. He was wearing my father's clothes, lying face down with the back of his head smashed in. It wouldn't have occurred to her that it was anyone else, would it?'

'That's what we'd like to ask her. By the way, where have you been this morning?'

'I had to go to London, to see a new owner.'

'Who was that, then?'

Charlie casually plucked from the air the name of the property dealer who had recently sent him a couple of two-year-olds. Ferrier noted it down.

'He wasn't there,' Charlie went on. 'Apparently he'd forgotten the date we made.'

'I see. I hear you still have a horse here that belongs to your father.'

'Willow Star? She used to belong to him. His lawyer sold her to a new owner, when we all thought my father was dead.'

'And who's the new owner?'

'A syndicate, run in a nominee name. I've never met them; we get all our instructions through the solicitors.'

'Isn't that rather unusual?'

'Yes, but it's not unheard of.'

'I see. Did you get on with your stepfather?'

'Not really. He was a very distant sort of a man. Of course he was away a lot when I was younger—he was in the army.'

262

'Yes. We do know that. I should think if he wanted to disappear from sight for a while, he'd know how to go about it.'

'I dare say,' Charlie said.

'But not your mother. Do you suppose she's with him?'

'I haven't a clue.'

'Listen, Charlie, if one of them gets in touch with you, you'll be committing an offence if you don't tell us, make no mistake.' Ferrier had abandoned his chummy tone and replaced it with a quiet, hard edge. 'So make sure you do, okay?'

Charlie watched him drive away. He wondered how convincing his lies had been, grateful, at least, that it hadn't been one of Sala Mahmoud's men asking the questions.

CHAPTER FOURTEEN

It had been a fine afternoon at Newbury but now, as the runners paraded before the last race, the sun was losing the last of its warmth. A slight chill descended, dampening the grass, and the casual racegoers found the Pimms Bar held more interest for them than a moderate staying handicap.

But for Persimmon Way this was a big occasion. It was going to be his first race since chipping a bone in his knee three months earlier. It had taken only a small operation to remove the tiny fragment, but Charlie had thought it wise to be extra careful with his recovery training schedule. He had no experience of a horse with this particular injury but common sense suggested that the joint should be subjected to

263

as little concussion as possible. He had asked Kate to take special charge of Percy, knowing that the gelding came second only to Willow in her affections. At sixteen hands two inches, Percy was a hand and a half taller than the filly, much more Kate's size. When she rode him out, she felt she was on a real racehorse.

Percy's re-training programme had started with long walks, always on the easier surface of the all-weather track and always when there were no other horses around to over-excite him. Gradually, Kate had started to hack gently over short distances, building up slowly until now they were cantering up to five miles a day. To this was added a daily swim in the local equine pool. Every afternoon, Kate led him down to the village for a work-out, rubbed him under a sun lamp until he was dry and then walked him back home. She was sure that he was fitter now than he'd ever been.

Charlie and Nick had invited Charles Gordon and his wife down to look at their fast recovering animal. As Percy walked round the paddock with muscles bulging under his shiny black coat, they all congratulated Kate on the wonderful job she'd done. She had never felt so proud.

On the peak of his form, the partners could have expected Percy to waltz home on this first outing since his recovery, but they were uncertain how much psychological damage the injury had caused. Some horses, having once suffered the pain of a chipped knee, were reluctant totally to commit themselves afterwards for fear of repeating the damage. Although Percy had always been a tryer before, Nick and Charlie wouldn't have blamed him if from now on he'd held a little in reserve. Jimmy Scaron, the jockey booked to ride him, was told that on no account was he to use his whip; whatever happened, Percy was to enjoy himself.

Charlie, Nick and the Gordons made their way to the front of the grandstand. Kate had gone off to the tote to have a small bet on her charge—just out of sentiment. The others had decided there were too many ifs about him to risk their money.

As she waited for her ticket, Kate sorrowfully reminded herself that now Nick was back, she would have to return to the Rescue Centre. She was going to miss the excitement of working at Oak Hollow. But she had made up her mind that she wasn't going back to manage the place. Working with the animals was what she enjoyed; if she had to take a cut in salary, so be it.

She rejoined the others on the stand just as the fourteen runners were coming under orders. The gates flew open and Kate raised her binoculars to focus on Percy's dark green silks. Her hands trembled with a confusion of emotions. She wanted him to do well, to be back to his best, but more importantly she prayed for him to come back sound.

Percy had been drawn on the inside and Jimmy Scaron kept him there. As the runners came round the bend in front of the stands for the first time, Kate cursed out loud. The horse outside Percy had cannoned into him, making him lose his footing for a moment. It was the sort of thing that happened in every race, but Kate didn't want it happening to Percy. She was like a mother worrying over a son in his first point-to-point. Jimmy Scaron took a tight grip on the reins and in a matter of strides had him back on an even keel. He kept Percy in mid-division until they started the long turn out of the back straight. Kate could see that some of the horses in front were tiring. Percy began to move through them slowly. His long stride seemed to be getting more powerful as the race developed.

They were heading for home and the pace quickened. When they passed the three-furlong pole, Kate began to jump up and down with excitement. Percy was going easily with his ears pricked and had cruised up to join the leaders.

Kate wanted to scream her encouragement but stopped herself before she made an undignified spectacle of herself. She compromised by giving Charlie a sharp jab in the ribs with her elbow. 'He's going to do it! He's going to do it!' Her gaze turned back to the track.

At that moment, Percy stumbled and almost fell. His nose crashed into the grass and then bounced up again. As Percy took his next stride to recovery, his jockey almost fell off and Kate stifled a desperate scream. Percy's near foreleg, which she'd spent months treating, was swinging limply beneath him. She turned to Charlie with wide, horrified eyes and grasped his arm with both hands. Her insides felt hollow.

Down on the course, Jimmy Scaron had pulled Percy to a halt and jumped off as quickly as he could. The magnificent animal stood bewildered, with his left knee outstretched and the lower limb dangling uselessly from it, like a weight on a crane.

In all her time at the Rescue Centre, nothing had prepared Kate for this. She had seen animals viciously burned, horses pulped in road accidents, any number of terrible injuries, but none of them came close to causing her the appalling anguish she felt now. Her closeness to Percy, all the time and care

266

she had lavished on him, added another dimension to the pain.

Once the initial, numbing shock had passed, she galvanised herself into running with the others down to the course where the knacker's van was already heading.

By the time they arrived, a dark, canvas screen had been erected. Percy's lad was in there, wet-eyed, holding the reins while the vet examined Percy's leg. It was, the vet knew, a mere formality. He didn't need to be told what the injury was, or what he had to do. But no matter how many horses he shot, coping with the animals' pathetic look of innocence and their complete confusion over what was happening to them never became any easier. They were always so proud; dying like this seemed so pointless.

Charlie made Kate and the Gordons wait some distance from the screen. Jimmy Scaron walked over and explained to them what had happened, though one look at Percy's leg had told them enough to expect the inevitable. As the vet took his humane killer from his bag, he nodded an apology for what he was about to do. Charlie joined him behind the screen and took the reins from the lad who was weeping uncontrollably now. The vet moved round to Percy's head. Charlie gave the broad, dark neck a last, loving pat. A second later, it was all over.

Charlie watched hopelessly, barely able to speak. Losing Percy was a disaster in its own right; coming on top of all the other events crowding in on him, it was as much as he could bear.

It would have to happen to one of Charles Gordon's horses, he reflected bitterly. Typical Sod's Law. This was the first time the Gordons had been to the races in months. It had taken him the best part of

267

a year to make it up with Mrs Gordon over the Flitgrove fiasco, especially when the filly went out and won three more races after Mike Dubens had bought her. And then Mrs Gordon had transferred her affections to the lovable Percy. Charlie grimaced at the unfairness of it, and braced himself to go and talk to her.

Later, after Kate, still fighting back her tears, had climbed up into the cab of the lorry with Kenny and set off for home, Charlie left the main enclosure and headed for the car park where he had arranged to meet Nick who was completing the formalities with the vet. He'd just reached the first line of cars when he became aware that a group of well-dressed, cosmopolitan olive-skinned men had fanned out behind and to either side of him. One of them, with a boyish face and a wafer-thin moustache moved against him.

'Come with us.'

Charlie felt a jab in his spine. If it wasn't a gun, it felt too like one to take a chance. Sweat prickled his torso. He looked around for help, but there was nobody nearby. He let himself be guided towards the back door of a black Mercedes. It was opened from inside and Charlie was firmly pushed in between two of the burlier Arabs.

As the engine started, Charlie wished he'd made a run for it. Now it was too late.

They drove on to the M4 and headed east through the late afternoon traffic. After a few minutes on the motorway, one of the Arabs spoke to Charlie.

'Sheikh Sala Mahmoud wants to talk to you.' He barked in Arabic through the intercom to one of the men in the front. The glass partition slid back, and the man in the passenger seat passed back a mobile

268

phone. The Arab on Charlie's right took it, spoke a few words and handed it to him.

Charlie took it apprehensively. Feeling slightly foolish, he said, 'Hello?'

'Your father has been a very stupid man. I trusted him.' The voice was deep, with a thick, throaty Arabic accent. 'Tell him he will not escape. I will not stop until I have found him and been repaid. If you are interested for him, you must tell him this. He should return my money to me.'

'W-what do you mean?'

There was a moment's silence. 'Perhaps you know; perhaps you do not. Just tell him what I say. And remind him, please, that unlike your police, my resources are limitless. We will find him. I wish you no harm, but if you get in my way, I will not be merciful. This is also true for your mother.'

There was a silence. Charlie didn't answer.

'Do you understand? I am a civilised man, but I will not be merciful.'

'I understand,' Charlie said flatly.

'Good.'

There was a click as the other end of the line was disconnected. Charlie slowly handed the phone back to the impassive man beside him.

At the next junction, the limousine swept off, swung through three hundred and sixty degrees and headed back the way they had come.

The man on Charlie's right turned to him. 'Where do you want to go?'

They dropped him where he asked, outside the pub in the village. Nick was there with Kate.

'Where the hell have you been?' Kate asked. 'We were beginning to get worried.'

Charlie, still recovering from what had happened,

nervously explained.

'What are you going to do?' Nick asked.

'As soon as I think it's safe, I've got to go and see Dad again. Sometime I've got to convince him it'll be far better for him in the long run if he gives himself up to the police. And, more to the point as far as I'm concerned, safer for my mother. And she didn't know until afterwards what had happened to you, Nick. My stepfather just took the chance when he saw it.'

'He's a callous bastard.'

Charlie nodded, thinking of the four men his father had killed.

'I hope he gets a taste of his own medicine.'

*   *   *

Charlie sweated it out for another twelve days. He was certain that someone was still keeping tabs on him, and he didn't dare risk leading them to Scotland.

Then two days before Willow Star's race at York, he answered the phone to hear the distinctive sound of his mother's voice. She was desperate to see him. Charlie didn't waste any time. Half an hour later, he slipped into the horsebox while it was parked in the yard.

He told the driver to stop for a moment at the roundabout in Newbury. When they reached it, the driver banged on the back of the cab and Charlie opened the side door. He nodded at the lad he left in there and let himself out. He walked briskly to the station, confident that no one who might have had the yard under surveillance would have seen him leave or followed the lorry.

He changed to the airport bus at Reading, going

270

through a couple of turns to check that he wasn't being followed, and did the same at Heathrow. He got a seat on the Aberdeen shuttle without any trouble and two hours later he'd hired a Ford Escort and was heading west out of Aberdeen. He had plenty of time to check again that he wasn't being followed. He left his car in the village and started plodding up the empty road, suitably clad in shorts and carrying a rucksack like any of the thousands of people hiking round the Highlands at that time of year.

Before he reached the point where the track down from the farmhouse gave on to the road, he turned off into the woodland and, for a third time, started to walk up the steep valley side to the hidden forest lodge.

Nothing warned him of the attack.

In a single motion, a hand covered his mouth, a knee was shoved into the small of his back and he was hurled to the ground like a day-old calf. As soon as he hit the ground, his attacker had a forearm across his windpipe and his arms pinioned behind his back.

The assault was so sudden, so efficiently achieved, that Charlie was beaten before he'd registered what was happening. As his mouth and nose were forced into the soft pine-needle mould, he knew he'd been jumped by a hardened professional. He felt the sharp pressure of a knee in the small of his back and didn't even consider trying to wriggle out of the hold he was in.

His head was lifted from the ground.

'Sorry. Boss's orders,' a throaty voice apologised. 'Are you Charles Patterson?'

Charlie nodded vigorously.

'I'm with your dad. Don't make a sound when I

271

take my hand away.'

The hand was removed and Charlie gasped for breath. He turned his head to see a large, craggy head topped with short, cropped grey hair and a beard to match. The dazzling blue eyes of a much younger man shone from a wrinkled walnut face. There was the same stillness in them that Charlie had seen in his stepfather's eyes.

'Who the hell are you?' he whispered.

'Shoosh.'

Charles did as he was told.

Without a word, and scarcely another sound, the man led him up through the woods to the house. When they reached it, he stopped outside and spoke in a low voice. 'Your father's expecting you.' He opened the front door and nodded towards the small sitting room on the left.

Charlie opened the door and went in.

David Patterson was sitting in one of the armchairs, reading a book. He looked up. 'You met Hutch, then?'

Charlie pushed the door shut behind him. 'Yes, if Hutch is the old soldier who jumped me in the woods.'

'He was one of the best squadron sergeant-majors in the regiment. No one'll get near us as long as he's around.'

'Come on, who are you kidding? You can't stay here for ever.'

Patterson looked at him coldly. 'I didn't want you to come, Charlie. You've been dragged up here for no reason.'

'I wasn't dragged. I'd have come whether Mum had phoned or not as soon as I thought it was safe. I've had people watching me, just waiting for me to

272

make contact with you.'

'I'm not planning on being here much longer.'

'Frankly, I don't know how you've survived so long with all the people who are after you. But that's your business. What I'm concerned about is Mum. She's put up with a hell of a lot all the time she's been married to you because she's a loyal woman. But this time you're asking too much.'

Charlie's stepfather made no reply.

'This operation's a fuck-up, and you know it. You're in danger of screwing the whole thing up and taking Mum with you. It's damage limitation time, Dad. You must see that.'

David Patterson still remained silent. He stared back at Charlie, not focusing on him, looking through him. He put a marker in the book he was holding, closed it and placed it on a table beside him. He lifted himself from the chair and walked across to look out of a small window at the thick evergreen woods that hemmed them in.

'There's no point your going on with this,' Charlie persisted. 'You've killed four people now.'

'More than that,' Patterson replied.

'What you did in the army was sanctioned. With these people it was straight murder.'

'What happened at the croft was self-defence. You can be sure that if they'd got to us first, they'd have killed us, whether or not they got the money.'

Charlie opted for another, less direct approach. 'Tell me about the money, Dad.'

'I told you, Mahmoud thinks I cheated him over some Linke furniture he bought from me—about a million pounds.'

'But you did cheat him. You told me the furniture was fake.'

273

Patterson shrugged. 'The pieces are so good, it's an insult to call them that. Very few people would ever know the difference. The cabinet-maker, Harry Thorndyke, specialises in Linke replicas and it so happened that he had quite a lot of what I wanted in stock, and he was prepared to pull out all the stops to make the rest. I think someone must have got to hear of it and tipped Mahmoud. I knew if I wanted to be left with anything at all for me and your mother to survive on, I'd have to disappear. I had no assets to leave, so if the money couldn't be found, there was no point in them suing the estate.'

'If things were so bad for you how could you afford to buy Willow Star?'

His stepfather took his eyes off the trees swaying outside to glance at his son. 'You have no idea how difficult that was to raise. But I knew it meant a great deal to you, with your plans for the new yard and everything.'

'But you never seemed that interested.'

'I may not have seemed it, but I was. I wanted you to have all the encouragement I could give you. I was really proud when you sent out your first winner.'

Charlie was amazed. His stepfather had never expressed an opinion or any particular interest in the performance of Oak Hollow. 'Who did you sell her to?'

The major put his finger to his nose. 'More than my life's worth to tell you.'

'Well, what will happen to the money that was paid for her?'

Patterson grinned. 'That'll all be a real mess, now they've dug up Tennent and know I'm still alive. I suppose the lawyers will hang on to it until they're forced to pay something to the hoard of creditors

274

wanting to get their snouts in.'

'Where's the money Sala Mahmoud gave you?'

'It's safe, where it can't be got at by any of the bastards who've ripped me off.' Patterson stood up and walked to the fireplace. He picked up a bronze sculpture from the mantelpiece and studied it. 'Bastards,' he muttered again.

'Who?'

'People I thought I could trust. Brother officers.'

'Helmsley-Barret?'

Charlie's stepfather looked surprised at hearing his name. 'You've come across him, have you?'

'I had lunch with him, after your "funeral". He was anxious to know if there was any money left in the estate.'

'He's already had a good bit of it.'

'How? He said you'd agreed to give some guarantees for a restaurant business which has gone bust.'

'That business may have gone bust, but the restaurants are still there and he still owns half of them.'

'But if he defrauded you, surely you could have gone after him in the courts.'

'That would cost tens of thousands, take years, and there's no certainty I'd get a result. He knows that, so he let the banks come after me for my guarantees. There seemed absolutely no end to it, and at the same time, every year since I became a Name at Lloyds, I've been asked to cough up bigger and bigger cheques. I paid them for the first two years— seemed fair enough. It was what I had agreed to, and put my name to. Now, of course, I realise it was all an enormous fraud to let the insiders off the hook,' he added bitterly.

Charlie looked at his stepfather and understood his resentment and what this kind of financial ruin meant to him. It wasn't just the money, or even mainly the money, it was the knowledge that he'd made so many bad judgements. David Patterson was humiliated and, under the laws of a practical world, defenceless. Now he was dealing with the crisis in the only way his instincts and his training enabled him to.

Charlie was beginning to understand but he still thought his father's course of action was wholly misguided.

'You can't win, Dad,' he said. 'You're wanted for murder and on the run from the police as well as Mahmoud's people. Sooner or later you'll be caught, and my bet would be on Mahmoud getting to you first.'

'I appreciate your concern, Charlie, but I'm not turning myself in, and that's final. When I've laid low for a while longer and things have quietened down, we'll slip away. I'll let you know in due course where we've gone. In the meantime, I don't think you'll have too much trouble from the police or Sala Mahmoud's men. Just give the impression that you'd like them to find me as much as they would. Shouldn't be hard.'

'But how can you be so sure I won't let it out?'

'I may have been a lousy stepfather and I'd probably deserve it if you gave me away but I haven't got a choice and I trust you.'

'Even after what you did to Nick?'

'That was no big deal. I thought they'd arrest him and maybe charge him, I admit it, but they'd have been hard-pressed to make it stick. And anyway, once I was out of the country, I was going to contact you to tell the police to exhume the body in my

276

grave.'

'There's no way you could have been sure that would have worked,' Charlie said, outraged by his father's complacency. 'The police found Nick's fingerprints on the poker. That's pretty damning evidence, though he said he couldn't remember touching it. Was that your doing?'

His father looked down guiltily. 'Yes, I swapped the handle of the tongs he'd used in the sitting room.'

'What about Brian Tennent? Why was he in the house?'

'Your mother first told me about him a long time ago. He was a complete bastard of a man but she'd tried to help him in prison. After he got out, about the time your girlfriend Kate found Willow Star, Pru arranged for him to come down and do a bit of decorating at the cottage. It was a very generous gesture of trust on her part but he never showed up; instead he got involved in a bit of chance burglary which went wrong.'

'Where was that? At your place?'

'Oh no. We never knew about it at the time. But last month your mother saw him in London. When she came home I could see she was worried, she said she'd noticed a watch he was wearing—a big gold hunter on a chain. She recognised it as old Cyril Barton's. The police had no way of knowing what was taken when the old boy was killed because he lived on his own and nobody had a clue what he owned.'

Charlie sat down at the desk opposite his stepfather. 'Are you saying Tennent murdered Cyril Barton?'

'I'm saying that he was supposed to come to our cottage that day. He must have got lost and found

277

Lodge Farm, vulnerable and rich in pickings, and I guess the old boy caught him at it.' Patterson gave a characteristic shrug of his shoulders, exonerating himself from his subsequent actions. 'After that, I had no compunction about his role in my scheme.'

'You'd planned it already?'

'More or less. Your mother had mentioned that he was about my age and build. It was easy to construct a plan to make it look as though he'd murdered me and gone.'

'But did Mum know?'

'She had to. It took a lot of persuasion, but I think she accepted that Tennent's life wasn't worth a jot, and she knew we had to get ourselves out of the mess we were in.'

Charlie didn't believe she would willingly have accepted any such thing. 'But she can't have agreed with you doing what you did to Nick.'

'No, of course she didn't. She wasn't even there when he came. I collected Tennent from the station at Hungerford. I drove him home and took him into the drawing room. I knocked him unconscious, tied him up and when he came to, I questioned him about Cyril Barton. He admitted what he'd done, said it was an accident. Then I hit him with the poker on the back of his head. He went straight down; I didn't have to do anything else.

'That was when Nick arrived and started lecturing me about how I should pay for training my horse. When I lost my temper, he was scared out of his wits. He started trembling and it suddenly occurred to me, if I could have leave him at the scene of the crime and get his fingerprints on to the weapon, it would give the police another lead to follow besides Tennent, and generally keep them from working out what

278

really happened. I went out, smashed a vase in the sitting room to sound as if someone had broken in, and called Nick for help. I just waited behind the door until he came in.' Patterson shrugged. 'After I'd messed up the study a bit and dressed Tennent in my clothes, I disguised myself and slipped out through the woods. I walked down to Marlborough and away. All your mother had to do was identify Tennent's body as mine. And that was that.'

Charlie looked at his father, shaking his head. Part of him admired the cold-blooded ingenuity of the scheme; part of him was filled with disgust. 'Well, from the way I see it, you've got no choice. For Mum's sake, you *must* go to the police.'

Patterson glanced impatiently at Charlie and walked across the room to stand by the window. After a minute, he turned. 'If I give myself up,' he said, 'I'll be in jail for the rest of my life. If your mother can't take what's happening now, maybe she should go to the police herself, to demonstrate her own innocence. I could get out of the UK now if I had to, but she wouldn't ever see me again.'

Charlie knew how his mother would react to this plan. She would be incapable of deserting her husband; it would be against all her instincts.

'It's her choice. We either carry on running, together, until we find a safe haven—which we will, with plenty of money—or I give myself up, take all the blame and let her visit me in jail for the next twenty years. Or does she go back, proclaim her innocence, and never see me again? Those are the choices. I've told her, and I've told her I want her to stay with me. She'll be safe with me, I can guarantee that.'

'You can't guarantee anything and it's not much of
279

a choice,' Charlie said sharply.

'It's all there is. I've got nothing more to say about it. And unless you want to be implicated, don't come here or try to find me again. Sooner or later you're going to lead someone here like you did to Loch Cluanie, and then there'll be trouble.'

'Look, if you give yourself up, with a good lawyer you could get as little as ten years, you might be out in seven.'

'What about Mahmoud?'

Charlie thought of what the Arab had said to him on the phone in the Mercedes. 'I will not be merciful.'

'If you gave him the money back, I think you could handle him.'

'If I gave him the money, I would be penniless. Your mother would never be able to cope with that while I was in jail.'

'You're underestimating her. And I'll be around to help her, if she needs it.' Charlie stood up and moved nearer to his father. 'Listen to me,' he said urgently, his anger bubbling just below the surface, 'if you're capable of listening to anybody. You're in a real mess! You need to resolve it. Now! You know it; I know it.' Charlie's voice became harsher. 'You're not on some SAS operation; you're talking about the life and feelings of a woman who's given you her life, for God's sake! You know what you have to do. Now bloody well do it!'

Charlie turned and walked from the room. He slammed the door behind him. There was no one in the hall. He went through the door opposite the sitting room. It opened into the kitchen where his mother sat at the table with Hutch. Behind him, he heard his stepfather walk through the hall and out of the front door, which he closed with a bang. Through

280

the kitchen window, they watched him stride towards the woods.

Charlie sat down next to his mother. 'Look, Mum, I don't know if I've got through to him or not, but if he doesn't come round in the next few days, I think you should come back home, to the cottage, and tell the police everything you know. That way at least they might not charge you, if you convince them you genuinely thought the body you found was Dad's. They'd find it very hard to prove otherwise. That might at least jerk him into action, one way or the other. But you can't go on with this sword of Damocles dangling over you. He must realise it. I spoke to Sala Mahmoud last week. His men picked me up so I could speak to him on the phone. He's not pleased, but I don't think he's a complete savage. If honour is restored, he'll leave us alone.'

'What about his men who were killed?'

'I guess he'll have to take that in his stride.'

Hutch nodded. 'Yeah. He's right. If the major crawls back with the money, Mahmoud will consider the slate clean.'

They all knew that the major would never crawl.

Pru looked at her son. 'Thank you for trying, Charles. I'll let you know if I'm coming back.'

Charlie stood up. 'I've got to go.'

'You can't go already,' his mother protested.

'I'm not hanging around to see him again. If I said anything else, I'd probably undermine what good I may have done. Anyway, I've got to get to York. Willow Star arrives there tonight. She's running her first big race of the season tomorrow.'

*   *   *

Charlie walked back down the valley to find his hire car parked where he'd left it beside the road. He was back in Aberdeen in time to check it in that evening. British Rail delivered him to York before eleven o'clock the following morning.

Resolutely he switched his mind to Willow Star. He found Kate and Nick with Titch at the stables. Willow Star had been perfectly settled since her arrival. She'd eaten up her small breakfast, been out for some light exercise, and now had her head over the stable door, ears flicking with interest, obviously looking forward to the outing she knew was coming.

One of her opponents, a light chestnut colt called Hit the Canvas, who was trained locally, was led into a stable opposite. He looked magnificent, at least a hand taller than Willow Star, full of confidence and with a bounce in his stride. Charlie immediately began to doubt Willow Star's ability to win, but decided not to brood on it. 'Come on, let's go and get a cup of tea,' he said brightly, and set off across the middle of the course towards the main buildings on the far side.

They were almost there when they bumped into Imogen, who'd been looking for them. Charlie wondered why she hadn't told him she was coming. He greeted her and turned with a grin to introduce her to Kate.

'Hello, Immy,' Kate smiled.

'Have you two already met?'

'Yes,' Imogen said. 'Several times.'

'When Immy's been to the yard,' Kate added.

'I didn't know you'd been,' Charlie said, surprised.

'Nick's asked me round a few times. You just haven't been there.'

'Nick?' Now Charlie was amazed. Nick hadn't said

a word about it.

Nick joined them and a smile spread across his face when he saw Imogen. She reached up and kissed him. 'How's your Star?'

'Well, aren't you the sneaky ones!' Charlie joked, quite taken aback by their obvious affection. He noticed the slight reddening of his partner's cheeks and not wanting to embarrass Nick he deftly turned the conversation to Willow Star's race.

Throughout lunch, in the Champagne Bar, they discussed little else. There had still been no communication from Willow Star's new owners. No one knew if they were coming to watch or not. Kate and Imogen decided that in their absence, they would deputise, so when Nick and Charlie walked down into the paddock, they followed.

The Duke of York Stakes was fourth on the card. Six furlongs straight, for some of the fastest horses in training. Apart from Willow Star and Hit the Canvas, there were eight other runners. They all looked fit, but Hit The Canvas just shaded them. His muscles ballooned beneath the glossy skin of his enormous frame.

It was impossible to be unimpressed, but Charlie and Nick were determined not to be put off. Instead, they convinced first the girls then Owen Williams that Willow Star could do it. 'The bigger they come the harder they fall,' Charlie said confidently as he legged the tiny jockey into the saddle. 'Try as hard as her and you'll win.'

Charlie gave Willow Star an encouraging pat on the neck, wished Owen and Titch good luck and then caught up with the others, who were making their way towards the front of the grandstand.

The commentator, perched high in his gantry,

watched the runners canter down to the start, checking that their colours corresponded with the crayoning in his ledger. He had them down in the order in which he would see them leaving the stalls. Below him, the stands were full. A short while later, as he watched the last horse being eased into the stalls and readied himself for the next seventy seconds of furious action, with every pair of eyes trained towards the start, Willow Star set herself like a spring ready to uncoil. Every sinew in her body was tensed, every muscle in her quarters bulged ready to thrust her forward the very instant that the gates holding her in began to part. Her delicate nose was now jammed against her chest as she braced her neck, the steel of the bit still firm across the corners of her mouth. The noise from the main road running only thirty yards behind her was suddenly drowned as the ten iron traps released them on their way. Owen Williams was thankful that he'd grabbed a handful of Willow Star's mane as she flew out of the stalls beneath him. She was eager to show everyone just how good she really was.

At home she always had to wait for the others, and in France, where she'd had her last race, she'd been running a temperature. Her entire body had ached so much she doubted her ability even to finish. Every stride of the race had hurt her. Now, she was in peak condition. Above her, Owen Williams could only sit and steer as she took control and blazed away down the long carpet of green that lay before them.

He couldn't believe that this was the same animal he'd ridden at Goodwood. It was as though Willow Star had been programmed to reach the finishing line like a missile locked on to its target. The furlong markers flew by with not so much as a glimpse of

284

another runner. He knew that she couldn't possibly sustain her speed, and about three hundred yards from home, for just a brief moment, he feared that she might be about to falter. Then, before he had time to react, and just as he sensed another horse at his quarters, Willow Star changed legs, picked up the bridle and was off again.

It was the most exciting feeling he had ever experienced. The sheer power of the horse sent a shiver down his spine. He glanced behind as the winning post flashed past. The others seemed a distance away. As he slowly eased her down, he lowered his right hand and patted her neck appreciatively. If she didn't turn out to be the season's Champion Sprinter he'd hand in his licence.

Kate rushed from the stand, taking the iron steps two at a time. She met Willow as they walked off the course towards the winner's enclosure and threw her arms around the filly's neck, hugging her as they walked, beaming like a child on a fairground ride, and kissing her wildly.

Charlie and Nick weren't far behind. As professional trainers, it wouldn't do to show as much excitement as Kate, but they were every bit as pleased. Nick had a lump in his throat and was pinching his leg to stop himself from crying.

The cheer from the enthusiastic crowd who packed themselves around the winners enclosure was deafening. Willow Star froze for a moment until Titch encouraged her to step forward into the limelight. Once she realised that the applause was for her, she jutted her head up proudly in the air and stood like a champion, allowing people to pat her and take her photograph.

There were no photo finishes or objections or

stewards' inquiries to cast a shadow over the result. Charlie bore in mind the instructions he had had from the lawyers acting for the anonymous owners. In the event of the filly winning, he was to nominate someone to accept the prize on the owners' behalf.

Kate was the obvious choice. She was so thrilled by the result, Charlie thought she might drop the trophy that went with the winner's prize of sixty-five thousand pounds.

'Kate, you look as though you won the bloody race yourself.'

She turned to him, beaming. 'I have—at least, I feel as if I have!'

'You mean you backed her well?'

'Yes, of course I did, but it's more than that.'

Charlie grinned at her. He thought he understood. She felt she was a fully integrated member of the Oak Hollow team now, and she was right.

CHAPTER FIFTEEN

They were in the members' bar opening a second bottle of champagne when Charlie heard his name called over the Tannoy. His mind instantly began scrambling for reasons why the race could be taken away from him. He'd watched the jockey weigh in and there had certainly been no interference then, so unless someone had actually objected to something it was difficult to know what else could have gone wrong.

More concerned than he cared to admit, he offered his apologies to the group and quietly edged his way out of the bar. When he reached the weighing room, he turned left towards the tiny communication booth. The operator recognised him. 'There's someone here to see you.' He nodded towards a man whom Charlie had just walked past.

He was about thirty-five, slightly built and wearing a cheap suit. Charlie's relief that he wasn't a steward was tempered by the look of concern on the man's face. He walked over and tentatively introduced himself.

'Hello. I'm Charlie Patterson.'

The man offered his hand and gave his name as Sergeant Kenneth Foreman from York Police. He led Charlie into a small empty room adjacent to the changing rooms.

'I'm afraid it's about your father,' he said eventually.

Charlie instantly had an image of his stepfather arrested and incarcerated; then his thoughts flashed to his mother distraught, humiliated and confused.

'Stepfather,' he said automatically.

'Sorry, sir. But he's been involved in an accident.'

'What? Where?'

'On the A1M. Just south of Scotch Corner. I'm afraid he died on the way to hospital.'

'What about my mother?'

'He was on his own.'

The news was so unexpected, so contrary to anything Charlie had been anticipating that for a few seconds he felt as if he'd been hit on the back of the head with a sandbag. When he had recovered, he asked huskily, 'How did it happen?'

The sergeant looked down at the notebook he had opened on the table in front of him. For a few moments he said nothing, then he cleared his throat.

'He was being pursued by a police officer at the

time. He had been reported speeding. The police driver was trying to catch up with him. He was travelling extremely fast along the raised section at Darlington when he left the carriageway and broke through the outer crash barriers. There's a drop of fifty feet to the road below. Fortunately, nobody else was involved.' He paused. 'I am sorry to have to give you such bad news.'

Charlie heard but he couldn't reply for a moment as he grappled with the image of his father being hounded by the police. What had been going through his mind? Where was he going? Could he have been coming to York? And if he was, why?

'How did you know how to contact me?' Charlie asked.

'From the front of his personal diary: who to contact in case of emergency. Durham Police rang your stables, and they told us you were here.'

'Can I see him?'

'We would like you formally to identify him. He's at Darlington. Have you got transport?'

Charlie knew that Nick would supply that. 'Yes. I'll go right away.'

*   *   *

Charlie left Kate, Nick and Imogen at the Post House in York. They were as shocked as he was and had offered to come with him, but he wanted to deal with this alone. When he told them he would be going straight on to Scotland to tell his mother, they agreed to go back to Lambourn in the lorry while Charlie took Nick's Subaru.

Charlie shivered in the hospital mortuary. A taciturn, white-coated official pulled out a body-

288

sized drawer and stood back. Charlie and the police sergeant who had met him at the hospital gazed at the pale, handsome features. Beyond a few small abrasions, there was no sign of the accident on David Patterson's face. His torso, the policeman said, had been completely crushed. The police surgeon's report gave the information that he had died in the ambulance on the way to hospital. Every means of revival had been tried, but the damage was too serious.

Charlie tried to divine from the set of his father's lips and his closed, bloodless eyelids what his intentions had been as he drove his car from the road. He tried not to face the possibility that it had been a deliberate act to resolve the impossible dilemma he faced.

Charlie wasn't looking forward to breaking the news to his mother. And he knew his own involvement wasn't over. Maybe Sala Mahmoud would not want revenge now, but he would still want his money. 'Would you mind coming back to the station with me, sir? There are a few things we need to clear up.'

Charlie carried on gazing at his dead, adoptive father and nodded. He wondered if the sergeant had any idea just how much there was to clear up.

Charlie was treated with deference and consideration by the police. Interrogation was preceded by polite sympathy. A lean, earnest detective inspector sat opposite him to ask the questions.

'There's something puzzling us about this incident,' he said slowly. 'The police vehicle pursuing your stepfather wasn't marked and the officer wasn't wearing a cap. There was no way he could have known it was the police after him, and yet the driver reports that he was definitely trying to get away from him, as if he was expecting somebody to be pursuing him.' The detective opened his eyes wide with inquiry. 'Any idea who he might have thought would be after him?'

Charlie looked blankly back at him. He imagined his father had assumed that Mahmoud's people were on his tail. 'No,' Charlie said. 'I don't know who he might have thought it was.'

'But did you know the Thames Valley Police were looking for him?'

'Yes. They told me.'

'Did you know where he was?'

'No. But he phoned me,' Charlie lied. 'To tell me he was coming to see me.'

'Do you know why that was?'

'Not for sure, but I had tried to persuade him to give himself up.'

'You're aware of why he was wanted?'

Charlie nodded.

The DI looked at him for a moment before he went on. 'Thames Valley want to see your mother, too.'

'They told me. I can't help, I'm afraid. She went off to stay with friends, to get over everything, then I lost contact with her.'

The policeman looked at him with frank scepticism. 'Where will you be going when you leave here?'

'Back to my yard at Lambourn.'

'Yes, you're a trainer, aren't you? I gather you had a good winner today at York.'

Charlie nodded.

'I imagine this has all taken the gilt from the
290

gingerbread,' the detective said with a hint of sympathy.

'Yes,' Charlie agreed. 'It has rather.'

'All right, we won't keep you here, but Thames Valley want to see you in the morning. There's one last thing, though.' The policeman flipped back a sheet of his spiral-bound notebook. 'When the driver of the police vehicle reached the car, he could see that your stepfather was still alive, but the car was so badly buckled by the fall that there was no way the ambulancemen were going to get him out on their own, so he called the fire brigade. They took a good quarter of an hour to cut him free before the paramedics could take over. While the fireman was working, Patterson spoke to him, quite lucidly. He asked him to give you this.' The policeman tore a page from his notebook and handed it to Charlie. 'He said someone should give it to you. That's not the original, of course, but maybe you can make something of it.'

Charlie stared at a strange list of figures, and a name:

60/60/24/7
ROGER.

After a few moments he looked back up at the detective, shaking his head. 'Doesn't mean a thing to me.'

'Maybe not right away, but I'd say he was trying to convey something to you in a way only you would understand. It may have no bearing on Thames Valley's inquiries, but if you can work it out, we'd like to know what it means.'

'My stepfather,' Charlie stressed the 'step', 'was an
291

eccentric man. We didn't have much in common and I don't pretend to understand how his mind worked, but if I think of anything, I'll let you know.'

*   *   *

Charlie drove the Subaru up the track through the pine forest south of Banchory. He was certain that no one had followed him from the police station in Darlington. He hadn't seen another car for the last five miles.

It was a black night and 2 a.m., little more than twenty-four hours since he had last been here. Now his father was dead. The police and Mahmoud had been deprived of their quarry, but while his death had done away with some problems, it had also presented new ones. Where, for instance, was the sheikh's money? His mother evidently didn't know, and if the slip of paper from his father wasn't a clue then the money could easily remain undiscovered forever. He'd studied the numbers from every angle for the entire journey, and still they meant absolutely nothing. He'd also started to worry about how best to break the news to his mother.

Charlie stopped the car and parked it in front of the barn. He walked briskly up the moonlit path to the house, hoping he would be able to rouse his mother.

He had gone a few yards down the track when he was dazzled by the light of a powerful torch.

'What the hell are you doing back here?' Hutch rasped from behind the beam.

'My stepfather is dead.'

There was a moment's silence before the light was clicked off. Hutch thought of the man alongside

292

whom he had fought for the past twenty years. The only person in the world he cared about.

As Charlie's eyes adapted to the moonlight again, he made out Hutch's bulky frame in front of the house.

'What happened?' the ex-soldier asked huskily.

'He drove off a motorway.'

Hutch turned and opened the front door of the house. Charlie followed him in. They went on into the sitting room where Hutch took a bottle of Scotch from a cupboard. He poured a glass for Charlie and filled one for himself. He took a gulp. 'Was he forced off?'

'No. It was an accident. The police were after him, but only for speeding. They hadn't caught up with him when he went over the side of the flyover outside Darlington.' Charlie took a drink of whisky. 'They said they couldn't see any reason why it happened.'

'He was going to York, to see you. Then he was going to give himself up.'

Charlie shook his head slowly, considering the irony of it all.

'I'll bet you that was no accident. People like your father don't have accidents.'

'But he was being chased by the police.'

'It was because you came to see him,' Hutch said accusingly.

'For God's sake, you can't blame me. I just told him what the choices were, for him, for my mother. He was living in a fantasy world, as if he was on some military operation, running from a bunch of Omani terrorists or something. He wasn't making sane judgements any more.'

Hutchinson's face twitched. 'He was doing what he knew best. He'd tried to play by the rules of the real
293

world and they let him down.'

'Didn't he think what it was like for my mother?'

'Yes, in the end, he must have done—you must have convinced him. But that left him no choice.'

'Is my mother still here?'

'Aye, she is. She's been fretting terrible since he left. He never told her he was going.'

'I'll go up and break the news.'

Charlie knocked on the door of his mother's bedroom. As soon as she saw him, she knew something had happened to her husband.

'Let me put on a dressing gown,' she said sleepily. When she appeared in the sitting room half a minute later, she looked at Charlie's face again and flung her arms round him.

'What happened?' she asked.

There was no easy way to begin. Charlie took a deep breath and recalled the bare facts of the accident. He felt his mother quiver against his chest. 'It was quick,' he lied. 'He didn't suffer. I saw him; he looked quite calm.' That at least was true.

His mother gave an uncontrollable shudder. 'Oh God! He could never have coped with prison, or penury, even for me. The poor, stupid man. He felt hunted, like a fox.'

'Hutch said it was my fault,' Charlie said.

'Don't even think that. Someone had to tell him. It's been like living with a boy obsessed with some private code of behaviour. Hutch understood it. I recognised it, too, but he knew I couldn't bear it.' Pru pushed herself from her son's arms and stood back. She tried to regain some dignity, wiping her eyes, dabbing at her nose with a handkerchief. 'I'll make us all some tea. Come into the kitchen and tell me exactly what happened.'

Charlie saw the grief, the deep lonely grief, and was amazed again by the strength of her love; his stepfather couldn't have been all bad to have retained the loyalty of a woman like her.

* * *

'I'm not sorry to leave that place behind,' Pru said as they waved farewell to Hutch and Charlie drove them from the house next morning. In the back of the car were the few personal possessions she and her husband had brought with them to the small lodge. Pru had no intention of going back there again. First they were going to the croft by Loch Cluanie to pick up David Patterson's things. It was a fine day for a Highland drive, but both of them were living in a kind of numb suspension of time, hating to look back, unable to look forward.

Charlie had heard his mother in the night, sometimes letting the grief take over in huge, gasping, desolate sobs, but in the morning she'd been determined to cope, to pull through and deal with the mess that faced her.

'I don't know what it is about men like that,' she went on. 'They seem to derive a kind of child-like satisfaction from hiding themselves away as deeply as they can. I suppose there's an innate insecurity about them.'

'But you wouldn't call Hutch or Dad weak men.'

'No, of course not, but a very strong man with a single weakness is a bad combination.'

Once they had settled into the long journey across Scotland, Charlie handed Pru the piece of paper the DI in Darlington had given him. 'Dad gave it to a fireman who was cutting him from the car. What do

295

you suppose it means?' He glanced at his mother.

Pru looked at it and shook her head. 'That's typical of him, obscure to the end. He loved all those lateral thinking games but I could never work them out. It's obviously a clue to where the money is.'

'Christ! What a mess!' Charlie exploded, as it sank in that if he didn't find the money, Sala Mahmoud would never believe David Patterson had gone without telling him where it was.

Pru put a hand on Charlie's arm. 'Please, don't blame him. He couldn't help the way he was. Do you think I'd have tolerated him if he could?'

* * *

Pru gazed with astonishment at the sparse, tidy contents of the croft in Glen Shiel. 'Until a few weeks ago, I had no idea this place existed,' she said. 'And then he only told me because he had to, in case of emergency. This must be where he used to come when things got on top of him.'

Charlie nodded. 'He would escape into another identity here, he told me. The locals thought he was just a romantic eccentric; there are enough of them around. No one ever bothered him.'

Charlie opened the drawers and began to remove the objects his father had kept there. Pru begged him not to bring the weapons, so he took them out and flung them into the loch. Together, they gathered up all Patterson's portable belongings—books, papers, pictures and a few small pieces of Victorian sculpture.

When the back of the Subaru was full, they closed and locked the door of the croft for the last time and set off for England.

They stopped for the night at an anonymous motel outside Manchester. They ate for the first time that day and bought newspapers. Several carried reports of Major David Patterson's death while being pursued by the police, with the additional information that he was wanted for questioning over the deaths of two ex-convicts, Brian Tennent and Miles Latimer. There was no mention of any missing Palestinians.

Pru read the reports bleakly. 'My gosh, it sounds so sordid.'

They set off for Wiltshire next morning. Pru intended to present herself to the police before they started looking for her. Despite the fact that all her instincts were those of a law-abiding, conscientious member of society, she let herself be persuaded by Charlie that she should offer a restricted version of events. 'They won't understand anything you might have done out of loyalty to Dad,' he said.

Everything was quiet at Birch Lodge when they arrived there after midday. The door lock had been repaired and the house tidied by General Sheridan's daily since the Palestinians' visit.

For a while, Pru sat in the drawing room where only a few weeks before Tennent had been killed. When she had plucked up the strength, she rang the police and was immediately put on to Inspector Ferrier.

'I'm very glad to hear from you, Mrs Patterson. I take it your son was able to convey the news about your husband?'

'Yes, yes. He came and told me.'

'We understood he'd be back home yesterday morning. We were getting worried. Where were you, Mrs Patterson?'

'In Scotland, at a friend's house. I went there after I thought my husband had been murdered to try and get over it.'

'I see.' He paused. 'Obviously, I want to talk to you.'

'Of course. When shall I expect you?'

'I'll be there in about an hour, if that's convenient.'

When Pru had put the phone down, she looked at Charlie sitting opposite her. 'Will you stay?'

Charlie nodded. 'I'll ring Nick and tell him I'll be home later.'

'Thanks,' she said. 'I'll see if there's anything in the deep freeze.'

She found enough food to make lunch, which they ate at the kitchen table. There was an air of reassuring normality to it after the crazy events and turmoil of the last few days. Charlie took from his pocket the piece of paper with Patterson's last message. Again they studied the numbers and the name that he'd left for Charlie, but they couldn't make sense of it.

Pru was clearing away the plates when the doorbell rang. 'That must be Ferrier.'

'I'll let him in,' Charlie went to the front door and opened it.

A large man came in as if he'd had his shoulder to the door, followed by two more who suddenly appeared behind him.

Charlie had time to see that while one was Arab, the first two looked English. It was one of them who hit him, an almighty, breath-killing blow in the lower guts.

He lay gasping on the floor of the hall as they stepped over him and went through into the kitchen to find his mother. He heard a stifled scream. They dragged her out and pushed her through to the

298

drawing room. Someone pulled Charlie up and propelled him into the room behind her and thrust him on to a chair.

One of the Englishmen pulled a small automatic from his belt and aimed it at Charlie's head. The other posted himself by the window that looked out on to the drive. Neither of them spoke.

The Arab stood opposite Charlie and hissed, 'Your father is dead, but he has not taken the sheikh's money with him, has he? Now it is you who has it, and you must give it back, or you will inherit the dishonour.'

Charlie recognised the man now as one of those who had picked him up in the Mercedes. 'Don't hurt my mother,' he pleaded. Then he was struck by a sudden thought.

'First, I should like to see the Sheikh Sala Mahmoud myself.'

The Arab narrowed his eyes. He was about to reply when the man by the window growled that a police car had arrived.

Within seconds the three men had disappeared, letting themselves out of the back door and heading straight into the woods.

Charlie made a quick decision not to mention their visit to DI Ferrier, who appeared at the front door with another junior detective. Charlie let them in. In the back of his mind an idea was forming.

'Hello, Mr Patterson. You've been very elusive over the last few days.'

Charlie shrugged his shoulders. 'I was racing at York. Durham Police got hold of me there and I went to identify my stepfather.'

'It was really him this time, was it?' Ferrier couldn't help saying.

'Your question is in poor taste, Inspector,' Charlie said. 'My mother's been through hell over what happened last time.'

'So you thought it was him, last time, did you, Mrs Patterson?'

'Of course I did. You were there. What can you expect? I came home and found a man, wearing my husband's clothes, same sort of size and shape and hair, lying face down on the carpet with his head bleeding.'

Ferrier looked at her and let his uncertainty show.

Pru turned away with her shoulders heaving.

'But why did you disappear, Mrs Patterson?'

'For goodness sake, Inspector, I was upset; I thought my husband had died. I wanted to get away. A friend in Scotland lent me a house, in a very quiet, isolated spot.'

'And now we're back,' Charlie said quickly. 'And I'd like you to tell me how the press got hold of the idea that my father was wanted for questioning over the death of this other man, Miles Latimer.'

'I don't think there's any doubt that your father was responsible for Tennent's death, though we have yet to find out why. It clearly had nothing to do with an attempted robbery. When Tennent's one and only friend, the only person who knew where he was the day he died, turns up buried in a skip, I think we have reasonable grounds for believing there might be a connection, don't you?'

Charlie sighed. 'I suppose so.' Conceding his father's crimes didn't much matter now. What did matter was concealing Mahmoud's involvement and ensuring that his mother wasn't implicated in Tennent's murder.

'Right, then. Your stepfather may be dead, but

300

we've still got to establish how these other two men were killed, so if you don't mind, we'll sit down and go through the whole thing again.'

Ferrier stayed for two hours. At the end of the session, Charlie still couldn't be sure if the detective suspected him or his mother of playing a part in the two murders, but he didn't suggest that either of them should be detained. When he and his constable had finally left, Charlie and his mother relaxed slightly.

'It's not over yet, Mum,' Charlie said. 'And you can't stay here in case Mustapha and his two heavies come back.'

'But surely we can't go to your house either?'

'No. But we could go to Kate's.'

Pru looked suddenly tired and defeated. 'I seem to have done nothing but run and hide for the last few weeks.'

'When we've worked out where the money is, we might get somewhere. And I think it would be worth going to see Sala Mahmoud in person.'

'But unless you've got something to give him, he's not going to make any concessions.'

'I'm not sure. Mustapha was just about to say something that might have been revealing when Ferrier turned up.'

'Thank God he did,' said Pru.

'I don't know. I'm not sure those guys had any intention of harming us. But we'll still keep out of their way,' he added hastily, seeing his mother's worried face.

Charlie phoned Nick and told him as cryptically as he could that he was going to go to Kate's cottage, and suggested he meet them there.

Half an hour later, after travelling round in circles, Charlie drove a hundred yards up a narrow track to

Kate's tiny brick and flint cottage. He parked the car at the back of the house and pulled an old green tarpaulin over it.

He let himself and his mother in. They were making themselves at home when Nick turned up.

'Kate couldn't come; she's flapping about a minute corn on Willow's foot. She said she'll be over later and she'll bring some food.'

Charlie nodded. He brought Nick up to date on everything since he'd last seen him in York, including his father's obscure message. 'I'll write down these numbers for you to have a look at, see if you can come up with anything.'

'I'll try. It was signed "Roger", you say?'

'It wasn't exactly signed. He just wrote the name, in capitals, under the numbers.'

Nick stared at the numbers for a few seconds.

'Well?' Charlie asked.

'I don't know, but I can't believe it's all that complicated. Is there a relation or an old family friend called Roger?'

Charlie looked at his mother, but she shook her head. The damned puzzle was beginning to irritate her.

CHAPTER SIXTEEN

Nick and Charlie were still talking when Pru came back into the kitchen. She had a piece of cheap, lined paper in her hand.

'I think this'll answer Ferrier's questions about Latimer. It arrived at Birch Lodge, and I passed it on to David.' She handed the paper to Charlie.

It was a scrawled note:

'B.T.'s dead. I know who did it. If you want to talk about it, come to the toilets on the corner of Warwick Ave and Clifton Gardens. Nine in the morning Monday or Tuesday. If you don't come, I know who to tell.'

Charlie read it twice. He nodded gloomily, his senses blunted to what his stepfather had done. 'You're right. This had to be Latimer.'

'He said he was going to ignore it,' Pru said.

'He couldn't,' Charlie said. 'I suppose we might as well give it to Ferrier, just to show willing.'

Pru agreed. 'There's no point in pretending David didn't do it, now he's gone. The quicker it's cleared up, the less there'll be in the papers about it.'

'Mum, you're going to have to face up to the fact that the media won't let go that easily. This story's a gift for them—an ex-SAS officer drives off the road while being chased by the police for speeding when it turns out he's already wanted for two murders? And he was buried a month ago with all pomp and ceremony. Now we've got to do it all again.'

'What happens to Tennent's body?' Nick asked.

'God knows,' Charlie said. 'Unless some relation appears, I suppose the state re-buries him at their expense.'

Pru was gazing bleakly out of the window. 'Charles, you're going to have to deal with that. I don't think I can cope with burying him twice.'

'But...' Charlie started to say, then changed his mind. 'Don't worry, I'll look after all that.'

Kate came later, with a clutch of grocery bags. She insisted on cooking dinner for them all. Nick left at ten—he had to be up for first lot—and Kate stayed. Pru took herself to bed.

303

Her husband had chosen his own solution to his problems. Although it had left Pru desolate, she would survive, and she would not have to tolerate the torture of her husband being either in hiding or in prison. And only they suspected that his exit from the flyover must have been deliberate.

That night, Kate and Charlie didn't sleep until the birds had reached the finale of their dawn chorus. Two hours later they were woken by a hammering on the back door.

Charlie stiffened, then relaxed when he realised that if it were Sala Mahmoud's men, they wouldn't be knocking on the door. Wrapping a towel round his waist, he went down to investigate. He looked through the kitchen window and saw Nick and, behind him, Imogen. He opened the door to let them in.

'What are you two doing here so early? Has something happened?'

'It's half past eight,' Nick protested. 'I've just sent out the second lot. Kenny's got everything under control. Immy came round last night and I showed her your numbers.'

Charlie turned excitedly to his cousin. 'Have you cracked it?'

She laughed. 'No, sorry. Not yet.'

'Oh well,' Charlie said, disappointed. 'I'd better make some coffee.' He started to fill a cafetiere. 'Dad had a weakness for cryptic things. I only hope he hasn't overfaced us.'

'What sort of cryptic things?' Imogen asked.

'Oh, I don't know,' Charlie said, trying to think of one. 'Oh yes. There was one about a man who had a square house with windows on all four sides and they all faced south. Where was it?'

304

Imogen laughed. 'That's easy.'

'Okay. So where was it?' Charlie said.

'At the North Pole, of course.'

'If you got that one so easily, why the hell can't you work out these numbers?'

Imogen sat down and wrote the numbers in a column on an A4 pad: 60, 60, 24, 7.

Nick leaned across. 'It's a question of finding a sequence.'

'There's definitely something familiar about them,' Imogen nodded. 'Just be quiet for a second.'

A moment later she shrieked. 'Got it! It's been on the tip of my brain since I first saw them. It's to do with time. Sixty seconds in a minute. Sixty minutes in an hour. Twenty-four hours in a day. Seven days in a week.'

Nick and Charlie stared at the numbers. 'That's brilliant,' exclaimed Charlie, hugging her. 'But what the hell was he trying to say?'

'I should think it's the word we end up with—weeks.'

'Weeks?' Nick said.

'Weeks and Roger. What's the connection?' Charlie asked. He stared at the paper and his head spun in frustration. Somewhere at the back of his mind among the charged grey matter of his memory cells, he knew there was a connection, but he couldn't get to it yet.

'Come on,' Nick said impatiently. 'Immy's right—weeks and Roger. Just think, will you?'

'I am bloody thinking,' Charlie protested. 'But I didn't get a lot of sleep last night.'

'I bet you didn't,' Nick said with a grin. 'But you'll have to try harder or those guys will smash you in the balls again and put a stop to your fun.'

305

'What are you all doing?' Pru's sleepy voice asked as she appeared in a white dressing gown. She rubbed her eyes and looked with some surprise at Nick and Imogen.

'Mum, Imogen's done it,' Charlie said, explaining the riddle to his mother. 'What we need now is a connection between "weeks" and "Roger".'

Pru sat down and poured herself a cup of tea from the pot Charlie had made. 'It could be a sound-alike—the weeks.'

'How do you mean?'

'Something that sounds the same but is spelt differently.'

'Weeks? Weaks—W.E.A.K.S.? Weekes! With an E!' Charlie exclaimed.

'What?' asked Nick.

'The sculptor! A Victorian. Dad's got a few of his.'

'Of course he has!' said Pru. 'We brought some with us from the croft.'

'Roger,' Charlie said urgently. 'Which of them is Roger?'

'That's easy,' his mother answered. 'Roger, Second Marquess of Hampshire. He's still in the car.'

Charlie and Nick rushed out of the house together. Charlie pulled the tarpaulin off the car and opened up the back. Buried among the things they had removed from the tiny Scottish dwelling was a small bronze bust. It depicted the Victorian marquess as a Roman emperor, complete with laurel wreath and toga. It was an undistinguished example of the work of the period, not rare, and not valuable. Charlie tugged it out and carried it back into the house. 'This is him, isn't it?'

'Yes, of course. It says so.' Pru pointed out a small inscription on the base.

Nick picked it up and turned it over. The underneath was smeared with some dirty brown wax which antique dealers sometimes use to 'age' their wares. He scraped at it with his fingernail until a clear circular cut in the bronze emerged. 'This must come out somehow,' he said.

Charlie, who considered himself more practical, took it from Nick. For some frustrating moments, there didn't seem any way of unlocking it, but by applying pressure and a little oil, he suddenly found that he was unscrewing it. When a neatly threaded circular panel dropped out, he was able to insert his hand into the hollow bronze. With his fingers, he felt some fine velvet cloth inside and extracted what turned out to be a small drawstring purse. His hands were trembling slightly as he opened the purse and poured the contents on to the kitchen table.

Fifteen stones of several pastel colours scattered in a glittering display on the worn pine surface.

'Shit!' Charlie said. 'That's it!'

'It looks like it,' Nick agreed. 'I don't know much about gems, though, what they are or what they're worth.'

'He went abroad, just before he disappeared. He must have got them then. What do we do with them?' Charlie asked.

'I'd turn them back into money if I were you. It'll be a lot simpler when you're dealing with Sala Mahmoud.'

Charlie shook his head. 'Maybe, but I'm not so sure. The first thing to do is to find out just how much they're worth.'

Three hours later, Charlie parked his car in Sydney Street, Chelsea. An old friend whom he trusted and who had, at the age of thirty, already made a name for himself as a reliable jobbing jeweller, had a shop close by in the Fulham Road.

Billy Wiseman emerged from the back office of his premises and greeted Charlie warmly. 'Don't tell me you've found some poor victim who'll have you?'

Charlie couldn't think what he was talking about for a moment. 'Victim?' he asked cautiously.

'Some innocent little creature that's been taken in by your specious charms?'

Charlie laughed. 'You mean am I getting engaged? Good God, no.' He stopped abruptly. 'At least, I don't think so. Anyway, that's not why I've come to see you. Can we go into your lair in the back?'

Billy Wiseman looked at the pile of stones Charlie poured on to the desk in his small private office. 'My goodness, Charlie, what have you been up to? I thought the only crime you ever committed was doping other people's favourites.'

'Look, Billy, these aren't mine, but I need to know how much they're worth before I pass them on.'

'Worth? That's an elastic term. We're talking markets and the variability of jewellers' eyes. But I could give you a figure within ten per cent either way.' Wiseman shrugged.

'That'll do,' Charlie said.

An hour later, he left the small jeweller's shop with the bag of stones, a list of their approximate values, and an invoice from Billy Wiseman for £200 for the valuation. Charlie felt fortified by the knowledge that the contents of the little velvet purse nestling in the inside pocket of his jacket were worth between two and three hundred thousand pounds more than the million the Arabs had said they were seeking.

He found his car and headed for Carlton House Terrace. When he managed to find a place to park

308

near the Turf Club, he slipped up to the room he had booked earlier in the day. He changed out of the jeans he had been wearing and went down to the bar where Nick was waiting for him.

'Where the hell have you been?' Nick asked nervously.

'You don't get a million quid's worth of stones valued in five minutes, you know.'

'I couldn't help thinking somebody had cottoned on to the fact that you're walking around with those bloody things and nobbled you. Where are they now?'

For an answer, Charlie patted the breast pocket of his suit.

'What are you going to do with them?'

'I'm going to repay Sala Mahmoud. At least I know what they're worth now. Dad seems to have bought them well.'

'The sheikh is going to want some kind of concession, too, for his men being killed,' Nick pointed out.

'I'll just have to hope he's civilised enough not to blame me for that and accept that the person responsible is himself dead.' Charlie wasn't at all confident that that would be the Arab's attitude to his missing men, but it was a risk he had to take. There was no other way to dispose of the threat hanging over him and his mother.

*   *   *

Kate arrived in London in time for dinner.

They ate in the club, the three of them, and talked about the horses at Oak Hollow. The two men found they were treating Kate as if she was a partner too. It was only when they were drinking coffee that the conversation turned to the business of Sala Mahmoud's million.

'So, what are you going to do now, Charlie?' Nick asked.

'I'm going to see Sala Mahmoud.'

'Face to face?'

'Yes. I think that'd be best.'

'Where are you going to see him?'

'I've got to find out where he is first.'

'I know his trainer's secretary. I may be able to find out through her. I'll try now.' Nick left the table to make the call in the lobby.

Charlie looked at Kate for a moment before he spoke. 'I wonder if you'd do me a rather big favour?'

Kate grinned and gave an exaggerated shrug of the shoulders. 'Sure. If you think I can do it, I'll do it.'

'I wouldn't admit it to Nick, but it's just possible somebody at Billy Wiseman's might have traded the information that I'm wandering about with a bagful of diamonds. I'd hate anybody to jump me and help themselves. I don't think I ought to leave here with them.'

Kate's eyes gleamed. 'I'll take them out, no problem.' Charlie gave her a look that made up for all the fear already bubbling in her guts.

'What a woman!' he laughed.

Nick had made his call and was walking back into the dining room. He watched his friends clasp hands across the table and grinned to himself. There was no pain in it now.

As he came closer, he gave an exaggerated cough.

Charlie looked up. He could tell that Nick had the information they needed.

'So what's the story?'

310

Nick sat down in his place. 'It looks as though you're off to Paris,' he said, 'or, to be precise, the Forest of Fontainebleau.'

CHAPTER SEVENTEEN

Charlie drove Nick's Subaru on to a late ferry from Dover to Calais. Before they had left the club premises, Kate had ordered a cab. It picked her up and took her to Waterloo where she bought a ticket for the next Eurostar to Paris.

Charlie drove off the ferry on the other side of the Channel and headed for the French capital.

He arrived as the birds woke and men were sluicing down the ancient cobbled streets in the early morning light. He found a cafe that was open, sipped coffee and drank in the unforgettable atmosphere of a city he'd always loved, until it was a respectable hour to turn up at the hotel where he had arranged to meet Kate. He had become accustomed to trying to shake off tails, and after a series of manoeuvres in London, he knew he hadn't been followed to Dover, let alone Paris. He was sure that he and Kate weren't at risk, at least until he exposed himself to Sheikh Sala Mahmoud.

Over an extended breakfast in a St Germain brasserie, he gave Kate a more detailed account of what had gone on over the previous two days. To her disappointment, he told her he would not take her to see the sheikh.

He knew roughly how to find Sala Mahmoud's mansion in the Forest of Fontainebleau, but when he reached the village of Bois-le-Roi, he had to ask for

311

more detailed directions.

From the locals' reactions, he gathered that it was a well-known and awe-inspiring place. He drove the last mile through the forest with growing trepidation.

He identified the opening in the trees that marked the start of a long private road that led to the house. He crept up it until he crossed a small bridge over a railway line, and covered another four hundred yards of dead straight road until he came to a fifteen-foot gate flanked by a chainlink fence topped with razor wire. The drive beyond curved away into the trees. There was no sign of the house. Charlie waited a moment; he had spotted a TV camera on top of one of the massive stone gateposts. When nothing happened for a while, he climbed out and walked across to find a small push-button beneath another camera lens, and a loudspeaker.

He pressed the button and stood back. After a moment, a disembodied voice addressed him in clipped Cockney.

'Who is it?'

'My name's Charles Patterson. I need to see Sheikh Mahmoud.'

'Do you have an appointment?'

'No. But if he knows I want to see him, I'm sure he'll agree.'

'Charles Patterson, right?'

'Yes.'

There was a click on the loudspeaker and the connection went dead. Charlie waited and wondered who he had been talking to.

The gatepost hissed back into life. 'Right. Leave your vehicle parked on the hard-standing to your left. Come in by the personnel gate and walk up to the house.'

Charlie got back into the Subaru and parked it. He climbed out and walked towards the gates. He heard a slight click as a smaller gate set in one of the main ones was unlocked. He pulled it open, stepped through. It swung back and closed behind him.

When he rounded the bend in the drive, he understood why his stepfather had described the place as one of the most magnificent in the forest. It was a fine example of nineteenth-century French architecture at its grandest and most elegant. While it wasn't the largest of the *fin de siècle* chateaux, it must have been one of the most beautiful and it was spectacularly set in its parkland, surrounded by the ancient forest.

On one side of the house, a lake, perhaps ten acres and edged with every kind of rush and full of lilies, gleamed and reflected the blue-grey tiles of the roof and the shimmering cream of the walls.

At the bottom of the long, double sweep of steps to the square pillared portico, a silver Rolls-Royce Phantom VI was parked; a liveried European chauffeur was yawning in the driver's seat, reading a paper.

Charlie walked across the expanse of fine gravel and up the steps. Before he had reached the front door it swung open and an Indian servant bowed him into a marble-floored hall. Apart from a pair of plain, upholstered benches, there was no furniture, but a couple of fine English equestrian paintings—Stubbs, Charlie guessed—hung on the walls to his left and right.

He was admiring them when a stocky, bald man in a light-weight fawn suit appeared, clicking metal heels on the floor as he walked towards him.

'Mr Patterson.'

313

Charlie recognised the voice which had spoken to him over the intercom. 'Yes. Good morning.'

'Morning to you.' The bald man held out a hand. 'I'm Bill Jackson, head of Sheikh Sala Mahmoud's domestic security.' The man's manner was almost welcoming. Charlie began to feel a little more at ease.

Jackson beckoned him to follow and spun on his heel. As he walked, he turned and looked over his shoulder. 'I was sorry to hear about the death of your father.'

'You knew him?'

'Of course I did. I was in his squadron, then he recruited me to the sheikh's team when I left the regiment.'

Somehow, Charlie had overlooked that the sheikh's personal security had been his father's responsibility for seven or eight years.

He was being led down a long oak-floored corridor now. He noticed that none of the furniture and fittings were of that garish, over-the-top bad taste which he had always been told was distinctively Arabic. He recognised some pieces of furniture as François Linke's designs, though presumably by the hand of Harry Thorndyke.

At the third door, Jackson stopped and showed him into a large room with full-length windows which looked out over the lake. 'Have a seat.' He waved Charlie to a high-backed oak chair. 'The sheikh will see you when he sees you. Don't hold your breath, though. I'll have some coffee sent in.'

Charlie sat where Jackson had suggested and tried to relax. Jackson had been friendly enough, but that was no guarantee that his master would be.

An Indian maid appeared after a few minutes with a tray containing a jug of coffee and a small cup.

314

When she'd gone, Charlie poured out some of the thick, dark liquid. He had taken only a few sips of the bitter brew when Jackson returned.

'Sheikh Sala Mahmoud will see you now,' he said, while his eyes communicated that Charlie was very honoured to be seen so fast.

Charlie followed Jackson out of the room, back to the central hall, up a wide curving flight of shallow marble stairs with beautifully wrought iron banisters. A rotunda above the stairwell illuminated the sheikh's huge English canvases to great advantage, though possibly not to their long-term benefit.

Charlie was led along a thickly carpeted landing corridor, through another room and, after a sharp knocking, into a second room beyond.

'Charles Patterson, effendi,' Jackson said, bowing from the waist in a way that seemed inappropriate to his undisguised Cockney accent.

Charlie found himself facing the man he had seen at the funeral in Putney Vale. Sheikh Mahmoud was half sitting, half lying on a silk upholstered sofa, wearing traditional Saudi robes, white, elegant, not greatly adorned. He had a short, well-trimmed and shiny black beard with eyes to match. He lifted one hand no more than an inch in greeting. Charlie felt impelled to bow slightly as Jackson had done.

'Good morning, Mr Patterson.'

Charlie was struck at once by his soft articulation. It didn't tally with the guttural tones he'd heard over the mobile phone in the limousine.

'Good morning, Sheikh Mahmoud.'

'I am glad to see the son of my old friend.' Charlie detected no sarcasm in the statement. 'Although I am sorry his death has been so, how shall I say, controversial?'

315

Charlie couldn't think of an appropriate response. He nodded.

'However,' the sheikh went on, 'having attended his first funeral, I will not be able to attend the second. But please pass my respectful condolences to your mother.'

'Thank you, sir.'

'And why have you come to see me?'

'About the furniture.'

'The furniture?' the sheikh said with surprise. 'The furniture of François Linke which your father collected together for me most efficiently?'

'Yes.'

'You can see it all around you.' He waved a hand at various pieces in the room. 'Doesn't it look magnificent?'

'My father told me it would be just right for the house,' Charlie ventured.

'Indeed, but that isn't why you came to see me, is it?'

Charlie couldn't tell from the Arab's voice if he was teasing him or genuinely didn't know what he wanted to talk about.

'No, sir,' he plunged in. 'I understand, though, that they are not genuine François Linke pieces.'

'What? What are you saying?' The sheikh sat up, his black eyes blazing. He swung his feet over the side of the sofa and planted them on the ground. He stared hard at Charlie, puzzled and angry.

'But surely, sir, you knew. Men came to see me to find my stepfather, saying that you were very angry about it and wished my father to return the extra profit he had made from selling it to you as genuine.'

'Men? What men?'

'They said they were your men, and I saw them

with you at the funeral. Then, after that, some others picked me up in your Mercedes and I spoke to you on the phone...' Charlie didn't finish the sentence. It was clear that this was not the man he had spoken to from the back of the car.

'I don't know what you are talking about, Mr Patterson. I have not been told that these pieces are not what your father told me they were. I am very pleased with them. I have sent no people looking for your father or you. The men you saw at the funeral were not my men, merely functionaries of my country's embassy in London—bodyguards and so on.'

'But they said you had sent them.'

'So you say, but I tell you I did not send them. What is this about the furniture? Did your father admit to you that he had cheated me?'

Charlie looked straight back into the glittering ebony eyes. 'Yes.'

'And why do you come now to tell me, when your father is dead?'

'I have come to repay the excess profit my father made, in accordance with what I understood were your wishes. I tried to persuade my father to do it before he died, but he wouldn't, although he believed you had sent your people to demand it. That's why he faked his own death, and to avoid paying hundreds of thousands of pounds he owed in England.'

'Your father was having such difficulties? Why didn't he tell me? I have great respect for him. He was a strong and honourable man.'

'He was far too proud to do that, Sheikh Mahmoud.'

'Then why did he cheat me?'

'He said you would never know that he had.'

317

'And I would not have done, nor has anyone who has been here and seen the furniture. We must find out how these people who posed as mine knew and who they are.'

'But the people in the limousine that picked me up at Newbury, they must have been your men.'

The sheikh nodded. He clapped his hands and a figure emerged from the shadows. Sheikh Mahmoud spoke briefly and the minion bowed and swept silently from the room.

A moment later, Bill Jackson knocked and entered.

The sheikh spoke to him in Arabic. Jackson nodded when he had finished and replied, apparently fluently, in the same language. During a further exchange, and the sheikh's issuing of a final command, Jackson betrayed no signs of his reaction. He acknowledged the sheikh's instructions, bowed and left.

'Mr Jackson will deal with them,' the Arab said briskly. 'So, you wish to repay the fraudulent profit your father made.'

'Yes, sir, in the interests of preserving our family's honour. Alternatively, since I have been able to locate the funds my father acquired through his transaction with you, I could repay you in full and take the furniture back.'

The Arab leaned back on his cushions and looked at Charlie through narrowed eyes. 'I do not understand why your father has done what he has,' he said.

'He was desperate; he didn't know how to deal with the prospect of bankruptcy. It must be hard for you to understand, but he had been tricked into a lot of obligations. He honoured some of these although

318

probably he could have proved he'd been deceived. He was a formidable soldier, a leader of men, but when it came to the real, corrupt world of business, he didn't know the rules.'

'But you, you can deal with it?'

'I don't know. My partner and I are trying to get our training yard off the ground. We took a few gambles to get started, but we always knew exactly what the downside was.'

'And now you are offering to return to me a sum of money, I don't recall how much, a million pounds or so, to recover your family's honour?'

'To be truthful, it was also out of fear of reprisals. These people who were after my father had turned their attentions to me now that he's dead.'

'I admire your honesty.' The Arab regarded Charlie with an enigmatic half-smile. 'Where are you staying?'

Charlie gave him the name of the cheap hotel where he and Kate were staying, not expecting it to mean anything to the sheikh. Sala Mahmoud repeated the name. 'My people will come for you. Please, stay in Paris until then. This is a serious problem.' Charlie was dismissed with a curt nod and a wave.

Jackson drove Charlie to the gates in a Mercedes which had been parked outside the front door. He and two more British ex-soldiers covered him as he climbed into the grimy Subaru. Jackson assured him that no one was following, apart from one of his own men. Charlie didn't doubt him.

When he arrived back at the hotel, Kate was sitting in the tatty old salon reading. She looked up and smiled with relief when she saw him walk in. 'What's the story?'

'I don't think the sheikh has any plans to neutralise me right away. I still don't have any idea if he wants his money back. He's bloody pissed off, though not with me. It looks as if someone on his own staff got hold of the news that the furniture was wrong, omitted to tell the sheikh and thought they'd go after Dad for the money on their own account, pretending they were acting for Mahmoud.'

'Did he know that the furniture was bogus?'

'No. Not at all. He was chuffed to bits with it. Still is, as a matter of fact. He bought the stuff to sit on, not as an investment. Still, I dare say he'll want his pound of flesh.'

'But what about those men who were after you?'

'There's nothing in it for them any more. Besides, I think he told Bill Jackson to deal with them—and that'll discourage them.'

'Who's Bill Jackson?'

'He's a man my father recruited into the sheikh's service, used to be in his squadron at Hereford. He's head of domestic security now and quite capable of quietly disposing of a few wayward henchmen without recourse to the law.'

'Thank God for that.' Kate gave a tremendous sigh of relief, and Charlie realised with a stab of guilt that she'd been a lot more worried than she'd let on.

They spent the rest of the day being tourists. They walked across the Seine, ambled up the Champs-Élysées, stopping to lunch in a small restaurant by the *rond-point*. Kate hadn't been to Paris before. She soon agreed that she wasn't immune to the legendary charms of the place, especially in the early summer sun. After lunch, she and Charlie took a taxi to see the race-course at Longchamps. They found an official who, on learning who Charlie was, allowed

320

them to walk the course.

'Just think,' Kate said, gazing at the empty stands, imagining the roar of the crowds it could hold. 'One day, we ... you,' she corrected herself quickly, 'may be unloading runners here for the Arc.'

'What do you mean, one day?' Charlie laughed. 'We'll find something to run here next autumn. Any excuse to bring you back here again.'

They fantasised happily as they strolled arm in arm back across the *périphérique*.

When they reached their hotel, footsore and pleasantly weary, they took a bottle of champagne up to their room. Charlie drew the curtains and lifted Kate on to the bed.

'At last!' she laughed, kicking her shoes to the ceiling and taking a quick gulp of champagne. 'Here's to Sheikh what's-his-name, whatever he decides to do to you tomorrow.'

That evening, before they went out to sample more culinary delights, Charlie telephoned Nick.

'What's going on?' Nick asked.

'I've seen Sheikh Mahmoud.'

'And you're still alive. That's good. Your charm worked then?'

Charlie filled him in. 'The main thing is,' he concluded, 'he'll put a stop to those thugs who've been threatening me. I should think he'll be in touch about the money quite soon. In the meantime, Kate and I are seeing the sights.'

'I bet that's not all you're doing. By the way,' Nick went on, 'I hope you'll be back here the day after tomorrow. Willow Star's owners are coming to see her.'

'Good Lord. At last. I thought that win at York might flush them out. Who are they?'

321

'I don't know, beyond the fact that they're two women.'

'Two women? One each, eh?'

'I should think you've got enough on your hands.'

'You could say that,' Charlie laughed. 'I'll ring you tomorrow, if I'm still alive.'

*   *   *

Charlie didn't feel very alive when he was woken by the phone beside his bed at ten o'clock next morning. He and Kate had left Regine's in an advanced state of euphoria at three that morning. Now he had some difficulty lifting his head from the pillow.

'Hello?' he croaked into the receiver.

L'auto de Sheikh Sala Mahmoud vous attend, m'sieur.

'What? Now?'

'Oui, m'sieur.'

Charlie put the phone down and looked at Kate. She was lying beside him, sleeping serenely. He slipped out of bed, showered, gulped down a fizzing glass of triple Alka-Seltzer and wrote a note for Kate. Downstairs, he was ushered into the Sheikh's Rolls-Royce.

Lounging in the back, Charlie wished he was in better shape to enjoy being driven through Paris like this. To his surprise, he found some whisky in a decanter in the drinks cabinet—he didn't think Saudis drank. But he rejected the temptation to swallow a hair of the dog and tried to concentrate on his imminent meeting with the sheikh.

The limousine eased its way effortlessly south along the autoroute from Paris. It turned off to glide through the great forest of pine and broadleaf until it

322

swept through the gate into the grounds of the sheikh's mansion and pulled up outside the classical portico. The chauffeur opened the door and Charlie stepped out at the bottom of one of the flights of steps up to the front door.

Again, the door opened before Charlie had reached it. He was ushered inside by an Indian servant and straight to the sheikh's salon.

Sala Mahmoud was sitting in one of the François Linke chairs, behind a carved walnut writing table. He lifted his head and smiled when Charlie walked in.

'Good morning again, Mr Patterson. I hope you are well?'

'Yes, thank you, sir.' Charlie walked across and stood in front of the table.

'Good. They tell me you have a good future in training horses.'

'We hope so,' Charlie mumbled, surprised by the sheikh's sudden reference to racing.

'I have some horses in England,' Mahmoud went on. 'Only twenty or thirty.' He made a gesture to demonstrate the paltriness of his string. 'Now,' he went on. 'I have thought about what you told me yesterday. I must tell you that I have been made very angry by what your father has done to me. But you have been honourable. You have told me, and you have exposed a traitor in my own household. I thank you for that. Do you have the money?'

Charlie's heart sank. He had been quietly nursing the hope that Sheikh Mahmoud wasn't going to ask for it. He had, nevertheless, come prepared. He took the small purse from his inside pocket and poured the stones on to the table.

The sheikh looked at the glittering display with apparent approval. He picked up one stone and turned it in the light.

'These are fine diamonds, but why do you bring me gems?' he asked Charlie.

'My father bought them with the money you paid him. Before he died, he left me instructions where to find them. I've had them valued. They're worth over a million pounds.'

'We shall soon see,' the sheikh said. He clapped his hands. A manservant appeared like a genie from behind a screen at the back of the room. The sheikh uttered a few words in Arabic. The servant slipped away silently.

Charlie gazed at the sheikh, trying to read his mind.

Sala Mahmoud rubbed his shiny black beard. 'You have said you will take back the furniture your father sold to me. I will decide and you will be told.'

Charlie knew enough not to ask when. He also understood that the audience was at an end. He bowed slightly. 'Thank you, sir,' he muttered and left the chamber.

The servant waiting outside seemed to know exactly what was going on and showed Charlie to the front door and into the Rolls which was waiting outside. He was taken back to Paris in silence. Only when the limousine drew up outside his small hotel did the chauffeur speak.

'Sheikh Sala Mahmoud will send a messenger.'

Charlie watched the car drive away. He had been gone for only two hours, but it was as if he had been to another world. He was brought down to earth by a New Age tramp asking him for money. He had nothing on him. He shrugged and walked into the hotel.

Kate was still asleep. He undressed, climbed back into bed and gently woke her.

*   *   *

Charlie drove the Subaru on to Le Shuttle at Calais late the next morning. When they reached Dover, he headed for the M2 and London.

He turned to Kate with a wide smile. 'Sorry we couldn't stay longer, but it's good to be back.'

'I can hardly believe so much has been settled in forty-eight hours.'

Charlie laughed. 'I think you'll find there's more to come.'

Kate nodded. 'You're right. Nick won't know what's hit him. How much did you say Mahmoud was sending?'

'Basically, he's giving me back half the money. He's decided to keep the furniture and he feels honour has been satisfied.'

'What are you going to do with it?'

'Give it to Mum. After all, he's promised us four yearlings for next season and he's paying their fees up front. We're doing very nicely out of it.'

'But that means you're not getting anything personally.'

'Women are so practical,' Charlie laughed. 'We'll have to break it to Nick gently. He's already fussing about where to put the extra horses; that's another reason why he was so keen for me to get back. Anyway, at least we'll be there in time to meet these women who bought Willow.'

'Yes,' Kate agreed. 'I wonder what you'll think of them. I bet you'll really fancy one of them.'

'Of course I won't,' Charlie laughed. 'At least, I'll try not to.'

* * *

Nick's greeting was predictably ambivalent. He was immediately concerned that there was no room for four new horses.

'Don't worry, Nick,' Charlie said. 'We'll find somewhere to put them. We'll build new boxes if necessary.'

'I'll believe that when I see it. It's a pity it's not the Sheikh who hands out planning permission.'

Charlie laughed. 'And when you check our next bank statement, you'll find he's already paid the four yearlings' training fees twelve months up front.'

Nick made a quick mental calculation. His jaw fell visibly. He didn't say anything for a moment, then he gulped, and shifted his feet. 'Good Lord. I owe you an apology, then.'

'Don't worry,' Charlie said. 'Am I in time to meet Willow's owners?'

'What? Oh yes, I'd almost forgotten about them. They haven't turned up yet.' He glanced at his watch. 'They're due any time now.'

They all walked back towards the yard, Charlie and Kate anxious to see the horses again. Kate made straight for Willow Star's box and made her usual fuss of the filly.

They hadn't been there long when Kenny shouted that there was a car turning into the drive. Nick and Charlie hurried to see who it was.

A new but extravagant Ford was creeping down the track. As it came nearer, Charlie saw that it contained only the woman who drove it. 'I suppose that must be one of them,' he said. 'Perhaps they're coming separately.'

They watched fascinated as the car drew up and a curiously dressed woman of about fifty let herself out and walked carefully towards them.

'Hello,' Charlie said.

'Hello. I'm Cora Lenigan,' the woman said with a broad Liverpudlian accent.

'Have you come to see Willow Star?' Nick asked doubtfully.

'Of course I have,' Cora chuckled. 'I own half of her.'

'Well, it's very nice to meet you at last,' Charlie said. 'But I thought there were two of you.'

'There are,' Kate's voice said from behind them. They hadn't heard her come out of the yard.

Charlie and Nick turned sharply, reacting to her tone of voice.

'What?' Charlie asked suspiciously.

'Cora and I are joint owners of Willow Star, fifty-fifty.'

Charlie and Nick gaped at her.

'Good God! Why on earth didn't you tell us?'

Kate met Charlie's incredulity with a grin. 'A girl likes to have some secrets, you know. Besides, I didn't want to say until I was sure we wanted to keep her at this yard, otherwise it might have been rather awkward, mightn't it?'

'But you do want to keep her here now, is that right?'

'Yes,' Kate said thoughtfully. 'I think she may as well stay here.' She paused. 'As long as I do.'

'That's blackmail!' Charlie protested.

'Yes,' Kate said with a grin. 'I suppose it is.'

'In that case.' Charlie fumbled in his trouser

327

pocket and pulled out his screwed-up hanky. He opened it. Inside, a pale violet stone, which he had kept from the Sheikh, glittered in the afternoon sun. 'I suppose you'd better tell me how you want this set.'